DABAR
PROMISES

MARGARET DOWRICK

Ark House Press
PO Box 1722, Port Orchard, WA 98366 USA
PO Box 1321, Mona Vale NSW 1660 Australia
PO Box 318 334, West Harbour, Auckland 0661 New Zealand
arkhousepress.com

Unless otherwise stated, all Scriptures are taken from The Holy Bible, New International Version®, NIV® Copyright 1973, 1978, 1984, 2011 by Biblica, Inc.™ Used by Permission. All rights reserved worldwide.

Cataloguing in Publication Data:
Title: Dabar Promises
ISBN: 978-0-6451657-3-9 (pbk)
Subjects: Fiction
Other Authors/Contributors: Dowrick, Margaret

Design by initiateagency.com

With heartfelt thanks to Glen, Don, Louise, Trevor, David, Hilary, Dixie, Jo-anne B, Ken, my dear sister Merilyn and all my friends whose encouragement and interest in this book so greatly assisted its production and completion.

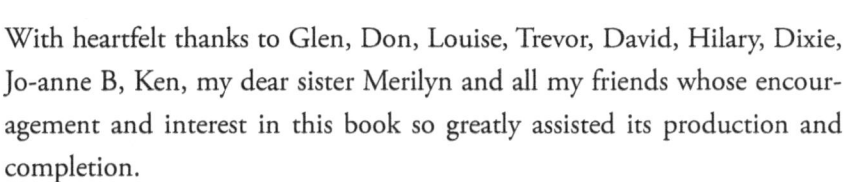

The writer would like to suggest the reader peruse the novel without referring to the biblical references provided. These have been implemented to assist those readers wishing to locate the biblical origins of the novel's contents.

List of Contents

PART ONE – THE EARLY YEARS

PART TWO – A DIFFERENT PATH

PART THREE – FULFILMENT AND EXPOSITION

PART ONE

THE EARLY YEARS

Chapter One

REBELLION REIGNS

T he scorching Judean sun sizzled down on the dry farrowed field with fizzling fervour. Oblivious to its intensity, and despite the beads of perspiration on their brows, twelve boys darted around chasing one another across the bare ground. Sounds of joy and laughter penetrated the seething air, for in their innocence their minds were on the pleasure of the moment and not the sun's ferocity.

"Catch me, Ananiah!" cried out one boy.

"No, catch me!" yelled another. Ananiah paused to review the situation. Of all the boys playing in the field, there was only one who was always too slow and clumsy in retreat and without any further exclamations from the children, Ananiah immediately ran towards Kaleb.

Kaleb's heart pounded; inwardly he knew that he would be Ananiah's prey – he always was. Escaping from the boy who was taller, faster, spiteful, and obnoxious seemed to be the plight of his young years. Secretly, Kaleb longed to befriend Ananiah but unfortunately, Ananiah was too head strong and arrogant, displaying limited pity to anyone - after all, he was the oldest of eight other children. His father Zuriel, a godly man, named his first born 'Ananiah' (Adonai answers) however, Kaleb and the other boys would often query the meaning behind this name wondering if Adonai could possibly have a streak of meanness that sanctioned the severity of Ananiah's harsh behaviour. This was often physically and emotionally hurtful.

"Let's play Olam (Hide) Sachar (Seek) Heez (Dare)!" exclaimed one of the boys. "Yes!" the other boys shouted. Kaleb's heart pounded even more. Olam, Sachar, Heez was usually a fun game, except when it was Ananiah who was in charge. The rules of the game were similar to "Hide and Seek" except for the additional task of daring which, when placed in Ananiah's hands was often cruel, mean and sometimes very painful.

The rules of the game were quite simple. One child would count to 100 while the others hid. Once found, you had to help the seeker find the remaining children. The very last person to be found was rewarded the opportunity of stating a 'dare' which all participants had to complete. The dare could be completed either before the next game or during the game itself. If anyone faltered on the dare by not completing it, or failed to fulfil the designated task, he would be eliminated from the next and subsequent games until finally there was only one person left- the ultimate winner! How Ananiah loved this game!

Kaleb flinched. Memories of the time when Ananiah dared the boys to stand on top of an ants' nest to see who could stay there the longest, flooded back to him. Of course, Ananiah did not participate in this task, but laughed loudly as the boys shouted in pain and anguish, jumping up and down in extreme agony as the ants' ferocious venom felt like acid dissipating through their veins. Needless to say, it was Kaleb who suffered the most distress even though he was the first to run off the angered ants' nest.

"What an excellent idea!" remarked Ananiah. "Because I was the last one in, during our last game, I will start this game with my own dare. Now let me see, what will the first dare be?"

≈   ≈   ≈

The Roman centurion's calloused hand powerfully hammered the public notice onto the Governor's Gate in the city of Yerushalayim (Jerusalem). The noise of the hammering echoed throughout the surrounding marketplace drawing the attention of the nearby crowd who pressed forward to see what the notice contained.

"Not another tax from those Roman hoarders!" someone murmured.

"I dread to see what this new edict says!" said another.

"No! No! No!" came from the disgruntled crowd.

As people pressed forward to see what was written on the declaration, Zév, a well-known Pharisee stepped up to the notice. After he hushed the crowd with his hands, he started to read aloud.

"Attention all citizens of Yerushalayim

His Excellency Titus, Governor of Judea, is abhorred by the increasing number of robberies and murders by a bandit group known as the Deliverers in the area surrounding the city. Upon receiving this notice, a new monthly tax of two denarii will be required from all citizens in Yerushalayim and the nearby areas. Two new companies of Roman soldiers will now guard the roads near the eastern and western gates of the city.

Any citizen knowing details of the whereabouts of these bandits must inform Palace Authorities. Any citizen found to be in collaboration with these law breakers will suffer the same fate of the members of the group - execution without trial".

Many of those present were fully aware of the Deliverers, a group of twenty to thirty men who rebelled openly against the Roman authorities and sought to return the governance of Isra'el (Israel) to its rightful owners. Over the years, there had been many different groups of antagonists, but this group proved to be extremely rebellious, completely unmerciful and malicious in their violent atrocities. Their terrorist acts often resulted in the shedding of innocent blood. It appeared that although the group originally claimed it would restore peace to Isra'el, their methods for achieving this were contradictory and extremely brutal. With recent attacks on communities outside of the city walls and the reports of many innocent men, women and children murdered during raids, there was a sense of relief that finally some steps were being taken to address the problems of the rebels' rebellion. However, as usual, when a country is governed by an unwelcomed captor, taxes only tended to fill the pockets of the captor rather than provide the relief they were intended to bring.

Exactly where the Deliverers resided or established their camp was unknown though some believed that not far from Yerushalayim were several caves with catacomb-like passages and small chambers. These would provide a perfect hideout for such a group. Believed to be the burial places of people who had lived many years ago, the caves appeared distant and unwelcoming to those travelling through the Yerushalayim area. So, the exact location of the robbers' den, if it was in these caves, was not known. As no one wished to confront the rebels face to face, it was firmly believed that should the exact location of the group's camp be found, this would be the last piece of earthly knowledge taken to the grave.

"This has become quite unbearable!" one man exclaimed.

"How long must we wait before the Messiah comes and relieves us from these oppressive infidels?" shouted another.

Several people in the crowd cried out aloud "It's been many years since He rescued us from Egypt and the desert - has Adonai forgotten us?". Many in the crowd concurred as unrest quickly started to spread around the marketplace. Once more Zév hushed the crowd with his hands and then when they had quietened down, spoke to the people before him.

"Dear friends", he replied, "does not Adonai's word tell us, that He will never forget His people? Has He not said that He has carved our names in the palms of His Hands?[1] No! He has not forgotten us, but we must remain faithful, firmly believing that the promised Messiah will come and when he does, he will overpower our enemies and rule this world with an iron rod and sceptre.[2] Then, as Adonai promised, the tables will be turned on our captors and we shall live a life that is free of oppression and fear. According to His promises, all Gentiles and infidels will bow down before Adonai including our Roman captors and they will be our servants".

The Pharisee's words appeared to alleviate the anxiety of the crowd which quickly dispersed as the people returned to the market. With avid interest Zuriel had been watching the crowd and the animated discussion that had preceded its dispersal. As a scribe like his father and grandfather before him, the words that he had so carefully copied onto the scrolls over the years had, in their own way, found themselves inscribed deeply into his

---

[1]   Isaiah 49: 14-16
[2]   Genesis 49:10; Psalm 2:9

heart. Perhaps it was the repetitious act of copiously copying each letter, each word, and each line of the Tanakh, that like his predecessors before him, Zuriel believed that the scrolls contained information about the coming Messiah which for some reason had not been fully understood by the people. Although the words were deeply imprinted in his memory, there was an even stronger conviction within his soul that the promised Messiah would do much more than just restore peace to Isra'el.

"That was well stated!" Zuriel said placing a supportive hand on Zév's shoulder. "You were quite right to encourage the people to be patient and wait for the Messiah". As Zév turned and looked at the face of the man encouraging him, he smiled. "Thank you, Zuriel" he replied, "but as Adonai's people we must not forget his promises to us, and we must hold onto the hope that only He has given us".

"I absolutely concur with you Zév, but I feel convinced in my heart, that when He comes, the Messiah will not just bring a political peace for our nation, but something else that we cannot anticipate", Zuriel stated.

Zév seemed a little puzzled by this remark so Zuriel continued, "I am not sure that the peace you proclaim He will bring, will mean peace just for Isra'el".

Zév smiled and looked straight into Zuriel's eyes. "Of course, it is just for Isra'el Zuriel for Isra'el is Adonai's one and only chosen people!"[3]

"Then tell me Zév," replied Zuriel, "why does the prophet Yeshaẏahu (Isaiah) also say that the Messiah will be a light for the gentiles?[4] Moreover, if the Messiah will reign over them with an iron rod, dare I say more harshly than we have been over the years, how could they possibly perceive him

---

[3]   2Samuel 7:8-11; Isaiah 44:1
[4]   Isaiah 42:6

to be their light? Furthermore," continued Zuriel, "Does not the prophet Yecherzk'el (Ezekiel) report of unity and no division under Adonai's rule?"[5]

Zév appeared quite stunned. "Dear Zuriel!" he said "Isra'el is Adonai's own chosen people! Why would He wish to embrace the godless gentiles? Your views are strange and somewhat outlandish! You remind me so much of your late father and dear Grandfather! Both had similar strange views but you, Zuriel, have an insightful gift which enables you to recall and recite Adonai's word so easily. You could in fact achieve a higher position, even possibly a chief scribe if you wanted to. Unfortunately, these unusual opinions of yours hinder you in any further aspirations so I do recommend that you keep these opinions exclusively to yourself...oh and by the way, you may want to have a good talking to that oldest son of yours. There has been much talk in the Sanhedrin about his rebellious and unholy ways".

"Unholy talk in the Sanhedrin!" thought Zuriel to himself, "I'm sure that my son's behaviour is not the only unholy thing discussed there!"

≈ ≈ ≈

Ananiah's sparkling azure blue eyes surveyed the surrounding fields. The farrowed field in which they were playing was the furthest field to the east of the farm and encompassing the whole eight fields of the farm were tall olive trees. These trees provided a boundary to the farm and were also the expressed limitation as to where the boys could play. With the recent concerns over the atrocities of the Deliverers, Ananiah's uncles who worked the farm were happy for the boys to play on the farrowed field because they could keep the boys under a watchful eye. It had been clearly stipulated to

---

[5]   Ezekiel 37:24-25

9

all the children that they must keep within the farm's boundary and under no circumstances were they to play beyond this.

Farther east beyond the olive trees in the distance were low lying boulders surrounded by trees and shrubs. Bored with playing in the familiar farm field, the rock outcrops to the far east looked captivating and intriguing and seemed to beckon Ananiah's desire for adventure and naughtiness at the same time. "The first dare will be" declared Ananiah, pointing to the east, "who will be the first person to reach the boulders?"

The children's hearts sank. This dare would mean that they would be disobeying their parents' requests that they play under supervision and within the boundaries of the farm. "But we have been told we are not to go outside the boundary of the farm under any circumstances!" one boy protested.

"And I promised my father I would not play outside the farm", added Kaleb.

"I promised my Daddy I would not play outside the farm", mockingly mimicked Ananiah in a babyish voice. "Honestly, Kaleb, you are such a baby at times!"

Tears started to fill Kaleb's eyes despite trying to prevent the others from seeing his hurt. Ananiah rushed up to him, struck him brutally across the face and watched as the tears that Kaleb was trying to hold back, started to flow freely down his cheeks.

Taking a deep breath Kaleb said, "I promised my father I would not go beyond the boundary of the farm and even you Ananiah, will not make me break my promise. Besides, the Deliverers have been sighted outside of the city. I do not want to, and I will not go!"

"The Deliverers have been sighted outside of the city!" mimicked Ananiah, "and I told my daddy I wouldn't disobey him! You're such a daddy's boy, Kaleb!" Then he turned around to the boys who were quite dismayed by his brutality, and their feet stuck to the ground unable to move.

In their hearts, they knew what Kaleb had said was true but the thought of receiving a similar outburst from Ananiah made them shudder with fear. "Anyone else afraid like this scaredy cat?" he demanded.

"Well, by asking us to disobey our parents, you are also asking us to disobey Adonai"[6] one brave boy responded.

"Adonai? Adonai? Who believes in Adonai? Has anyone seen him? He's just a figment of our parents' imagination! He doesn't even exist! Now, let's see who is willing to accept the dare and be the first one to reach those boulders!"

Four boys including Kaleb stayed behind in the field whilst the others hesitantly then gradually ran faster and faster, heading towards the distant rock outcrops.

≈   ≈   ≈

The news of the boys' perilous adventures was soon discussed in homes scattered throughout Yerushalayim and it wasn't long before the news of the youth's rebellious activities reached the ears of the members of the Sanhedrin. The Head Cohanim (chief priest), Zarid, a Pharisee, called 23 of the elders to discuss the stance the Sanhedrin should assume on the matter. Should the rumours be true, the fathers of the rebellious boys should institute fair punishment to deter the boys from offending again. If the rumours were found not to be true, the people needed to be warned again of the dangers of the current times.

Although it was an informal meeting, heated debate arose in the Royal Stoa. One side, not wishing to anger the Roman authorities any further, argued that this was a Jewish concern for what had occurred was in direct

---

[6] Deuteronomy 5:16

rebellion against the laws of Adonai, including a total disrespect for the parents concerned.[7] On the opposing side, was the view that the recently nailed notice on the Governor's Gate indicated that this issue was under Roman jurisdiction as the Roman government was taking responsibility for eradicating the problem of rising insurgents. The proponents of keeping the situation in Jewish hands replied that this was a very good reason why the punishment and retribution of the offending children needed to be dealt with by the laws of Adonai and not the cruel, unyielding and heartless administration of the Romans. By handling the situation themselves, the parents with the recommendations of the Sanhedrin could administer the necessary punishment and keep the boys alive. There was, however, a consensus that the Sanhedrin did not wish to anger the Roman authorities, particularly as relationships between the two groups were always on shaky ground.

After much discussion and debate Zarid rose from his chair and spoke. "My fellow servants of Adonai", he said, "before we can discuss what form of punishment can take place, we need to call all the parties in this matter so that we can ascertain the exact truth of what has happened. Therefore, I propose we send the temple guards to the houses of all known participants and bring them back to us with their fathers accompanying them. Then, after each boy has been given an opportunity to tell us exactly what took place, we shall be able to determine what the punishment should be. After we have done this, we can confidently say to the Roman authorities, that because we consider this to be a Jewish matter, we have swiftly and immediately addressed the issue and therefore believe that with the punishment delegated and implemented, it shall not happen again". The group concurred wholeheartedly.

≈   ≈   ≈

---

[7]   Exodus 20:12

Chapter Two

SUMMONED BY
THE SANHEDRIN

T he twelve fathers with the twelve boys involved in the incident
were individually brought by the temple guards to a small room
located within the basement of the temple. As each pair arrived,
the temple guards gestured them to go into the room and immediately,
after they entered, the door was firmly shut. All the fathers were totally
unaware as to why they had been all so abruptly summoned to attend the
Sanhedrin and the fact they were asked to bring their child made things
even more bewildering.

Upon sighting Ananiah's presence in the room, a few fathers immediately assumed that the children must had been led by this known rebellious
child to do something of a delinquent nature. "Why have they brought
us here?" one father asked but the only response he received was the silent

shaking of several heads. After twelve men and their sons were in the room, the door opened and a temple guard spoke sternly, "Follow me".

Ananiah was pleased to get out of the small room which had no windows but fortunately twelve oil lamps, three on each wall provided sufficient light to the room. Even though the room was well lit, the air within the four walls had gradually become quite stifling and stale. Two temple guards led the group down a narrow, elongated corridor which seemed to have no exit point and if there was such an exit it must have been very deep within the surrounding darkness at the end of the corridor. On the left-hand side of the passage were several rooms no doubt like the one they had just exited. Once again oil lamps flickered on the right-hand wall of the corridor. After what seemed a long time, the group was finally led up a flight of twelve cold stone steps - the stairway lit with more brightly burning oil lamps. When they had reached the top of the steps, the group welcomed the fresh breeze that brushed across their faces, all happy that they had left the uncertainties found in the dungeon-like room below, yet they increasingly became more fearful of what was lying ahead.

Zuriel looked around and realised that the group had been brought to the portico of the temple which surrounded the eastern Court of the Gentiles. Four long porticos surrounded the whole temple area on the northern, eastern, western and southern sides. The northern, eastern and western porticos each had a total of ninety strong ten-foot high stone pillars. On the southern-side however, the portico's mighty columns were twelve feet high and on top of these pillars was the Royal Stoa – the place where the Sanhedrin met. This was to be their destination but the journey to their place of judgement seemed to be an eternity away.

When they came to the end of eastern portico there was a large wooden door. One of the temple guards knocked heavily three times on the door which slowly opened. Moving into a small room with yet another large door, the group hustled together to fit into the room's tiny perimeter. The same temple guard again knocked three times on the second door which slowly opened.

As they were led along a much larger portico (with the supporting columns at least twelve feet high), Zuriel realised that they were near to their destination but Ananiah totally unaware as to what was going to soon happen, was intrigued by the beautiful large white polished stones that were on the floor. Each white square stone, had a striking black star and inside the star was a small white circle. The floor had a glossy covering of absolute elegance and Ananiah wondered if he was in the palace of a king. Walking swiftly down the centre corridor with the others, he noticed on his right-hand side was a large court and behind this court, on the northern side was a large building which appeared to take up most of the width of the complex. The building seemed to taunt Ananiah as his eyes were transfixed on its magnitude. Unknown to him was the fact that this was the Temple – the Living Place of Isra'el's Holy God. Finally, when they came to the end of the corridor which was at the western side of the temple complex, the group went up a flight of twenty steps. Once again, polished oil lamps lined the walls at the side of the stairs.

When the group had reached the top of the stairs, Ananiah gasped in astonishment as he observed the splendid surroundings before him. The group had finally entered the Royal Stoa and on the top floor of this building was a large basilica – an oblong hall with three walkways to the eastern end of the building. The stones on the floor of the Royal Stoa were even more beautiful than those on the lower floor; each marble tile had shades of pink, grey, black and white delicately intermingled and the glossiest covering which reflected the light emitting from the burning oil lamps that surrounded the large hall. The whole area radiated an ambiance of importance, dignity and sovereignty. As they walked to the eastern end, Ananiah saw that there was a very large apse impressively located at the far end of the Royal Stoa.

As the group moved closer towards this area it became apparent that an important meeting was taking place for behind a large, ornate and delicately designed arch were 24 men all sitting side by side in a semicircle encompassed by the tall-sided walls. At the back of the apse was a tall yellow curtain approximately twelve feet in width and twenty-four feet in height. There were also two men, one seated on the right and one on the left just behind the arch. Each man had a small writing easel on which there was a scroll of paper and a feather, pen and ink pot.

Ananiah had heard his father and his great grandfather talk about the Sanhedrin many times so he knew that included within the group of those seated was a high priest, some acting high priests, Pharisees and Sadducees, chief scribes and elders who acted as a council which looked after civil jurisdiction of the implementation of the Jewish law and its requirements. The body attempted to liaise closely with the Roman authorities and as the Sanhedrin had authority of life and death in Jewish law[8], it held many powers. It could order arrests by its own officers of justice[9] as well as judge cases which did not involve capital punishment. Capital punishment cases required the confirmation of the Roman procurator.

There was a hushed silence as the twelve boys shaking to their innermost core stood in a row. Behind each boy stood an anxious father. The chief priest rose from his chair and spoke in a firm voice. "As this is an unofficial meeting of the Sanhedrin, we shall not require the scribes so gentlemen, please take your easels, writing materials and leave us". The two scribes seated on the left and on the right, picked up their materials, stood

---

[8]   Matthew 26:59; Matthew 26:66
[9]   Matthew 26:47

erect before the group and bowed their heads before departing. The chief priest then continued:

"You have been called here because it has come to the Sanhedrin's attention that three days ago a group of boys was sighted playing outside of the eastern side of the city in the perceived dangerous territory of the Deliverers rebel group. The Roman authorities over the months have placed numerous warnings on the Governor's Gate which have advised all citizens of the destruction and devastation these bandits have brought to our area. We need to know the truth behind these rumours that have been brought to our attention so that we can determine the punishment the offending children must suffer before there is Roman intervention of a more severe kind".

Addressing the boys, he continued; "It is the requirement of Adonai's Law that you speak to us providing us with only truthful answers. If you lie before us today, not only will your punishment be doubled, you will incur the wrath of Adonai Himself who is the only one who is sinless and without fault". Zév, who was seated next to the chief priest arose from his chair. Immediately, the chief priest sat down. Then addressing the twelve boys Zév asked, "Do you swear by Adonai that the words you speak here will be the truth and that you will use no lies in your speech?" The boys with their knees still shaking nervously quivered "We do".

Zév sat down and another member of the Sanhedrin rose and asked the boys "Were all of you playing on the fallowed field on Zuriel's family farm three days ago?" The boys nervously nodded their heads. "And were there any other boys who are not here today, playing with you in the field?" he continued. The boys timidly shook their heads. "We can't hear you" pressed the inquirer. "No sir!" was the unison response. The man then sat down.

Another man on the opposite side of the apse rose to his feet. "Can you, the boy in the middle, tell us what happened that day?" The boy took a deep breath and shared how he and the boys had been playing a game of tag in the field as they had often done before. He added that when they get bored they would change to another game and that day they had decided to play Olam (Hide) Sachar (Seek) Heez (Dare).

An old man seated to the right of gentleman speaking, stood up and in response the previous inquirer immediately sat down. "Please forgive my age and ignorance" he commented, "but Olam and Sachar I often played as a boy, but never did it involve a 'Heez'. Can you enlighten me and those of my colleagues present, what the dare entailed?" The boy continued "A dare could involve any challenge you wanted. You could make it a single dare before the game or include it within the game itself. A dare I made involved us all playing hide and seek by hopping on just one foot. Everyone had to hop, those who hid as well as the seeker. Even if you were trying to hide or even if you were the seeker, should you be forced to put your other foot down, you are out. Boys are eliminated one by one until finally there is only one person left, and it could be either the seeker or the other boy".

One member of Sanhedrin rose to speak and once again, in respect, the old gentleman retired. "What happens if the seeker stops hopping and there are still a few more people to find?". Quite a few members of the Sanhedrin immediately glared at the inquirer as it was obvious that such a question would not provide any insight into what had transpired on the day in question and after all, that is why the meeting, even though it was unofficial, was taking place.

Another boy, who by this stage was feeling a little more at ease, resumed the conversation. "He has to go out but before doing so he has to delegate another player to be the seeker".

"Well, that does sound like a lot of fun and these dares, that are made up, are all of them fun?" the inquirer asked. There was a definite pause from the boys, most of their eyes stared at the floor. "Look at me!" the inquirer shouted. "Answer my question! Were all of the dares made by the group, fun?"

"No Sir," responded another boy, "In fact some of the dares could be sadistic and painful".

"Please give us some examples", the inquirer demanded.

"Well one of the more awful dares before the game commenced involved us having to steal eggs from a bird's nest and smash these into the ground. One time, we had to walk across a long stretch of prickly grass without wincing. Then there was the time we had to see who could stand the longest on an ant's nest and then there was the time…"

"Enough!" interrupted the inquirer, "I think we get the picture! Which boys present here would develop such a dare?"

When Ananiah cockily (with more pride than shame) admitted that he was the sole author of such dares, Zuriel's heart sank. He had no idea that his first-born son had such a merciless, cruel and callous heart. Moreover, Ananiah showed no degree of remorse, in fact it appeared by the smirk on his face, he thought the dares he had given were quite clever and humorous. The inquirer sat down as another man arose from his chair. "Tell us," he asked, "Did you provide the dare to your friends when you played in the field three days ago, and if so, what did you dare them to do?"

The faces of those seated in the semi-circle around the twelve boys as well as the fathers grew stern as Ananiah unashamedly explained that he had provided the dare and what the dare was. When he was asked why he decided to use that dare, Ananiah answered by shrugging his shoulders. This made his father's heart sank even more and as embarrassment crept in, Zuriel also felt a certain degree of anger at his son's open rebellion. Then, he became ashamed that he had failed his son but more seriously, he had failed Adonai in raising him.

When another man seating on the edge of the semi-circle stood up the current inquirer sat down. "Tell us", he queried and randomly selecting Kaleb, "Did you think this was a funny dare?"

"No, Sir" replied Kaleb as he told them of his insistence that he would not participate in the dare.

"Why didn't you want to complete the dare?" his inquirer asked.

Nervously, Kaleb explained that he had promised his father that he would only play on the farm and not go any further outside its boundaries. He knew that it is was thought that the bandits had their camp to the east of the city and that made him scared. Furthermore, he insisted that by breaking his promise to his father, he was also breaking his word to Adonai and there was no one who was going to make him do that.

"Well spoken!" remarked his inquirer "And were there any others who felt the same way?" Some nodded their heads. "Step forward those who refused and did not participate in the dare", he demanded. Four children including Kaleb stepped forward. "You four boys did not participate in the dare?" the inquirer asked.

"No, Sir", the boys replied.

There was a long pregnant pause as the members of the Sanhedrin collectively looked at one another, their eyes conveyed a consensus of opinion. Then the chief priest rose. "We see no further reason to detain these four boys and their fathers any longer. Before you go, may I just say to the boys who have stepped forward that serving our gracious Adonai is not easy yet His laws are clear. You have honoured them as your father and forefathers have taught you and it is always wise not to follow an alternative path to the one that Adonai has so graciously provided[10]. Keep your heart set on His laws and you will not falter for in His faithfulness, He will uphold you[11]. Now go in peace and remember Adonai's blessings". The four boys and their fathers bowed their heads and swiftly exited down the main corridor

---

[10] Psalm 119: 105-112
[11] Psalm 41:12; Isaiah 41:10

of the basilica - so swiftly one of the temple guards had to run to catch up to them. Relieved, they were shown the exit of the Temple.

The remaining boys and their fathers anxiously stood before the Sanhedrin. Most of the fathers felt fearful for their boys but the most apprehensive heart belonged to Zuriel. For many generations, his forefathers had served Adonai faithfully professing their love and servitude to Him. So faithful were his forefathers that a few generations ago, Zuriel's grandfather Obadiah (Faithful to God) had pledged an oath to Adonai, that in the years to come one of his descendants would serve Him by writing and recording His words and preserving them for future generations. Consequently, although the family were farmers, the successful produce of their farm ensured that at least one person completed this task and ever since Obadiah's oath, one person from each generation had worked as a scribe. This was considered by the family as a true blessing for although there were no Levites in their lineage, Adonai had faithfully blessed the farm. From only two fields, the farm had now expanded to eight. Zuriel dreaded the thought of telling his grandfather what was occurring before him. He felt ashamed but most of all, he felt increasingly disheartened.

Summoning the remaining temple guard, the chief priest arose and told the group of fathers and sons standing before them to go to the end of the Royal Stoa and wait for the Sanhedrin's decision. The guard moved the group of the eight fathers and their sons to the western end of the building. Relieved to be out of the confrontation and awkwardness of the recent interrogation, Ananiah breathed a sigh of relief however looking at the far end of the Royal Stoa, he could see, though not hear, the members talking fervently.

The thirty minutes that passed during the time of heated discussion seemed like an hour but finally, the group was summoned to stand before the Sanhedrin once again. Ananiah felt a fear of dread as they stood once again with the boys in front of their fathers. The room fell silent as the chief priest arose to speak. "Would the eight offending boys please step forward".

"It is the decision of the Sanhedrin that your actions of three days ago left you all in a vulnerable and dangerous situation. You are all fully aware of the recent concerns regarding the Deliverers bandit group which has been increasingly reported around the Yerushalayim area. Your fathers have no doubt warned you about the concerns of the Roman authorities regarding the safety of the citizens of the city. Are you aware that there have been several sightings of this group in the area you chose to perilously play? Are you also aware that this group has mercilessly murdered over 100 people; included in that number are forty children – boys and girls of your own age? If the bandits offered no mercy to all those poor people who had innocently crossed their paths, do you really think that they would offer any mercy to you?"

"Your acts were not only serious for your own safety but the safety of your friends. They were also undertaken in complete contradiction to what your father and families have told you. Despite the sacred teachings that have been brought down to us all, you in your self-centeredness and stubbornness, had totally disregarded your father and your mother's demands of you[12]. In your selfishness and stupidity, you have dishonoured them and yourselves but the most unforgivable thing you have done in this situation, is that you have dishonoured Adonai who watches over all".[13]

"It is the decision therefore of the Sanhedrin, that all eight boys will be punished for their disobedience. Not only have they been disobedient to Adonai but also their fathers, themselves and their friends. Our law instructs us that you must be disciplined for your rebellion[14]. Moreover,

---

[12]   Proverbs 1:8
[13]   Psalm 33:12-15
[14]   Proverbs 3:11-12; Proverbs 19:20.

the law states that by sparing our children from discipline, we are in fact preventing our children from learning what is right[15]. Hence it is our decision that each child here shall receive at the hands of his father ten swift thrashings which shall be undertaken using either leather straps or hickory sticks. Each blow must be of equal power to the preceding blow and the reason for each blow must be spoken before the blow is implemented".

"The first blow is for the boy's blatant and precarious sin against Adonai; the second is for the boy's rebellion against his father's authority; the third is for himself and the perilous path he chose to take; the subsequent seven blows will be for each boy who was included in his rebellion. Each boy's name should be spoken aloud before each blow takes place so the offending boy can remember the names of those whom he has caused to suffer in the foolishness of his sinful actions".

"Do the fathers of the boys standing before us agree to undertake the punishment as directed?"

"We do", the fathers responded.

"And do the boys standing in front of their fathers before the Sanhedrin agree never again to disobey Adonai and their fathers or put themselves or their friends in spiritual or mortal peril?"

"We do", was the united reply.

"Then go in peace and never forget the vows you have made this day" concluded the chief priest and the boys with their fathers swiftly left the building, pleased to get out of the trauma but dreading what was to come.

---

[15] Proverbs 13:24

—————— *Chapter Three* ——————

PUNISHMENT
AND PAIN

Z uriel placed three large sacks of flour on top of each other on the bare barnyard floor. This was the barn in which all threshing, winnowing and sieving implements were stored and where all the winnowing and sieving of the grain took place. In seasonal times, the grain was usually sieved daily, six days a week and the resulting flour placed in large sacks. Most of the daily produce was taken to the markets and there were always extra sacks that were piled in the barn during the time the family were selling their goods in the market place. By Adonai's grace there were always spare sacks of grain even in pre- and post-season periods.

The barnyard floor was clean and all that was left in the barn were the instruments and the latest season's sacks of flour. Ananiah watched his father stack the sacks and then go to the farm instruments and taking a strong, long piece of narrow leather, return to the pile. "Come over here, lower your pants and bend over the pile" Zuriel ordered his son. Hesitantly Ananiah came over to the pile and did as his father commanded him. He knew in his heart that his actions had affected his father and in some way, he was sorry to have caused his father and his family such displeasure. He was also disappointed that his mother, Hannah, had not agreed to his father's desire to complete the beating with Ananiah bending over the table where the family ate their meals. But as his mother had insisted the table was made for eating and not beating, Zuriel decided the beating should take place in the farm barn.

"Ananiah," his father began, "in your stubbornness and selfishness, you have brought much disappointment to your mother, your family, your friends, to me and most of all to Adonai. As instructed by His law and the directions given to me by the Sanhedrin today, you will receive ten lashes". Zuriel raised high his right hand which held the leather strap. "One, is for turning away from Adonai's laws" – down came the strap and slashed painfully across Ananiah's bare buttocks. Excruciating pain seared throughout his body; it was like no pain he had experienced before -its intensity did not dissipate, but rather seemed to increase and lingered even more.

Raising his right hand again, Zuriel continued: "Two, for disobeying Adonai's law and not honouring your family particularly your father". Down came the lash so quickly. The result was that the agony currently writhing through his body was now superseded by a far greater pulsation of pain.

His right hand raised again, Zuriel stated: "Three, for letting yourself down and not remembering right from wrong". Loudly the lash came down, tearing both the swelling and red skin causing blood to seep from the wound. Ananiah thought that his heart was about to burst for the pain increased even more with each blow. Although he was listening to his father's words, pain overwhelmed his body and he began to wish that it would soon be over. But there was more to come.

Zuriel then gave seven more strong lashes, stating the boy's name who had been entrapped by Ananiah's wicked ways. With each slash, the wounds on his buttocks were widened, blood oozed and his skin was red, raw and extremely painful. At last the final boy's name was stated the lash came strongly down, delivering such excruciating pain as the nine lashes before.

Silence filled the barn. "Get up", said his father. "Think about what you have done and seek Adonai's forgiveness".

When Ananiah looked into his father's eyes, he saw the deep disappointment in regard to his recent behaviour and realised that this had been in complete defiance of his father's faith. Although this made him feel ashamed for what he had done, he still muttered to himself, "Adonai! Adonai! I don't believe in Adonai!'

≈ ≈ ≈

When Ananiah entered the house by the back door he saw his mother busily preparing the family's meal. As she turned and saw him in the doorway, he pouted his lips and looked very sorrowful. Although he had mastered this look over the years and it usually worked well, this time it received no response. Instead, his mother paused and then unmoved, went back to the task at hand. No response from his mother! Ananiah was indeed in a sad and sorrowful place! Slowly he walked through the house, his buttocks feeling as if they were on fire with non-extinguishable pain. Exiting the front door, Ananiah found his great-grandfather Obadiah, sitting on a wooden chair on the front porch of the house. Located next to the house were their surrounding farm and the houses of the members of the family who were also farm workers. Situated about a kilometre from the walls of the city, the farm and its surrounding area was nurtured by fertile soil supplemented by good annual rainfall.

Obadiah had seen many years; his face etched with oldness and his frail body advanced in years. He was the patriarch of a large family who grew up strong in its faith. Even though Obadiah's family were farmers through many generations, he held an immense love for the law of Adonai. So much so that he had promised that if Adonai blessed his land, he would allow one person from his family to become a scribe. Many generations ago, the role of scribes and priests had been allocated to the Levites by Adonai when His people were in the desert[16]. Over time, more people assumed this role, though it usually meant no wage and the upkeep of the family member who was a scribe, was subsidised by the wider family.

His eldest son, Uriah (God is my light) and his grandson Zuriel had faithfully taken on this role. Uriah, Zuriel's father, had died five years earlier and with sadness still within his heart, Obadiah prayed earnestly that the task Adonai had so graciously allowed his family to complete, might continue in the newest generation of his family. Alas, as this role was usually undertaken by the eldest son, there was increasing uncertainty that the task would be completed by Ananiah whose young days seemed to be filled with trouble and rebellion.

The old man lifted his head and turned to Ananiah and asked "Punishment over, Ananiah? Pull that chair over next to me and sit down". "I would rather not", replied Ananiah still feeling the throbbing of his bleeding buttocks.

"Ah yes!" said Obadiah, "The strength of a father's leather lash speaks loudly, doesn't it? Ananiah you will learn when you are a man and have your own family, that one thing you must do whether you like it or not, is

---

[16]   Numbers 1: 44-54

to discipline your children. For without discipline, how can a child learn 'right' from 'wrong'?"

Ananiah said nothing but walked to a post supporting the front porch and gazed at the golden barley fields before him. Obadiah continued. "Ananiah, no matter what you do you must know that Adonai is a God who loves you and has promised you and all your family, that He will oversee your life if you trust in Him". Still staring out on the barley fields before him, Ananiah said softly but vehemently, "I don't believe in Adonai!"

"You don't believe in Adonai?" his great-grandfather exclaimed. "Then tell me Ananiah, how come you are standing on this porch near the great city of Yerushalayim? How did your family get to be here when it is known that many, many generations ago, your ancestors lived a cruel and agonizing life in the ancient land of Egypt? How did your people escape from their slavery and suppression?"

As there was no answer forthcoming, the old man slowly raised himself out of his chair, and deliberately moved his tired limbs across the wooden floor, grasping the other supporting post of the porch, he placed his old feet on the ground below. Then, he lowered his aged body down until he was sitting on the floor of the porch. Calmly leaning forward his old hands picked up a small stick on the ground. "Come over here, Ananiah" he said, "I want to show you something". Ananiah moved over to where his great-grandfather was and watched him as he drew deliberately in the sand, illustrating each point clearly as he spoke.

"Here was Egypt, a great land with fertile plains and pastures. It was a long distance from where we are now over here on the outskirts of Yerushalayim. Now tell me Ananiah, how is it possible that your forefathers before you, travelled from here to here? Don't forget that separating Egypt from the surrounding countries is the Red Sea which is here. Past the Red Sea is the wilderness where there is neither water nor food. Once again, how could your ancestors find their way from the cruel and brutal Egyptians to the place where we live today? First, how did they get across the Red Sea?"

"They could have got there by boat" retorted Ananiah who didn't quite know where this discussion was leading.

"By boat!" exclaimed Obadiah. "Do you know how many boats would be needed to transport all those people? We know that approximately two and a half million people left Egypt with Moshe (Moses) and that doesn't include their animals! Now if a boat could contain ten people, how many boats would be needed to take all our people out of Egypt? Don't forget that Pharaoh was not happy with this arrangement and immediately chased after the exiting people to force them to return. Wouldn't it take too long for all the boats to load up with eight people, take them across the sea and come back to pick up eight more people, until all the two and a half million people and their animals had been saved? No, it couldn't be by boat, Ananiah, that would be too impossible! And how could they survive for so long in the desert? How did they survive wandering for 40 years in the wilderness? What could they eat in the desert which would keep them alive for 40 years?"

"They could have eaten ants" replied Ananiah who was in his usual 'won't give in' mood.

"Exactly how many ants would you have to eat until you felt satisfied and while there are lots of ants, there probably wouldn't be enough for two and half million people, not to mention their animals? No, besides ants would probably bite you all the way down your inner passage and do you think you could survive on just eating ants? If they killed and ate their animals, there would be no animals left for all those people to eat! Where could they find water in such a desolate place?"

Ananiah remained silent for the questions that had been presented before him were just too complex to solve. But this did not stop his great-grandfather from continuing. "Tell me Ananiah, how can two and a half million people leave a land that is surrounded by the Red Sea, travel through the desert for forty years and now reside in land thousands of kilometres away? How is that possible?"

Obadiah looked deeply into Ananiah's eyes. Obadiah's blue eyes gleamed and his face appeared transformed as he placed one of his old hands on Ananiah's shoulder. "Only by a miraculous hand could our people be saved from the depths of the waves of the Red Sea to the struggles of a barren land without food or water. Faithfully Adonai heard their cries and faithfully He answered them[17]. Despite sending ten plagues to weaken the stubborn and defiant heart of Pharaoh, the Egyptians made our ancestors' lives even more unbearable until Adonai sent a final plague killing the first-born sons of the Egyptian captors. Then, as Pharaoh relented, our people's mammoth exodus brought them to be trapped by the Red Sea".[18]

"What seems impossible to man, is no problem to our great and mighty Provider. Miraculously, for only by a miracle could our people be saved, Adonai parted the deep waves of the Red Sea to allow his people to travel to land safe from their enemies. Tell me, Ananiah, how do you part the waves of the seas? And furthermore, when all His people were safe on the other side, He caused the parted waves to return to their original place. Tell me, Ananiah, how do you make waves that have been parted, join together again? Is this not miraculous? All these things have been recorded in the scrolls. All of this is true!"

"Then, our people in their stubbornness forgot the miracle of Adonai's protection during the next forty years and rebelled again and again in

---

[17]   Exodus 16:11-36
[18]   Exodus 12:29-50; Exodus 14:26-31

the desert. Yet they were fed with quail and manna and their thirst was quenched by water in the desert.[19] How? Only by Adonai's Hand! It is only by the Hand of Adonai, Ananiah, that our people were brought from the land of Egypt to the Land of milk and honey. It is only by Adonai's hand, Ananiah, that His people were saved".

Several minutes of silence passed as the boy looked down on the drawing before him. He did not know the answers to his great-grandfather's questions but he could see by the old man's conviction, that his family's beliefs had been passed down each generation. He wondered if his great-grandfather's beliefs could possibly be true?

The old man continued. "Ananiah, when I was a young boy about your age, my great-grandfather gave me a precious gift and I would like to give it to you. He instructed me that should I ever feel afraid or be in any danger, I would confidently say this prayer which is based on His promises found in the Tehillim (Psalms)[20]: '*El-roi, El-roi! You delivered your people from the waves of the Red Sea and from the scorn of Egypt, deliver me, your child, for death is before me and I am doomed. Remember Your promise to Your people'.*

"What does El-roi mean?" Ananiah asked. "It means the strong one who sees" replied his great-grandfather. "Adonai has many different names because of His greatness and we need to remember that He sees all. Repeat the prayer with me". Ananiah stumbled as he repeated the prayer with his great-grandfather. When Obadiah asked him to repeat it again, he did so until he was confident he knew it word for word. "Now promise me, that when you are ever in any danger or if you are ever fearful, you will say this prayer to Adonai" the old man requested.

"I promise I will, great-grandfather". And he meant it.

---

[19] Exodus 17
[20] Psalm 3:4

Chapter Four

HEART AND SOUL
YEARNINGS

he conversation ended, Obadiah sat alone on the front porch
of the house. His timeworn eyes wandered over the ripening
barley crops. By Adonai's blessing on Obadiah's faithfulness, the
acquisition of additional land over the passing years meant that not only
could the farm's profits increase but also the farm was able to diversify its
produce. By the sixth month of the year, both the barley and the wheat
were harvested and gathered. Crops of flax and millet were harvested and
gathered in the seventh month whilst the expanding number of bordering
olive trees around the expanding farm, always provided a bountiful crop
of ripe, delectable olives in the tenth and the eleventh months. So fruitful
was the produce that additional workers were always sought during harvest
times, providing income not only for the family but also to other men and
women as well.

Adonai had indeed been faithful. While the sight of the growing crops delighted and pleased Obadiah, just one more thing brought him pure joy. Because the family was financially able to support a member to undertake the duties of a scribe, each generation was involved in studying and producing the word of Adonai. Each person had become so absorbed in what he was transcribing, many words had found a place in their collective hearts. Often each man would come home after a hard day's work and eager to share with the menfolk what had been found that day when transcribing the words of the Tanakh.

Obadiah sighed as he remembered his time as a scribe. For forty years, he had served Adonai and each year he became keenly interested in the Torah (the five books of Moses) and the Writings (which included Psalms, Proverbs and Job). One day he was asked to transcribe a scroll from the prophecies of Yesha'yahu (Isaiah) and it was from that day, his heart became increasingly excited and curious, particularly when he was transcribing the sections that spoke of the coming Messiah. Thus, Obadiah agreed wholeheartedly with the teachings of the Pharisees that the Lord (Adonai) would restore the faithful remnant of Isra'el to inhabit the kingdom when the Messiah came[21]; Isra'el's enemies would be defeated, and Adonai would protect his nation[22]; Isra'el would return to a position of world pre-eminence[23] but also life would be so peaceful[24]. When a nation is invaded, and stripped of its sovereignty and powers, its people will always long for a better time to come. Over many centuries, Isra'el had been invaded and defeated many times and the Jewish nation had not only been devastated but also scattered across many lands. The promise

---

[21] Isaiah 10:20-21
[22] Psalm 5:11; Isaiah 66:13
[23] Isaiah 66: 20
[24] Isaiah 9 :7

of a mighty and powerful redeemer brought hope to many an anguished and despondent heart.

Obadiah was both pleased and proud that his eldest son Uriah (God is my light) willingly pursued his father's footsteps. Even as a young child Uriah was interested in his father's discussions about what he had learnt that day and therefore it was no surprise that when the time came for Obadiah to retire, his son eagerly participated in the tradition of scribing. Obadiah was delighted that the promise he had made to Adonai was continuing and in his heart, he knew that this would please his faithful Lord.

The seed that had been initially planted, that is the interest in the words of the prophet Yesha'yahu (Isaiah), expanded even more over the years. To his delight, Uriah found many passages written by some of the prophets revealed more information about the coming Messiah. Finding new information caused the family to believe that the viewing, reading and writing of Adonai's word, was such a great privilege.

After thirty years of recording the words of the prophet, Uriah passed away in his sleep. His son, Zuriel like his father before him, gladly stepped into the role of serving as a scribe for Adonai. Although only five years had passed since Zuriel had assumed the role of scribe, he had become engrossed in the passages that suggested that there was going to be some form of rejection and rebellion from the people. This concerned him greatly for like his grandfather before him, Zuriel believed that the Messiah would be such a welcoming saviour to a very dispersed and unhappy people.

And now, after many years, Obadiah wondered about the future of the promise he had made to Adonai in providing a member of each generation to serve Him in this way. Maybe one of Zuriel's seven remaining sons might assume this responsibility because at this point in time, the rebellious heart of Ananiah exempted him for any form of consideration. Yet he knew, Adonai was all-knowing and had everything in control[25].

Just as Obadiah was thinking about these things Zuriel walked out of the house onto the front porch. Without saying anything, he wrapped his arms around a supporting post on the right-hand side of the porch and rested his head on his arms. Surveying the fields before him, he sighed deeply. Obadiah felt the heaviness of his grandson's sigh and said, "Disciplining his child is one of the hardest things a father can do. It can be so painful".

"Yes, it is hard", replied Zuriel "but what is more heart wrenching and agonising is his rebellion not only against me, but Adonai".

"Well in all my years, I believe that it is only Adonai who can deal with man's stubbornness and rebellion. But Adonai is a great and merciful Lord. Didn't he deal with the stubbornness of our ancestors before us? Why, their numbers must be countless as the stars in the sky! With the number of rebellious hearts our Lord has dealt with over time, surely the heart of a small troubled boy can be just as a grain of sand! Have faith! Just ask Adonai to break through the stone walls surrounding Ananiah's heart. If Y'hoshua and his army with Adonai's help can bring down the stone walls of a city[26], how much more will Adonai be able to remove the stubbornness of an eight-year old's heart? Pray for him!".

"I already have Grandfather" replied Zuriel.

"And so have I!" Obadiah said.

≈   ≈   ≈

Once again, the sound of loud hammering noises rang through the market place. A Roman centurion drove the nails into the wood securing the

---

[25]   Jeremiah 29: 11
[26]   Joshua 6 1-21

latest announcement from the governor who had decided after the latest incident, to put this abominable, arrogant, fanatical race of people in their place. Although the intentions of the Sanhedrin were primarily to protect the offending boys from the cruel and unmerciful hands of the country's captors, it seems that their decision to ascribe guilt and punishment ruffled the feathers of the governor (who must have been having a bad day).

All those in the marketplace gathered around the latest message hung on the Governor's Gate. "What does it say?" the people asked. A man got up to read the notice as the crowd began to hush. He turned to the people and related the message. "It has now been decreed by His Excellency Titus, Governor of Judea, that as from this day all actions relating to the bandit group the Deliverers will be under Roman control. Any information concerning this rebel group must be immediately reported to the centurion at the Governor's Barracks. The order is in effect immediately".

"Thank goodness the Sanhedrin intervened when they did" said one woman, "who knows what punishment those boys would have received?"

"They seem to take offense at any actions we take", replied another.

"Well I thought the Sanhedrin treated the boys justly, who knows what could have happened to them if their paths fell in the way of those terrible bandits" said another.

The topic of the boys' foolishness and their punishment had been the source of much gossip over the past few days. There was not one home in Yerushalayim which had not heard of the events of the preceding week. There was also not one person who didn't have an opinion about the way in which the situation had been resolved.

Kaleb's father Nosh witnessed what had just happened in the marketplace and overheard the conversations that followed. These were certainly difficult times not only for his family but also the Jewish race. Like many others, he longed for the coming of the Messiah so that the chains of bondage would be broken and his people could live in peace again. As he looked at the people around him, his eyes fell on Zuriel who was in the marketplace selling his grain. Walking up to Zuriel he said, "Shalom Zuriel, we don't usually see you in the marketplace".

"No", replied Zuriel, "but it is a busy time for all the family preparing for the reaping and the threshing of the next crop, so to allow as many of the family to be engaged on the farm, I help them out here at times. What can I do for you, Nosh?"

Looking deeply into Zuriel's eyes Nosh saw a man who was struggling to hide his hurt. "Zuriel" he said, "I am so sorry that our sons have taken a wayward path and that we found ourselves before the Sanhedrin as we did, but this embarrassing and awkward situation does not impede the respect and friendship I have with you. I pray you feel the same".

"Of course, I do!" exclaimed Zuriel, "but it is I who should be apologising to you, not you to me! My son Ananiah has been such a handful and I am deeply disappointed in his disrespect for Adonai. But he is my challenge and I do love him. You have been such a good friend to me Nosh and I am very grateful for this. Please let us continue to be friends no matter what our sons might throw in our way!"

Chapter Five

HARVEST AND ADVENTURE

uriel's farm was a hive of busyness. The two fields of the wheat crop as usual, matured before the barley and this meant that workers could reap and collect its harvest almost immediately before it was time to take their scythes to the barley crops. The week before had seen the last bag of flour placed in storage in the barn as the workers cleared the barn preparing this for the coming barley harvest. Now it was time for the barley to be reaped!

Three groups of ten men worked busily in three barley fields cutting the stalks of grain and removing from the bounty any weeds which were set aside to be burned. The left-over grain was then tied in bundles and taken to the threshing floor where twenty women had the arduous task of separating the grain from the chaff. To separate the mixed-up pile of grain, stalk and hush required the winnowing fork. The women would scoop the pieces of the crop and throw this up into the air. The lighter pieces of the stalk would fall to the side, while the grain, which was both heavier and roundish, fell immediately down.

Therefore, over time, there would be three distinct piles of material; the good grain which had fallen immediately down, the larger pieces of stalk or "straw" had blown away to the side and smaller pieces of the stalk known as chaff had been blown even further away[27]. The straw was set aside to be placed in sacks for fodder for horses and other farm animals. This would be sold at the markets and assisted greatly in the farm's takings. Once the grain was placed on the threshing floor, the women would stomp over the grain or an unmuzzled oxen [28] would be driven back and forth with their feet threshing out the grain. Sometimes the farms' donkeys were used in this process. Large round grain sieves were then used by the women shaking a small amount of grain until unwanted refuse was removed and the good grain came together in the centre of the sieve.

Not only were there lots of people working on the farm but many strangers as well. Keeping to the law of Adonai, the paid reapers had been instructed that they were not to glean or pick the stalks at the ends of the fields but rather they had to leave these intact so that the poorer people could gather food for themselves[29]. Nor could they glean any seed which may have fallen away as they reaped. This seed and the seed in the far end of the fields was left for poorer people who gleaned a good way behind the reapers. Everyone on the farm was very busy.

Also busy on the perimeter of the farm, was a group of nine young boys playing chasey among the bordering olive trees. Completely absorbed in the fun they were having they had not realised that they had chased one

---

[27]   www.truthortradition.com
[28]   Deuteronomy 25:4
[29]   Leviticus 19:9-10; Leviticus 23: 22

another around the entire perimeter of the farm. Happy to rest on the eastern side of the farm, not so far away from them were the daunting hills that had enticed them months before. Of the four boys who on that previous day refused to accept Ananiah's challenge and leave the farm, only one was present this day – Kaleb. All boys knew however, that they had promised their fathers that they would no longer play with Ananiah whose ways they were told, would led them on a downward path. Yet this promise had been completely overlooked by all the boys who sat in the shade of the surrounding olive trees.

Recuperating in the shade, as the soft breeze brushed across their flustered faces, the boys' eyes were drawn to the surrounding hills which once more seemed to be enticing them to have even more fun in an unfamiliar but unforgettable place.

"Weren't there lots of wonderful rocks to climb over there?" remarked one of the boys.

"So many different places to hide!" responded another.

"There really wasn't any danger there!" protested another and most of the boys agreed.

Ananiah looked around him. As both the barley and wheat fields were on the western side of the farm, most of the workers were hard at work there and the only people he could see were the gleaners and they too, were quite a distance away. "Anyone willing for a real challenge?" he asked. "Let's go and play there and have some fun climbing those rocks!" Whether it was because he had no-one to support him or whether it was because he too was intrigued by the hills in the distance, Kaleb voiced no concern over what had been suggested. The brutal and anguishing pain of the ten lashes were completely forgotten by the offending boys as were the promises made to their fathers. Caught up in the excitement of the challenge nine boys sprang up on their feet and ran quickly to the hills beckoning them from the distance.

Surprisingly it was Kaleb who was the first to reach the base of the hills. As he surveyed the surrounding rocks at the base of the hills which seemed to stretch on for miles, he understood all that had been said about this place was true. There were different sized rocks and boulders, some on top of each other, and some just beside each other widely scattered across the base of the hills behind them. Upon reaching the site, the boys immediately climbed some of the rocks and crawled between the boulders. It was so exciting finding paths across the rocks particularly when the path taken allowed the boys to gain height and lord it over their peers below.

"I think I can get to the top of that hill!" a boy shouted and immediately scaled up a steep incline and then stood on top of a hill which had a very flat top. As the others quickly climbed up to join him, the boy ran on further to yet another hill, and then another. The boys all followed him gleefully. This was such fun!

Suddenly they heard the leading boy shout "Wow! Come and look at this!"

The boys followed eagerly as they knew something exciting must have been found to promote such enthusiasm. As they grouped together on the top of another higher hill, they looked down below them. They were on the edge of a very sharp precipice and quite a steep distance below them was a narrow winding sandy valley. The valley curved its way around the surrounding hills and despite the steepness of both sides of the canyon, it seemed to go on for miles and miles.

"Wouldn't it be great to go down there!" someone said.

"I think we can", replied Ananiah. "Follow me!"

Like a colony of ants, the boys made their way carefully down the precipice holding onto vegetation growing on the slopes and placing their feet strategically on protruding small rocks on the canyon's steep side. Finally, when they reached the base of the valley, they were quite astounded.

The width of the valley was in fact quite broad even though there were parts when the valley curved, there always seemed to be a good distance between the sides of the canyon. "Oi! Can anyone hear me?" shouted Kaleb. The boys laughed as they heard his amplified voice echo around them. Then, joyfully, they all joined in making many weird and boyish sounds. Following the canyon as it meandered between the surrounding high hills, the boys felt jubilant and resilient.

Engrossed in their fun, the boys paid no attention as to the direction they were taking nor of the time that was passing. Finally, the valley appeared to come to a circular shaped cul de sac where there were many large boulders and rocks; the valley continued south ward, but the shade was cool, and they were happy to have a spell before continuing further. One of the boys started to investigate what seemed to be a narrow passage on the northern side of the valley. "Hey, come and look at this!" he shouted.

To their complete surprise and delight, there was indeed a much narrower passage which seemed to go on for a short distance. It was quite well hidden behind the escarpment that surrounded them. Perhaps it was big enough for one horse to ride through but because of their size, the smaller passage presented no problem for the boys. They all proceeded to follow the passage until finally they came to yet a large semi-circle of what seemed to be multi-storied caves. These caves were in fact burial chambers that had been carefully hewn within the surrounding rocks. Six chambers had been hewn into the stone on the left and right side approximately six feet off the ground. Then six feet above each row was another set of six chambers. In the middle, there were only three chambers six feet off the ground and above them was another set of three chambers.

The boys could not believe their luck! What a fantastic place to play! However, it was at that moment Kaleb noticed the dying embers of a recently used fire right in the centre of the cul-de-sac. Then his eyes went to the rope ladder descending from the first level of the chamber; it had carelessly been left hanging in full view for all to see. Kaleb's heart sank! "This must be where the bandits live!" he exclaimed and as fear overwhelmed him, he cried "I'm not staying here! This is too dangerous! We must go now before the bandits get back!"

"Oh Kaleb!" Ananiah groaned, "Just when I thought you were finally showing us you were not a girl in boy's clothing, you now reveal your true colours! Well, if you want to go, go! We don't play with girls! Go back and find some girls to play with! Get out of here! Go on! You're no longer welcomed here!"

Kaleb wiped away the tears which were flowing so freely from his eyes. He had enjoyed himself so much up to this point but a feeling of danger suddenly overwhelmed him and he knew he had no choice. Turning back into the narrow passage he started to run as fast as he could. His father would be very disappointed this time and Kaleb started to worry about what would happen when he got home. By the time he had reached the circular shaped cul-de-sac, he had decided he would tell his father the truth and face his punishment although the thought of ten strong lashes on his bare buttocks caused him to dread doing so. Kaleb sat down on a large rock and sobbed continuously for he realised that he was in so much trouble. It was just then he noticed something strange. There was a soft noise which seemed to get gradually louder and louder and it was if the ground was calling out to him. Placing his ear to the ground, Kaleb listened carefully.

He soon recognised the sound. Horses were being ridden down the northern side of the valley! It must be the bandits returning to their lair!

Full of fear, Kaleb hid behind a large rock. He dared not go ahead or they might find him so he decided he must remain behind the rock in the hope that they will eventually go to their camp…their camp! His friends were in such danger!

Kaleb's heart seemed to be pounding so loudly he was afraid the sound it was making could cause the bandits to find him hiding behind the rock. The pounding of the horses' hooves on the dirt soon appeared to be deafening until finally they arrived at the cul-de-sac where all the riders stopped their horses. Kaleb swore he could hear the horses breathing and if he could hear the horses breathing, surely the bandits could the pounding of his heart!

Then, one by one, the bandits rode through the narrow passage of the cul de sac. It seemed to take ages before they were all gone. Kaleb started to panic. He had to return to the place where the boys climbed down into the valley! But would he be able to find the exact spot where the boys had descended into the valley? How would he manage to ascend that steep climb? The boys helped one another going down but now he was alone and the escarpment was so precipitous. It was then he realised that if the bandits had ridden their horses through the valley, there must be an access point that is accessible for the animals to enter. All he had to do was to follow the valley back to where that entrance point would be. Once the bandits had all entered the narrow valley, Kaleb ran as fast as he could; in fact, in his young life, he had never run faster!

Caught in the moment of intrigue and adventure, the young boys eagerly explored the exciting playground before them. One boy ascended the rope ladder finding himself in one of the burial chambers. "Wow! you should see this!" he was heard to exclaim. The other boys quickly climb up the dangling ladder which was a challenging obstacle course. Alighting from the ladder, each boy found himself in a small three by one-point five meters hewn cavity laden with human bones of various shapes and sizes, all placed aside in a large heap at the side of the chamber. There were skulls, knee bones and thigh bones all collectively piled in one big heap – but none of the boys wanted to touch the bones. All they could do was peer in awe.

Another boy who found a one-point five-meter tunnel which connected the chamber they were in to another, beckoned them to see what he had found. The boys moved into the narrow tunnel and on each side, hewn into the surrounding walls were two platforms. Layered on each platform were more human bones. The tunnel extended into the next chamber where once again, there were more bones piled in a heap at the side of the cavity.

"You're not going to believe this!" called out another boy who had proceeded further along another tunnel to the chamber they were in. Excitedly the boys ran to see what caused the boy to call them. When they arrived, they were astonished to see a small flight of narrow winding stairs leading up to the next floor.

After extensive investigation, the boys had realised that they had before them a honeycomb of chambers and tunnels in which they could hide. Moreover, the tunnels on each level were designed to allow a person to proceed completely around that level from one side of the catacombs to the other. The small stairwells between the lower and higher levels were on the left and right side of the catacombs. Once you were on the lower level, you could transcend to the next level anywhere in the catacombs. The exception was in the central area of the catacombs for there was no set of stairs there. It took some time for the boys to become accustomed to the terrain.

With thirty chambers, twenty-eight tunnels and four stairwells, the catacombs proved to be a honeycomb of fabulous fun and ecstatic enjoyment.

—— *Chapter Six* ——

HELL ON EARTH

A lthough they had not been in the catacombs for long, it seemed to the boys that the time they had spent discovering the layout of the structure had taken most of the day. Entrapped in their enjoyment, they moved playfully in, through and around the structure. Never in its whole existence had such gleeful sounds echoed through its strong walls. No one, it seemed was aware of a gradually increasing thundering sound of horses' hooves or of the imminent return of the bandit gang.

When the bandits had all returned to their hideout, they did not notice at first that they had unwelcome visitors. Dismounting their horses, they made their way towards the rope ladder on the right side of the rock. It was only when the first bandit climbed up the rope, he noticed the scared, frozen face of a young boy peering at him from a chamber on the first floor in the centre of the catacombs. "We have company!" he shouted and immediately the bandits assumed battle position clenching their swords and knives.

Within minutes at least twenty of the Deliverers had scaled the rope ladder and entered the chasms and tunnels of the catacombs. Unlike the boys who had just discovered the catacombs, the bandits knew every inch of their hideout and because of their numbers, were able to search each chasm and tunnel in less than five minutes. For the young boys, there was no hope.

When the boys became aware that they were not the only people present, their hearts immediately sank. Terror filled their bodies and all they could do was attempt to hide from the bandits. It soon became apparent that they were not able to do so, when the piercing scream of a young boy shattered the silence. There was no way the boys could hide from their captors despite fleeing down steps and hiding behind piles of bones. Terror ran amok.

When Ananiah heard the first of many excruciating and agonising screams, he realised what had happened and his heart pounded with fear. The bandits took to the catacombs like hornets to their nest and from his chamber which was placed on the top of the left-hand side of the catacombs, Ananiah observed several bandits scurrilously searching the twelve chambers on the right-hand side. Without thinking, he scampered to the centre top level of the catacombs. There, he had found a small crevice in the rock behind a large pile of bones in its corner.

Ananiah's heart pounded loudly within him as he heard the bandits moving from chamber to chamber. Curling himself into the smallest ball he could, he could hear the bandits cursing and shouting directions to each other. Finally, one of the bandits was in the room where he was. Ananiah had to close his eyes for he could not bear to see the face of his discoverer. He could hear the bandit's footsteps and the loud sound of brittle bones being moved. "There's no one here!" he heard the bandit call. The sound of heavy footsteps gradually faded and Ananiah realised that the bandits were now on the left-hand side of the complex. Scurrying as fast as he could, lowering his body, Ananiah ran from chamber to chamber, stopping for a few seconds in each tunnel, peering through the chamber to the levels opposite to ensure no bandit could see him. At last he came to the stairwell. From there he dashed between the lower level tunnels as he had done before until he finally came to the first chamber with the rope providing his only exit.

Looking down on the ground below him, Ananiah could not see a bandit in sight. Scampering down the rope ladder he made it to the ground and when turning around to his complete horror, his eyes confronted the sight of a bandit mounted on his horse. There was no sympathy or mercy in the man's eyes as he raised his sword into the air and started to move his horse swiftly towards Ananiah.

It seemed barely a second had passed when Ananiah saw the whites of the man's evil eyes, piercing into his soul. Then, immediately Ananiah saw the sun reflect on the blade raised before him and heard a harrowing sound which left as quickly as it came.

≈   ≈   ≈

The families of the boys supposedly playing on Zuriel's farm became anxious when the boys did not return home for their tea. Inquiries were made from door to door in Yerushalayim, had anyone seen the boys? As night descended, Zuriel called a meeting of the boys' fathers to see if they should look for them in the morning or tell the Roman authorities. Both tasks would be difficult as no-one seemed to know where the boys were. All the fathers were anxious and fearful for their sons.

To the group's astonishment, Nosh stood at the door of the room with his young son Kaleb at his side. Kaleb's face was white and sorrowful. "It's much worse than we have thought" Nosh told them. "The boys have found their way to the bandits' hideout and the bandits returned!"

"How can this be?" asked one of the fathers. "My son promised he would not go beyond the farm, nor play with Ananiah. How could this possibly be?"

Nosh motioned to Kaleb who was still shaking and fearful to stand in front of him and tell the men what has happened. Kaleb told them what had transpired that day and as he spoke, the men's hearts began to sink within them. Kaleb told them about everything: playing chasey amidst the olive trees, the race to the hill, the climbing of the rocks and hills, the passage way, the hideout, his rejection, the horses' hooves, the long trip back through the valley, his long trek back to Yerushalayim. Each man thought to himself "All is lost!"

"I fear it is too late to search for the boys this evening", said Zuriel "but first thing in the morning, we should go to the centurion's barracks and let the authorities know what has happened. Most probably they will send out a search party to look for the boys".

"This is a dangerous and hopeless situation", one of the fathers said. "I fear it is highly unlikely that the boys will be alive and this will be a body recovery mission. I too, would like to go with the soldiers to the location of the hideout. If my son was killed there, I must bring him home". There was a consensus from the group that all the men present wanted to do the same.

The heaviness and hopelessness of the situation weighed heavily within the room. There were comments of disbelief, sadness and astonishment from within the group. Zuriel called the group to silence by saying "Brothers we should seek Adonai's guidance in this for only He is able to sustain us". As the men started to bow their heads in prayer, disbelief and amazement came upon their faces for there once again, standing in the doorway was a child – Ananiah had returned!

His whole body shaking, Ananiah mumbled to himself "Adonai has delivered me! Adonai has delivered me!"

"He calls on Adonai!" said one man. "Adonai has certainly delivered him!"

"Let the boy speak!" shouted another but the only response the group could hear were the words, "Adonai has delivered me!"

Despite many attempts by the men to gain information by multiple questions, not one was successful. Ananiah's mother Hannah who was present in the room, came forth and spoke to the group. "The child is obviously traumatised by what has happened", she said. "He needs to rest and when he wakes first thing tomorrow, we will hear from him. As you can see, we shan't get much from him tonight in this state. Let's hear what he has to say, the first thing in the morning". Hannah's loving arms embraced her son as she took him away from the group. Everyone had to wait until the morning to hear what Ananiah had to say.

Early next morning the group of fathers once more assembled in Zuriel's house. Ananiah had recuperated from the night before, and spoke clearly to the men eagerly seeking more information about the fate of their sons. Describing the events as Kaleb had the night before, Ananiah recounted what had happened the previous day. Pausing for a moment, he told them of the fear and dread that filled his heart once he knew that the bandits had returned. Ananiah told them in detail how he had managed to escape from the bandits as they searched for the boys, the horrendous cries of his friends, and his utter disbelief when he saw the bandit on his horse, with a sword raised to kill him.

"It was then I realised that I was going to die" recounted Ananiah "yet some-how I remembered the words of my great-grandfather's prayer. I quickly said the prayer several times and each time I repeated it, it sounded more believable - '*El-roi, El-roi! You delivered your people from the waves of the Red Sea and from the scorn of Egypt, deliver me, your child, for death is before me and I am doomed. Remember Your promise to Your people'.* As I repeated the prayer, I became aware of a powerful presence. Immediately, I knew in my heart that Adonai was real! He was there listening to me! A complete calmness came upon me and I have never known such peace. The last thing I remember is the sight of a shining sword descending down upon me. Then, as if I was somehow taken out of the catacombs, I found myself walking home near the hills, repeatedly saying the prayer. I could not believe that I had been rescued and I kept saying aloud 'Adonai has delivered me! Adonai has delivered me!'"

The room was silent. "Why did Adonai choose you instead of my son?" one father asked. Ananiah looked the man directly in his eyes and said, "Sir, I do not know why Adonai chose me over the other boys. What I do know is that for some reason He chose me. I am here only because Adonai delivered me!"

Once more, the room was silent.

≈　　≈　　≈

The Roman centurion and five other soldiers were standing over a detailed map of the Yerushalayim region which was sprawled across a large table. "Go and bring old Ori (My Light) here" he ordered. Old Ori was eighty-five years of age and because of his expertise and knowledge of the area, he had often been used by the soldiers in their missions around the city. All the men perused the map carefully yet they failed to determine where the hideout of the bandits could be. Only half an hour before they had been informed by the centurion in charge that they would be sent on a body recovery and if possible, a bandit execution. The mission would entail crossing the rugged surrounding hills on the eastern side of the city.

Seven of the boys' fathers together with Kaleb and Ananiah waited outside the room where the soldiers were planning a strategy to retrieve the boys' bodies. Suddenly they saw Old Ori accompanied by two Roman soldiers walk towards the room. One of the soldiers knocked on the door and the three entered. The fathers were relieved when they saw the old man for he was well known in Yerushalayim for his knowledge of the surrounding area and if their boys were to be found, Ori would be the person who would be able to accurately direct the search party.

≈   ≈   ≈

Old Ori approached the captain and glanced at the map spread out across the table. He listened intently as the captain explained the situation. Ori reported that there were two sets of catacombs in the hills; one to the north and one to the south. To determine which of the catacombs was the bandits' hideout, he needed more information. It was then that the order was given to bring in the men and the two boys.

The men and the two boys anxiously entered the room. When asked by the Roman centurion in charge about the exact location where the boys had played, both Kaleb and Ananiah stepped forward. "This is a map of the surrounding hills where you played" commented the centurion. "Show us where you think that was: here is your father's farm and here are the hills. Where did you play?"

Ananiah's fingers nervously moved from the olive trees on the side of the property towards the eastern hills, where the boys had found a precipice, the winding valley, the cul-de-sac with its hidden passage and then the catacombs. "Is this correct?" the Roman centurion demanded of Kaleb. Kaleb nodded his head.

"As I have said there are two sets of catacombs in the small valley that runs across the surrounding hills" Ori stated. "One is the southern end and one the northern end. By the boys' description I believe that the bandits were hiding in the northern catacombs. The canyon near the cul-de-sac which leads to the hideout is narrow, so if you are thinking of bringing a dray it will need to be left in the cul-de-sac. You might like to bring one or two donkeys to help in the recovery of the bodies. It might be possible that the bandits have delayed their flight from the hideout so perhaps a small legion of soldiers might be able to continue to the southern site as they may in their arrogance, believe they would be safe there".

The Roman centurion gave his orders: one small dray and a battalion of fifty soldiers on horse-back plus twelve blankets, ropes and other stores were to be ready in fifteen minutes. "I have a donkey we can use!" stated Zuriel. His comments drew a bewildered response from those present but in particular the centurion in charge, the captain. One of the soldiers whispered to the captain who looked at the beseeching faces of the fathers before him. As a father himself, he empathised with the men who were still ignorant of their children's fate. "You may come with us" he said, "but you are under my authority and must comply with my orders. Bring your donkey and remember this is a dangerous mission. Remove the two boys. They have had enough adventure to last them a life time. Meet us in the quadrangle in fifteen minutes."

Chapter Seven

AN ARDUOUS TASK

T he long train of soldiers, most of whom were mounted on horses with two driving a narrow dray drawn by two strong horses, nine anxious fathers, and a donkey trailed behind Ori who rode ahead of the group. Riding beside him was the captain. As the group made its way towards the unwelcoming hills on the eastern side of the city of Yerushalayim, Ori's eyes peered at them intently for it had been quite some time since he had travelled as a boy to the northern and southern catacombs. He hoped that he would be able to recall the entrance which would lead them into the northern passage yet he remembered the entrance was often difficult to find. Moreover, the passing years had probably ensured that the vegetation surrounding the hills may have changed, so he prayed in his heart that Adonai would assist him in finding the entrance which by now may have become completely overgrown.

Half an hour later, at the base of the hills which was completely encompassed with rocks, trees and bushes, Ori halted his horse. "This must be very close to the entrance", he thought to himself but as he surveyed the surroundings, it was now evident that the entrance had become camouflaged by the surrounding terrain. Scrutinizing the terrain even more intently, his eyes came across some odd-looking bushes. Dismounting from his horse, he walked towards these and pushing their branches aside, Ori heaved a sigh of relief. There, well hidden behind the bushes was the entrance to the valley. The bandits had cleverly left the bushes intact so that to the naked eye, the entrance to their hideout was well hidden from view.

Ori turned and signalled the captain who steered his horse towards the bush and the entrance. Summoning a soldier to come and remove the bushes, the captain signalled to the group to stop and wait. Once the bushes had been completely removed, the branches quickly hacked and cores uprooted, the party began to pass through the entrance.

Surprisingly, there was enough room for all members to travel through and as they progressed through the chasm, all the men were in awe of the steep rising cliffs on each side of the canyon as the path took them deeper into the hills. It was so much cooler in the canyon and as they were walking along, the fathers surveyed the difficult terrain of rocks and bushes on the right-hand side of the valley. They wondered how on earth vegetation could grow in such a hostile and forbidding domain. More deeply they wondered (for they just could not understand) how the boys managed to safely find their way down to the floor of the canyon with the terrain so steep and treacherous.

Half an hour later the party reached the cul-de-sac which was exactly as Ananiah and Kaleb had described it. The captain halted the group as Ori looked for the concealed passage to the hideout. It too was hidden by bushes like the first entrance. However, it didn't take as long for the bushes to be removed to reveal the concealed entrance. Leaving the train behind them, the captain, Ori and one other officer, singly rode down the narrow entrance. Upon reaching the hideout, the captain motioned to his officer to dismount and go to the fireplace in the centre of the clearing. Placing his hands on the black coals, the soldier turned to his captain and said. "There is still warmth in these embers, Sir! The bandits may not be far away!"

Ori looked at the captain. "It might be possible that the bandits have fled to the southern catacombs for if they had exited the catacombs, we would have met them in their retreat", he said. "The southern tombs are not as concealed as these, but they are nevertheless just as suitable for hiding. In their arrogance, they may believe that they are just as safe there, as they were here".

Pausing for a moment, the captain nodded his head and together with the two men he returned to the remaining group packed into the cul-de-sac where the fathers were so anxious for any news. The captain spoke to an officer "Take forty soldiers to follow Ori to the southern catacombs", he commanded. "Ten soldiers will remain here with the fathers as we search for the boys' bodies". The fathers' hearts stopped when they heard the word 'bodies' for although it seemed impossible, there was always hope that their sons may have avoided the bandits by hiding in the catacombs. Could they still be alive?

Ori and forty soldiers continued down the valley heading towards the southern end of the hills.

Ten soldiers with their captain singly rode through the narrow passage to the bandit's hideout. The captain had left orders that the dray would remain in the cul-de-sac as the passage was much too small for this to pass through. Last to enter the passage way were the fathers and the donkey; their hearts full of fear for what lay ahead.

Coming to the clearing, the group saw the surrounding hills had been hewn into catacombs and the whole structure was semi-circular in shape with two levels of chambers high above the ground. The ladder which had previously been left by the bandits was no longer there and the men wondered how the soldiers would be able to climb up the catacombs to search for the boys. The commander turned to a soldier and commanded that a rope ladder be made. One soldier who had removed the ropes and other tools from the dray before entering the narrow passage, swiftly wove the pieces of rope together and made a ladder. Winding this around his shoulders, he then mounted his horse and moved towards one of the chambers. Manoeuvring his horse close to the chamber, he then stood up erect on his horse and pulled himself up into the chamber high above the ground. Hewing two places in the rock with a spike and hammer, he secured the rope ladder and flung this over the side.

The soldiers climbed up the ladder and began searching the catacombs. As they stooped low going through the connecting tunnels, their eyes searched anxiously for any sign of life. It wasn't long before a voice was heard. "I have found one!"

"So, have I!" exclaimed another.

The soldier stared at the lifeless body of the small boy before him. Surely the child was no more than eight years old! Mercilessly the child had been stabbed in the centre of his heart and the blood that oozed out of his body completely covered the whole pile of bones on which his small body had been thrown. "What cruel and callous hands caused such an injury to an innocent boy!" he thought as he cursed the bandits feverishly.

Another soldier searching in a tunnel spied what appeared to be a tiny hand under many bones collectively stacked on the lower shelf of the crypt. Removing the bones, the soldier found the body of a boy whose throat had been slit from side to side. At least this child had been spared a painful death, he thought. His fellow-soldiers searched all levels of the catacombs, on all sides - dreading what they would find but assuming an air of indifference as Roman soldiers were reputed to have.

It seemed like an eternity to the fathers who waited patiently in the shade at the entrance to the catacombs. They could see the soldiers searching vigorously through the different levels of the catacombs. Then, when they heard that a boy had been found, their hearts dared to leap in expectation. Could it be possible for the boys to be found alive? Their eyes observed one Roman soldier scale down the ladder and run over to the captain. There seemed to be some extensive discourse before the captain finally looked towards the men who were waiting so anxiously. Walking over to the men, the captain's expressionless voice said "Two boys have been found but I am afraid they are dead. As my men bring each one down, if you could identify if the body is your son's, I will have one of my men take the body to the dray using the donkey".

"If you please", ventured Zuriel, "I will lead the donkey out of the passage. I know how to handle him as he can be stubborn. Perhaps each boy's father can accompany me as the child is removed to the dray".

Nosh replied, "I too shall go with the first father and remain with him at the dray so that the fathers can have someone with them as they mourn their sons".

"These pesky Jewish rabbles!" thought the captain to himself, "Just who do they think is in control here?"

One quick nod of the head indicated the captain approved the notion. The sight that confronted his men and the gruesome reports of the children's injuries should be kept well away from a father's eyes. As soon as all the bodies of the children had been found, they could all leave this godforsaken place; its air was cumbersome and unpleasant.

The fathers watched as two soldiers from one of the lower chambers lowered a small body, swaddled in a blanket from head to toe, slowly to the ground. Using two ropes, the body was gently lowered until it came to the arms of a waiting soldier. Holding the bundle tightly in his arms, he waited for another soldier to untie the two ropes secured around both ends of the wrapped body. Once the ropes were loosened, the soldier walked over to the group of fathers whose hearts were barely beating. When he reached the men, one of the fathers nervously peeled back the blanket to reveal the boy's face. One of the fathers gasped. "That's my son!"

Zuriel gently took the wrapped body from the soldier who then returned to the catacombs to continue the search. After securing the boy's body on the donkey, Zuriel, Nosh and the boy's father who was now in tears, made their way back to the dray. Although it wasn't far, it seemed like an eternity as the men and the donkey, escorted the child away from the place where his life had so cruelly been taken.

Lifting the body reverently from the donkey, Zuriel placed the child in the narrow dray. The father entered the dray and attempted to unwrap the blanket so that he could hold his son's hands for the last time. Nosh quickly called out, "Do not touch his body lest you become defiled!"[30] With large sobs, the father fondled the outline of his child's body and pressed his hand into what he thought was the lifeless hand of his son. In silence, Nosh went up to the father and placed his hand on the man's shoulder. Any words of comfort were suppressed by the overwhelming sadness of the tragedy. Wretchedly there are times when words provide no comfort at all.

After returning to the open area of the catacombs, Zuriel saw a second body being lowered to the waiting arms of another soldier who then brought the wrapped body over to the waiting fathers. A gasp of horror revealed the identity of the child, whose body was gently placed and secured on the donkey. Zuriel embraced the mourning father and brought

---

[30] Numbers 19:11-13

him to the donkey and they then proceeded through the narrow passage to the dray in the cul-de-sac.

The fathers watched as they saw the soldiers relentlessly searching for the boys on the various levels. Meticulous in their searching, for many chambers were searched more than once, the soldiers never seemed to stop in any one place at any time. Little did they know what was transpiring.

Suddenly, a soldier climbed down the ladder and walked quickly towards the captain. Both the captain and the soldier were in deep conversation but the men were unable to hear what the discourse was about.

"Captain", the soldier said, "we have found the decapitated body of a young boy but despite five of us searching throughout the tombs, we have been unable to find his head!"

"Such bastardry!" replied the captain. "I refuse to ask a father to identify his son's headless body! Keep the body well-hidden and then, after all the other children have been identified, bring the body out as the final corpse. Make sure it is bound completely so that the father cannot see the life-less remnants of his son". The soldier bowed his head and placed his right hand across his chest. Then he went back to the ladder to do what he had been ordered.

Not long after this, two soldiers began to lower the wrapped body of another child down into the arms of an awaiting soldier. Bringing this over to the men, a father tentatively pulled the covering aside. "It's Jaden!" cried one father. Once again, Zuriel who had returned from the dray with his donkey, gently laid the corpse across the donkey's back. Jaden's father, numbed with grief, placed his hand securely on his son's swaddled body as the donkey moved through the small passage.

Once again, while the group of anxious awaiting fathers grew smaller as boys' bodies were found, the soldiers continued their search. At this point, four bodies had been placed in the dray and the fathers believed that three bodies remained. A soldier came down the ladder and moved quickly toward the captain. Once again, a deep conversation took place unheard by the watching fathers.

"Captain", the soldier reported, "we have found another headless body!" "Is there anything on either body that may help us with the identification? Search the two bodies carefully and let me know" ordered the captain.

Returning quickly to the ladder the soldier scaled it swiftly and disappeared into the catacombs. Not long afterwards, another soldier descended the ladder and moved across to the captain. "We did find this on one of the beheaded bodies, Sir", he said. There, in his hand, was a small brown shema bracelet with the words 'Adonai is my Protector' delicately sewn around its outer side. The captain nodded and commanded that the bracelet be shown to the remaining fathers. Going over to the small group of men, the soldier asked if anyone recognised the bracelet. "It's my son's! My wife made it for his last birthday!" a father cried.

The soldier gave the bracelet to the bereaved father and returned quickly to the captain. "Bring down the body of the boy who owned the bracelet" he commanded. "Make sure it is wrapped tightly and bound. Ensure that it looks like a whole body". Nodding his head, the soldier placed his right hand across his chest and went up the ladder.

Moving towards one of the tunnels, he relayed the captain's demands to another soldier who was starting to wrap the headless body in a blanket. That soldier questioned how it could be possible to make this misshapen body look like a complete body. The other soldier seizing a small nearby stone the size of a human head, placed it on top of the child's body. Immediately, the other soldier discarded it quickly and reaching across to nearby pile of bones, picked up a small skull and placed this on top of the body where the boy's head should be. Once the body had been wrapped in a blanket and secured tightly with ropes, it was taken to a chamber where it was lowered down.

Calling to two nearby soldiers the captain gave instructions for them to accompany the father and Zuriel to the cul-de-sac and remain there until all the bodies had been recovered. He insisted that no father see the butchered body of his son and the soldiers were to make sure that all the children's bodies were kept wrapped in the dray.

By noon, five small bodies lay still in the dray in the cul-de-sac. The hot sun beamed down on the fathers who remained near by stunned and traumatized by the sight before them. One of the soldiers realising he was thirsty grabbed his water bottle, a leather container filled with watered down wine, and took a swig. Glancing across the cul-de-sac he saw the grieving fathers and realised that these men had, for the whole day, been without any food or drink and so he walked over to them offering them his water container. At first the men and the fellow officer stared in disbelief that a Roman soldier could offer anyone such compassion. Encouraged by the soldier, each father gratefully took a swig from the bottle. Their parched lips were refreshed, but their bodies remained numb.

Just then, the sixth body wrapped securely in a blanket was lowered down to the ground. Immediately the captain summoned a soldier still searching in the catacombs. When he stood in front of the captain, he was given the order. "Bring down the unidentified body now. His poor father should not have to bear anymore anxiety and pain". Saluting his captain, the soldier returned to the ladder and after a few minutes brought the final body to the chamber to be lowered down. Once again, the soldiers had ensured that the body appeared to be intact. Just as before, the blanket was wrapped around the body and tightly secured with ropes.

It was a solemn and silent trip back through the ravine and the only sounds that could be heard were the sound of the horses' hooves on the dry ground of the cavern and the creaking wheels of the dray. The captain leading the group reflected on his many years of service in the Roman army and despite many brutal battles before, this, he believed was one of the most gruesome operations he had undertaken. He had seen many cruel and brutal actions over the years both in his own regiments and by his enemies, but surely, the bastardry and cowardice of the monstrous, merciless murder of these seven innocent boys, must be the harshest memory of all.

Chapter Eight

A TIME TO MOURN

I t was not until the small party had exited the passage and was making its way back to Yerushalayim that the captain turned around and noticed a small speck behind him in the distance. Stopping to see what this was, he signalled the group to keep moving. Peering intently, he saw the form of several men on horses and realised that this was the rest of the battalion who had been sent to the southern catacombs in the hope of capturing the bandits. As he tried to estimate the number of horses in the distance, he saw one soldier galloping towards him.

Several minutes later, a wounded soldier was reporting back to his captain. Despite the blood trickling down from his head and several open wounds on his body, the soldier began: "Sir, we found the bandits hiding in the southern catacombs as Ori suspected. We had a long confrontation with them until they finally surrendered to us. Five of the bandits were killed and twenty-one of the group were taken prisoners. We suffered no fatalities, Sir, though a few of us have the battle scars to prove they did not surrender willingly. Ori was hurt but it is not serious. He insisted Sir, that he would help us fight the bandits. We were going to slaughter their animals but decided to use these to bring the remaining bandits back to Yerushalayim to face their punishment, as well as those who were killed in the battle".

"Good move!" replied the captain, "When the men have returned to the barracks, make sure that the bandits' horses are not killed but sold. The money received for all the horses you have captured must be equally divided and given to the families of the seven boys whose bodies we have retrieved. Ensure each man in the operation today receives a double portion of rum tonight!"

The messenger saluted the captain and then returned to his company. The captain rode on to catch up with the company of soldiers ahead of him. Riding up to the group of fathers who were at the back of the train, he told them that the murderers of their sons had been captured; some of whom had already been killed by his battalion. When one father asked if the remaining bandits would be hanged as punishment for their atrocious crimes, the captain immediately replied, "Hanging's too good for those bastards! They should be crucified!"

≈   ≈   ≈

The small group entered the city gates on the eastern side of the city. News of the boys and their failure to return home the night before had spread quickly through the city and the fate of the boys was on everyone's lips both in the streets and at the market place. There was a solemn air to the procession as it moved through the cobbled streets of the city. People on the sides of the streets stared at the small league of soldiers and when they saw the sight of the dray and the neatly wrapped bodies placed side by side, there were quiet gasps from the crowds. It seemed that the prayers of the people had not been heard; the boys were returning but not in the way the people hoped.

As the group passed by the market place, a solemn hush grew over the area as traders and buyers turned to watch the passing procession. The gasps which had greeted the group were repeated and often these were followed by long cries of anguish from the women folk. The wailing of women, children and men accompanied the procession to the barracks. Outside the barracks, waited the mothers of the boys who failed to come home safely. When they saw the load in the narrow dray and the agonising faces of their husbands walking behind the dray, the women knew that the worst had happened.

After entering the barracks the group moved towards a large building and was brought to a halt. The fathers were told by a soldier to stay where they were while the rest of the soldiers on horses rode to the nearby stables. "We must bury our sons as quickly as possible" the fathers lamented. Immediately Nosh stepped up onto the dray and spoke to the men.

"My dear brothers" he began, "Our law states that our dead must be buried right away[31] and should not be left overnight to await their burial. Our sons have been cruelly and mercilessly abandoned by their murderers for one whole night but this was not our fault. It is, therefore, most crucial to have your sons prepared for their burial immediately. Our law also states that anyone who touches a dead body must be set apart, be cleansed and return to their families on the seventh day. It is most important that you bury your sons into the earth from which they came[32] and grieve their passing with your wives and families. Therefore, Zuriel and I, who have been with your sons all day will prepare them for their *Taharah* (purification) on

---

[31] Acts 5:1-10
[32] Genesis 3:19

your behalf. All we ask is that you provide us with oil and perfume, nard and myrrh, graveclothes, sudariums (face burial cloths), shrouds, candles – all the things we need to do right by your sons. Zuriel and I will stay with the boys so that they will not be left alone[33]. We shall work as thoroughly as we can and Adonai willing, you can come and take your sons once we have prepared them".

Just as Nosh was speaking, a soldier returning from the stable, walked up to the men. He informed them that the captain would allow them to use the long room in the building next to them to prepare the bodies for interment. As he was speaking, another soldier came up and unlocked the door of the building next to them. Once in the room he lit the many candles on the surrounding walls. As he was doing so, soldiers brought in seven large jars of water which were placed alongside a wall. There was a large table in the middle of the room. On this, were two large wash basins and a jug. One soldier motioned the men to enter the room and as Nosh and Zuriel looked around them, they realised that they must start their preparations immediately.

"But Nosh" responded Zuriel, "how will we know which boy is which?"

Nosh replied, "I remembered each boy's name in the order they came to the dray. Unbeknown to each father I took seven stems from a wild bramble bush and carefully removed the thorns from each stem until I had seven stems with a specific number of thorns. So, when the first body came, I placed the bramble stem which only had one thorn into the blankets' folds: likewise, for the second which had two thorns, and so one. The boys' names and the order in which they were brought to the dray have been etched into my brain".

---

[33]   www.jfedgmw.org

Just as they were speaking, some soldiers carried in the corpses and placed these on the floor. In a short time, there was a line of seven wrapped blankets and Zuriel and Nosh began their work. Gently folding each blanket back, Nosh removed the bramble stick he had concealed on the child's body without the father knowing. Finding the number of thorns on each bramble stem, the men then placed the bodies in their order of discovery. The bramble bush sticks were then carefully placed above each head.

≈   ≈   ≈

The battalion of soldiers who had fought and captured the bandits made a particular point by returning them to the western gates of the city. Before the gates was the unquarried, cold terrain of Mount Gulgolta (Golgotha) – a small barren hill of stone quite close to the place where thieves, murderers and bandits were crucified. Then, as they entered the city by the western gate, the people in the street stopped and watched the procession of horses with the soldiers, the captured outlaws, and the dead bandits laid across their horses move through the cobbled streets of the city. Once more, the only sound in the streets was the horses' hooves treading the cobbled stones. Occasionally, when the people realised that these were the bandits that had wreaked havoc and mercilessly murdered and plundered innocent people, there were blasphemous shouts, insults and curses hurled at the Deliverers.

The insults and abuse that were thrown at the outlaws as they moved through the city seemed to have little to no effect as the group of bandits sternly gazed ahead as the procession moved towards the barracks. Their faces reflected the coldest of hearts, un-affected by any human sentiment or women's tears. But it was the leader of the group who appeared the most arrogant. Nothing this rabble of Yerushalayim could throw at him would cause him to show any form of timidity or weakness. That was, until the procession passed through the gates of the barracks.

Standing alongside the gates was a large crowd of men, women and children and it was there, in the midst of this huge crowd a pair of haunting blue eyes of a young boy caught his attention. The rebel leader's eyes were transfixed on the child as he realised that this was the child he thought he had slaughtered! A chill went through his whole body as he recalled riding up to the blue-eyed boy in the compound, raising his sword and viciously bringing this down only to find the boy had disappeared. How could this be the boy? Perhaps it had not been his imagination! He stared in disbelief at the boy as the procession moved into the barracks. Fixated on the sight of the boy, the leader received a brutal blow from an accompanying soldier. "No use you looking backwards you atrocious rebel when you have an execution to look forward to!" the soldier shouted.

≈ ≈ ≈

Nosh and Zuriel looked at the row of shrouded bodies lying across the floor. Each now had a candle above its head and the bramble sticks removed.

It had been an arduous task which the two men had faithfully completed. Ensuring that each body was washed, oiled and wrapped according to their Jewish traditions, the men worked swiftly but reverently giving each boy the love and respect required.

There were two incidences that startled the men in their ritual preparations. When the fifth body was lifted, placed on the table and unwrapped, a large sound was heard on the hall's floor. As Nosh looked down to see what had fallen, to his surprise was a small human skull. In disbelief, he revealed the skull to Zuriel who then peeled back the blanket to reveal that the body before them was completely headless. The men swooned as they realised what had happened to the boy and immediately understood why the soldiers wanted to mask this horror from the boy's father.

Nosh asked what they should do with the skull – should it be placed back on the body, or should it be discarded? The men concluded that as it had been previously kissed, washed and purified with oil, the skull was not unclean and should therefore accompany the body as it was presented to the father a few hours before. To the men's complete horror, this was not the only body which had been so viciously treated. Nevertheless, the white shrouds tightly bound and lying neatly on the floor and the candles flickering above each head, indicated that now the boys were at peace.

_____ *Chapter Nine* _____

A LONG JOURNEY
BEGINS

B usily preparing the family meal, Hannah was surprised to hear loud knocking on the front door of the house. As she opened the door, there standing before her were seven men, their faces stern, like flint.

"What is it that you want?" she asked.

"We have come from the Sanhedrin" the men replied. "May we come in?"

Hannah had just begun to open the door further so that the men could enter the house, when they briskly brushed past her. When they were all in the front room of the house a spokesperson for the group informed Hannah that they wanted to speak with the boy who had been saved by Adonai during the recent catastrophe.

"But his father is still in the process of purification!" Hannah protested "and he cannot be with the boy when you cross examine him!"

"We are not here to cross examine the boy! We are here to hear what took place", the spokesperson claimed.

"The boy should not talk to you without his father being present" Hannah insisted.

"I will be by the boys' side" offered Obadiah who was also present in the room. "Call the boy so that he can share with our brothers the wonderful thing Adonai so magnificently has done".

Hannah went and brought Ananiah to the group of men assembled in their home.

"Come over here and stand by me" Obadiah said to his great-grandson, "and share with these good people from the Sanhedrin what took place when Adonai delivered you from your recent peril". Ananiah went and stood confidently by his great-grandfather. Although he had repeated the tale many times during the past few days, he never tired of sharing the wonder he had experienced in the realization that Adonai was real and not a figment of his imagination. Moreover, how wonderful it was to be assured Adonai truly loved him.

Word by word Ananiah recounted the tale of what had transpired that fatal day in the catacombs. Listening intently, the men were amazed that when the boy talked about Adonai, he spoke so passionately. They were impressed how the child's voice, so unquivering, confidently shared with them the miraculous response of his great-grandfather's prayer. For two hours, the men asked many questions and Ananiah answered them clearly and directly. Finally, the spokesperson concluded: "Adonai is indeed great! And in His mercy, He has looked upon you favourably, Ananiah. You have been well and truly blessed! Adonai must have a great and wonderful task for you in His Plan. May you complete this with your whole heart and soul!" Then the men left the house.

It didn't take long for the news of the men's visit to circulate through the homes of the people who lived in Yerushalayim and it soon became acknowledged by many that this was a miracle performed only by the Hand of Adonai. Because of the stories circulating, Ananiah was soon identified as the boy "whom Adonai saved". Whenever he was sighted, in the marketplace or synagogue, people gazed at him from a distance and wondered why it was this boy over all the others who were at the catacombs that day, Adonai chose to bless.

There were others, particularly those who sons had previously suffered at the sadistic hands of Ananiah, who wondered how such a child known for his bullying and cruelty could find such forgiveness in Adonai's eyes. Some of these men and their sons chose to reserve their judgement about the complete and dramatic change in Ananiah's behaviour. Yet the boy's demeanour, his attitude and outlook on others but more importantly his love of Adonai, totally surprised them all.

One day, while he was in the marketplace, helping his family sell bags of grain from the latest harvest, a familiar face came up to him. "Shalom Ananiah!", Kaleb said. "I have longed to tell you that I am so grateful that Adonai graciously saved you that day when we were at the catacombs."

"As He did you!" responded Ananiah. "I, too, am thankful for this. O Kaleb! I have had much to ponder over the last week or so, and I am so sorry for all the terrible things I have said and done to you! Please forgive me!"

Kaleb smiled as he responded. "Ananiah, if Adonai has so graciously forgiven you all your sins, and let's face it, they are many, who am I not to forgive you for just a few?"

It was from that moment that the boys became the best of friends.

≈   ≈   ≈

Obadiah and Zuriel sat on the front porch of the house discussing the bounty of the recent harvest as they watched the receding sun in the colourful red and gold evening sky. Zuriel's youngest son Bogdan (Given by God), aged two was seated at the feet of his great-grandfather contently playing with blocks of crudely shaped wood. Some of the blocks were larger than others; all were off cuts from a carpenter's floor. While they were talking Ananiah came out of the house and sat down on the floor of the porch. "And how has your day been, Ananiah?" his father asked.

"Just fine" replied Ananiah gazing at the picturesque sunset before him. "Oh my!" he exclaimed. "Isn't that a marvellous scene!"

"Yes" responded his great-grandfather, "Adonai's creation is a beautiful thing!" Pausing a moment, his eyes still fixed on the dusk scene before him, Ananiah thought to himself how differently he perceived the world since that day Adonai rescued him from certain death. His heart had been so deeply touched that whenever the thought of there being a higher deity interested in him; this cheered him to his very soul.

His father Zuriel then commented, "It's almost as if creation is celebrating the Messiah's coming! Do you think he could be coming tomorrow?" Obadiah laughed and commented that wouldn't it be wonderful if he did. His attention captivated, Ananiah eagerly asked his great-grandfather who was the Messiah they were talking about. His question caught his father's attention as Zuriel glanced across to Obadiah. There was a slight smile on Obadiah's face as he recalled to his great-grandson, the promise and hope of his people.

Obadiah explained that Adonai has always loved his creation, right from the beginning of time. Yet the stubborn heart of man has resulted in much rebellion against His Words and Laws. Once man had betrayed Him in the Garden of Eden, Adonai promised that He would send a Messiah, someone who would help us overcome the Adversary (Satan)[34]. Despite man's continued resistance and rebellion against Adonai, He vowed that the Messiah who would be an offspring of Avraham (Abraham)[35], Yatz'chak (Isaac)[36] and Ya'akov (Jacob)[37]. Moreover, this Messiah would be heir to King David's throne[38] and because of this, when he came to save Isra'el from its enemies, he would establish his kingly throne and reign forever; bringing the peace to the people of Isra'el sought and longed for over many, many years.

"We firmly believe" continued Obadiah, "that these promises are so special, we have called them our 'Dabar Promises'".

"But what do you mean by 'Dabar Promises'?" inquired Ananiah.

His father then continued. "'Dabar' comes from an ancient Hebrew word which specifically identifies that when Our Living God speaks, the very words that directly proceed forth from His mouth also have life and therefore, because of their source, they are extremely powerful. So authoritative are these living words, that like Their speaker, they have height, breadth and great substance (volume). But more importantly, they have purpose[39]. So powerful are the spoken words of Adonai they powerfully permeate throughout creation, touching and affecting lives of those they touch, returning to their initiator in absolute and perfect accomplishment.

While the human ear can hear someone repeat Adonai's words and the human eye can see them written down on parchment, it is only with your spiritual ear you can hear and fully understand what the Lord is saying. The

---

[34]   Genesis 3:15
[35]   Genesis 12:1-3
[36]   Genesis 17: 7
[37]   Genesis 46:1-3; Numbers 24:17
[38]   2Sam 7:12-13
[39]   Isaiah 55:10-11

scripture tells us that Adonai is Spirit[40] and we believe this why we need spiritual ears to understand what he is saying".

"But where do we find these Dabar Promises?" asked Ananiah. His father continued by telling him that in the Tanakh, there were many recorded words of Adonai. For example, in the Torah were five books of Moshe (Moses), B'Resheet (Genesis), Sh'Mot (Exodus), Vayikra (Leviticus), B'Midbar (Numbers) and D'Varim (Deuteronomy). When scribing over the years, Obadiah, Uriah and Zuriel had come across some of the Dabar Promises in these old writings. Likewise, in the writings of early and later prophets, the menfolk had encountered what they believed were promises though many times they were not sure as to what exactly the promises meant.

They were however inwardly convinced that in His promises, Adonai was telling His people that there was much more involved in the Messiah's coming and that the reasons for His coming were far deeper than man could comprehend. Many times, when seeking wisdom and clarification from the leading scribes and teachers, family members scribing were often harshly rebuked for their perceived foolishness. Often they were ridiculed publicly by the leaders for attempting to comprehend what Adonai meant only for the men in 'higher positions' to understand. Because of this, the men found it difficult to share their findings with others.

Eagerly Ananiah asked "What exactly is believed about the coming Messiah?"

Obadiah told Ananiah that the Messiah would be born of a virgin[41], in Bethlehem[42], from the line of David, Avraham, Yatz'chak and Ya'akov. He

---

[40] Genesis 1:2; John 4:24
[41] Isaiah 7:14
[42] Micah 5:2

would be formed in the womb and it was believed that he could be called a Nazarene.

It was also believed that the Messiah would ride into Yerushalayim[43] where He would establish His own kingdom where He shall rule mightily[44]. Defeating Isra'el's enemies[45], He would rule with an iron sceptre[46] and all people would bow down before Isra'el[47]; not only would Gentiles bow before Him but also all people of the world, Adonai's own creation. World peace would exist in this kingdom[48] and men would enjoy long lives[49] with no sorrow or mourning[50]. In fact, even the wild animals would be tamed[51]; can you imagine the lion lying down with the lamb! Yerushalayim and Isra'el would rise to great prominence in the world[52] and the knowledge of Adonai would be worldwide[53].

Ananiah's heart beat loudly as his great-grandfather related the promises to Adonai's people and they seemed to resound more loudly when Zuriel turned to his son and said "What Adonai has taught us over the years, as we have faithfully studied and transcribed His Word, is that there are some important aspects we need to know. For example, my father Uriel found that even the gentiles will seek the Messiah and He will be their light too[54]. Now you know that many gentiles worship Adonai in the Temple today but isn't it amazing that Adonai delights in them seeking Him, too? You

---

[43]   Zechariah 9:9
[44]   Isaiah 9:6-7
[45]   Isaiah 9:4; Isaiah 61:8
[46]   Psalm 2:9; Numbers 24:17
[47]   Isaiah 49:23
[48]   Isaiah 9:7
[49]   Isaiah 65:20
[50]   Isaiah 60:20
[51]   Isaiah 11: 6-9; Isaiah 65:25
[52]   Micah 4:1-2
[53]   Zechariah 14:16
[54]   Isaiah 42:6; Hosea 2:23

also received His mercy when He saved you from the rebels. The grace He showed to you reflects how great His mercy and love is".

"That is so true", Ananiah thought to himself. He always knew he was a stubborn and rebellious child and yet after being saved, he felt as if the strong arms that safely delivered him were still securely wrapped around him. He knew that Adonai was so strong, Adonai would never let go of his hand. Ananiah firmly believed that Adonai's great mercy and love, though totally underserved, was unconditional.

Silence fell upon the three as they each reflected upon the passing conversation. Bogdan continued playing with his blocks unaware of those around him. Then, Zuriel's face grew stern.

"Just the other day", continued Zuriel "I came across a passage that deeply troubled me. I have come across the phrase so many times and it never seemed to leap out before me. But the other day it did".

"What phrase are you talking about?" inquired Obadiah.

"Remnant!" replied Zuriel.

"Remnant of Isra'el!" said Obadiah. "Yes, that is scattered throughout the Tanakh. But why should that cause you concern?"

"I found a section written by Yesha'yahu (Isaiah)" continued Zuriel, "which clearly states that Adonai will restore the faithful remnant of Isra'el[55]. But then I told myself a remnant is only a portion and not the whole of Isra'el! And furthermore, just how big will that remnant be?"

"Well, a remnant is just a part!" Obadiah interrupted.

"But is that part large or small?" asked Zuriel.

Zuriel continued – his voice more emphatic and anxious. "It troubles me that even after the miraculous parting of the Red Sea with the waves as walls around them[56], the people passed through safely and even with

---

[55]   Isaiah 10:20-21
[56]   Exodus 14:21

the cloudy pillar of Adonai surrounding them day and night[57], knowing they were encamped in the strong arms of Adonai, yet they stupidly made an idol to nothing and worshipped it![58] I mean, Adonai was with them; surrounding them, and yet they did not see or even acknowledge this. And moreover, they broke the very first commandment![59]"

"Will it be that when the Messiah comes, our people's hearts will be like their predecessors and will they stubbornly refuse to see the Messiah for who he really is? How terrible it will be if it is just a small remnant that remains faithful. This makes me fearful that the people might be stubborn as they have been in the past and fail to recognise the Messiah when He comes[60]. I dread to think of what evil things they might do in their rebellion!"

"What might they do?" asked Ananiah. The two older men shook their heads.

"Who are we to determine the size of the remnant that is to remain? Man's heart has always been stubborn" replied Obadiah, "So what we must do is make sure all our kin are aware of the Tanakh and what it says about the Messiah. We must never let our children's minds be closed but always opened so that they may see the handiwork and purpose of Adonai".

"I would love to be able to read the word of the Lord" said Ananiah. "Do you think I would be able to come and see what you do each day, Father? Would I be able to come, see and touch the parchments on which Adonai's laws are written?" Zuriel's heart rose in excitement. He never thought that such a request would ever come from his eldest son's lips, but Adonai is faithful, and his son's request was a wonderful answer to his

---

[57] Exodus 13:21-22; Exodus 14: 18-20
[58] Exodus 32:4,8
[59] Exodus 20: 1-4
[60] Isaiah 6:10

prayers. Obadiah was also thankful; from this request he knew in his heart that there would be yet another generation of his family who would undertake the duties of a scribe and fulfil the promises he had made to Adonai so many years ago.

The sound of clinking and falling blocks resonated on the floor of the porch. Bogdan played on, captivated by the task of tower building but oblivious to the conversations that were taking place. Leaning forward, Obadiah bent down and picked up a small cube discarded by the young builder and spoke to Ananiah.

"Take this cube" he told his great-grandson "and remember that it symbolises the Dabar Promises about the coming Messiah the Lord is showing us. Our words are futile. We speak them, they last but a moment, and after this they are no more. But Adonai's words are far greater. As they come from Adonai's mouth, His words breathe life and power. He has told us His words will never return to him void but they will accomplish exactly what He desires and achieve their purpose[61]. Therefore, His words are so much powerful and deeper than ours".

Turning the cube in his fingers Obadiah explained: "Like Adonai's words which have many meanings, levels and facets, this block with its area, volume, width and depth reminds us of the complexity of His words. As the block's width and breadth combine with its heights to give us its volume, so too has Adonai carefully linked his promises together to solidify and perfect His will. To man these promises are complex and unconnected. But Adonai, in His infinite greatness has structured each one carefully in its place, and he has unified them altogether for His own purpose".

Handing the small block to Ananiah, Obadiah continued "Some of the Dabar Promises we already know relate to the restoration of Isra'el to

---

[61] Isaiah 55:11

Adonai; some others relate to the genealogy of the Messiah, and we are still discovering others which we find difficult to place in Adonai's plan. Pass this block onto your children who Lord willing, may also be able to study His word and follow His path. With each generation of scribing, may Adonai graciously give to each wisdom and knowledge of His complete and perfect plan. Then, when all sides are revealed with His purposes, your family, and their families to come, will know that Adonai is always faithful and what He has promised to do, He will do".

Ananiah took the small cube from his grandfather's hand and from that day on, he kept it in his chabit (purse) tied to his belt.

PART TWO

A DIFFERENT PATH

—— *Chapter Ten* ——

A VERY LONG DAY

On the day after the Sabbath, Ananiah woke early his heart full of excitement for the approaching day. His father had success-fully asked if Ananiah might be able to observe the day of a scribe, and the elders firmly believing that Adonai had a special purpose for this child, gave their consent. Both Obadiah and Zuriel had spoken at length to the boy about what would be required and rather than the boy repeatedly asking questions during the day, the day's whole ritual was clearly revealed to him.

As scribing was a means of serving Adonai during the day there would be times of complete silence. Zuriel knew that for a boy who loves to ask endless questions, this might prove difficult in the boy's eagerness to learn more about his God. So, each of the day's activities was fully explained and as Ananiah heard the purpose and the requirements for each duty, his heart beat excitedly. Surprisingly, the silence required in some of the tasks did not deter him. What made him most excited of all, was that while he was observing and joining in with others, he would be worshipping Adonai and serving Him. He was so eager to do this and the day would provide him with such a wonderful opportunity for him to do so.

As they made their way to the Baths, which were located close to the Synagogue, both Zuriel and his son walked briskly along the old city's streets. His mother had insisted that he leave his chabit at home as his tunic was unfastened, Ananiah kept in step with his father who re-iterated key instructions along the way: 1) Don't interrupt anyone working; 2) Speak in a soft voice; 3) Remember your tasks are an act of service; 4) Speak only when spoken to and 5) All questions will be answered at home tonight. It wasn't long before they came to a set of steps which led down into a narrow passageway under the street. The passageway was lit with oil lamps along the right-hand side of the wall and Ananiah had to adjust his eyes to the darkness as they made their way downwards.

Coming to a medium sized room there were several men undressing, removing their clothes and placing these into a large wicker basket situated in the centre of the room. There were a few words of greeting spoken between those present but that was all that was said. There were also a few stares at the young boy whose presence was unusual at the bath which was specifically available for priests, scribes, Pharisees and Sadducees and others who served in both the Synagogue and the Temple. Ananiah chuckled to himself (and almost found it difficult to do this quietly) at the odd shapes and sizes of the bare buttocks before him but maintaining his composure he disrobed and placed his clothing into the large wicker basket. He also realised why his mother had insisted that he not take his chabit with him that morning for surely it would have to be discarded and its contents – that little precious cube his great grandfather had given him would have gone forever. Walking along side of his father, he proceeded through the door on the other side of the room which led into the Mikveh (bath).

The Mikveh was approximately three by four metres in its perimeter and the water was provided by a local warm underground spring which made it pleasant to use in the colder months as well as the warmer. Several oil lamps lighted the area and the baths had a cleansing yet soothing atmosphere. Ananiah noticed, just as his father and great-grandfather had told him, the men entered the water using the left-hand side of the descending steps. The men in the bath who had completed their bathing ritual ascended the steps on the other side. As he descended into the water by his father's side, he remembered his great-grandfather's words: "Go down sinful; come up cleansed!"

Following his father's previous instructions and noticing how his father completed the cleansing process, Ananiah prepared himself for purification in the warm water. Then, following his father, he came out of the bath on the alternative side of the entrance steps and picked up a clean towel from a large stack neatly placed on a bench at the back wall of the bath. Wrapping the towel around their waists, the two walked into a room where there were rows of clean clothes, neatly stacked on tables surrounding the walls.

Towelling themselves dry, they then walked towards the clothes on the surrounding tables. Zuriel looked through the clothes and found something for his son to wear. Of course, the men who came to these baths were all different shapes and sizes but no one had been as small as Ananiah. Finding the nearest size suitable for his son, Zuriel handed Ananiah clothing which he could wear. While he was dressing in a garment (which still was very over-sized), Ananiah realised that this was the reason his father would come home from scribing in clothing that was different to the clothing he wore that morning. He also remembered his father telling him, that everything body, soul and mind, must be clean before Adonai when scribing and he knew that while the body had been cleaned with new unblemished clothing on his body, it was now time for his soul and mind to be purified.

Moving with his father through an open door in the dressing room, Ananiah went up a flight of seven steps and entered a large room which had several small rugs placed upon its floor. Once again, the room was alight with oil lamps placed on the surrounding walls and the men who had preceded them into the baths were bowing on the mats and praying- sometimes aloud and sometimes to themselves. There were other men present as well doing the same – praying to their God.

Going to a mat at the back of the room where he had a clear view of his father, Ananiah bowed his knees. Some of the men assumed a similar position whilst others lay prostrated on their mats. Words of blessing and adoration often were heard as each man talked to his God. At one stage, several voices called out in worship: "Elohim (God's power and might)[62]", "Adonai (Lord)[63]", Jehovah-Adonai (God's Salvation)[64]", "Jehovah-Shammah (The Lord who is present)[65]", "Jehovah-Rapha (The Lord our healer)[66]", "El-Elyon (the Most-High God)[67]", "El-Shaddai (God Almighty)"[68] and "El-olam (The everlasting God)[69]". At first this greatly confused Ananiah but then he remembered his great-grandfather telling him that the God who had so graciously saved him from death, was such a great God who can do great and mighty acts. It was not surprising therefore, that He should have many names.

A spirit of peace and joy filled the room. Sometime later, the two large wooden doors on the eastern side of the room opened widely and when this happened, the group ceased their prayers. Rising quietly the men stood

---

[62] 2 Samuel 7:20 (Complete Jewish Bible)
[63] Malachi 1:6 (CJBible)
[64] www.smilegodlovesyou.org; Isaiah 12:2 (CJB)
[65] Ezekiel 48:35 (CJB)
[66] Exodus 15:26 (CJB)
[67] Genesis 14:17-20 (CJB)
[68] Genesis 35:11(CJB)
[69] Isaiah 40:28 (CJB)

silently for a minute with their heads bowed, then they moved towards the wooden doors. Outside of the doors were two passageways: one to the left and one to the right. The passageway on the right led to the Temple whilst the passage to the left led to the Synagogue. Together with his father and a few other men, Ananiah took the passage to the left for the place where the scribes worked was adjacent to, though separate from the Synagogue itself. Walking down the well-lit corridor, he could see a closed door at the far end of the passageway. When they had reached the door, one of the men loudly knocked three times.

The sound of a key entering the lock, turning and releasing the mechanism resounded. Then, the door was opened. There stood an old man who bowed his head as the group proceeded through to another small hallway where, at the eastern wall a flight of stone stairs spiralled upwards. "What a boring task! Fancy having to do that every day!" Ananiah thought but soon corrected himself when he remembered something his old great-grandfather had told him: "I would rather be a doorkeeper in the house of my God than dwell in the tents of the wicked"[70]. Inwardly, he felt ashamed for he immediately realised that even the humblest of tasks is honourable to Adonai and this elderly door keeper in his old age, was faithfully serving Adonai in a lowly but highly acceptable way.

When they had reached the top of these stairs, Ananiah knew that they were on the ground level of the Synagogue. A further passageway lay ahead of him and on the eastern wall of the passage were two exits, quite a distance apart. Glancing through the first archway, Ananiah saw the stoned cobbled courtyard of the school. It was here that many boys his age attended from the age of seven where they were instructed in both Aramaic and Greek as well as learn how to read, write and speak in the Hebrew language. Half

---

[70]   Psalm 84:10b

way up the passage was a hallway on the western side. Entering the hallway which suddenly turned to the right, he realised that this was where the Head Scribes and all the scribes worked. A large wooden staircase led down to a large lower room which was filled with large tables, writing materials such as animal skins, papyrus, sharpened reeds and quills, the black ink made from a special recipe and cutting instruments.

To the left was a large open room which had six large desks equally spaced in two rows. On each desk was a brightly lit candle and a small sheet of papyrus and located nearby, a small stool. On the western wall of the room were three large windows which let in the bright sunshine and each window had shutters attached so that when it was raining, these could be closed. Well-lit with oil lamps spread uniformly around the room ensured that there was sufficient light for the scribes to successfully complete their work. To the front of the room there was a longer desk which belonged to the Head Scribe, and this faced the neatly aligned desks. Behind the desk of the Head Scribe were two large cupboards one on the right and one on the left. On the shelves in the cupboard on the right (the cupboard located nearest to the Temple) were the original scrolls that were currently being transcribed whilst on the shelves in the cupboard on the left were the semi-completed scrolls. These were placed in the exact position as their originals in the other cupboard.

The men entered the room and went to a specific desk. Located in the corner behind Zuriel's desk (which was in the back row of the lined desks) was another stool which had been placed specifically so that Ananiah could closely observe his father and vice versa. Standing by their individual desks, the men paused as the Head Scribe entered the room. Acknowledging them with a nod of the head, the Head Scribe sat down at his desk his eyes perusing the room. The men did not sit down but all of them leaned over to a small sheet of paper which had black etched recordings of their work documented; with such information as the name of the scroll they were transcribing, its number in the Torah, the record of the transcript's width and length as well as the number of words and spaces that had already been transcribed. Individually each man entered the cupboard on the right-hand side to retrieve his scroll. Returning to his desk, each placed the original scroll on the right-hand side of his desk. Then, each proceeded to the left-hand side cupboard to retrieve his work to continue transcribing this.

Seated on his stool, Zuriel carefully unrolled the original scroll and then the transcript on his left; he did not immediately begin to start writing, rather he meticulously re-counted the number of words and spaces he had previously completed so that he would be re-commencing the transcription in its exact place as found on the original scroll. When he was certain that he was in the correct place to continue, he picked up the sharpened reed, dipped this into the ink pot and began writing. Breaking the silence as if it was in unison, was the etching sound of pen on paper which echoed around the room accompanied by the voices of each man who would say aloud the word he was writing.

There was such reverence in the room, each scribe attentively acknowledging the awesome responsibility of transcribing the word of Adonai carefully so that generations to come would still know of His existence and His will for His people, Isra'el. As the men continued their work, Ananiah remembered the rules of transcription his father and great-grandfather had related to him: each column of writing could have no less than forty-eight letters, and no more than sixty lines; the letters, words, spaces and paragraphs had to be counted and the document would become invalid if two letters touched. If a mistake was made, this could be remedied by carefully cutting into the paper however, if the error could not be remedied, the scroll was removed and stored, later to be buried in a genizah for no document containing Adonai's word could be destroyed. Other rules went through his mind but Ananiah's eyes were firmly on his father.

After a while, Zuriel placed the sharpened reed in the ink pot and looked at the final word he had written. Waiting for a few minutes for the ink to dry, he started to recount the letters, words, spaces and paragraphs of his transcript and once again, picked up the reed once more, and filled in the final numbers of his tallies on the small sheet of paper on his desk. Rolling up the original and then the copy scroll, Zuriel took his work and gave this to the Head Scribe who was seated at the front of the room.

Scrutinising the copy scroll, the Head Scribe picked up a large book which recorded the correct tallies for all the original scrolls. Confirming that Zuriel's scores were correct, the Head Scribe stood up and took the original scroll, placing this also on the right side of his desk, and then opened the scroll. He then took the transcribed scroll and placed this on the left side of the desk and opened this as well. Then meticulously he examined the document for quite some time. Finally, the Head Scribe nodded his head and upon gaining the Head Scribe's approval, Zuriel rolled up the original scroll and returned this to the right-hand side cupboard. Returning to the table, Zuriel rolled up the second scroll and took this to the cupboard on the other side.

Upon returning to the Head Scribe's desk, Zuriel waited as the man picked up another book on his desk, opened it and ran his fingers down a page. Then, after writing the name of the number of the scroll Zuriel was to transcribe next on a small piece of paper, the Head Scribe handed him the piece of paper. Zuriel spoke quietly to the Head Scribe who appeared to listen intently. Then, Ananiah noticed that the Head Scribe nodded his head. Zuriel took the small piece of paper and then moved to the cupboard on the right-hand side and not long afterwards, returned with the original scroll to his desk where he placed down the small sheet of paper that had been handed to him. Turning to his son, who had been patiently sitting on the small stool, Zuriel beckoned with his fingers for his son to come to him. Without saying a word, Ananiah went to his father and together they moved towards and down the large staircase which led to the lower room; the original scroll held safely in his father's hand.

When they came to one of the many large tables within the room, Zuriel carefully opened the scroll his eyes measuring the width and length of the document. Moving over to two large jars filled with different sized measuring sticks, he studied the selection carefully selecting four lengths before returning to the document and then determined which of the four sticks accurately represented the perimeter of the parchment. One stick was correct so Zuriel placed this carefully on the right-hand side of the table, and moved the incorrect sticks making a pile on the left-hand side. Then, returning to the jars he attempted to find four more sticks which were then used to find the exact remaining measurement of the scroll. Once this was found, all the remaining sticks that were of incorrect measurement were returned to the jar.

On the far side of the room were rolls of papyrus paper and Zuriel selected the nearest one. Carefully placing this on the table, he unrolled the paper to the approximate measure of the original scroll. Then using the measuring rods meticulously found the exact area of paper to be cut with the sharp razor left on the table. After this had been completed, voluntarily, Ananiah carefully rolled up the remaining papyrus roll and returned it to where it originally had been placed. Turning to his father, he saw his father's fingers once more beckoning him. When he came to see why his father had called him, his saw his father's fingers move right to left, line by line down the scroll he was to be transcribed until they stopped. As he stooped over to read what the passage said, Ananiah read the following:

"But you, Beit-Lechem near Efrat (Bethlehem Ephrathah) though you are small among the clans of Judah, out of you will come for me one who will be ruler over Isra'el, whose origins are from old, from ancient times"[71].

His father mouthing clearly without speaking, said "A Dabar Promise!" Ananiah's heart skipped a beat as he realised the excitement his father, grandfather and great-grandfather must have experienced when they came upon such an historical promise from Adonai. Although there could be days, weeks or even months before sighting such a verse, the period of waiting grew insignificant to the joy of finding the promise itself.

Moving up the stairs, Zuriel returned to his desk and Ananiah to the stool in the corner. Once again, his father counted all the letters, spaces, words, lines, paragraphs in the section he was transcribing and recorded these on the small piece of paper he had been given. Only after all these aspects had been recorded could the transcribing begin.

Ananiah's composure and interest in the work being completed was quickly noted by the Head Scribe who, at first felt uncertain as to how long a small boy would be interested in such a protracted task, realised that this boy was different. Concerned that the boy should at least be able to stretch his legs, he motioned one of the older scribes in the room to come to him. "The three sections of the prophet Y'hoshua (Joshua) urgently requested for the Temple are now completed. Please take these to the Temple and take the boy to help you carry them. If he asks you questions, answer him quietly" he said. The old man bowed his head, turned to Ananiah and beckoned him. Together they went into the left-hand cupboard where the

---

[71] Micah 5:2

old man perused the shelves and found the three scrolls from Y'hoshua. Giving one to Ananiah, he quietly said to him "Follow me".

The scrolls seemed if they were as tall as the boy but carrying the one given to him width-wise, proved far more manageable. The two left the room, proceeding down the hall, the corridor, the stone steps and came once again to the old man sitting by the locked door. Once again, the old man stood up, bowed his head and reaching into his pocket produced a large key which was then inserted into the locked door. The two continued down the lighted passage way soon passing the closed double doors of the prayer room and continuing for quite some time until they finally came across another locked door. Without hesitation, Ananiah knocked three times on the door which after a few seconds finally opened. What lay ahead of them seemed like an endless corridor but to the eastern side of the wall was an archway and under this archway was a staircase which gradually rose upward to the ground level of the Temple.

When they reached the top, Ananiah found himself in a totally different part of the Temple. The long underground staircase had led them up into the Court of the Priests. To his left and right were several rooms but central to them all was a place that seemed hauntingly familiar as its very presence immediately drew Ananiah's attention causing him to immediately stop in his tracks. "Come on son" said the old man as they continued across the court to one of the rooms on the right-hand side of the court. The room they had entered was like a larger version of the cupboards in the scribing room and once again, each of the scrolls they were carrying had a specific location on the shelves. When they left the room, Ananiah's attention went straight to the centre of the court and a feeling quite familiar drew his face to the curtained feature before him. That feeling was one that he would never forget: the exact feeling that came to him that fatal day when he called on Adonai and that Adonai, in His grace, had answered so faithfully.

"What is that place?" he found himself asking the old man. "That, my boy, is The Holy Place" the old man whispered. "Adonai is there" proclaimed the young boy. "I can feel His presence".

The boy's response startled the old man who had heard of the boy's deliverance and the emerging rumour that Adonai had a special purpose for the child who had begun his life as a rebellious rebel. Compelled by the desire within him Ananiah began walking towards the curtained room only to be quickly pulled back by the old man. "No! No! only the Chief and High Priests can enter the Holy Place and when they go there alone, they must wear the rope of gold tied around their waist so that if anything happens to them when they are in the Holy Place, other priests may safely pull them out". As he was talking the old man pointed to a large golden rope, entwined with large segments of golden cordage, wrapped around a bronze hook on a column closest to the Holy Place.

The boy looked confused so the old man explained further that the Holy Place before them was just like the Holy Place in the original tabernacle outlined to Moshe in the desert so many years before. Everything contained within the veil and beyond it was exactly as Adonai instructed. It was decreed a Holy Place where only High Priests might enter and only at certain times. As Adonai Himself lives there, here on earth with His own people, it is Holy ground and therefore if anyone unclean (as we all are) entered, that person must be put to death because they have disobeyed Adonai's instruction about His Holy dwelling, defiling His Holiness by their impurity and sinful presence[72]. Also, the Torah revealed no-one has seen Adonai's face and lived to tell the tale[73]. Ananiah peered intently at the dwelling before him but it was too far away for him to see what was inside.

---

[72] Numbers 18:7
[73] Exodus 33:20

"Please, may I go closer?" he pleaded, "I promise I will not go into the Holy Place but I do want to see where the God who saved me lives". The old man relented for the boy's faith seemed so refreshing and sincere and if this was the boy Adonai chose to save, He must have had a very purposeful reason for doing so. Slowly the old man took off his sandals and motioned Ananiah to do the same. Then, placing his old hands on the young boy's shoulders the couple drew near to the Holy Place.

At the front of the Holy Place was a beautiful large mauve transparent curtain and inside a shining light on the left-hand side, emitted such brilliant light, enabling Ananiah to see inside the place where Adonai presided. "That is the lamp of gold" whispered the old man. "It is also called 'the lamp that never goes out'. Every morning and evening a High Priest will come and tie the rope of gold around his waist and enter the Holy Place to refill the oil in the golden lamp. It is believed that even when Aaron came to refill the lamp's oil, the lamp itself would never completely be out of oil[74]. And do you know, to this very day, this is what the high priests have found to be true!" As the old man continued to tell the story about the lamp, Ananiah examined as keenly as he could its delicate structure and detail.

The lampstand (menorah) was a work of extraordinary beauty and seemed to be like a tree; from the base and the single shaft, six branches curved outward and upward; three branches on one side and three on the other and with the central branch in the middle had seven branches in all. The base, the shaft, the branches and the ornate bowls shaped like almond blossoms for the oil, and flowers were all made from one piece[75]. It was the most beautiful thing Ananiah had seen.

The brilliant light from the golden lamp reflected around the room. On the right-hand side was a golden table and on the golden table were

---

[74] Exodus 27:20-21; Leviticus 24:1-4; www.hebrew4christians.com
[75] Exodus 25:31-40

twelve loaves of unleavened bread. "That is the table of showbread[76]" con- tinued the old man. The rim of the table was finely decorated and the gold painted table together with the two golden plates on which the twelve loaves were placed (six on each plate), glowed in the lamp's light. "The twelve loaves represent the twelve tribes of Isra'el" continued the old man. "They are made to a special recipe. On each Sabbath four priests come and eat the bread, having sweet fellowship with Adonai. They replace the bread with fresh bread which remains in the Holy Place until the following Sabbath. Only priests can eat the holy bread and this can only be eaten in the Holy Place".

"But wouldn't the bread be stale?" asked Ananiah. "No", replied the old man, "It is made with a special flour and it is placed in the presence of the Living God". Between the golden lamp and the golden table was a small golden altar where incense was burning. "That is the altar of incense[77]" the old man pointed out. "It is meant to remind our people that prayer must be the centre of our lives and we are to pray continually to Adonai for He loves us and delights in hearing our prayers. When the High Priest comes to tend the golden lamp in the morning and evening, he also brings more incense to burn. I just love it when I come to worship for the aroma of the incense permeates throughout the Temple and it is as if Adonai Himself is saying to us all through its odour 'I hear your prayers…I will answer them'".

Totally absorbed in the vision before him and the old man's descriptive words, Ananiah's eyes were drawn to the large thick curtain, hanging on several golden hooks, at the back of the Holy Place[78]. The curtain was made of finely twisted blue, purple and scarlet yarn and embroided upon it with thick golden threads were some cherubim which appeared to protect the

---

[76] Exodus 25: 23-30
[77] Exodus 30: 1-10
[78] Exodus 26:33b

sacred place and contents behind the curtain. The light from the golden lamp emanated around the room, making all things golden reflect with such brightness. The golden threads that embroidered the cherubim flickered and brilliantly glimmered. It was behind there, in the Holy of Holies the old man explained once a year, the High Priest would come and make atonement for the sins of the people[79]. Ananiah gasped in awe. The very sight before him, the appreciation of where he was, and the very presence he was feeling, became so overwhelming, tears filled his eyes.

Gently pulling Ananiah away from the outside of the Holy Place, picking up their sandals, the old man returned to the top of the stairs that would return them to the corridor under the Temple. Ananiah touched the old man's arms and said softly "Thank you so much!". On his way back to the room where his father and the other scribes were still working, Ananiah's mind was racing with thoughts and praise.

It was approximately mid-afternoon, and since returning from his excursion to the Temple, Ananiah sat patiently on his stool still enraptured by what was being undertaken in the room. For some, this might appear as a monotonous sight of men diligently writing but not for Ananiah. The Head Scribe, over the day, had been intrigued by the boy's composure and interest. Then, gaining the boy's attention, he motioned for him to come to him. When Ananiah came to the Head Scribe's desk, he heard the man whisper "You have been very attentive and it has been a long day for you. Would you like to go home and catch up with your father there?" "If you don't mind, sir" replied the boy, "I would like to stay".

---

[79] Exodus 30:10

Chapter Eleven ————

FRIENDSHIP GROWS

few days after Ananiah's long day, as Zuriel was making his way home after scribing for eight hours, he felt a hand lightly touch his right shoulder. Turning around to see who it was, Zuriel saw the familiar face of Zév, a well-known Pharisee. His face smiling, and keeping his hand on Zuriel's shoulder, Zév explained how the Sanhedrin believed that Adonai had a definite plan and purpose for Ananiah's life and his conduct a few days ago in the scribing room was greatly admired by many people who were excited by his enthusiasm and desire to learn more about Adonai's laws. As there was a school next to the Synagogue which taught young boys of Ananiah's age about the law, religious beliefs and language of the Hebrew nation, would Zuriel consider sending his son there?

Like many other families in Yerushalayim, Zuriel's children had been taught at home and knowing that Ananiah was a bright boy who acquired new concepts quickly, the thought of him receiving further education by the rabbis from the Synagogue excited him. "And how much would this cost?" Zuriel asked. "There is a growing consensus from the Sanhedrin", Zév replied, "that as it is evident Adonai has a purpose for this boy, there should be no fees. This offer would appear therefore, to be a sign of the Sanhedrin's blessing on your son".

Zuriel responded by saying that he would give the suggestion further thought and prayer and would get back to Zév with the family's decision. Hurrying his steps, he couldn't wait to get outside of the city to return to his small collective and share this news with his wife, Hannah.

As he said he would do, Zuriel had deep discussions with his wife, his grandfather and Ananiah whose heart leapt in excitement at the prospect of being able to learn more about Adonai. In fact, it didn't take long for Zuriel to believe that this offer would be a blessing to his son who could learn so much more from the teaching of the experts of the law than what he was currently receiving. And so, it was that shortly after this, Ananiah attended the Synagogue school where he expanded his knowledge and appreciation of Adonai's laws.

On his first day of school, Ananiah walked to the Synagogue with his father. As they walked across the stone pavement in the school court-yard, Ananiah was feeling quite excited as he did not know what to expect as no one in his family, or through the generations of his kinfolk, had attended school. Yet, there also was within him, a niggling feeling of anx-iety, of uncertainty as to what the future was going to bring. Around the courtyard were several arches and within the arches were rooms of ten squared metres. Each room had paved stone floors with large mats on which the students sat in a semi-circle with the rabbi (teacher) facing them. Sometimes the rabbi would be seated on a chair, but he was usually seated on the floor.

Between each room on both side walls were doorways which led into the nearby classroom. Without interrupting the rabbis, Zuriel and Ananiah were taken through three classrooms by a tall man who finally brought them to the school room where Ananiah would begin his studies. There, seated in a semi-circle around the rabbi was a familiar face.

Upon seeing Ananiah the rabbi stopped speaking and motioned him to come and join the group on the mat. Kaleb, pleased to see his friend, shuffled to his left to allow Ananiah to sit beside him. Kaleb's smile was so welcoming, it helped dissipate Ananiah's anxieties.

This was the place where Ananiah would learn about the Book of Vayikra (Leviticus), the Nevi'im (Prophets and the Tehillim (Psalms) whilst learning to read, write and speak in the Hebrew Language. He would attend this elementary school for three years and in the following three years he would study in the advanced school where he would be required to commit to memory deeper teachings of the sacred law.

Some days later, when the classes had recess, the two boys were out in the school courtyard sitting under a shady shittah tree planted right in the courtyard's centre. Playing around them were several boys from their own class and boys from an older group. One of the boys was rather large for his age and quite fat in his appearance. He did not let his size deter him but rather used it for his own benefit to tower over the smaller boys. In today's terms, he would be called a 'bully' for he relentlessly tormented the children around him.

"I find I am struggling when writing our Hebrew Language" confessed Ananiah, "it is just too complex!"

"I used to think that at first" replied Kaleb, "but soon found that after much practice, it was much easier. Would you like me to help you, Ananiah? I used to practice on an old piece of slate my grandfather gave me. I am happy to help you, but it does come at a cost".

"What cost?" Ananiah asked.

"You know that skill you have to ricochet small stones to catch a target unaware? Would you teach me how to do that?"

"What like this?" asked Ananiah picking up a small pebble off the ground and throwing it so skilfully it deflected from the tree to a near-by wall and landed target centre of the large bully's broad, bent over backside, causing him to call out in pain.

"Yes, just like that! Can you teach me?" replied Kaleb.

As the bully turned around to see who had dared to do such a thing, it was exceedingly difficult for him to determine just who the culprit was; for around the courtyard all children present had the biggest grins on their faces as laughter repeatedly echoed across the enclosure!

≈   ≈   ≈

Every afternoon, after school and during the school breaks the two boys could be found sitting in the shade of the olive trees encompassing Zuriel's farm. Diligently, Kaleb proved to be an effective teacher, very patient and kind to his pupil who often struggled with the sophisticated application of Hebrew writing. To assist his pupil, Kaleb had different strategies to the ones the boys encountered at their school.

His main strategy involved Kaleb showing Ananiah the letter of the Hebrew alphabet by writing this on his piece of slate. Tracing over the chalked letter at least three times, Ananiah then would write this in the air three times. Satisfied that his pupil was ready to write, Kaleb would wipe the slate with a rag and giving the cleaned slate with the piece of chalk to his friend, watch as Ananiah wrote the letter carefully.

As there are 22 letters, five of which have different forms at the end of the word in the Hebrew alphabet[80], the teaching sessions went for a couple of months until Ananiah, because of his keenness and the ability of his tutor, improved to such an extent that when the teaching sessions were completed, he could write in small sentences. At the very end of the tutoring, Kaleb gave him the following blessing to write:

Barukh ha'melamed et yadi le'sapper et ha'otiyot

Blessed is the One who taught my hand to scribe the letters!

As he carefully and correctly wrote each letter and then showing this to his tutor, Ananiah said "You are aware, aren't you Kaleb that this blessing acknowledges Adonai as my teacher?"

Kaleb smiled. "But of course, my dear friend, every good thing comes from above![81] However, Adonai used me to help you! Now a bargain is a bargain! It's your turn to teach me a skill I have so longed to have!"

It was at that moment when the academic skill of writing was replaced by the physical art of throwing, but not just ordinary throwing, learning how to make a small rock ricochet from one surface to another with surprising accuracy.

Although Kaleb was a willing learner, the skill he was seeking to acquire was difficult and required several lessons, but his instructor was patient, and it wasn't long before Kaleb had successfully mastered the skill that enabled him to make a small pebble ricochet across two surfaces. Often, however, after the second collision of the stone, the exact target was missed. It was not, his instructor informed him, just a case of hitting two objects

---

[80] En.m.wikipedia.org
[81] James 1:17

before his final target, it was important that each impact was using the right angle to secure the successful passage of the stone to its specific target.

After many practices, although the ejected stone often came remarkably close to the original target, the skill of successfully completing the task seemed to be unachievable. One day, when Ananiah was teaching this skill, he drew out from his pocket a leather sling. "Now, I am not sure whether I should tell you this" he said to his friend, "but a year ago, I heard the story about David and Goliath and that David slew the mighty giant with a sling.[82] After making one for myself I found that not only did it improve the speed at which the pebbled travels but because of this increase in speed, where the pebble lands ensures it has a much wider impact area. For example, see that pomegranate over there on that tree. If I use just my pebble as a missile, it might just bruise it but if I use my sling, it is destined to be removed completely from the tree".

Placing a pebble in the sling, and repeatedly swinging this around and around, Ananiah's eyes were fixed on his target. When the pebble ejected from the sling, it flew directly at the targeted pomegranate which upon impact, fell to the ground below. Kaleb was quite in awe and taking his turn, practised and practised until finally one of the many pomegranates fell to the ground. "Was that the one you were targeting?" asked Ananiah. "Of course, it was!" replied Kaleb.

≈ ≈ ≈

When Ananiah reached the age of ten he went to the next level of his education which required deeper insights into the books of the Torah and other duties. One of those duties required all the senior boys to attend the

---

[82] 1 Samuel 17:26-50

Synagogue each Sabbath. This was always a joy for Ananiah who loved to join in with the others in praise, prayer reading of the Scriptures, as well as teaching and preaching. The time of worship would always begin with by reciting the Shema (a confession of faith) followed by a reading of from the Torah, which was penned by Moshe and an explanation of the passage. Then a second passage and explanation would follow.

One Sabbath as they were waiting on the steps of the Synagogue for their fathers, Ananiah and Kaleb were talking when a young girl, accompanied by her mother walked up the steps. Her presence caught the immediate attention of Ananiah though why, he did not know. "Shalom, Rachael!" Kaleb said but his greeting received a cold stare from Rachael's mother for it was not the custom for strangers to greet unknown women, particularly at the Synagogue (which was not a social venue, but a venue of worship), especially on the Sabbath! As they passed by Ananiah and Kaleb, Kaleb turned to Ananiah and whispered, "Pretty, isn't she?"

"Well actually I think my mother's prettier" replied Ananiah, his tongue in his cheek.

"No! I meant the girl!" said Kaleb.

"Actually, I didn't notice" responded Ananiah.

Although there were other Synagogues in Yerushalayim, this was the largest. Upon ascending the flight of seven steps from both the northern, eastern and southern sides of the building, one entered through the three large doors into a large, stoned foyer. On the northern and southern sides at the end of the foyer were two flights of steps which ascended to the second floor of the Synagogue where there were two balconies, one on the right-side of the building and the other on the left. This was where the boys from the school and other young boys would sit. On the second floor, each balcony had two long rows of benches so when the boys were seated, they were not only facing one another, they had a splendid bird's eye view of the Synagogue below.

On the eastern side of the foyer were two large arches, one on the right and the other on the left. The latter arch was where the women entered, and they would always sit on the three long rows of benches at the back of the building. The men would sit on two long rows of benches under the two balconies at the sides of the Synagogue, and like the boys, they would be facing each other. Poorer men folk would sit on the floor of the Synagogue which also had a Bimah (table where the scrolls would be read) and the Ark (a large cupboard where the Torah scrolls were kept).

From the tall ceiling above hung twelve bronze flat bowls each suspended with three long wires. The three long wires met together and were joined by a small ring which hung on an even longer hook from the ceiling. Contained within each bowl were seven candles and eighty-four candles in all, allowed plenty of light for the worshipers to see.

Upon reciting the Shema that day, Ananiah felt as if someone was watching him. He glanced across to his father sitting down on the opposite side of the Synagogue, but his father was in deep prayer. Then glancing across to the very back of the Synagogue, his eyes met those of Rachael. "She is kind of pretty" he thought to himself before entering deep and reverent worship.

≈   ≈   ≈

The very next wheat and barley seasons produced bountiful crops and Ananiah was helping his mother Hannah sell the produce in the markets. The marketplace was filled with the sound of merchants and pedlars selling their wares and people loudly bargaining for the best price. As Ananiah put the tendered money into his purse he glanced up to see a familiar face smiling at him. Rachael moved towards him and greeted him "Shalom Ananiah", she said.

"Shalom, Rachael" he replied, "What can I do for you today?"

Placing a square cloth of fabric on the trading table, Rachael explained that she was doing some baking for her mother and ran out of flour. She did not need a large amount, only about two shekels worth. As Ananiah took the measuring cup and took the small amount of flour out of the bag, he turned his back to his mother behind him and quickly added an extra scoop. Wrapping this up quickly in the cloth provided, he said "That's two shekels of flour!". Rachael gave him the money, smiled, and then disappeared into the crowd.

"Who was that girl who just bought some flour?" Hannah asked her son.

"Her name is Rachael" answered Ananiah while serving another customer.

"She's rather pretty, don't you think?" his mother asked.

"I haven't really noticed" replied Ananiah.

≈   ≈   ≈

When Rachael's mother Sarah (Princess) went to the cupboard to get some flour for the day's baking, she was surprised to find an extra portion of flour in the pantry. "Does anyone know where the extra flour in the pantry came from?" she loudly inquired.

"I put it there", replied Rachael.

"But why would you buy extra flour when we already have enough for two weeks?" her mother asked.

"Well,", replied Rachael, thinking on the spot, "I thought I would try to make some special bread for the harvest but was unsure if it would turn out OK and so, not to waste the existing flour, I bought some more, just in case".

"My daughter is going to make a very prudent wife!" Sarah thought to herself.

≈   ≈   ≈

Just before the next Feast of the Harvest Ananiah upon turning fourteen was at the point in his life where he would finish his schooling. It was always thought that as he excelled in all areas in the Torah, that he, like his father, grandfather, and great grandfather before him would become a scribe. But his father insisted that his son choose the profession he wanted for his knowledge of the Jewish law gained while attending the synagogue school, would positively assist him should he wish to become a lawyer. However, Ananiah's first choice of profession was made several years ago, when he observed his father at work. He wanted to be a scribe. So, it was no surprise, that when he declared this to his father and the elders, he should begin his working career assisting the scribes and completing minor scribing duties.

On the Sabbath, he and Kaleb went to the Synagogue as was the usual practice. Before the worship began, Ananiah searched the congregation of people assembled in the Synagogue to see if he could find that familiar face and, as usual she was sitting in the back row with her mother Sarah on her right.

During the service, the new priest Ezra provided a long, detailed description of his interpretation of the passage that was read. He spoke very boorishly for what seemed to be hours and because of the length of his interpretation, it became very apparent to Ananiah that the attention of quite a lot of people in the Synagogue was wandering far away from the topic. Ezra elegantly robed in his priestly garments seemed oblivious to the apparent boredom - possibly that was because he was enraptured by his new position and enjoyed being the centre of attention.

Kaleb's attention was also distracted and spying Rachael sitting next to her mother, pulled out a small pebble for his pocket. Calculating the angles of the stone to be ricocheted to Rachael's lap, he threw the small stone which hit two columns side by side before abruptly hitting Sarah on the left side of her covered head. Immediately Sarah, sensing that some-thing must have been projected from the left side of the room, scanned the left-hand balcony for any possible culprit. As most of the boys on that side of the Synagogue seemed to be totally disinterested in what was being said, Sarah looked to the right and her eyes came directly in line with Kaleb's. Sarah's frigid stare was enough to cause Kaleb to gulp as he heard a voice whisper to him "Angles of projection need to be more acute". Then, following his friend's advice, Kaleb threw another pebble which hit both columns on the opposite side of the Synagogue before landing on Rachael's lap.

Unlike her mother, Rachael knew that the projectile's path originated on the other side of the room and immediately looked up to the right-hand balcony. Shaken by his previous failure, Kaleb's sight focused on Ezra but Ananiah wanting to see if his friend's second throw was successful, was looking directly at Rachael. Sarah, noticing her daughter smiling at a boy sitting in the right-hand balcony, lent forward to see who this was only to find that her eyes once again, were staring directly at Kaleb who had bravely decided he had better look to see if his target had been reached.

≈   ≈   ≈

The Festival of the Ingathering (harvesting of the fruits) was always a joy-ous occasion and the city's marketplace was alive with people selling their wares and buyers busily bargaining. In the centre of the marketplace were young girls dancing joyfully singing and playing their tambourines. At the western side of the marketplace were two three by two metre open drays which the farmers would use to move their seasonal produce. The two drays were placed together and as they had no upright sides, they made a large rectangular platform.

Raised above the crowd this platform allowed a priest to be in full sight of the crowd whilst he gave the festivities his blessing. Stacked carefully on the second dray were colourful boxes of pomegranates, figs and grapes. Carefully tiered in rows with the tallest row about one metre above the head of the speaker, all boxes were stacked slightly tilted, exposing the bounty of the harvest. The containers of the colourful fruit provided a rich background of plenty.

Rachael joined her friends in the dancing for she loved this time of celebration and joy. Beating her tambourine in time with the small band of musicians who were accompanying the dancers, she glanced around at the people in the surrounding crowd. Seeing Ananiah, who was watching her with Kaleb, she received a reciprocated smile. It was not until the third time round the circular dance that Kaleb spoke.

"Oh, my heart is broken in two, Ananiah. I have just realised that each time I believed Rachael was smiling at me, she was really smiling at you!"

"Whatever do you mean?" asked Ananiah who truly was oblivious to his friend's statement.

"It's obvious, dear friend" replied Kaleb, "that it is not my ugly face that Rachel likes, it's yours!"

"Do you think Rachael likes me?" inquired Ananiah.

Suddenly, the noise in the marketplace quietened and the priest, Ezra clothed in his fine priestly attire, made his way up the make-shift steps to the floor of the first dray. Reaching the centre of the dray, waiting for the crowd to be completed hushed, he opened his arms out wide and began:

"My dear friends, it is such an honour to be with you, this day…" In his usual style, Ezra began speaking enjoying the moment to the fullest. A man in the crowd was heard to say "My friends! My friends! How does he have the nerve to call us his friends. He doesn't even know our names, nor does he know the names of our children! He knows nothing about us!"

Another was heard to say, "If he was my friend, he would greet me in the marketplace not walk by without speaking like he usually does!"

In his usual form, Ezra spoke for what seemed hours as the hot Judean sun burned down on the heads of those gathered in the marketplace. Ananiah and Kaleb had moved to a shaded section close to where Ezra was speaking. Scrutinizing the rows of pomegranates behind the gabbling speaker, Kaleb asked his friend which of the many pomegranates placed in the tilted boxes did Ananiah believe to be the most vulnerable. It didn't take long for Ananiah to sight the pomegranate on the third row from the top, third from the right. Kaleb could see that this pomegranate almost seemed to shake when warm breezes blew around the courtyard. Reminding his friend, that the stronger the propulsion, the wider the target area, Ananiah was not surprised to see Kaleb bring out his faithful sling. Unseen by the crowd, Kaleb swung his arms around and around and once the small stone secured in the sling was released it speedily made its way to its mark. Whizzing by Ezra's left ear, the pebble impacted the wavering pomegranate so quickly, it toppled down accompanied by other pomegranates which, in turn, quickly brought the whole contents of the other boxes teeming down the stage.

Like a huge tsunami wave the cascading fruit together with the contents of the boxes of figs roared swiftly down the makeshift stage. This happened so quickly, the last thing the people would see was the sight of Ezra being swamped and carried down by the fruit, feet first onto the ground below.

After the roar of the cascading fruit ceased, just for a moment there was complete silence before members of the crowd ran forward to help Ezra to his feet. But, alas, several pomegranates had split completely open on the cobbled-stone ground and needless-to-say, as people eagerly moved across to save Ezra, many of them slipped and fell on the slithery terrain.

Unfortunately, Rachael was one of them so Ananiah rushed to her assistance offering her his hand. Just for a moment, he felt as if there was an extra pull from Rachael which made him unexpectedly fall on top of her. "You did that on purpose!" he exclaimed. Finding his feet, he once again offered her his hand. Just as she was about to be raised onto her feet, Ananiah released his grip but slipped in the process. "You did that on purpose!" Rachael exclaimed. The next few moments saw the two trying to get to their feet, laughing loudly attempting to hold on to each other in the process.

As the marketplace started to roar with laughter at the sight of people trying to get back onto their feet, two pairs of maternal eyes witnessed the entire goings-on. Sarah on the right side of the marketplace was relieved that her daughter was laughing with a boy who was not that troublesome Kaleb, whilst Hannah on the opposite side of the marketplace thought maybe it was time to think of a bride for her eldest son. Also thinking to himself and most perturbed was Ezra: - "Do pomegranates stain?" he wondered.

—— *Chapter Twelve* ——

A DARK VALLEY

After finishing her house chores, Hannah sighed deeply. For the past few weeks she had seen a significant change in her husband Zuriel who wasn't sleeping well and always appeared to be overly tired. He had lost interest in his food and was looking lean and frail. He was usually the first in the family to rise in the morning and would keenly set off to Yerushalayim once his chores were done. But the enthusiasm for his work seemed to wane and it appeared as if he was becoming disinterested in life. Several times she had attempted to find out what was troubling her husband but the conversations never went very far.

Hannah had asked Obadiah if he might speak to his grandson, but once again, little came out of the conversation. Beginning to feel desperate Hannah asked his best friend Nosh if he could find out what was troubling his friend. Nosh said he would drop by the farm house the next morning (which was the Sabbath) and just as he had promised he turned up mid-morning to find Zuriel seated on the front porch of his home with his grandfather. There was a brief smile in his greeting to his friend yet Zuriel appeared to be quite tired and forlorn.

"I have brought you a present, my friend, made by my own hands" said Nosh. "I hope you like it". Nosh, a very skilled tanner, handed his friend the leather shema bracelet. Neatly and delicately inscribed around the outside of the bracelet were the words *'They cried out to the Lord in their trouble, and he brought them out of their distress*[83]. For several seconds Zuriel seemed deep in thought as he intently read the inscription, and then, smiling at his friend, he thanked him. The two friends had seen many troubles between them and no matter what the circumstances, they were always there for each other and this day was no exception. The inscribed words seemed to provide some release for Zuriel. Seeing that his friend was in anguish, Nosh pleaded with him to lighten the load on his heart. Surely the weight of his burden couldn't be that bad? It didn't take long for Zuriel to start unburdening his soul.

Just before the Ingathering Festival, he had been summoned by the head scribe and was informed that following a recent meeting of the Sanhedrin, it had been decided that some of the scribes should be allocated to specifically write all the Laws of Adonai. Of course, these laws were scattered amongst the readings in the Torah but because of the sinfulness of the people, the Pharisees and elders made additional laws. It was decided that as so many people could not remember the additional laws that were made, specific scrolls recording the additional laws should also be written. Two other scribes, together with Zuriel, were identified as excellent recorders for the task. A lover of Adonai's word and laws, Zuriel was honoured to do this task as he thought a closer investigation of Adonai's laws would be beneficial to his walk with Him.

---

[83] Psalm 107:28

However, it did not take long before intense frustration began to accompany this task. Unlike the words from the scrolls which Zuriel found so easy to remember each day when scribing, from many of these additional laws Zuriel could only remember a few. It became apparent to him, that even though Adonai left only 10 laws (commandments) with Moshe, the rebellious nature of man was such that the laws needed explanation, verification and elongation. Subsequently, Zuriel calculated from just those 10 laws, there were hundreds and hundreds of additional laws! No wonder his people had difficulty remembering all the laws that had been given to them! After all, ten laws are easy to remember but laws that number in their hundreds are not![84] Experiencing both a deep personal guilt for his own lack of knowledge and for that of his fellow men, Zuriel concluded that due to man's foolishness, other laws which attempted to clarify what had been introduced, only complicated, and confused the people even more. The only people who understood the additional laws were the Pharisees as it was this group that had made the supplementary laws. Zuriel became concerned that the people could not obey such laws as there were too many to comprehend and in his ignorance man would be further removed from Adonai.

Such concern caused Zuriel to be low in spirit and despair. It didn't take long for him to lose interest in scribing for each day after he left his work behind him, he felt that little had been accomplished. But, continued Zuriel, the thought that caused him most concern was that the people, in their stubbornness and attempts to obey Adonai's laws, might be blinded in their ignorance when the Messiah comes. His people, well known for their rebellion against Adonai, might just refuse to acknowledge the Messiah for who he is.

---

[84] There were 613 commandments given to the OT people in the Torah citing.

Obadiah looked benevolently at his grandson. As Zuriel exposed his soul and the dilemmas he was facing, Obadiah's heart weakened. He could see the heartbreak his grandson was going through but failed to provide any words that might be of encouragement to him. "I can see you have been most troubled. Much of what you are worried about, makes sense" he said. "Would you be willing to go and speak to a Pharisee about your concerns? A Pharisee is probably more equipped to counsel you on these. Is there any particular Pharisee you feel you would be happy to talk to?"

"Well, Zév, seems a decent man" responded Zuriel.

"I think that is an excellent idea" added Nosh. "If you like I would be happy to go with you".

"As will I" added his grandfather.

Sometimes when you are down at the bottom of the deepest pit, you must look upwards for the only way out is up. When you are doing so, it is foolish to ignore any outstretched hands of support. While a listening ear is always of some comfort to the troubled soul, it is within the help of friends, that one finds support and sustenance.

≈   ≈   ≈

It had been decided that Nosh would find Zév and request on Zuriel's behalf, to spend some time with the Pharisee who was so respected for his knowledge of the Torah. Informing Zév of both Nosh's and Obadiah's interest in Zuriel's dilemma, it was also requested that Zév might be able to advise the three, particularly Zuriel, as to how the identified difficulties might be resolved. Zév was only too happy to find the time for the three and as this appeared as a counselling type of meeting, he wondered if they would mind if he included a new young Pharisee he was mentoring in the discussion. So, a meeting at the Temple on a specific day at a specific time was determined.

When the day came, the three men arrived early and found Zév waiting for them at the Golden Gate entrance to the Temple. Upon greeting them warmly, he led the way into the colonnade that surrounded the temple on its western side. Continuing down a set of stone steps, Zuriel realised that down the long corridor that stretched out before them were rooms like the ones, he had been confined on that dreadful day he and Nosh and the other fathers had been called to address the Sanhedrin. "I have left my colleague to set up the room for us", Zév informed them. "He is looking forward to meeting you".

Finally, they came into a small room where they saw a man placing two chairs at one side of the table, and three chairs on the other. When the man turned to greet them, they realised he was Ezra. The formal placement of the furniture appeared to be a little unsettling to Nosh who, before anyone could take a seat said: "Unfortunately, Zuriel's grandfather is becoming a little hard of hearing and he isn't seeing so well, do you mind if we bring our chairs over here next to the oil lamps so that he can hear and see us more clearly?" Despite the startled glance he immediately received from Obadiah who promptly replied "Well, I heard that!", Nosh started to place the chairs in a cosy circle quite close to the lamps.

The oil lamps along the surrounding walls where Nosh was placing the chairs, enabled the room to be brighter and as the men sat down on the wooden chairs, Zuriel heaved a loud sigh. This less formal setting was conducive to listening and sharing and therefore allowed Zuriel to look at the faces of the men with whom he was sharing his story. Obadiah noted there was a surprising difference in the two men's faces. Zév appeared to be deeply interested, sometimes nodding his head as Zuriel spoke, sometimes slightly smiling as if in agreement. Ezra on the other hand had a solemn, expressionless face and all the time Zuriel opened his heart regarding his concern, appeared unmoved by the dilemma.

It was clear to all who were present that Zuriel in unburdening his many concerns, revealed that he had suffered much internal quandary about all the things that were laying so heavily on his heart. From his knowledge of the Torah and the nature of Adonai presented in his revelations, it was also evident that this was a man who passionately loved his God and was serving Him faithfully. Nosh noted that his friend's thoughts were presented more logically and succinctly and believed that as Zuriel had been given chances to express his concerns, the opportunity to express these openly to others was a therapeutic option.

After Zuriel had finished, silence filled the room. Ezra, feeling uncomfortable with this stillness was just about to speak, when Zév gently placed his hand on Zuriel's arm and said:

"My dear friend Zuriel – I say 'dear' for you have a love for the Living God that I too, share. I call you 'friend' for friends share their hearts openly despite revealing their warts and all! There are just two things I need to say to you".

"Firstly, you are indeed correct in your recognition of the rebellious nature of man. The heart of man has always been defiant of Adonai's holiness even from the beginning of time, in Noach's (Noah's) time, in Bavel (Babylon) and even till now. Why should now or the future be any different? Yet this problem of Adonai's people rebelling against Him was not caused by you and therefore you are not responsible! Why immerse yourself in a difficulty or problem that only Adonai alone can handle? Is He not able to solve these problems himself? Does he call on you to help Him? No, Zuriel! The problem of man's rebellion through time is such a big problem that the only one who can solve this, is Adonai Himself – no mere mortal man is capable! So, the first thing you must do is 'let go!' and 'Let Adonai' solve this as He wills".

"Secondly, you may or may not be correct in believing that when the Messiah comes, he will be rejected. But this I do know. Throughout our history, from the beginning of time, Adonai has given His people a free will; the choice of choosing right from wrong. Even if it is true that His own people shall once again reject Him, and even if it is written that this will take place, Adonai is still in control of this world and He will turn all history into good for His purpose[85]. So even out of the rejection, He will bring perfection to His plan. If the people's rejection is part of His plan, there is no man on earth who will change that. So, my second piece of advice to you is 'accept that Adonai's will has been included in all His promises'!"

The room seemed to resonate with the wisdom that had been given and all the men nodded in agreement. Ezra, not wishing to be excluded from the wisdom once again prepared himself to speak when Obadiah, believing a memorable moment should not be spoiled by human folly exclaimed "Praise be to Adonai for His Goodness to His people and may all that has been spoken here today remain in our hearts and in our thankfulness to Him - He who holds, watches and controls the wonderful world in which we live!"

And all the men said "She'y'h'ye!" (Amen)

---

[85] Romans 8:28

Chapter Thirteen

BETROTHAL

Although the subject had been raised several times, it was not until Ananiah's sixteenth birthday that his parents thought definite decisions and steps needed to be taken regarding Ananiah's future bride. As was the custom at the time, many parents often chose the bride for their sons as it was believed, and often found to be true, that love would come after the marriage vows. Furthermore, the love that grew from the marriage was very strong and unifying. However, Zuriel had always believed, that his father Uriel's decision which allowed him to personally choose his young bride Hannah, had greatly enhanced the love the two shared over the years. So, he hoped that Ananiah might have some input into this very important life changing decision.

And hence it was, two days later that the three were sitting at the table discussing Ananiah's future. It was the custom that most of the boys, by the time they reached the age of 18 would be betrothed or married, and now was the moment to make this important decision. To be truthful, Ananiah had often thought about who he would like to be his wife yet there was always only one face he could see, Rachael's. Ever since the laughter that was exchanged during the 'day of the pomegranates' (a term they often referred to and devised by themselves) the two had grown to learn more about each other, their likes and dislikes, their characteristics, their joys and pains. The more they learnt about each other, the more they seemed to be unified and although Kaleb was a dear friend, Rachael had become more than a friend to Ananiah. So, it wasn't a surprise to his mother when asked the question if there was anyone Ananiah felt would make him a good wife, his answer "Rachael" was immediately accepted.

To find out whether Rachael and her parents would be interested in such a union, Zuriel would have to go and speak to Rachael's father who would in turn, speak to his daughter to see if any further arrangements could be negotiated. Once either Rachael's father and/or Rachael had given consent, the preparations for a marriage contract could begin.

Immediately, for there was no time like the present Zuriel, made his way to Rachael's home which was in the eastern section in Yerushalayim. Knocking loudly on the door of the house, Zuriel was praying that his son's choice for a bride was also that of Adonai. The sound of knocking of the door made Rachael and her mother Sarah peer from the upstairs window down into the street. Rachael thought it looked like Ananiah's father whereas Sarah was certain it was Zuriel himself. Rachael was oblivious to the reason for his calling but Sarah, in her wisdom was not. Pulling her daughter out of view from the street she instructed her "Do not appear to be over keen; calmly answer but please be truthful!" Informing her daughter to stay in the room, Sarah moved quickly down the steps only to find that her husband Boaz (swiftness) had opened the door.

A portly and likable man, Boaz was known for his excellent breads and rolls which were always quickly sold at the local markets. As a baker, Boaz was a faithful customer of Zuriel whose crops of wheat and barley were the main ingredients in his wares. After formal greetings were exchanged, Zuriel was invited into the house. Standing in the front room of the house, Zuriel came straight to the point; his eldest son Ananiah had just had his 16th birthday and in anticipation that one day he would marry. Would Boaz's daughter Rachael be willing to become Ananiah's bride? Boaz immediately responded that both he and Rachael's mother would approve such a union, but the choice must lay with his daughter and turning to Sarah, Boaz asked her to summon her daughter.

Sarah moved slowly across the room to the steps but in ascending these, her pace grew faster. Whispering her previous advice to her daughter, she allowed Rachael to descend the stairs and enter the room where the two men were waiting. Rachael nodded her head in greeting Zuriel and then listened carefully to her father. "Rachael, my dearest daughter, Zuriel's visit to us today is for a very special reason. His oldest son Ananiah, whom I believe you know, has reached an age when he must consider wedlock. He has chosen you to be his bride and as you are also of a marriageable age, this may take place if the request has your consent. So, dear child, would you be willing to become Ananiah's wife? Please answer honestly. You are under no compulsion!"

Heeding her mother's advice, Rachael replied by calmly saying "Yes, father, I am willing." The men and Sarah could not contain their happiness at the young girl's decision with smiles beaming from ear-to-ear, joyously praising Adonai; this was a very proud and happy moment for them. Yet Rachael remained calm, bowed slightly and returned to her room up the stairs. Closing her door calmly behind her, she let go of her calm composure and throwing her hands into the air exclaimed, "Yes! Yes! Yes!"

With Rachael's consent the adults set out to discuss the dowry and plans for the wedding, which in accordance with tradition would occur only after the formal proposal by Ananiah himself. Ananiah would have to go to the bride's father to request her hand in marriage. When the bride-to-be gave her consent, a ketubah (a marriage contract) would be signed by Boaz and Ananiah.

His heart full of praise and happiness, Zuriel returned home. Upon sharing the good news with his son and his wife many tears of joy and happiness flowed. It was such a relief to hear the sound of happiness again in the house, for only fourteen months before, Obadiah had sadly passed away in his sleep at eighty-one years of age. For all his life, Ananiah's great grandfather had lived in the same house and as he played such a stalwart part of the family throughout many a crisis; the porch, the dining table and the house always seemed so much emptier without him. He wished in his heart that his great grandfather could be here to be part of the celebration.

It was Hannah who suggested that great grandfather's room at the back of the house could be made into a wonderful huppah (bridal chamber) for Ananiah to prepare for his bride and as this room was large enough for them to be their home, they could use this as such if they so desired. The day seemed to be moving so quickly but there was nothing but pure joy in Ananiah's heart. Many times, quite spontaneously in his heart, he thanked Adonai for his goodness and asked Adonai to bless his future wife and themselves as a couple.

His father took him by the shoulder and led Ananiah to the large room at the back of the house which was still filled with his great grandfather's belongings, a narrow bed, a small table and chair. As the two looked around the large room both felt confident that Ananiah would be able to alter the room and make this the perfect bridal chamber for his bride.

Zuriel related the wedding customs of his people that had developed over the years. Ananiah was to go back to Boaz to formally request his daughter's hand in marriage. He must take with him a contract that will state that the wedding is to take place after Rachael's dowry, which had been stated by Boaz, is paid. The contract will also state what assets (if any) Rachael may have e.g. land, property or revenue. After formally asking Rachael to become his wife, when she formally agreed, the two will drink a cup of wine together to signify their blood union. The couple shall then be considered betrothed but the marriage must not be consummated before an agreed time. Hopefully, within a year, preferably around Harvest time, it will be time for the marriage to be consummated and the wedding feast to be celebrated.

Ananiah carefully penned the proposed wedding contract as set out by his father and Boaz. As his father dictated to him the terms that had already been discussed, Ananiah reflected how much his scribing skills had advanced since Kaleb had tutored him under his father's olive trees. He strongly felt that Adonai had given him these skills not only to record His precious words but also the very words he himself was scribing in his own marriage contract.

It took a few days for the dowry price to be collected and together with proposed contract, as Ananiah set out to Rachael's house, his mother insisted that he wash his face, hands and feet and change into his better clothes. After all, he did not want to appear to his in-laws as an untidy, unclean person! When he finally left his house to make his way towards Yerushalayim, Ananiah felt excited yet a little fearful. Throughout his years after being saved from the bandits he had undertaken many fearful situations, such as the many discussions of what had transpired to members of the Sanhedrin and some of the priests. Even some of the elderly rabbis at the school would often have such a glassy stare and threaten sever punishment if tasks were not completed properly, but the fear that he experienced then seemed nothing compared to the beating of his heart that day. What if things went wrong? What if Boaz changed his mind?

Before he knocked on the door of Rachael's house, a passage from Mishlei (Proverbs) entered his mind. Repeating this to himself *"Fear of man will prove to be a snare, but whoever trusts the Lord is kept safe"*[86], he composed himself and knocked on the door. Rachael, who had not seen Ananiah for some time, anxiously peered from the upper room window but her mother pulled her aside and told her to remain where she was until she was called.

When the door opened, Boaz with his wife beside him, greeted Ananiah and invited him into their home. Casually glancing around to see if he could see his bride, Ananiah handed the dowry and the penned contract to his future father-in-law who began to carefully read its contents. Boaz nodded his head before placing the contract on the table: everything that was contained therein was exactly what was determined in the previous meeting he had with Zuriel. "You certainly have fine penmanship skills" Boaz commented. Sensing Ananiah was a little ill-at-ease and remembering how he himself had felt when he formally asked Sarah's father for her hand in marriage, Boaz said to Ananiah. "Ananiah, I have always wanted a son and today, if Rachael is willing, Adonai has given me one! This will make my wife and myself very happy for we see in you a very special young man whom we believe will bring our daughter much happiness".

Ananiah wanted to assure Boaz and Sarah that he would faithfully look after Rachael because of his love for her but as so many of the older generation believed that marriage usually precedes love, he decided he needed to assure his future in-laws in another way. "I do assure you sir, as Adonai is my witness, that I will honour all aspects of His laws in our

---

[86] Proverbs 29:25

marriage". Nodding his head in agreement, Boaz asked his wife to fetch their daughter.

Rachael gracefully ascended the stairs with an air of regency and grace. Her face was beaming and to Ananiah, she looked like a queen. Upon seeing Ananiah she lowered her head and eyes and then, looking up into his blue eyes, the eyes she had grown to love, greeted him. His heart beat so strongly and loudly, he thought that everyone in the room must have heard it yet despite this, he went up to her and asked her if she would be willing to become his wife. Her response needed no rehearsing as immediately she responded, "I will".

Placing a sharpened reed in an ink pot on the table, Boaz asked Ananiah to come and sign the wedding contract and after Ananiah raising the reed, gently tapped this against the inside of the ink pot, signed his name, he offered the pen to Boaz who dipped this once more into the pot and wrote his name on the paper. Sarah returned from the kitchen with four cups of wine on a wooden tray and her husband took the first, Ananiah the second, Rachael the third and she the last one. "We drink this cup as a sign of the marriage between Ananiah and Rachael and acknowledge this as a blood agreement between them" Boaz said as the couple were toasted.

After they sipped the wine, Ananiah said to his bride, for now, by law they were legally married. "Rachael, Adonai, with the consent of your parents, you have been given to me in marriage. You are so very special to me and I know that our union will be blessed. Now, as tradition ordains, I must leave you for a while so we both can prepare for our wedding feast. I must return to my father's house where I will make you a bridal chamber, a place where we may be truly united in our marriage. So, I must leave you and prepare a place for you[87]. Be ready for me my dear wife, for time quickly passes".

From that day on Rachael adorned a veil which demonstrated to those around her that she was betrothed. Society would call her 'set apart', consecrated by the price that had been paid for her in her dowry; she belonged to another and her life was no longer her own. As she gathered her trousseau and her wedding attire, she would have to wait each night for her bride groom to come. Not knowing the exact hour, she needed to be ready and to help her in this venture, ten young girls were chosen as her bridesmaids. As no one knew the exact the time of the bridegroom's arrival, except for the bridegroom's father, it was essential that Rachael remain home at night lest her bridegroom come and find her not there.

---

[87]   www.biblestudymanuals.net/jewish_marriage_customs.htm

—— *Chapter Fourteen* ——

EVERYONE LOVES A WEDDING

A fter their betrothal was announced, planning and preparation of the bridal chamber began. Once more taking his son into the large room at the back of his house, Zuriel said: "You must make this room into a wonderful chamber to bring your bride to on her wedding night. While its preparation is all your responsibility, I am sure that your mother will also help you, for after all, she is gaining a daughter in her family! And what a beauty she is, Ananiah! Once you have made the room a suitable dwelling for your bride, you must inform me and after I have given it my blessing, you must then go and formally bring Rachael and her wedding party back to our home and the celebrations will then begin! Oh, this is going to be a busy time for us all and your mother is just going to love it! Our first son is getting married! Our eldest son will soon become a man!"

≈   ≈   ≈

The following months were busy ones for Ananiah for not only was he assuming part-time responsibilities as a qualified scribe, he was also working part-time on his father's farms and now he had the responsibility of preparing his bride's huppah and his wedding. When discussing what furniture should now be placed in the back room of the house, Kaleb said that he would renovate the old chair that was there, obtain another similar one and begin to work on these turning them into two fine looking chairs with beautiful padded leather cushions. His father Nosh was willing to assist him in the process.

≈   ≈   ≈

One day, when the traders came to Nosh's shop with their merchandise, included among their wares was a beautiful large bear skin with a soft, luxurious coat. "This will make a wonderful mat for Ananiah's bridal chamber" Kaleb thought moving his hands across the animal's soft fur. His father, noticing his son's interest in the hide, said to the trader, "How much for the bear hides?"

"Eighty silver coins" was the response.

"I will take two for one hundred!" replied Nosh. The trader was hesitant. "And I'll throw in this luxurious sheep's hide which I have fleshed, broken and smoked!"

Now Nosh was well known for his tannery skills and the sheep's hide in question had been beautifully treated so the trader, realizing this could prove a valuable piece of merchandise, agreed.

"Why buy two, Father?" Kaleb asked.

"Well, one can be for Ananiah, and the other for you. Your mother and I want grandchildren, so you had better start thinking about a wife, too!"

"A wife!" thought Kaleb to himself. "Who would want to be my bride?" But his father's request started to persistently nag him and somehow the thought never seemed to be able to exit his head.

≈   ≈   ≈

At the end of the following harvest, Zuriel looked in amazement at the renovated room before him. In one corner of the large room was a double-sized bed which Ananiah himself had built. On the bed were beautifully embroidered cushions (no doubt Hannah's handiwork) and a beautiful bear skinned covering. Kaleb, under his father's watchful eye, had skilfully cut the completed tanned bear hide so that there was sufficient textile for both a bed cover and a floor mat which lay attractively on the floor in another part of the room.

On both sides of the bed were two small bed tables which Ananiah made to match the bed that he and his wife would share. The bed and the bed tables were welcoming and everything looked extremely comfortable. In the corner of the room were three large wicker baskets, one to hold soiled clothes and the others to store Ananiah's and Rachael's clean clothes respectively.

On the other side of the room was a small stove – a place for Rachael to cook and prepare their meals for the five days they would not be seen by their wedding guests. Nearby was a pantry cupboard and a narrow table which stretched across the side wall of the room. In the middle of the room under a window was a small table with two chairs. Each chair had a soft leather cushion adding a touch of luxury and comfort to the room. On the floor between the kitchen fire and the table and chairs, was the large comfortable bear skin rug.

Candles were placed symmetrically on the long table whilst three oil lamps were placed strategically around the room; one on the small table and one on each of the bed side tables. Their light illuminated the room but the most eye-catching moment of all was when Zuriel sighted in three sections of the room; on each of the two bed side tables, on the small table near the window and on the long table at the other end of the room - four small delicate vases and within each vase, an exquisite arrangement of lily of the valley. It didn't take long for Zuriel to turn to his son and say: "Well done! Go and get your bride!"

≈   ≈   ≈

That night, for the bridegroom always sought his bride at night, Ananiah in the finest clothes his mother had made, together with his best friend Kaleb and several of Ananiah's friends took off from the farm with torches blazing in the night. As they entered the city of Yerushalayim, the party began shouting "The bridegroom is coming!" With their cries echoing throughout the streets, it wasn't long before the waiting bride and her bridesmaids heard the shouting. The bridal party had been organised by Kaleb who was at his friend's side rejoicing with the others.

As was the custom, Rachael together with her ten bridesmaids spent every night waiting for the groom to come and ensured that all the lamps the bridesmaid had (for it was very dark in the streets at night) were well trimmed expecting the groom's imminent arrival. The shouts that were emerging from the streets were gradually becoming louder and louder, so immediately Rachael who was just preparing for bed, quickly adorned her wedding dress and veil while her ten bridesmaids quickly went down the stairs to wait outside for the approaching bridal party.

Boaz and Sarah also quickly stopped what they were doing and began to adorn themselves in their finest clothes. It did not take long for the bridal party to reach the house and find the bridesmaids waiting. Then, as Rachael, followed by her parents came out of the house, the crowd that had gathered joined in with the young men and sang the traditional song:

> *Young men, singing traditional songs and shouting,*
> *"Behold the bridegroom is coming!"*[88]

Upon receiving a blessing from her parents, Ananiah took Rachael's hand, and with Rachael still heavily veiled, the party moved through the streets of Yerushalayim with much merriment and excitement. As the wedding party exited the city and made their way to the barn on Zuriel's farm, the moon shone brightly on the surrounding countryside, the soil of the fields tilled and bared with most crops no longer there, yet the topography of the land at night could plainly be seen by all.

As the bridal party made its way to the farmhouse, everyone was joyful and excited for the young couple who were now man and wife. Zuriel and Hannah warmly greeted their son's new bride and as the barn had been cleared of all farm utensils and equipment, tables richly laden with dates nuts, raisins, milk cheese, eggs, cucumbers, melons, roasted lamb, honey, breads of all kinds and other delicacies surrounded its inner perimeter. This was the place where the festivities would take place. Large vats of wine were located around the barn and the oil lamps placed around the building added to an atmosphere of celebration and festivity.

Then, when the musicians commenced quietly playing young people, including the bridesmaids and some of the young men in the groom's party

---

[88] Matthew 25:1-13

began joyfully dancing and singing. The young couple did not remain long in the barn but with Rachael's hand in his, Ananiah led her towards the farmhouse and the bridal chamber awaiting them. As part of his responsibilities as 'ruler of the feast' and best man, Kaleb walked behind them and once the couple had entered the bridal chamber, his responsibility was to stay at the door to ensure that the newlyweds were not disturbed while the marriage was being consummated. Once the bridegroom called through the door that this had taken place, Kaleb would make the announcement to the guests celebrating in the barn.

When they entered the bridal chamber, the happy couple were taken by surprise. Around the kitchen area and spread along the large narrow table were items of delicious food left for them to enjoy over the next five days. Wine and beverages were also in abundance and the room looked enticing and welcoming. It was here they formally gave themselves to each other, just as Adonai had ordained.

While Kaleb was fully aware of what was happening behind the closed door, and curious in some ways, he waited patiently for the news from Ananiah which would allow him to return to the festivities. He was eager to catch up with one of the bridesmaids, he believed to be Rachael's cousin. Captivated by her on that day of the Ingathering Festival when there was dreadful calamity with the stacked fruit on the dray (and his targeting skill finally excelled), he found it difficult to get her out of his mind.

It was only a few seconds after he realised that the smiles he believed he was receiving from Rachael at the Ingathering Festival, were actually intended for his friend. Immediately after this realisation he noticed that the girl dancing beside Rachel was smiling directly at him. By the time the dancers had circumnavigated three circles, Kaleb was smitten. He was overjoyed that very evening when he saw the same girl waiting at Rachael's house with the other bridesmaids in the bridal party. Her lamp held high reflected her maturing beauty revealing that she had changed somewhat, but in a more alluring way.

≈   ≈   ≈

After a while, Ananiah informed his friend through the closed door, that now he and Rachael were truly man and wife in the eyes of Adonai. Hastening to the barn which was located a small distance from the house, Kaleb informed the guests of the announcement which caused all the festivities to begin. After shouts of joy of acclamation and applause, the musicians increased the volume of the music and the celebrations truly began. As was the custom, neither the bride nor the groom would be seen for at least five days and during the festivities, food and wine was expected to flow freely[89].

By the fifth day, Ananiah and his bride, now no longer wearing a veil, came to the barn where the wedding feast celebrations continued. It was obvious to all who were present, that this was a couple who seemed very much in love and very contented. A person who was not so contented was Kaleb's mother who had become quite anxious for, apart from the first evening, she had not seen her son. Her husband Nosh instructed her not to worry but after several days, tiring of her anxious questions, turned to her and said "You do want grandchildren, don't you? Our son is Ananiah's age and he, too, should be thinking about a wife. As to his exact whereabouts I am totally unsure". (But as with whom his son was in company, Nosh was absolutely certain!) Kaleb's constant presence in the company of Rachael's young pretty cousin several times during the entire festivities provided

---

[89] John 2:2-10

Nosh with immense satisfaction that the conversation the two had several months ago, was now being considered seriously by his son. And after all, everyone loves a wedding!

---— *Chapter Fifteen* ---—

A NEW FAMILY

reat-grandfather's former room had been totally transformed
into a splendid home for the newlyweds whose early days of
marriage were extremely happy ones. Everything so lovingly
placed within the room was so successful in making this a home within
a home. There were times when the couple shared their meals with the
family and times when they shared a meal in the quietness and solitude
of their own home. Rachael had proved to be a blessing for her husband's
family for she brought a wonderful range of bread making skills. She also
brought to the family the gracious duties of a daughter and it was probably
no surprise at all, that Hannah grew to love her daughter-in-law just as if
she were her own.

Ananiah's skills and knowledge of the Torah were well appreciated
amongst the scribes and priests of the Temple. He was delighted that not
long after his wedding feast, he was given the honour of being a full-time
scribe and in that capacity, was often asked to provide explanations of pas-

sages read at the Synagogue meetings. His exposition of the Torah was well known - this was not at all surprising to many of the people, who still referred to him as "the one Adonai saved".

One day, he provided an explanation which warned those present at the meeting not to be stubborn like their forefathers before them. Because it was so important that they were ready to recognise the Promised One when he comes,[90] Ananiah challenged the people to be ready for the Messiah who may come at any time. Reminding the people of the rebellion of their race throughout time, he passionately urged them not only to listen with their ears but also with their hearts. Adonai was a God who loves and honours a willing heart.[91] As Ananiah talked fervently and directly to the people, Ezra, dressed as always in his fine clothes, sat directly near him in the finer seating of the Synagogue.[92] Staring intently at Ananiah who spoke clearly and with conviction, Ezra's heart grew callous and cold. "Who does he think he is!" he thought to himself. "Is he inferring that I, a Pharisee, do not know Adonai as well as he does? That young man needs to be put in his place!"

After the meeting, Ezra made a point of coming up to Ananiah who was surrounded by a small group of men who were eager to know more about the Promised One and the need to be ready for his coming. "It has always been the concern of my father and my late great grandfather, that the rebelliousness of our forefathers, even in the presence of Adonai in the desert, seems to prevail throughout our history. Man's heart has always been obstinate and to look to one's own needs and neglect the will of Adonai is unacceptable! We are turning our backs on the Living God as we pursue our own vain and selfish interests!"

---

[90]   Isaiah 6:10
[91]   1Chronicles 28:9
[92]   Luke 11:43

"I do hope that you are not including the priests, Sadducees and Pharisees in your comments for surely these people are the holy ones of Adonai! We are all well trained in His teachings and laws and fully aware of what He requires us to do. Surely you do not think we are stubborn like the people?" Ezra asked as he interrupted the conversation.

Immediately Ananiah replied, "You may have high privilege in your servitude for Adonai, Ezra, but you are a man and have a heart, a mind and a soul just like the rest of us. Man's heart is sinful and has the capacity and ability to be selfish and that is why, no matter what a man's calling is, all men must willingly put aside their pride and look to the Lord for wisdom and understanding". This answer seemed to cause Ezra's mouth to remain closed and his resentment of this young man to publicly proclaim that all men are sinners, especially himself, started to progressively grow.

≈   ≈   ≈

As Ananiah and his father sat on the front porch of the farmhouse, they commented how they missed those wonderful conversations they had with Obadiah about what each was learning about Adonai's word. The two men had come across several more Dabar Promises in their scribing and each strongly believed that the verses in question related to the Messiah himself. As they were talking, unknowingly Ananiah's fingers played with the small cube in his pocket, turning it round and round, forward and backward. Suddenly, he stopped and taking the cube out of his pocket, he turned to his father and said, "Do you remember when great grandfather gave me this?

Zuriel smiled. He was surprised his son still had the small cube and that it was still intact after all these years. Ananiah recalled how his great grandfather believed that Dabar Promises were always multi-faceted and as the number of passages that were coming to their attention was increasing, maybe it would help them to see what aspects or themes were emerging. As the cube had six sides, perhaps they should purchase six sheets of parchment and transcribe all the passages onto these? There were, Ananiah pointed out, some distinct themes that had emerged such as those that related to the Messiah's return to Isra'el, those that related to his genealogy, his rejection and the recent belief that he would be a suffering servant[93] . The men decided that each time they found a revelation about the Messiah, they would write this on a specific sheet. They would place the promise alongside those of similar content. Maybe this would help them grasp the enormity and importance of the promises. So, six pieces of parchment were purchased and Ananiah carefully transcribed all the Dabar Promises they had encountered over the years as Zuriel recalled those his father and grandfather had also found. With each documentation, both men were convinced that the Messiah to come would do something wonderful but when he comes and what he will do, was going to be completely different to the current interpretations of this wondrous event. They fully understood that such a belief left them on vulnerable ground but as their hearts were completely convinced, they knew they must firmly hold onto their beliefs.

As all mothers know once their fledglings leave the nest, the home can become a somewhat empty place, and this was certainly the case for Sarah and Boaz. Rachael was their only daughter and although Adonai had graciously blessed them with their only child, they did not realise, until she was married, how much her laughter, smiles and singing had filled their home over the years. This had not gone unnoticed by Ananiah who realised that the joy his wife brought not only to himself but his family as well, was bound to be missed by her loving parents. And so, he insisted that every

---

[93] Isaiah 53:4-5

time after the couple went to the Temple, they would visit her parents. Boaz and Sarah were extremely pleased when this happened and each time the couple visited them, they felt so re-assured that their daughter was very happy in her new role as a wife.

One time, when Ananiah and Rachael came to the house, Boaz was taken by his daughter's radiant face. "Are you well?" he asked Rachael.

"Do you really need to ask that question?" her mother responded. "Your daughter is absolutely a picture of health!"

But there was a reason for Boaz asking that question for as he looked upon his daughter in her happiness, remembering the same look so many years ago, when her mother's face was just as radiant - when she was carrying their only beloved daughter.

"I am fine, father", Rachael insisted.

Sometime later, when Rachael's figure began to grow, Boaz's expectations were realised. Ananiah was quite beside himself. Although he had given plenty of thought concerning the prospect of Rachael being his wife, he had not extended his thoughts to include children in that plan. Yet to know that his child was growing within his wife's womb proved overwhelming to him. In preparing for the baby, he started to make a crib. Before he had even started to cut the wood, his mother told him "Make sure it is large enough to hold two babies for I had just started to wean you when I conceived your brother. Often he was placed in the crib with you and it usually was a tight fit especially as you both grew so fast".

Ananiah was dismayed! How could his mother possibly be anticipating the next baby when the thought of extending his current family by one, proved to be a demanding challenge! Nevertheless, he heeded his mother's advice and made a beautiful crib for two which their mother could gently rock.

The following Sabbath, word had come to Ananiah and Rachael that her parents would like them to visit. As they were at the table, Boaz took hold of his daughter's hand. "My dearest daughter" he began, "Your mother and I are so delighted that you and Ananiah are having our first grandchild. We know that you are both very happy living with Ananiah's parents, but we realise the room in which you currently live is suffice for two, but not so for three".

"You are no doubt aware that when your dear grandfather passed away, he left your mother, his only child, the two-bedroom house he owned in the western side of Yerushalayim. Although we have rented the house over the years, your mother and I have decided that this house is too big for us, what with three empty bedrooms. Therefore, we plan to go and live-in grandfather's house and leave this house to you both so that your future family will have plenty of room in which to grow. We also believe that as this house is not far from the temple, this will be so much more convenient for Ananiah, particularly as he has now become a full-time scribe. Instead of having large distances to travel to and from home, he will be closer to you and your child during the day. Also, we will be able to visit you more often. We hope you will accept this offer as it would mean so much to your mother and I".

Ananiah looked into his wife's pleading eyes and replied: "This is such a kind offer, Boaz, and we are very grateful. We have talked about how we would cope in our small present abode. With my family's support, we have no worries however it is true that it would be reassuring for me to know, that if Rachael needs me during the day, I can get to her as quickly as possible. I also know that she misses you too, and that by us living here in the city, we would be blessed to have you so close by. Therefore, we accept your kind offer".

Overwhelmed that their offer had been accepted, Boaz and Sarah arose from the table and enthusiastically hugged both their son-in-law and their daughter. It was anticipated that the current tenants in their grandfather's house would be given one month to find an alternative dwelling. This meant that within the next month all aspects involved in the transloca-tion of both parties could be planned. It also meant that when it was time for Rachael to have her baby, this would be born, just as she was, in the same house.

The month went quickly and Ananiah dutifully helped his in-laws in their move to their new house in the western part of the city. Together with his friends, he transported furniture from both theirs and his own dwellings to their new homes. It was such a busy time for them all, espe-cially for Kaleb who was now in the throes of organising his own wedding. Yet it all took place and in the transference process, surprisingly no break-ages occurred!

Sometime later, as Ananiah was at work, a messenger came running into the room and went up to the head scribe whispering what seemed to be an important message. The head scribe nodded his head and the messenger immediately left. Gaining Ananiah's attention, the head scribe revealed with a smile, "Ananiah please finish the line you are now writ-ing and go to your house. Your first child is waiting to be born!" Swiftly, Ananiah finished the line he was transcribing; counted each word, line and space he had written that day, recorded these on his record sheet, returned both scrolls to their appropriate cupboards and left the building, his heart thumping within his chest. His first son was about to be born!

Very thankful of the decision to move his family into Yerushalayim, he rushed down the streets to his house finding his father and Boaz in the front room. Both Sarah and Hannah were with the expectant mother upstairs and just as Ananiah started to rush up the stairs to the bedroom, his father pulled him back. "Leave the women to do women's business" he advised his son and placing his arm around Ananiah's shoulders, led him to the empty chair in the room. Now and again, when Rachael's screams were heard, Ananiah would jump up out of the chair only to be consoled by Zuriel and Boaz. After what seemed hours of waiting (and Rachael screaming) a baby's loud cry filled the house.

"I have a son!" Ananiah exclaimed.

"Or a daughter!" said Boaz, "Daughters can be blessing too!"

"Ever since I knew that Rachael was expecting, I felt deep within me, that she was carrying a son. I feel so convinced about this – I believe this has come from Adonai Himself!"

Suddenly, there was yet another sound of a baby crying. Zuriel looked at the astounded face of his son. Then, there was silence. Unable to contain himself any longer, Ananiah rushed up the stairs two at a time. Nervously, he knocked on the bedroom door.

After waiting for what seemed an eternity, the door finally opened. His mother stood by the bed as she said "Ananiah, meet your two sons".

There, in the bed was Rachael, her face beaming as she held in each of her arms, two swaddled infants. Seeing the happiness and amazement of her husband's face, she looked at the child on her right. "This is your eldest son" she informed him. "When he entered this world, he made a terrible noise. He was so white and pale, though now he is gaining a little more colour".

"Then, let us call him Laban" said Ananiah "for that means 'white'".

Turning to the child she held in her left arm, Rachael continued. "This is your second son, who almost immediately came into the world after his brother. Crying together they made such a noise until your second son reached across and touched his elder brother, and immediately their crying stopped!"

"Then he shall be called Naban for that means 'comforter'" the new father proclaimed.

"Laban and Naban, won't that be a little confusing?" Sarah asked. But Rachael gazing into the eyes of her delighted and proud husband declared, "Their father has given them their names. Laban and Naban are our sons".

≈   ≈   ≈

A few months after the twins were born, after a very bountiful harvest, Ananiah assisted his mother in selling their produce in the Yerushalayim market on their busiest day. All members of his own and extended families were involved clearing up the last harvest and preparing for the next and so, although his obligations as a scribe were expanding, Ananiah was pleased that he could help his mother and his sister sell the family's goods.

Nosh's tannery skills were the among the finest in Yerushalayim and it wasn't long before his reputation as a tanner spread around the city. So much so, that he found it beneficial to sell his produce in the local markets and use his shop for the preparation of the hides and skins he had purchased. Kaleb and his father Nosh were busily selling their wares on the stall adjacent to Ananiah's but there unfortunately was little time for the two friends to chat. As the marketplace echoed with the sounds of buyers and sellers completing their business, in the background, once again, a hammering noise could be heard.

As many people had gathered around the edict nailed to the Governor's Gate waves of disapproving remarks were heard around the marketplace. Suddenly a sea of discontentment rose within the crowd. Leaving his mother and sister at the stall, Ananiah made his way towards the notice and after reading this for a short time, returned to the stall. "It is an edict from Caesar Augustus", Ananiah explained. "It appears that there is going to be a census taken of the entire Roman Empire"[94].

"Why would they want to take a census of the empire?" Hannah inquired.

"Why to see how much they might raise taxes!" stated Kaleb who had heard the whole conversation.

"It is stated that everyone has to return to his own town to register. Thanks be to Adonai that we were all born in Yerushalayim!" Ananiah said.

"Thanks be to Adonai that your wives have also safely delivered your sons" Hannah remarked to both Ananiah and Kaleb, "and they don't have to suffer a burdensome saga of travelling long distances either with children or with child!"

---

[94]   Luke 2: 1-3

—— *Chapter Sixteen* ——

ONE UNFORGETTABLE NIGHT

I n the between hours of night and morning, Ananiah's sleep was abruptly disrupted by the sound of a loud anguished cry. Not wanting this to disturb his wife sleeping beside him, he arose from his bed and went over to the crib where his son Naban, swaddled in a warm shawl his grandmother Hannah had made for him, was wailing loudly. Small tears of anguish fell down his tiny face and so Ananiah, not wishing for his wife's sleep to be broken, picked the baby up and cradled him in his arms. "Oh Naban, will not your brother comfort you?", he said. As he cradled the baby close to his heart, he looked at the sleeping twin, totally undisturbed and oblivious to the disruption. "How could anyone sleep through your crying?" he asked his second born. And then, his thoughts ceased as he stopped in absolute amazement.

Although it was in the darkness of night, Ananiah could see everything in the room so clearly - just as if it was day! - the tears down his small son's face, his twin brother Laban sleeping sweetly in his swaddled clothes, his wife's beautiful face as she lay slumbering, the furniture in the room! It was as if the room was alight with daylight itself! Glancing towards the stone stairs that led up to the top flat roof balcony of their home, even more light radiantly streamed down from the top of the stairs. So, together with his son who had now ceased his crying, Ananiah walked up the stairs onto the roof only to find that the brightness came from a star shining brilliantly in the sky. That faint, familiar feeling he experienced that fatal day in the catacombs started to seep through his body. He knew in his heart that the bright shining star before was created by a mighty hand; but what was its purpose?

"Greetings Ananiah!" he heard a voice say. "Did the light awaken you, too?"

Looking across his roof he saw his next-door neighbour gazing at the sky. "It certainly is a glorious star! I have never seen anything like it! It's like it is heralding something great!" the man said.

"But where do you think it is located?" asked another voice, coming from his neighbour on the roof of the house on the other side. It was evident that the brightness of the star had interrupted the sleep of many people in the city. Exquisite in its radiance, the light clearly exposed all the houses roof tops and streets in Yerushalayim. Everything could be clearly seen; the light much brighter than moonlight - but softer than day.

"Well, it is definitely in the south but what town or city would that be shining directly over?" one man asked.

"The only town that it is that direction is Beit-Lechem (Bethlehem)" replied the another.

"Beit-Lechem!" thought Ananiah. "Could it possibly mean the Messiah has come?"

Not knowing whether it was the return of that joyous feeling that only Adonai gives, or whether it was the mention of Beit-Lechem or the star shining so brightly in the night, or even a combination of all these things, Ananiah felt deeply compelled to sight the scrolls once again to confirm what he thought was happening. So, he turned to go down the steps to return to the bedroom where he gently lay Naban, who was now contented and quiet, back in the crib. However, as soon as he was laid on the blanket beside his brother, Naban's cries seem to increase all the louder. There were moments when he stopped as he was picked up and comforted by his father but as soon as his tiny body touched the blanket in the crib, Naban started crying. After a while, his father concluded, that to prevent his wife and other son from wakening, he must take Naban with him.

Exiting the house quietly and moving down the brightly illuminated street it wasn't long before they came to the Temple Baths. Ananiah believed that he, at the age of 8, was the youngest person ever to use these baths which were specifically designated for priests, scribes and other temple servants. Now his six-month old son was going to go through the process of purification even though he would have no idea of what was going on. It was not surprising to find the baths opened, for priests and temple workers complete different tasks at different times of the day and night. Yet, when Ananiah undressed himself and Naban, no one was present. Discarding his own clothes and the shawl wrapped tightly around his son into the large basket in the centre of the room, Ananiah said to his son: "Please, please be good and please don't do anything you should not do while we purify ourselves!"

Making their way naked down into the baths using the left-hand side of the steps, the couple immersed in the calm warm water from the natural spring. Naban shouted in glee and delight as he and his father completed the purification ritual and then, finally, his father quickly immersed the child entirely under the water. Immediately bringing Naban up out of the water and holding him in the air with both arms outstretched, Ananiah lowered his head completely under the water. Arising to find his son continuing in joyous laughter, Ananiah brought him out of the pool by walking back up the steps of the baths on the alternate side. Reaching for two towels, he went quickly into the next room where he dried the child and himself.

Looking at the arrangement of clothes on the table in the dressing room while it was easy for Ananiah to choose what he could wear, his tiny son proved much more difficult and so he ended up swaddling Naban in the towel which he had used to dry him. Picking up the largest outer garment he could find, he proceeded up the stairs to the prayer chamber, which like the bath was completely void of any person. Ananiah with his son to his chest, prayed for guidance from Adonai to lead him to the truth of the night and the meaning of the star. Going through the large doors, moving quickly down the corridor towards the Synagogue, he was shocked to find that after knocking on the door at the end of the corridor many times, there was no answer.

Realising that there was no door keeper, he rushed back down the corridor, through the empty prayer room across the back of the baths and up the steps to the street. The Synagogue and its surrounding buildings were not located far away and once again the star-lit streets of Yerushalayim made travelling easy. Hurrying down the streets, Ananiah finally made it to the Synagogue, then crossing the courtyard, he walked through an arch way which led to the long corridor in the colonnade.

When he arrived at the scribing room, he was pleased to see that this was also well lit by the surrounding starlight. Hesitantly, he placed his swaddled child on the floor before lighting the small candle on his desk. Then, unwrapping the baby, he secured the large garment between two narrow columns at the side of the room, near to his desk, Ananiah made a hammock. Lifting Naban up off the floor, he placed him across the middle of the makeshift hammock so that Nathan could see his father and what he was doing. Instructing Naban to watch him, he made his way to the right cupboard near the chief scribe's desk. Once again, this was locked but fortunately Ananiah knew where the key was kept. Opening the small decorated box on the chief priest's table, he took out the key and returned to the cupboard. As he opened the cupboard door, light filtrated the storeroom, revealing shelves upon shelves all stowing the original scrolls. Determining where the scroll of Mikhah (Micah) was, he reach for this and took it back to his desk. Grateful that Naban was not crying, he stretched out the scroll. Moving his finger carefully across the parchment from right to left, his eyes eagerly searched for a specific verse until he came across the words that were echoing in his mind. Here, the resounding words confirmed his hopes and aspirations:

> But you, **Beit-Lechem** (emphasis added), Eprathah, though you are small among the clans of Judea, out of you shall come for me one who will rule over Isra'el, whose origins are from of old, from ancient times.[95]

After reading this aloud, Ananiah rolled up the scroll and returned it to its place in the cupboard. But where did the other verse that was going around his head come from? He was certain he had read it somewhere! Moved by a strong feeling that the mysterious verse came from one of the books of the Torah, he glanced at the inscriptions at the ends of the assorted scrolls. Without realising what he was doing, he found himself reaching

---

[95]   Micah 5:2

for the scrolls of B'midbar (Numbers). Believing it was in the middle section of the book, he took three scrolls down from the shelves and returned to his desk.

After he had rolled out the first scroll, he quickly read from right to left only to be unsuccessful. Closing the scroll, he picked up the second. Once again as he read quickly through the scroll, he could not find the verse he was looking for. However, when he came to the third scroll his eager fingers stopped as the lines appeared:

> A **star** (emphasis added) will come out of Jacob; a sceptre will rise out of Isra'el.[96]

Reading this out aloud he turned to his son and pointing to the light shining through the side windows stated "Now that's what I call a star! Don't you think?" Naban smiled at his father. "And," added his father joyfully "another Dabar Promise!"

Returning all three scrolls to the cupboard, quite by accident, another scroll fell to the floor. Picking this up, Ananiah noticed that it came from the book of Yesha'yahu (Isaiah) and as many of the prophecies about the Messiah came from this book, he took the scroll to his desk to read what it contained. Once again, as his fingers moved across the parchment, they immediate stopped when he came to the verse which said:

> For unto us a **child is born** (emphasis added), unto us a son is given, and the government will be upon his shoulders, and he will be called Wonderful, Counsellor, Mighty God, Everlasting Father, Prince of Peace.[97]

---

[96] Numbers 24:17
[97] Isaiah 9:6

Reading this more loudly, most excitedly Ananiah looked up at the star and then turned to his son. "Naban, our Messiah has finally come! A Dabar Promise fulfilled!" Naban babbled loudly and joyously. Ananiah's heart was stirred. The One for whom Isra'el had longed for had finally come! Yet would Adonai's nation be ready for him and most importantly, would they give him the reception he deserved? Returning the scroll to its original place, Ananiah locked the cupboard, put back the key in its box, picked up his son, removed the hammock and blew out the candle. "Time to go home", he said.

Woken by the brightness of the morning sun, Rachel looked across the bed where her beloved was soundly sleeping. So, as not to wake him, she quietly moved across to the crib to greet her precious babies, who like their father were sound asleep. Before she had finished saying "Good Morning my precious boys!" she was perplexed by the attire of her second son. Wrapped very strangely in a garment she had never seen before, she wondered where her husband (who obviously was the cause of this confusion) had obtained such an unusual vestment. No doubt he would tell her when he was awake.

≈　　≈　　≈

That morning when Ananiah woke he explained to his wife what had happened the night before. Oblivious to the light and the interruptions, she had slept most soundly. Her husband, on the other hand appeared so animated and excited and it wasn't long before he left to tell his father about what had happened the night before. Although the distance from Yerushalayim to their small farm on the outskirts of the city was not far, today it seemed to take an eternity to get there. Finally, when he reached the farmhouse, he found his father sitting on the front porch.

Zuriel listened intently as his son told him of all that had happened. Excitement filled Zuriel's heart as his son revealed he believed that the longed-for Messiah had finally come. When Ananiah told him of the confirmation he had received from the Holy Word, Zuriel's heart was filled with praise. Together father and son prayed to Adonai giving thanks to His faithfulness in the fulfilment of His promises to the people. To think that very soon, Isra'el would be delivered from her evil captors and the Jewish people free from the bondage they had endured since the beginning of time!

≈   ≈   ≈

Several days later father and son sat on the farmhouse porch in deep discussion over what had just transpired. In the distance, they saw a man approaching the farm who seemed to be in a hurry. It wasn't long before they discerned that the emerging figure was Nosh. Approaching the two on the porch, Nosh greeted them and then sat down on the floor of the porch quite breathless. He wanted to share with them some rumours he had heard whilst attending the temple. It was reported that approximately ten days after the first sighting of the star in the south a couple had brought their first born to the temple [98]as was the custom. Old Shim'on (Simeon) was there that day and it was rumoured that upon seeing the child, the old man took the child in his arms and began blessing him for being 'the light of revelations to the gentiles'. As Shim'on was getting on in years, despite being well known, his attendance at the Temple seemed to be getting less and less. Yet on the very day he attended the temple, he offered dedicated praise to Adonai for the affirmation of the Promise. Moreover, it was said that the

---

[98]   Luke 2: 25-35

Prophetess Hannah Bat-P'nu'el (Anna), who constantly went daily to the Temple began praising Adonai for the one that is to come[99]. "Could this be true?" asked Nosh. Then the men talked about all that had happened and all three believed that the time for fulfilment had come and now, Isra'el will finally be redeemed.

---

[99]   Luke 2: 36-38

── *Chapter Seventeen* ──

HYPOCRISY IN
A MIRROR

One day Nosh had the task of watching the stall at the market together with his youngest son Micah, while Kaleb, whose skills were also gaining recognition, worked in the shop. Nosh witnessed the strangest of sights. As he was busily selling his wares in the marketplace which, as usual was a thrive of bustle and activity, his ears heard the strangest sound. Looking up he saw entering the marketplace and moving across the courtyard a large caravan of camels. At the front of the convoy were several men robed in fine clothes entwined in golden and silver threads. On their heads, they wore turban-like hats which were in the finest of colours, mauve, blue, red and green. Holding their heads erect as they rode, it was obvious that these highly-distinguished men were also of high degree. Each of the camels on which they rode, had beautiful mats across their humps and attached to the mats were tiny silver and gold bells.

As the camels gracefully strolled through the marketplace, the melodious sound of tiny bells rang across the courtyard. Behind the men were several camels, each stacked with lots of boxes carefully tied across the camel's backs. The sight of the procession caused many people to cease what they were doing and watch the spectacle before them.

Nosh told his younger son, to mind the stall and rushed up towards the men who led the caravan. He heard someone in the crowd speak to one of the visitors in Aramaic asking them where they were from. Nosh could not believe his ears when he heard one of the visitors reply that they had come from the east following a star which they have found from the astronomical charts, which heralded a new born king. They believed that this king was the King of the Jews. This news startled the crowd and many became troubled by the presence of these foreigners[100]. As the procession made its way towards Herold's Palace, Nosh informed his son he would be back and then proceeded as quickly as he could, leaving the city and making his way to the farm house where he related to his friend Zuriel all that had transpired.

Hearing his friend's words, Zuriel responded. "Surely, Ananiah is correct when he says that the Messiah has come! As you were telling me, the verse 'May all kings fall down before him!'[101] sprung immediately into my mind. I don't know if these visitors are kings but they sound very regal indeed. Did you say they made their way towards Herold's Palace? I doubt whether any good will come from that. We must relate this news to Ananiah. He will be most encouraged to hear it".

One Sabbath, after Ananiah had once again provided an explanation to a passage read during the meeting in the Synagogue, he and his father were making their way to the Temple. Meeting Nosh and Kaleb on the way, the four made their way towards the Court of Isra'el. Whilst walking under the

---

[100] Matthew 2:1-2
[101] Psalm 72:11

western colonnade, they saw Ezra walking quickly towards them. Although he had anticipated that he would talk to Ananiah privately, the fact that there was company present did not deter him. After all, Ananiah's companions were foolishly following his downward path. Ezra was convinced that someone should inform Ananiah his incorrect and farfetched ideas about the coming Messiah, particularly as Ananiah's ideas transgressed far from the learned teachings of the Pharisees. Looking forward to pulling Ananiah down off the pedestal he had made for himself, Ezra would be able to, as it has been said, "kill two birds with one stone" – but in this case, it would be four. Without any formal greeting, Ezra walked straight up to Ananiah and said "I want to talk to you Ananiah, about what you have been stating publicly in the Synagogue. Your words are quite foolish and are leading people astray".

"Which of my words are foolish?" Ananiah asked, "and how are these leading people astray?"

That was the exact cue that Ezra had anticipated and so, as he had rehearsed his response many times before the meeting, he continued to address the young man. Ezra pointed out the responsibility for interpreting and teaching Adonai's word lay with His appointed priests and the leaders of the Jewish people and not with the untrained farmer who has only had a tiny glimpse into the law of Adonai. Ananiah should therefore not present himself as an expert publicly or in conversation with Adonai's people but leave the interpretation of the Torah to those that Adonai has appointed to serve in the Sanhedrin.

Secondly, in assuming the pretentious role of a priest, Ananiah did not speak to the people at their level, but rather at a level above their understanding and hence, he made no connection with the people he was attempting to teach. Thirdly, he was making all people in the Synagogue feel as if they were complete sinners and had no right to the forgiveness of Adonai. By making them feel so repulsive, they would never be able to receive Adonai's forgiveness. Finally, Ezra concluded that if Ananiah knew the law of Adonai, he would understand that He totally forbids us to add or subtract to His Laws[102].

Before he had time to respond, Ananiah heard his father say "You are correct when you say that we have been forbidden to add or subtract from the word of Adonai, Ezra. But tell me, why is it that the priests and law makers of our people have added so many more laws to the number of laws Adonai gave to Moshe (Moses)?"

Totally taken back by this question, Ezra retaliated in a very callous tone, "I am talking to Ananiah, not to you".

"Then allow me to answer your comments as a dear brother in the family of the Almighty Adonai" Ananiah replied. "First, I do not consider myself an expert in Adonai's law for that honour must go to my learned brothers who have trained so very diligently over the years. All I know is that when I am scribing, Adonai's word is such a blessing and by His grace, these are often written not just on the paper before me, but etched within my heart. Does not the word say that if the law of God is in your heart, your feet do not slip?[103]" Ezra did not answer but just stared at the man before him, his face pale and expressionless.

"So, I believe, because they are etched within my heart, that I am not adding to or subtracting to Adonai's word. I am just sharing with my brothers and sisters what I believe. Secondly, as so many of my brothers have come to me after the meetings to discuss what I have said, I am not sure whether I have been speaking in a language which is alien to them but your comment is a valid one, and one that I shall endeavour to keep in mind when I continue to share my heart with others".

---

[102] Deuteronomy 4:2
[103] Psalm 37:31

"Thirdly, I do believe we are all sinners; Does not Adonai's law ask, "Who can say, 'I have kept myself pure: I am clean and without sin?'"[104] Are you without sin, Ezra? Are all the priests, Pharisees and Sadducees without sin? Of course, not! For when we are disrobed of our fine clothes or poor rags, we are just men in the sight of Adonai."

"Are you telling me" continued Ezra "that Adonai Himself has told you all these things?"

"Yes" replied Ananiah, "I believe He has".

"Do you mean He has chosen to do this with a poor farming boy and not the learned priests whom He has chosen to serve Him?" demanded Ezra.

"Why Adonai has chosen to teach me these things, I do not know but I do know that His ways are not at all like mine[105]. However, as His child, I gratefully accept whatever He may choose to teach me. Don't you feel the same way, Ezra?"

"How dare you attempt to lecture me!" retaliated Ezra in anger and immediately turned his back and walked off in a high-hearted huff leaving the four men totally amazed. They stood aghast for a minute till Zuriel broke the silence. "Tell me, what just happened? The whole time he was talking I kept on saying 'What a fool!' and then immediately sought Adonai's forgiveness[106]. His tongue was as cruel as that of a cobra's, his words as venomous and poisonous without a shred of love! Does he not realise that his actions and the way he spoke reveal more about himself and that is not pleasing to Adonai? Does he not realise and know His God lives within him? Does he not realise that he failed to reveal Adonai to us in the manner he spoke? The man lacks compassion and shows no love of Adonai!"

---

[104] Proverbs 20:9
[105] Isaiah 55:8-9
[106] Matthew 5:22

"If you don't mind a word of advice?" came from a voice of someone standing nearby. Turning around they saw the familiar face of Zév who had watched the whole proceedings. Speaking directly to Ananiah, he said: "I have met many people in my life and I have sadly come to two conclusions – I have had a similar conversation with your father a few years ago. Throughout this world, there are many different races and people. Unfortunately, no matter what race, Adonai's people included, there will sadly be a group of people who will just not listen no matter how patiently you plead or talk to them. They have closed their ears and hearts to anything that may be said and consequently, they will not move away from their stubbornness. These are the people that you cannot change and only Adonai can, if they allow Him to do so. Therefore, do not press them anymore, and allow Adonai to change them. Only Adonai can break through their stonewalled hearts. You cannot. So, hand them over to Him; they are not your problem, but His. Finally, our God is so great and His promises are true and there is nothing that can prevail against Him. What He has promised, He will deliver. You must believe this truth".

"Thank you for your kind words of wisdom, Zév. Once again you have brought peace to a troubled soul" remarked Zuriel.

"It is strange that the word 'fool' came to your mind as Ezra was speaking", Nosh said to his friend. "The whole time he was speaking, one word came to my mind repeatedly."

"What was that?" they asked in unison.

"Pomegranates!" Nosh replied.

Chapter Eighteen

Two special promises on a terrible, terrible day

The sound of ink being etched on paper filled the room where all scribes performed their duties with deepest concentration. This familiar noise had resounded through the room for the whole day and now it was late in the afternoon. So deeply entrenched in their tasks the scribes were not aware that a messenger came quickly into the room and whispered to the chief scribe whose face whitened in disbelief. The messenger left as quickly as he came and with a deep breath, the chief scribe told all the men to stop their work and return to their homes immediately. All men stopped, counted the tallies of the day's work before folding both scrolls and returned these to their respective cupboards. "What has happened?" asked Ananiah but the head scribe in disbelief could only shake his head.

He had only just reached the courtyard near the Synagogue when the sound of a woman wailing came to his ears and as he turned the first corner, the sound seemed to amplify. "What has happened?" he asked as he stopped a man walking down the narrow street. When the man turned to look at Ananiah, tears were flooding down his face as he spoke the words that were like arrows in Ananiah's heart; "Those bastard Romans have slayed every young male babe in the city![107] Not one boy under the age of two is alive!"

"Laban! Naban! Laban! Naban!!" exclaimed Ananiah, "My sons! My poor sons!" he cried as he started to run towards his home on the western side of the city.

But suddenly, the noise of wailing became too overwhelming and he stopped in his tracks. As the cries of people near and far resounded through the streets of the city, for some unknown reason he found himself saying aloud "Rachael is weeping for her children!"[108] For just a moment, the world seemed to stop. What does this mean he thought to himself? Could this be a Dabar Promise that he and his family had overlooked? What about the child Messiah? Has the one Adonai sent been maliciously murdered by the cruelty of man?

Turning around, Ananiah ran as fast as he could. He would not go to the scribing room for he knew that the words he had just uttered came from the prophet Yirmeyahu (Jeremiah). Instead, he believed there was only one place where he could receive an answer from Adonai; so, instead of completing the purification process again, he headed straight for the Temple. Entering via the Golden Gate he quickly ran down a set of steps

---

[107] Author's Note: Matthew 2:16 states "Bethlehem and its vicinity", as Jerusalem in approximately 5 miles from Bethlehem, it has been included within this story.

[108] Jeremiah 31:15

which lead to the long corridor with its many rooms under the base of the Temple ground. Then, recalling which flight of stairs he needed to take, he rushed quickly up these and found himself in the Court of the Priests. The curtained area that seemed to call him so many years ago, as a small child, was nearby and yet again', it seemed to entice him to draw near. Once more, Ananiah sensed that the Mighty hand that extracted him out of danger in the catacombs, was again close by. Hesitating for only a second, he took the large golden rope that was hanging on the bronze hook on the wall and tied this securely around his waist. Walking up to the curtain, he took off his shoes and taking a deep breath, Ananiah brushed the veil aside and went into The Holy Place.

Immediately without any effort on his own part, he found himself face down, flat on the floor. His heart beating so loudly in his chest, Ananiah drew all his courage yet faintly murmured, "The child – is the Messiah child safe?" A voice which sounded like rushing winds and waters replied, "The child is safe in Egypt". Overwhelmed by the Holy Presence of Adonai, the wondrous voice he had just heard and his love for this God who had so willingly saved him, Ananiah found himself saying out loud, "Out of Egypt, I called my son[109]" Then, his body shaking nervously Ananiah proclaimed "I have looked so forward to seeing Him!" To his dismay, the voice that sounded like rushing wind and water replied, "Not with thine eyes shall you see Him but your very soul. And, after all has come to pass, you shall see Him for who He truly is".

Suddenly out of nowhere, Ananiah found himself extracted from The Holy Place and at the feet of a priest standing over him, his face full of anger and rage. The end of the golden rope was secured in his hands. Untying the golden rope, the priest roughly pulled Ananiah to his feet and slapped

---

[109] Hosea 11:1

him sharply across the face with one of the sandals Ananiah had placed outside the veil. In complete numbness, all Ananiah could say was "Rachael is weeping for her children: Out of Egypt I called my son".

"Don't you realise what you have done? You have done the unthinkable! You have against Adonai's word, entered The Holy Place! The punishment is death!"

"Rachael is weeping for her children: Out of Egypt I called my son" was all Ananiah could say.

Slapping him once more across the face, the priest disclaimed "Ananiah, you have desecrated The Holy Place where only priests can enter. Don't you realise what you have done?"

"Rachael is weeping for her children: Out of Egypt I called my son" Ananiah replied.

Slapping him even harder with the sandal, the priest angrily scrutinized Ananiah's eyes and at last he seemed to be attentive. "You are absolutely correct when you say, 'Rachael is weeping for her children' for your dear wife Rachael is at home mourning the dreadful loss of Laban and Naban. I will not cause any more grief to her on this terrible day by taking her husband from her, too. So, you may go home and comfort your wife and console her tonight. But, in the morning, when the temple guards arrive at your home you must go with them to the Sanhedrin where you will be trialled and punished. You have brought your own death upon yourself. You have been told that it is unlawful for anyone who is not a priest to enter The Holy Place, yet you chose to defy this. You had best go home quickly and may Adonai have mercy on your soul".

As Ananiah rushed towards his home, his heart was confused and tormented as feelings of anguish seemed to merge with feelings of peace. He did not think it possible that the two emotions could accompany one another but his head, his heart and his soul were all in total disarray. He felt such joy and relief that the Messiah child was safe and realised that just as Zév had recently said, Adonai was in control. He also reflected with joy on the promise he was given. He would see the Messiah one day but not with his eyes, his very soul. Why not with his eyes? He found the second part of the promise complexing; what was meant by 'seeing him for who he really is'? Isn't he just the Messiah; the one Adonai chose for His people! As these thoughts were running through his head, Ananiah stopped still and began sobbing loudly.

His beloved sons! – only two years of age and so innocent! Sweet Laban and Naban who had been such a precious gift and blessing to Rachael and himself; cruelly slaughtered and slain so mercilessly! And for what reason? Whatever could be the reason of slaughtering defenceless children who had done no harm to anyone but whose only purpose in their brief lives was to bring joy to their parents? "So many questions" thought Ananiah to himself, "so many unanswered questions!"

When he entered his front door, he found his father and mother together with Boaz and Sarah attempting to console an anguished and decimated Rachael whose loud sobs filled the room. Beside herself in grief, there appeared to be no consolation or words that could be said to comfort her. Seeing her husband standing in the room, Rachael fled straight into his arms and the two together locked in grief, cried oceans of tears; each firmly holding onto the other, they grieved the loss of their sweet innocent boys who were so cruelly taken from them; the boys they were unable to protect but loved so devotedly.

Chapter Nineteen

DELIVERANCE ONCE MORE

Waking before the cock crowed the next morning, Ananiah's thoughts were interrupted by the sound of loud banging on his front door. Scanning down into the street, he saw below his house a small group of temple guards. Glancing over to his wife who was woken by the noise, he told her that there was a meeting of the Sanhedrin, and he had been summoned. Passionately kissing his wife on her lips, he said farewell and left.

Once again mixed emotions and thoughts rattled incoherently through his brain and the past twenty-four hours seemed like an endless nightmare. Yet as the morning sun shone on his face as the party walked down the street, he knew that this was not a dream and that what lay before him was very daunting – so much so, that he became extremely anxious.

The temple guards took him directly to the Royal Stoa and as they crossed the lower floors Ananiah recalled the day when he and his father stood before the Sanhedrin. This time, however, his attention was not drawn to the fine tiles on the floor yet the building on his right which he knew was the temple, still seemed to draw him. The comfort and the closeness of Adonai in His Temple the night before was not forgotten by Ananiah and so it was with mixed emotions the young man was led up the stairs to the higher floor.

At the top of the stairs to his complete surprise was another small group of temple guards with his father, Zuriel. Ananiah's heart sank. He dreaded the thought that the man he had loved so dearly would witness his trial and the pending judgement which would bring total shame upon his family. When the guards who were accompanying Ananiah met their peers, they seemed to be in deep discussion before eight of the company left, leaving one guard to remain with the bewildered son and his father.

"Do you have any idea why we are here?" his father asked. Ananiah just could not bring himself to inform his father about what had happened. His father would be so disappointed and recognising the fear growing inside of him, he repeated the prayer that his great-grandfather Obadiah had taught him. Facing yet once again the certainty of death, all he could do was place himself in the strongest of hands: '*El-roi, El-roi! You delivered your people from the waves of the Red Sea and from the scorn of Egypt, deliver me, your child, for death is before me and I am doomed*'.

Upon being summoned by the Sanhedrin who were meeting in the far end of the Royal Stoa, the men walked together as they had done so many years before but unlike the previous time when Ananiah felt fear, this time the words of his great-grandfather's prayer were once again so meaningful. This time when he repeated the words, Ananiah said them not just hoping there was a God who could save him; but in full assurance that Adonai was his friend, his king and lord and would, if he so wished, answer his heartfelt prayer. As they were approaching the council, Ananiah noticed that there were only twenty-two men present and on the right side of the semi-circle of the seated members, was one vacant chair which stood out so clearly like a missing front tooth in a smiling mouth. It didn't take long for Ananiah to realise that the priest who had interrupted him the night before was not present. That caused him to wonder when the Head Priest rose from his chair and addressed the men before him.

"Greetings Zuriel and Ananiah!" he began. "Thank you for coming to our meeting so promptly. The council has been in urgent consultation for together with the tragic and devastation occurrence yesterday, last night something wretched happened in the Temple. You may be aware that we have an empty chair and that chair belonged to Tzion, a faithful priest of many years".

"Sadly, last night when he went to trim the Golden Lamp and burn the incense on the altar in The Holy Place, Tzion was called to Adonai. He was found early this morning by another priest with the golden rope firmly secured around his waist just outside of The Holy Place.

Our laws require another to take his place and we have elected Ezra to be a high priest in the Lord's service. But this, as you see, leaves a space on the council which needs to be filled. The Sanhedrin has discussed this vacant position and this morning caste lots to find the man to fill the position[110]"

"Zuriel, you have always served Adonai most faithfully as have your forefathers before you. We ask that you continue to serve your maker by joining us in the Sanhedrin where your knowledge and expertise in Adonai's word will provide the direction we need. Are you willing, Zuriel, to serve your God in this capacity?"

---

[110] 1 Chronicles 24:31

Zuriel immediately thought of his father and grandfather who had hoped that one day one of their sons would be able to sit in the Sanhedrin. Although he knew it would be a difficult task, Zuriel believed that with Adonai's help, he might be able to provide some input into the decisions that the Sanhedrin made, hopefully ensuring that the decisions were honouring and in accordance with Adonai's law. "With His help, I am willing", Zuriel replied.

"Then come and take your seat and may Adonai bless you and give you wisdom and strength to serve Him faithfully, bringing Him the glory". And all the men seated around the apse said, "So be it!" and applauded loudly.

Turning to Ananiah the Head Priest said: "The Sanhedrin requested that you witness the honour that has come to your father, Ananiah, because we believe that you, like him you have become a faithful servant of Adonai. It is our hope that one day we shall be offering such an opportunity to you. God speed."

Ananiah, in total disbelief, struggled to comprehend what had just taken place. Extremely proud of his father, he was so pleased to have witnessed what had happened. And as to how Adonai had transformed the previous night's situation into one that seemed not to have taken place bewildered him. Once again, El-roi had seen his dilemma and once again, saved him from the jaws of death! Again, he re-affirmed to himself, that Adonai had a specific task for him to do and not knowing exactly what this could be, he once again placed his life into the caring hands of his Lord.

Hannah felt in turmoil as her excited husband told her his news. She could see by his face that he was delighted with the opportunity to serve his Lord in this way, but not forgetting the hopelessness he had recently faced by means of man-made decisions in Adonai's business, she felt unsure.

This was the same feeling his best friend felt as, upon hearing the news, Nosh ran to see his friend. Although Zuriel appeared to be excited by the decision, Nosh was not so certain. Privately, he talked to his friend as they sat on the farmhouse front porch. "Are you sure this is what you want to do?" he asked. "Do you think you are strong enough to take on the obstinacy of the Sanhedrin?" Zuriel thanked his friend, appreciating his concern and then replied: "Nosh, I have served Adonai faithfully for many years and my body tells me I am getting older each day. As Ananiah is now a full-time scribe, I am no longer scribing; his brothers are capably managing the family farm, but I still feel that I can serve Adonai somehow".

"When I was in the Royal Stoa, yesterday, as the High Priest was talking, I looked around at the 22 men seated before me and I realised that while there were some who had their own agendas in being on the council, there were several other good men there – men of faith and good intent. Just as I was thinking this, I was asked if I was willing to serve Adonai in this capacity. Of course, I will! I realised then, that I would not be alone providing what I do honours Adonai in my service to Him. The political or personal ambitions of those that served were not my concern, but Adonai's. I know I may not change their selfish hearts, but I can stand up for what I believe to be true and so, it is for that reason, I will meet this challenge! Zév's words are etched deep within my heart, just like the marvellous words of Adonai. Through all the trials and difficulties that lie before me, He will be my rock!"[111]"

When Ananiah returned to his house immediately after he left the Temple, he found his wife crying in the kitchen. Wrapped in the grief she bore for her murdered children and deeply missing her husband, she felt very much alone. Cradling her strongly in his arms, he kissed her forehead and told her all would be well. Securely wrapped in this loving embrace, they once more consoled each other but the morning's reprieve was dead

---

[111] Psalm 31:3

locked within his heart. Despite Ananiah's wicked and ungodly actions, Adonai had once again intervened! Yet Ananiah had done so many sinful things without even thinking- he entered the Holy Place defiled and uncleansed; he entered the Holy Place where he should not have gone, and his sin totally condemned him. But for some reason he had been delivered, yet again! He vowed to himself, that what he had so wrongfully done the night before and the amazing rescue that had taken place must remain his secret – one he would take to his grave.

PART THREE

FULFILMENT
AND
EXPOSITION

Chapter Twenty

THE IN-BETWEEN YEARS

A lone on the farmhouse's front porch, Ananiah's tired eyes struggled to peer at the harvested countryside around him. Fondly he remembered with great joy the many times he had such elongated discussions with his father and great grandfather on that very porch. "Those wonderful days!" he thought to himself – days which seemed like yesterday, but in truth occurred twenty-eight years ago! Those twenty-eight years had turned his brown hair grey, his blue eyes dim and now he felt alone, yet the memories of the passing years kept flooding back to him.

He pondered on the devastation that came to Yerushalayim on that dreaded day when young, helpless male children were so cruelly executed and vowed they would never be forgotten by the residents of that great city. It did not take long for the word to spread around Judea, that the decree to slaughter all innocent male children under the age of two came from

Herod himself [112]. The visit by the men in the large caravan seeking a newly born King of Jews had challenged Herod's insecurity. Over the years, many rumours circulated about the declining mental health of this ruler but his decision to slay all the innocent babies in Bethlehem and places within its vicinity, was deemed most horrible. And so, it was several years later when Herod died, there was hidden satisfaction in the hearts of many in Judea.

For Rachael and Ananiah, their two little boys were never forgotten. It was such a blessing that two months before the first anniversary of their passing, Rachael gave birth to a son. Her pregnancy and delivery went unusually well and Ananiah believed that the child in her womb was a sign of Adonai's faithfulness to them and so, when the baby was born, Ananiah called him Joel (Adonai is God). Joel had the exact facial features of his father and brought the couple and their parents great joy and pleasure. Two years later, another son was born. Unlike his brother before him, the child had given his mother extreme morning sickness and a nine-month pregnancy in which there was much discomfort. His father named him Daniel (God is my judge). Two years later, Rachael gave birth to another son. As the child was small and well rounded this reminded Ananiah of his father-inlaw, Boaz, Ananiah decided he should be called Jethro (Abundance). Rachael wished that the child would be called after her father but took her husband's naming as genuine rather than jesting about the stature of her dearly beloved father.

So, five years from the dreaded day, Ananiah's and Rachael's family had increased to three children. Yet the size of the family was due to increase even more. Following Jethro was Seth (Appointed) and then, Jabin (Perceptive). After twelve years of marriage, the couple had five children aged between 12 months and nine years. Just after Jabin was born, tragedy

---

[112] Matthew 2:16-18

struck the family when Zuriel, aged fifty-three, died. How Ananiah missed his father's company! During the later years of her husband's life, Hannah had become concerned about his health. Although he enjoyed his time on the Sanhedrin council, she believed it gave Zuriel additional unwanted stress. Confronted by many incidences where pressure, division and stress fell upon him, it was his composure and faith that carried him through. Zuriel was adamant that he could serve Adonai among this collective of learned men and felt in his own heart there were many times when he had successfully obeyed his Lord; and times when his efforts had some impact on the many meetings' outcomes but also times when Zuriel believed he had sadly failed.

Ananiah had a more objective appraisal of his father's efforts in the Sanhedrin as some of those efforts considered unproductive in his father's eyes, were in fact victories. Three specific incidences of his father's efforts in the Sanhedrin came to Ananiah's mind.

There was the time when the Sanhedrin wanted to increase the taxes of the sellers of the temple who offered pigeons, doves, sheep, and other sacrificial animals for those people who had travelled far to the temple for the Day of Atonement and other festivals. This was done every year, so it was not long before the temple grounds were overtaken by buyers and sellers. Only Zuriel spoke out vehemently stating that he wanted the council to note his concern was not so much for the increase of the tax (which he did not support), but the very presence of the sellers on holy temple grounds. The worldly activity of buying and selling on such a holy site, was a desecration of the earthly dwelling place of such a holy God. It was reported around the city that his father spoke with great passion before the council and yet the resolution was passed. Then, not long after this, when the temple taxes were counted, it was suggested that the Sanhedrin might put some of the money towards more comfortable chairs as often meetings went well into the night. Zuriel, once again, spoke against this motion and suggested that the money go towards the repairs in the eastern section of the Court of the Gentiles where there were many broken tiles. After all, Zuriel informed the group, the money is for the maintenance of the Temple of the Most-High and not for men's aging and sagging buttocks! Despite Zuriel's objections, while the former resolution seeking the tax increase passed, the subsequent resolution, which proposed that money from the Temple taxes should go towards more comfortable chairs was amended to addressing the repair of a broken tiled area in the Court of the Gentiles.

There was the time when a resolution was proposed that the scribes who spent long hours recording all the events of the meeting, should only record the resolutions made by the collective. Zuriel was strongly against this and when he rose to debate the issue, it was said that he was both confident and persuasive. He reminded the meeting, that this group was responsible to Adonai himself and as such the records of all who spoke and what transpired at each meeting needed to be an honest, historical, and accurate record of the event. Also, if any questions arose which sought to determine what took place at a meeting, the records would be open and informative. The records of the meeting Zuriel argued should remain as they had been in the past. The proposed resolution failed. and this was one time when Zuriel felt as if Adonai Himself had interceded.

As the years went by, the friendship between Ananiah and Kaleb fortified and strengthened. After marrying Rachael's cousin Tayla (dew from God), Kaleb had six children, all sons. As the children were born at similar times to Ananiah's family, and because of the family connections between Rachael and Tayla, plus the friendship between the two men, their sons grew very fond of one another. Both Rachel and Tayla would laughingly comment that they each felt as if they had eleven children in their families!

Ah yes! Those were happy years but not so, with the passing of his dear father whom he missed so much. Then, there was the dreaded day he remembered so vividly. A year after Zuriel's passing, Ananiah was transcribing on the sheets containing the Dabar Promises passages he believed should be recorded. How he missed his father in this task! Gazing at the sheet before him, he realised that the line he had just written, appeared quite blurred. Moving his head backward and then leaning forward, he peered intently at the paper but still he could not see clearly exactly what he had written. His heart collapsed within him. As he was thinking to himself that it could be the limited light in the room which must be hindering his sight, Joel aged ten at that time, came through the door.

"Is everything alright, Father?" he asked.

"I am having trouble seeing what has been written on the paper!" Ananiah exclaimed.

"Then, let me write the words down as you dictate them to me!" Joel said. And so, it was from that day forth, that the pilgrimage of writing the Dabar Promises proceeded to yet another generation. Although Ananiah was delighted that the work of his forefathers was continuing through his eldest son, he inwardly lamented the fact that his eyes were failing him. Could this mean that his eyes would not be able to behold the sight of the Messiah? As the years passed, his sight deteriorated so much so that when Joel was twenty-five years old, Ananiah could no longer read and therefore, he could no longer complete his beloved task of scribing. He was happy that his son had continued doing the work he and his forefathers had undertaken so faithfully.

Although Ananiah and Rachael offered to take their widowed mother into their home in the city, Hannah expressed her wish to remain in the farmhouse where she had spent all her married life. Of course, all her chil-

dren were married and living in homes scattered in the area, but the farmhouse was where she wanted to live out her days.

Hannah was always delighted when Rachael brought the children to her
for a visit and they found the farm and its surroundings a wonderful place
to play, just as their father did. "Oh, it is lovely here" declared Rachael one
day. "I too, have many pleasant memories living in this house".

"Then why don't you return?" asked Hannah.

Rachael said she would ask her husband and see how he felt about the
idea. When she mentioned this to Ananiah that night as they lay in bed,
he said "Let's not decide about this now, but discuss this in the morning".
He knew his wife so well and understood by the way in which she spoke,
Rachael was very keen about the idea.

Weighing up all the pros and cons the next morning, it was decided
that at that time the family would not move immediately but perhaps move
later. Five years later, when to everyone's surprise, Rachael found that she
was pregnant again, it was decided that the family would move to the farmhouse where all their six children could live more comfortably in the wider
spaces of the countryside. By this time, his eldest son Joel had excelled in
scribing and was, like his father before him, working alongside the scribes
and elders in the Temple. To everyone's delight, when it came time for her
eighth child to be born, Ananiah's only daughter Abigail (My father is joy)
was welcomed by all her relatives.

Then, there was the passing of his beloved mother not long afterwards.
Hannah had insisted that when the family moved back to the farm, that
Zuriel's bedroom should become Ananiah's and Rachael's and she would
live in the back bedroom where great grandfather used to sleep. But Rachael
replied as that as the grandfather's room was the room she and Ananiah had
made their own, and a room where there were such happy memories, they
would sleep there and Hannah would remain in her own room, the one she

had faithfully shared with her husband for so many years. After all, this was still her home.

≈   ≈   ≈

Now, almost twenty-eight years from that dreaded day when innocent young male children were so cruelly slaughtered, Ananiah conceded Adonai had so greatly blessed him and his family. Joel, his eldest son was now a father himself, as were Daniel, Jethro, Seth and Jabin. All sons now were no longer residing in the large farmhouse but lived nearby. Joel became a chief scribe in his mid-twenties; Daniel, Seth and Jabin all worked on the family's farms with their cousins, while Jethro to his mother's delight took over Boaz's bakery. They were all fine men, of good moral character and all had inherited their father's love for Adonai; all knew his story of deliverance and all were eager to honour their Lord. Now, in his 'retirement', Ananiah was well looked after by Rachael and his dear daughter Abigail in whom he took such delight.

As Ananiah was immersed in these thoughts, Abigail brought him a cup of water. "Mother said you must drink this for the weather is warm" she said. Ananiah's eyes struggled to see the form of his daughter's face and once again his eyes failed him. He knew that she had splendid beauty inside and outside for at fourteen years of age she had inherited her mother's good looks and her grandmother Hannah's gentle nature. Peering intently into the distance, Abagail saw a small contingent of men moving towards the farmhouse. As they drew nearer, she realised that the three men were her uncles. "Uncle Adam, Tomas and Bogdan are coming to see you" she informed her father.

Approaching Ananiah, the men seemed a little flustered and out of breath. Coming up to him, they greeted him and said "Shalom dear brother! We need to speak to you".

"What is the problem?" inquired Ananiah.

"We fully appreciate that the harvesting is now over" one of the men replied, "but four days ago, while we were tidying up the barn three of Kaleb's sons came excitedly onto the farm to look for Daniel, Seth and Jabin who left immediately with them, and we have not seen them since".

"We understand and accept that as Joel has been called by Adonai to be a scribe, he cannot scribe and work on the farm at the same time. Yet, we feel, it most unfair that your three sons should be paid for work they have not completed. We call upon your honesty and wisdom to see our point of view" stated another.

"Where are Daniel, Seth and Jabin?" Ananiah asked.

"We have no idea!" the men replied, "Neither do their wives and children!"

"I promise you that as Farm Manager I will speak to my sons and if they have left for any illegitimate reason, I assure you they will not be paid. Leave this with me. I will act upon it".

Ananiah's brothers, content with this answer, left and returned to the farm. "Where do you think Daniel, Seth and Jabin are?" asked Abagail.

"I have no idea!" her father replied.

≈   ≈   ≈

Around mid-day, as Ananiah, Rachael and Abigail were finishing a small repast inside the farmhouse, Daniel, Seth and Jabin boisterously burst through the door. Their faces were flushed with excitement as they blurted out to their father, "We have found him! We have found him!"

"You've found who? Who have your found?" their mother inquired.

"The Messiah! We have found the Messiah!"

— *Chapter Twenty-One* —

COULD THIS
BE THE ONE?

C losely seated around the table, the family listened intently to every word that was spoken. Their hearts soared as they listened to what had transpired over the past four days – could this really be true? Is the man the brothers have found truly be the promised one? Daniel began the conversation. The second born was a handsome man with wavy dark hair and dashing green eyes. He told the group that four days ago, when they were tidying up the farm after the last harvest, Nosh's sons Rafe, Micah (named after his deceased uncle) and Tomas came to see them. In great excitement, his friend Rafe told them that the men had just witnessed an amazing sight near the Yarden River.

That very day, as Kaleb's three sons were fishing from the banks, they saw many groups of people moving towards the northern part of the river. Realising that there must be something happening up ahead to draw so much attention, they decided that as the fish weren't biting, they too would journey up the river to see what the attraction was. Quickly gathering up their gear, the brothers followed the crowd which seemed to grow bigger as they headed north. When they saw quite a few friends along the way they became even more curious as to what could be happening up ahead that demanded so much attention.

When they came to the place where the crowd was at its thickest, they still couldn't see what was going on so they moved even closer, gently moving ahead of the people who had gathered there. When they came to the banks of the river to their surprise, in the middle of the river was a man, unshaven and wearing camel skins for clothing, with a leather belt around his waist[113]. Speaking to the people, the man's voice could be clearly heard above the crowd. It was such an unruly sight for the man, dressed in such strange attire with such an unkempt appearance, spoke boldly and with such conviction that their attention quickly drew away from his attire and centred on the words he was saying.

In a strong, commanding voice the man preached about the coming Messiah, telling the people that the Kingdom of Heaven was near and employing them to be fully prepared. The man's mission, so he claimed, was to make sure that the people were ready for the advent of the Messiah, so that when he made his appearance, they would be able to recognise him and accept him for who he was. Yet as the man called for people to repent of their sins and return to Adonai, the man did not speak of a political restoration for Isra'el! This puzzled the brothers. So, the brothers immediately returned to Yerushalayim and to the farm to tell their friends what they had seen.

---

[113] Matthew 3:4

Knowing full well of their forefathers' beliefs about the coming Messiah, Daniel said that immediately, without any hesitation, he and his brothers left the farm with their friends and went to witness for themselves the man preaching so convincingly by the riverbanks.

Seth continued the tale. His brown eyes flashed with excitement as he told the family seated at the table that it didn't take long for the group of friends to reach the Yarden River and to their delight, the man preaching along the river, was now moving closer towards Yerushalayim. Finding many people gathering as the crowds grew, Seth stated that it was almost like groups of ants being drawn from the wilderness to travel home to their nest. As they had done before, the men gently edged their way to the banks of the river where the man stood, preaching the message they had heard before.

The message the man in the river spoke was not of unification and peace, but rather of separation, separating the faithful remnant of Isra'el from the stubborn rebellious others[114]. Moreover, the man claimed that the people who in their rebellion had become purposeless for Adonai, would be burnt in a scorching fire! [115] Then the man claimed that the people should not feel that as they were physically descendants of Avraham and Yitz'chak (Abraham and Isaac), they would automatically have access to the Kingdom!

So enrapt were the group of six men that they stayed with the man for a few days before returning home to tell their fathers their news. Jabin interrupted his brother reporting something else the party of men had observed. The youngest of Ananiah's sons Jabin was eighteen years of age and had recently become a father. Of all the sons, his was the quietest nature and often, as his name suggested, very perceptive about the world around him.

---

[114] Matthew 3:10
[115] Matthew 3:12

Jabin told the group how the man, seeking the people to repent of their ways by returning to Adonai, asked them to come into the river and be baptised. Baptism, he related was not something uncommon to the Jewish people for their laws were steeped in the washing required for purification and preparation[116]. Yet he believed that while the washings involved in the old laws brought restoration to a previous condition, the baptism offered by the man in the river was one which would be in preparation for something far greater than the purification from the water of a river. Jabin felt that there was something more wonderful to come though he did not know what that could be.

Silence filled the room. Interrupting this, Daniel quickly rose from the table and turning to his brothers said, "We should go to our wives, they must be anxious about us after all we have been gone for a few days. Then, we shall return to the river to learn more about this man who could be the Messiah".

"Before you go to your wives, there is something else you must do" ordered Ananiah. "Go to your uncles and apologize for leaving them as you did. Tell them you shall not be returning for a few days. If they ask why, tell them you are on your father's business". Kissing their mother and sister goodbye the three sons hurriedly went on their way.

Not long after the sons had departed, Ananiah's eldest son Joel appeared at the door. He had run all the way from the city to the farm. His heart was pounding in his chest as he breathlessly asked, "Is it true what I have just been told? Daniel, Seth and Jabin have found the Messiah?"

"Whether they have met the Messiah or not, I do not know" replied Ananiah. "But he does sound an unusual man".

---

[116] Leviticus 14:8

"This is something I have to go and see for myself" replied Joel. "I will go to the river, tomorrow".

"And so will I" replied his father. "I must see this with my own eyes!"

"What will you see with your failing old eyes?" asked Rachael as she gently kissed her husband on the top of his head. "You had better travel with him Abigail and look after him well. Don't let him overdo things as he often does – oh! You had better take Zimra with you. She may prove of use to your father, if the journey gets too tiring".

"Oh no! Not Zimra!" objected Abagail. "Why can't we take one of the other donkeys?"

"You will take Zimra with you!" insisted her mother.

"But mother!" protested Abagail, "She stinks!"

Ananiah and Joel laughed aloud and agreed. "Yes, she surely does stink! But Abagail by now you should know the three 'Nevers' when it comes to Zimra: one, never let her drink water in your presence; two, never, never tickle or twitch her right ear and third, never, never, never be down-wind of her!" Raucous laughter filled the room.

≈   ≈   ≈

Early next morning, the three set out for the river Yarden. Rachael had prepared food and beverages for the journey and Joel also came early to prepare Zimra. Now Zimra was often the butt of many a cruel joke and despite her faithfulness in working for the family on the farm, she unfortunately had a noteworthy aliment. To say it was extreme flatulence might not be an overstatement. For some unknown reason or reasons, when the animal drank water her flatulence increased. Also, if you patted her head and caught her right ear in the process, once more the most horrible smell would waft on the air. When she was working, such as threshing the grain or in the fields, one always had to be ahead of the beast or else suffer the dreaded consequences.

Farewelling Rachael, the group travelled along western side of Yerushalayim. This was not Abagail's favourite trek for the narrow road passed by the unquarried area of Gulgolta (Golgotha) where criminals were executed. This was an excellent deterrent to anyone passing by the city of the cruelty and authority of the governing Roman Empire. Every time a traveller would pass by this area, cruel wooden crosses with poor unfortunate souls could be seen in the distance. To avoid even looking in the direction of the poor bodies hanging lifeless on the crosses, Abagail began to make endless chatter. Asking several supercilious questions, she failed to realise that in doing so she had fallen behind her father and her brother, and Zimra. Just as she was about to ask yet another senseless question, she exclaimed "Pooh! Oh Zimra!"

"Up-wind, Abagail, up-wind!" replied her father and brother in unison.

≈   ≈   ≈

It didn't take very long for the three to see small groups of other travellers moving towards the river which was on the eastern side of the city. Gradually, the numbers of people moving towards the river increased and Joel stated, "I understand what Seth said when he remarked that the people were all like trails of ants streaming towards their home. I think that the man must just be up ahead for the crowd is thicker there".

To Joel's delight he caught sight of his brothers Daniel, Seth and Jabin who were with their friends Rafe, Micah and Tomas. The six men came up to greet them, quite surprised yet very pleased to see the small trio of travellers. "We will need to get as close as we can to the man in the river" Joel said, "as father isn't seeing too well these days".

"But his hearing is excellent!" retorted Ananiah.

Gently the group edged their way closer to the bank of the river but there was still one line of people in front of them.

"I cannot see" said Abagail, so much shorter than the others with her.

The group was near a tree to their right on the bank which provided splendid shade and it was obvious that the men at the front of the crowd weren't going to lose their position right in front of the man in the river. Immediately Joel moved Zimra into the shallow water of the river. "There, Zimra" he was heard to say, "You've had a long journey – have a drink!" Without any hesitation, the donkey went down into the river and drank. Sounds of people sniffing could be heard, but for some unknown reason, the people remained where they were, holding securely the ground they had claimed. Noticing this, Abagail, stooped down, picked up a small pebble and with amazing accuracy, threw the pebble onto the side of the tree. Its second projectile flew a hair's breadth by Zimra's right ear which began to flitch nervously. "Where did you learn to do that?" Joel asked her.

"Father taught me" was her reply.

A few seconds later, the people at the front of the crowd immediately moved away and placing their headdresses around their faces (particularly covering their noses), the group of nine moved to the front of the crowd where they could not only see what was happening, but also, they heard every word the man in the river was saying. Moving Zimra out of the water and placing her behind them, they listened to the man who began to say:

"Repent! Repent! For the Kingdom of Heaven is at hand! Turn from your wicked ways and return to Adonai!"

"Are you the Messiah?" an old man asked.

"I am not the Messiah!"[117]

---

[117] John 1:20

"Who are you?" a man from the crowd asked.

"I am the voice of one calling in the wilderness, 'Make straight the way for the Lord'".[118]

Ananiah's heart stopped. "He quotes a Dabar Promise from the prophet Yesha'yahu (Isaiah)!" he exclaimed.[119]

"Be quiet!" a man behind him said "We can't hear him while you are speaking at the same time!"

"Oh, people of Isra'el" the man in the river continued "Look how sinful we have become in our foolish ways! We have turned our backs on Adonai and He is greatly offended. I urge you now to come and be baptised as a visual sign of your repentance! As you come into the water, leave your sinful ways behind you and return to Adonai! I baptise you with water for repentance. But after me comes one who is more powerful than I, whose sandals I am not worthy to carry. He will baptise you with the Holy Spirit and fire. His winnowing fork is in his hand, and he will clear his threshing floor, gathering his wheat into the barn and burning up the chaff with unquenchable fire[120]".

Joel gasped. His memory helped him recall the words he had scribed only the day before. For some reason, the words etched themselves securely into his brain. Those words came immediately to him:

> *"You have rejected me," declares the Lord. You keep on back sliding. So, I will reach out and destroy you; I am tired of holding back.* ***I will winnow them with a winnowing fork*** *at the city gates of the land".*[121] *(emphasis added)*

---

[118] John 1 :23
[119] Isaiah 40:3
[120] Matthew 3:11-12
[121] Jeremiah 15:6-7

"He's quoting from Yirmeyahu (Jeremiah)!" Joel whispered to his father. The man in the river urged the people to come into the river as a sign that they wanted to repent and after giving this call several times, people slowly came down to the river and went into the water to be baptised. Each time, the man in the river would ask "Do you repent and desire to return to the Lord?" After affirmation of his desires, each man was pushed down into the water. Ananiah listened intently to the words that transpired as each man was baptised. In his heart, he knew that Adonai was such a loving God and He desired his people to return to His ways. While he was considering these thoughts the feeling that he felt so long ago, when he was delivered from death in the catacombs increasingly disseminated within his whole body. It was also like the same feeling he felt that day when he committed the unforgiveable sin of entering the Holy Place. Ananiah was convinced that the One who delivered him, was once more very close at hand.

"Behold the Lamb of God, who takes away the sin of the world!" the man in the river exclaimed.

Then Ananiah heard rippling sounds of parting water as a man entered the river. But it sounded as if the man in the river did not want to baptise the man who had just entered the water. "I need to be baptised by you, and yet you come to me?"[122] Ananiah heard the man in the river say.

"Let it be so now" the stranger replied, "It is proper for us to do this to fulfil all righteousness". The man in the river consented and the stranger was baptised. Immediately Ananiah heard the voice from the Holy Place – the very one that sounded like rushing wind and water announce "This is my Son, whom I love; with Him I am well pleased".[123]

When he recognised the voice, which resounded from the sky, and being overwhelmed by the sense of His spiritual presence, Ananiah gasped. He

---

[122] Matthew 3:13
[123] Matthew 3:16-17; Isaiah 42:1a

turned immediately to his sons and their friends beside him and vigorously urged them, "Follow that man!"

"Which man?" they inquired.

"The one that has just been baptised!" replied their father. "Didn't you hear that voice?"

"What voice?" they asked.

"Never mind, just follow that man!" Obeying their father and in the company of their friends, the sons immediately followed the stranger.

"What did he look like? The man who just got baptised, what did he look like?" Ananiah anxiously asked his daughter.

"He was just a man" she replied. "He had no extraordinary features – he was just a man."

Immediately, without hesitation Joel stated, "He had no beauty or majesty to attract us to him, nothing in his appearance that we should desire him!"[124]

"Do you think the man in the river is the Messiah?" Abigail eagerly asked her father.

"No, I believe that the man in the river is Adonai's promised messenger[125]", her father replied. "But the man who has just been baptised, I believe that he could be the Messiah!"

As the man in the river continued to move downward and began talking to the crowds again, Ananiah turned to his son and daughter and said "I think we should head home now. I give praise to Adonai for such a wonderful day! How wonderful to think the Messiah has come!"

Before he had finished speaking, Ananiah heard a voice he recognised. "Do you believe that this man in the river who preaches repentance is the coming Messiah, Ananiah?" the voice asked. Peering intently with his eyes,

---

[124] Isaiah 53:2b
[125] Isaiah 40: 3-5; Malachi 3:1

Ananiah failed to see the elderly man behind him but recognising his voice, replied, "Shalom Zév! No, I have just told my children that I believe that he was the messenger that Adonai promised He would send. The Messiah, I think, was the man who got baptised".

"Quite a few men were just baptised!" exclaimed Zév. "Which one was the Messiah?"

"The one you would least expect!" answered Abagail.

Realising how much his dear father's friend had aged, Ananiah offered him a ride back on Zimra to Yerushalayim and so it was, as they headed back towards the city, there was much joy in their conversation as they discussed all that had taken place by the river that day. As they recalled the various sections of Adonai's word that had been fulfilled before them, they anticipated many exciting things would soon be happening. Now, it seemed, was the time when Isra'el as Adonai's people would be redeemed and restored to her maker. Adonai's people had waited for so long and finally, the time of deliverance had come!

— Chapter Twenty-Two —

A SHREWD
MANAGER

J oel's pen moved carefully and meticulously across the sheet of paper.
A small candle's light provided the room with ample luminance.
Ever since his father's sight began to deteriorate, Joel had kept the
six sheets pertaining to the Dabar Promises at his home. He had main-
tained the decision to simply write each promise on a sheet of paper and
surprisingly there were still some empty sheets of parchment. Yet, today,
several passages had been drawn to their attention and so Joel made a
point of carefully adding these to the collection they had already recalled.
Excitedly, when he added the quotation about the Messiah which related
to his appearance, he placed this on an unused sheet. While it was a slow
process, Joel believed that this was a valid thing to do as each promise in
the collection brought further insight into the role of the coming Messiah.

His wife, Zohar came into the room with some light refreshments. "It's been a long day for you, Joel. Why don't you stop and have something to eat?" she asked. Joel looked up from his writing and saw the smiling face of his beloved wife. Zohar always seemed to be there when he needed her and as he was quite hungry, he did what scribes never do. He stopped what he was doing and gladly ate the refreshments set before him. "This has been a special day, Zohar" he told his wife. "Today we witnessed some of the Adonai's promises about the Messiah coming true before our eyes. I believe that what my father says is true - the man in the river is the messenger He promised but there is something about the other man father appeared so interested in. He was such a plain man, but the scriptures tell us that this is true about the Messiah".

"That man may or may not be the promised Messiah" Zohar replied, "but if Adonai wants you to know the truth, He will tell you". "Zohar, my darling" replied her husband, "no truer words have ever been spoken!"

≈   ≈   ≈

It had been several days since Ananiah, Joel and Abagail had trekked to the Yarden River and every day Ananiah attempted to recall all the promises that had been written on the sheets of paper. Once again, as it often would do, the sacred promise that he heard that day in the Holy Place echoed through his mind: "Not with thine eyes shall you see Him but your very soul". Although he had never doubted this promise, the many long years that had passed seemed to prolong the hope that he would personally meet the Messiah. Now although his eyes were failing, and the fact that yesterday he could not see the man who entered the water and was baptised, he felt assured within himself that the man who entered the waters was known to Adonai Himself. He marvelled at the difference between the physical ability of being able to see what it is in front of you, and the spiritual sight of knowing what is around you but not seeing this physically at all[126]. Could it be possible, therefore, that though his eyes were failing him, he would still be able to meet and know the blessed Messiah?

As he was pondering these thoughts, his three sons Daniel, Seth and Jabin came through the door. Their appearance was ragged, and it was obvious from the tone of their voices, that they were troubled by what had happened. Sadly, it seemed although the six men followed the man who was baptised in the river, after a very short time, they somehow lost him. The six men had decided to break into groups of two and travelled around the area but to no avail. "It was just as if" panted Jabin, "he disappeared into thin air!"[127] The men had spent several days looking for him, but alas they could not find him. But all was not completely lost for the brothers and their accompanying friends had requested that some of the people they had met with in their travels would send word to them should this man return.

Ananiah thanked his sons and sent them immediately home to their families, requesting that they return to the farm the next day to work with their relatives. "How unfortunate!" Ananiah said to himself; yet he was not worried for his heart kept telling him that Adonai is, and always will be faithful.

≈   ≈   ≈

The stiff bones of all those men sitting around the semi-circle in the apse in the Royal Stoa ached. For four long hours or more the Sanhedrin had discussed a lot of aspects and now, as the men listened to the current speaker, quite a few older men regretted not purchasing the more comfortable seats

---

[126] 2Corithians 4:18
[127] Luke 4:1-13

suggested many years ago. When it looked as if the council would finally be finished for the night, a member stated that there should be some discussion about the man who had been baptising in the Yarden River. The subject of this man had been raised at several meetings before and as some of the members now had themselves investigated what the man was doing, this was the time to report their findings back to the Sanhedrin.

Ezra, now aged in his late fifties, rose and suggested to the President, Caiaphas, who was the chief priest at the time, that perhaps the scribes need not record the discussions that were to take place so that the matters raised within the meeting would be held in strict confidence between members. Responding immediately to this recommendation, Zév suggested that if the purpose of the scribes being present was to provide a complete and historical record of the meeting, then everything that was raised during the coming discourse should be accurately recorded, for as Zév stressed, 'We have nothing to hide'. Momentary discussion and arguments regarding the inclusion of the transcription in meeting notes interrupted the procedure of the meeting.

Rising to his feet, the chief priest Caiaphas spoke clearly as he announced. "Let the minutes of meeting record that much discussion about this man took place, but as for what is individually reported about him, let those comments remain within the boundaries of this committee".

One man stood up and looking around the apse acknowledged that there were many men seated in the room who had been to the Yarden River so that the meeting would be able to have a valid discussion of the man's activity. Who was this man? It had been rumoured that people were calling him "Yochanan the Immerser" because he was preaching around the Yarden River and Judea, calling for people to return to Adonai. Why was he asking the people to do this? The main purpose of his preaching was to prepare the people for the coming Messiah and accept him when He comes.

Another man stood up and reported to the group that while the man in the river wanted to prepare the people for the coming Messiah, he wanted them to recognise that they had become sinful with many turning their backs on Adonai. Preaching both repentance and return to Adonai, the man urged all the Jewish people to be kind to one another, to practice virtue and be pious to their God. Surely, the man asked, this is what Adonai wants?

Another man rose to speak. It was not what the man in the river said, that concerned him but rather what he did not say. He did not talk about deliverance from Isra'el's enemies, nor about the judgement that was to befall upon their captors – in fact the man did not talk about justice for the Isra'el nation at all.

Yet another man stood up and reported that the man in the river didn't talk about justice, but he did talk often about the coming Messiah separating the wheat from the chaff, the good from the bad. The good, he believed, were all those who believed in Adonai whilst the bad were all those who refused to listen to His words.

Another man rose to his feet expressing his concern that he felt the man in the river was quite antagonistic towards the scribes and his Pharisee colleagues who had accompanied him to the river. "He had the audacity to call us snakes! It was if he believed we had poisoned the word of Adonai! His comments were quite disrespectful and rude"[128]. Ezra rose again. He claimed to concur with his fellow colleague who had just spoken as he said that he was shocked to hear the man preaching say that just because the Pharisees and the people claimed that Avraham (Abraham) was their father, this would not allow them immediate access into the Kingdom. From this it was implied that there were some people sitting around the Sanhedrin

---

[128] Matthew 3:7-10

that very night who would not be entering the coming Kingdom. Loud scoffing and laughter sounded through the room.

Throughout the night many people spoke. The man in the river had vehemently denied that he was the Messiah, Elijah or the Prophet.[129] But when he did respond to who he was, the man quoted the prophet Yesha'yahu (Isaiah)[130]!

Another man rose from his seat. Telling those present that many of the people were turning to this man and quite a few believed, despite his denial, this man is the coming Messiah. One elderly man stood up and questioned whether it would be worthwhile to seek Ananiah's advice for his advice like his father Zuriel's before him, was full of counsel and wisdom. Another commented that when he went to see the man in the river, he saw Ananiah and his sons were there. Ezra stood up again and salaciously commented that Ananiah and Zuriel's wisdom was not completely faultless and perhaps Ananiah himself would state, like some have already, that the man in the river was the Messiah himself! Scoffing and ridicule arose from the men seated around the room.

Immediately, Zév rose to his feet and said unequivocally that for Ezra to state Ananiah would think such a thing does Ananiah a great injustice. Moreover, such a remark revealed more about the accuser's character than Ananiah's. Zév affirmed to the group that he had heard Ananiah state on several occasions, the man in the river was not the Messiah.

The Chief Priest rose from his chair. "It is late and although we have learnt a lot about this man who is called 'Yochanan the Immerser' nothing which has been said here tonight demands any intervention on our part. So, we will just wait and see what happens. I have heard it said by some people that when he speaks about the moral corruption that has deeply

---

[129] John 1:19-21
[130] Isaiah 40:3

engrained itself into Judaism, he also speaks of Herod's and Herodias' adultery![131] If he continues down that path, it just might be, that Herod will ensure his fate for us. This meeting is dismissed".

≈   ≈   ≈

Ananiah's brothers Adam, Thomas and Bogdan moved swiftly towards the farmhouse. Their hearts were pounding inside their chests but as they were on a mission of equality; unitedly they had joined together once more to confront their eldest brother on what they perceived to be a total injustice. Entering the house through the backdoor, they found Ananiah and Rachael seated at the table near the kitchen. "We wish to talk to you, dear brother" demanded Thomas. "Shalom to you all, dear brothers" Ananiah immediately replied, "Now, please sit down and tell me what is causing you such concern".

The three brothers sat down, each one looking at the other two. "Perhaps I can give you a drink?" offered Rachael. But the men declined.

"We have come here today to ask you, once again, where are your sons Daniel, Seth and Jabin?" asked Adam. "What do you mean, 'where are my sons?'- did not Kayin (Cain) say to Adonai 'I am not my brothers' keeper'?"[132] replied Ananiah.

"Are you telling us, your brothers, that you have no idea as to the whereabouts of your sons who like us, are all workers on the family farm?" Bogdan asked angrily. "They left abruptly yesterday afternoon only to tell us that they were going to do their father's business. Now, it seems that you do not know where they are. How can they go on your business if you don't know where that takes them?"

---

[131] Luke 3: 19-20
[132] Genesis 4:9b

"If my sons say they have gone somewhere to do their father's business, what is that to you? In truth, I do know exactly what they are doing but I do not know where they are just now. May I remind you that as the oldest son, I am the Manager of this farm, and as manager, I do not need to pass my decisions by you to make sure that these are reasonable and acceptable. But tell me, what is the real reason you are here today?"

Adam spoke sincerely to his brother. The three brothers (together with their children and other family members who worked on the farm) felt very unhappy that Daniel, Seth and Jabin were being paid the same wage as all the family workers, despite their erratic attendance on the farm. It was not, they purported, fair that Ananiah's sons should receive the same wage when they had not contributed the same amount of work hours as the others.

"Is it my understanding" inquired Ananiah, "that you refused to accept my decision to allow my sons to do the specific tasks I have set them?"

"Are the tasks farm related? What specific tasks have you asked your sons to do?" inquired Thomas.

"That is none of your business!" Ananiah promptly replied.

"But dear brother" pleaded Adam, "Do you really think it is fair for them to receive wages for working on the farm, when they have done little to no work at all?"

"And furthermore" said Thomas, "With the poor helpers who are paid even less than us, despite their lower wagers, they are being paid for the work that your sons are not doing! This is not right, Ananiah. For a Godly family, this is not right!"

"How kind of you to speak on behalf of your fellow workers" thought Ananiah to himself but somehow the brothers' concern did not appear to be sincere. In his many long hours of thinking he had thought about the absence from the farm by his sons and so, unknown to the three brothers he began to present them a previously well thought through solution.

"We all know that for the past four generations of this family, this farm has been managed by the eldest son after he has completed his scribing duties. This is the way the farm has been managed since Obadiah's agreement with Adonai. Throughout these years, it has always been accepted that for each year, one-fifth of the farm's income would be set aside for costs of seed and farming equipment, one-fifth would be set aside for the payment of the management including the wages of the manager and the son who is scribing and allowing for investment and expansion. The remaining three-fifths would go towards the cost of paying the workers. The son in charge of the farm would set aside a sum for the family workers and the remaining money would be used to hire helpers during the busy seasons. The farm manager has always provided his workers with food and beverages at no additional cost. This cost has been covered by the Manager himself. I have never objected to this before but as you speak about equity and fairness, perhaps the terms under which we work the farm should be changed".

"As I understand from what you are saying, you are no longer happy with this arrangement and wish it to change. Consider what I am proposing. In terms of the farm's yearly income, one-fifth shall continue to be set aside for outgoing expenses and one-fifth shall be set aside for payment to the management, the son who is scribing, as well as allow for opportunities of further expansion as before. The remaining three-fifths will still go to the salary of the workers, but the condition of payment will change".

"It seems you are seeking equality for all your workers in your request. After all, if no work is done, why should a person who has not done any work receive any payment? As the hired workers therefore do the same work as the family workers, each person will be paid the same amount per season -whether hired or family. All workers will give to the farm manager

5% of their salary for the cost of food and beverages and this will be the same for all workers".

"This is my new offer to you. Whatever one you accept will be implemented hence forth and never rescinded under my management. After this meeting, the subject will be raised no more. Offer one, we maintain the existing system as it is without any changes. Offer two, the wages for all who work will be the same, with all workers contributing 5% of their earnings for food over the season they work. This will be given directly to the farm manager. Which offer do you choose?"

The brothers looked at each other, trying to do the maths in their heads but provided no answer.

"You have come to me with a problem that has obviously been weighing you down and consuming you with the feeling of unfairness to all your workers. I have offered you an alternative which may appease your dilemma, please give me an answer" Ananiah said to his brothers.

"We choose the second option," said Adam.

"So be it!" replied Ananiah.

The brothers acknowledged one another as they said farewell. As they were returning to the farm both Thomas and Bogdan looked perplexed. "Don't you understand?" Adam asked them, "that we accepted the option where Daniel, Seth and Jabin will no longer be paid!" "So, we have won!" exclaimed Thomas.

≈   ≈   ≈

"Do you think they will soon realize that they haven't won?" Rachel asked her husband as she observed the jubilant nature of the brothers' departing gaits. Ananiah did not speak a word.

"Ananiah" replied Rachel more sternly, "You are still going to pay for the worker's lunches aren't you – just as the farm manager has always done?" Ananiah gave no reply.

"And the workers' five percent tax will be set aside to cover the cost of our sons and their families as they continue to follow the man from Galilee, won't it?" Still there was no response from her husband.

"Oh Ananiah, you are a clever manager!" Rachel exclaimed.

"No, my dear, not so much clever, but definitely shrewd", her husband replied.[133]

---

[133] Luke 16:1-9

— *Chapter Twenty-Three* —

FOUR BROTHERS
REPORT

T hroughout each year, while there were many festivals of thanks-
giving for the Jewish people, many would religiously attend the
three major feasts:- Hag Hammassôt (the Feast of Passover)[134],
sometimes called Pesah (the Feast of Unleavened Bread) celebrated the people's deliverance by Adonai from their cruel masters in Egypt; the Feast
of Weeks[135] which also included Hag Sabuot (the Feast of the Harvest)
celebrated Adonai's bountiful provision to his people; hag hassukkôt (the
Festival of the Tabernacles/Booths)[136] celebrated that while delivered from
the cruel hands of the Egyptians, Adonai physically dwelt among his people

---

[134] Exodus 12: 1-29; Leviticus 23:4-5
[135] Exodus 34:22; Leviticus 23: 15-17
[136] Leviticus 23: 33-36

in the wilderness[137] and faithfully provided their every need[138]. Included within this period was the Yom Kippie (the Day of Atonement)[139] which occurred once a year when special sacrifices were made by the priests for the people's sins. It was no surprise, therefore, that during these times, Yerushalayim was a hive of travellers and worshippers from many parts of the land.

Ananiah believed that if this man was a man of Adonai, he would return to Yerushalayim for the festivals, particularly the Passover which was a most important time for the Jewish people. So, while he often thought of his three sons and their three friends, Ananiah believed it would not be too long before he would see them all again. He pondered in his heart the stories that they might tell about the man. He was hoping that they would return soon for Passover was swiftly approaching. For his people, this celebration did not just involve the acknowledgement of Adonai's faithfulness to his people in Egypt, but it also provided hope for a new beginning, another year. It was rumoured that people from all over the land were now coming to Yerushalayim so in his heart and in his many thoughts, Ananiah was happy.

Rachael was delighted when she looked out the window of the farmhouse and saw three men running towards the house. It was the day before Passover and as she gazed up at the men moving quickly towards her, she thanked Adonai for returning her sons Daniel, Seth and Jabin safely home to her for this important Jewish festival. Overjoyed, she ran out to meet them and finally when they came together hugged and kissed each one passionately. Although she had spent many hours wondering where they were and whether they were safe, she kept her concerns to herself not wanting

---

[137] Exodus 13:21-22
[138] Exodus 16: 1-35
[139] Leviticus 23:26-28

to burden her husband who by now, had become completely blind. It felt so wonderful seeing them return home not only to her, but also to their families who missed them terribly while they were away. "We've so much to tell father" said an anxious Daniel, "Even though it hasn't been a long time, from what we have seen so far, we are convinced the man father told us to follow is a wonderful man of Adonai. Where is father? We are so excited to tell him what we have seen".

"Your father is with Abagail who has travelled with him to Joel's house in the city" Rachael informed her sons. "Do let me give you all refreshments before you move on. It is so wonderful having you home again and you all look so flustered from your running". The sons, always obedient to their mother, welcomed some refreshments before leaving for the city in search of their father. They had travelled with the man and his ever-widening group of followers to Yerushalayim for the Passover Feast and therefore this was an excellent opportunity to provide feedback to their father about him.

Leaving the farmhouse, they moved quickly towards the city, entering by the western gate which provided the quickest route to their brother's home. All the streets were packed with people yet the brothers managed to quickly edge their way through the crowds to their brother's street. By the time they entered Joel's house the three brothers looked just as flustered as they had previously. Immediately recognising his sons' voices as they greeted Zohar, Ananiah unexpectedly arose from the chair and exclaimed that his boys were home again. Bursting into the room, the boys greeted their father, brother and sister warmly. After joyous hugs and kisses, the three men told their father although they hadn't been away for very long, they had become in awed with the man whom they told was called Yeshua of Nazareth.

"Nazareth?" queried Joel. "But 'Nazareth' means branch" interrupted Ananiah "and the prophet Yesha'yahu (Isaiah) states that out of the line of David's father Jesse, would come a branch!"[140]

"He is thirty years old and he has lived with his mother, brothers and sisters as a carpenter. His father, Joseph is deceased. We learnt from his mother that Joseph was from the line of David[141]" continued Daniel.

"His age is about right" Ananiah thought to himself. Daniel continued to tell them that upon hearing word that the man they were searching for was sighted near the Yarden River, they had left the farm fields once again and went to Galilee. It was by the river's waters that they saw some local fishermen who told them about the man who had just travelled by the lake and called some of the local fishermen to stop what they were doing and follow him. The men the stranger had called were well known in the area but the most complexing thing was that they completely left all their property aside on the lake, and simply followed the man[142]. The brothers believed that as K'far-Nachan (Capernaum) was such a busy thoroughfare where there was a Roman garrison on a major road, this would be a possible place the man might be. Despite searching the large town, they could not find the man though there were rumours of him being seen in the district. Most despondent, they agreed to return home.

As the next day was the Sabbath, the brothers decided that they would not return until the following day. So, on the Sabbath, they went to the local synagogue where to their delight, when they were participating in the worship, who should they see there but the man himself! When the man began to teach, he spoke with such authority and knowledge and everyone in the synagogue was amazed. Jabin declared he had never heard such con-

---

[140] Matthew 1:1-17
[141] 2Samuel 7:12-13; Isaiah 16:5; Matthew 1:1-17
[142] Matthew 4: 18-22

fident and interesting teaching yet he was particularly drawn to the humble nature of the man. There was another man in the synagogue who was obviously not mentally well who cried out in a loud voice "What do you want with us, Yeshua of Nazareth? Have you come to destroy us? I know who you are - the Holy One of God!"[143]

The brothers said they froze as it was obvious that the man with a demon recognised the man Yeshua they had been searching for, and the man actually knew Yeshua's name! Moreover, the demonized man stated that the man Yeshua was the Holy One of God! Seth then continued the tale by telling them that the man named Yeshua spoke sternly to the spirits and then, the man shook violently as he screamed loudly. His tormented screams were agonizing to the soul and pierced them all to the core. After this, in the silence that immediately followed, the man appeared to be fine but all the people present were so amazed and shaken that Yeshua's teaching was so authoritative even evil spirits obeyed him! This it seemed was one of many miracles this man Yeshua was reported to have done. The three brothers concurred that they probably would not have believed it had they not seen what had happened with their own eyes.

The brothers managed to join the large collection of followers the man Yeshua had accumulated – these had come from different walks of life. After staying at K'far-Nachan for a few days, Yeshua with his followers made their way to Yerushalayim for the Passover Feast. As soon as the brothers reached the outskirts of Yerushalayim with their group, they left them to rush to their father to tell him all that had happened. Ananiah told his sons that he was so pleased that they had found the man Yeshua but instructed them to please their elderly father by not going into the city to remain with this

---

[143] Mark 1:21-28

man for the duration of time he was here in Yerushalayim, but rather go immediately to their families who had been waiting so patiently for them.

"It seems apparent that he is a godly man who obeys our holy days and festivities and that he will be coming to Yerushalayim at least three times a year. So, whenever he returns here, one of you should come and inform me of all that has happened and then return, like the others to your families. I am very happy that you are finding out so much about this man but I realise that your task takes you away from your devoted wives and children. They must never feel that you have forsaken them, so I ask that you complete my request to honour me and your families". And so, it was from that day forth, each time the brothers returned to Yerushalayim with the followers of the man named Yeshua of Nazareth, one would report all that had happened to their father as the other sons would spend a short period of time with their young families before embarking on another trip.

It was during the very first visit to Yerushalayim by the man named Christ and his followers, that many rumours started to filtrate the city. On the first day of the week after the Passover Feast, Ananiah and Abagail visited Jethro in the city. To his mother's delight, Jethro had worked alongside her father Boaz in the family's bakery and upon Boaz's passing ten years ago, Jethro took over the family business. Unlike his tall, dark haired and good-looking brothers, Jethro's appearance was short, robust with ginger curly hair. It was a family joke as to whether Jethro's genes came from his blue eyed, formerly dark haired (but now very grey) father or his beautiful brown eyed, brown haired mother as his appearance was so contrasting to all the members of Ananiah's family. But Jethro had the most jovial and likeable personality. Friendly and kind to all, it was no surprise to find that he was one of the most liked persons in Yerushalayim. As they entered the shop, Jethro's already kind face sparkled even more. "Ah! My dearest father and my favourite sister, Shalom!" he cried, throwing his arms into the air and quickly leaving the counter to go and embrace his loved ones vigorously. "How can I be your favourite sister when you only have one?" asked Abagail. "Maybe that's why you're the favourite!" Jethro laughingly replied. Taking his father by the hand and leading him to a chair which was located against a wall nearby, Jethro continued.

"I really am pleased to see you father, for there is so much I want to tell you." Just as Abagail went to go on with the shopping, leaving her father in her brother's care, as she usually did each week, Jethro said that he had made something special for Abagail. Leaning underneath the counter, he pulled out a freshly baked loaf of bread. He had been experimenting a week ago, and to his delight, he had come up with a different type of loaf which he had filled with raisins, currants and figs. Inside the loaf, he had added a little honey and the result of his efforts resulted in him calling his creation, an 'Abigail bun!' He had named it after his sister because she too, had lovely, good things inside her. Handing her the loaf, Jethro smiled as a customer entered the shop. As she was leaving, she heard her brother say to the man, "An Abagail bun? Sorry, the last one has just been taken".

When the customer left the shop, Jethro came up to his father and told him about what the people were saying had taken place in the Temple just before the Passover. Apparently, a man who has been reported as doing many good things, got very angry when he saw the vast numbers of stalls and sellers peddling their wares in the Temple grounds. Making a whip out of cords it was reported that the man drove them all out of the temple area, both sheep and cattle![144] Overturning the tables of the money changers he cried out that they had all turned his father's house into a marketplace!

As Jethro was sharing what had taken place with his father, Ananiah immediately thought to himself "Zeal for your house consumed me!"[145]

---

[144] John 2:13-25
[145] Psalm 69:9

Moreover, Jethro added that when the people asked just who did he think he was to do such an action, this man replied that if they destroyed the temple, he would raise it up again in three days. "Three days? Three days?" queried Jethro raising his hands high in the air. "Jonah was in the whale for three days" replied his father, "and what a miracle took place there!"[146] From almost out of nowhere, Ananiah remembered how the expansion of the numbers of stalls in the temple groups greatly upset his father who spoke several times during Sanhedrin meetings about why the traders and their tables should be removed from the temple grounds to a location that was close to, and near by the temple. But despite Zuriel's comments, it seemed no action had been taken by the leaders of the people.

As time went by, the problem greatly increased with no resolution in sight. Babbling to himself that he had heard many people believe this man to be a good man, very gentle and kind, Jethro commented that he, himself had seen the man in the streets who appeared to have just that - a very peaceful and calm demeanour. While his son continued in his habit of talking without taking one single breath, Ananiah's thoughts turned to what had recently transpired in his life and his heart rose within his chest. "Surely" he thought to himself, "the moment we have all waited for has finally arrived!"

Just then, another customer came into the shop. "Shalom Nichodemus! What can I get you today?" inquired Jethro

"I so enjoyed your Abigail bun last week; do you have any left?"

Jethro sadly shook his head. "Well… any loaf will do" the customer replied.

Always a source of chatter, Jethro shared with his customer how the two men had just been discussing the man they call "Yeshua of Nazareth" and

---

[146] Jonah 1: 1-17

what he had been doing in Yerushalayim over the past few days. Jethro then asked what Nicodemus thought of the man. Nichodemus paused. "Well, many say that he has done miraculous things and as Adonai is only capable of doing such things, you might believe that this man truly does come from Adonai. But I have heard it said that he has strange beliefs which need our discernment. He apparently has said that to enter the Kingdom of Heaven, one needs rebirth! Now that's a strange concept, isn't it?"[147]

"Perhaps we need a spiritual rebirth!" added Ananiah who was listening to the man whom he knew was a wise Pharisee who served on the Sanhedrin. "Perhaps, perhaps" said Nicodemus as he paid Jethro for the loaf and then left the shop.

Seven days after Passover, the man Yeshua and his growing body of followers left Yerushalayim for Galilee. Despite their absence, the city was often ablaze with rumours of great and miraculous things the man had done. This man like the man Yochanan the Immerser (John the Baptist), stated that the people needed to repent their foolish ways for the Kingdom of Heaven was near.[148] This man, like Yochanan the Immerser did not seek people but rather they sought him and many were following him from town to town.[149] There were also reports that as he travelled the countryside and met so many people, he performed many healing miracles. There was one time it was reported that in the town of Cana, a royal official (who was probably from Herod's household) came to see the man because his son was very sick in Cana.

It was thought that the child was going to die. The official went to the man and begged him to come and heal his son who was at the point of death. Then, this Yeshua of Nazareth dismissed the official, telling him to

---

[147] John 3:1-12
[148] Matthew 4:17
[149] Matthew 4:25

return home for his boy was going to live. While the man was returning home, his servants came up to him, seeking him to tell him his boy was better as the fever had left him. When the official asked what hour they fever had left the boy, to his astonishment he was told that the fever had left the boy the same hour as Yeshua had told him, the boy would live![150]

Who was this man? He displayed a righteous anger in the Temple during the recent Passover and now, he was showing such compassion as he travelled around speaking about Adonai and how much Adonai loved his people.[151] Many people believed he was the promised Messiah for no one had ever performed such miraculous things whilst others were not so sure. Surely, when the Messiah was to come, he would redeem Isra'el from the cruel and tyrannous hands of its conquerors?

Ever since his brothers return, the incident in the Temple and the circulating rumours about the man people began calling 'the Christ', Joel's heart was stirred and unsettled. He, like his father, believed that the Messiah's coming would be different to the way the teachers of the law were proclaiming. He had always thought there was something much deeper and complex to the coming of the Messiah and now, his heart was perplexed because it seemed that this man and his behaviour was somewhat different to that of a conquering deliverer. Yet the man seemed genuine and Joel longed to find out more. On the spur of the moment, he went to the senior scribes and informed them that he would not be coming to work for a few days as some important family business demanded his attention. Joel knew that while there wasn't any difference between a 'white' and 'black' lie, there was an element of truth in what he was saying: seeking information and facts about the coming Messiah was indeed family business and had been for at least five generations. Asking his wife to pack some refreshments for

---

[150] John 4:45-54
[151] John 3:16

him, he left home and headed towards Judea where it was rumoured that the man Yeshua of Nazareth was preaching.

A few days later Joel had found himself near the Sea of Galilee and as he was looking into the distance, he saw what seemed to be large crowds moving towards the lower plains of the surrounding hills. Once again Seth's words came to his mind: 'ants' busily returning to their homes for comfort and peace. Catching up with the crowd, he moved gradually through this seeking to get closer to the man who had drawn such a large number of people. Finding his way to the commencement of the crowd, he saw the man whose persona and humility had so greatly attracted him. At this point he wished he had brought Zimra along so that he might be able to get even closer but as it appeared that Yeshua was mostly talking to his disciples who were seated on the ground near the feet of their master, Joel remained at a distance. To his complete surprise, he could hear every word the man spoke and as the man began speaking, Joel's heart beat strongly within him.

The man Yeshua spoke with such authority and appeared to be fully versed in all the words of Adonai. Moreover, he claimed he came not to abolish Adonai's Law but to fulfil it.[152] As the man spoke to the crowds for quite some time Joel soaked up every word, mentally storing what was said locked within his brain. Afterwards, when the man had finished, Joel did not even stop to see if he could sight or catch up with his brothers and their friends. Instead, he left quickly, going over in his mind all the things that the man Yeshua had said, placing importance on all the words that had been spoken. Joel was convinced that there was great importance in the words that the man said. Yet, he also believed, there was also importance in knowing where these man's words came from. Travelling as quickly as he could, he made his way back to Yerushalayim. When his greatly relieved

---

[152] Matthew 5:17

wife saw him enter their house, Joel quickly embraced her and asked her to fetch a writing reed, some ink and a parchment for him. Immediately he sat down and wrote feverishly, recalling all the comments made by the man who had talked to the crowds. Then, glancing at what he had written, Joel sat back and sighed. Once again, he found his heart was pounding. He could hardly wait to share with his father what he had recorded the man saying but for now, he must share with his wife what he had learnt.

Afterwards Joel took the transcript in his hand and hurriedly made his way to his father's house. As he moved through the narrow street ways towards the city's gate, his mind was rushing ahead of him. He had locked so much information there and once it was released on the transcript, Joel's thoughts extended beyond the words and what their meaning was. There was something about the man who spoke with such gentleness and authority and as he physically moved swiftly out towards the farm, Joel's mind was thinking of many things. When he arrived at the farm, he saw his sister feeding the farm animals. He greeted her warmly, then told her to stop what she was doing and come and hear what he was going to tell their father. So, Abigail stopped doing her chores and followed her brother into the house where her father and mother were talking in the kitchen. Both parents were pleased to see the safe return of their son who had unexpectedly left the city and had not been seen for several days. Upon greeting both his parents, Joel sat down at the table and asked them to join him. Then, he revealed to them what had transpired over the past few days.

Joel explained that since he had heard about the events in Yerushalayim and the widening rumours about the man they saw baptised in the Yarden River, his heart was greatly stirred within him. So, on a whim, he decided that he would try and find this unusual man and hear what he had to say for himself. Joel related how it didn't take long to find the man who was preaching to his disciples near the Lake of Galilee. There were, Joel reported, large crowds of people from all over Judea, Yerushalayim, and from the coasts of Tyre and Sidon who had heard of this man and had come to see for themselves.[153] Revealing to his family how the words of this man as he spoke resounded in his heart and how he kept each of the man's words etched in his memory, Joel began to read the transcript of everything he recorded the man saying.

His family listened with great interest and it was apparent as the words were read, they too were enrapt with the message the man was conveying. Quite some time later, when he had read the last sentence on the parchment, Joel stopped and looked at those seated around him. After a moment of silence, it was Rachael who spoke; "What an amazing man!" she said. "But father" continued Joel, "don't you find it interesting that when he speaks, he is talking about our *spiritual* wellbeing and all that he has told us to do relates to our own restored relationship with Adonai! Don't you think it is wonderful how when he talks about our poverty, our grief, our hunger, our mercy and our love, he is not just talking about our physical being but rather our spiritual relationship with Adonai?[154] As long as I can remember, when I first learnt about the future Messiah, I have always believed with my whole heart, that there was much more than a physical restoration for Isra'el, and now, I believe this man has revealed that this is so! The man called Yochanan the Immerser was the messenger who came to prepare the way for the coming Messiah, and I believe that this man the one that is called 'Yeshua of Nazareth' is indeed a man sent from Adonai".

"What I find so interesting" Ananiah added, "is that he corrects the additional teaching of the Pharisees and teachers of the law![155] I remember my father once telling me of his concern for all the additions man has

---

[153] Luke 6:17
[154] Matthew 5: 1-10
[155] Matthew 5:31-48

added to the Laws of Adonai and how these laws provide stumbling blocks to the faithful. What this man has said, confirms my father's beliefs which I feel laid heavily on his heart. Those aspects he mentions: our anger, murder [156], adultery [157], divorce[158], and retaliation against our foes[159]- all are caused by our sins. But not just one sin, for from one sin further sin grows, causing us more grief and pain! Sins weighs us down taking us further away from the laws of Adonai who, being a God of Love encourages us to love our enemies.[160] Everything, the man spoke of evolves around Godly love and mercy. If Adonai gives this to his people, how much more should his people give this to those around them? In all of man's ways, sin is the thing that brings him down and removes him from the loving grace of Adonai".

"Oh! And what I forgot to mention" added Joel, "Including within his dialogue were several parables! [161] Did not the prophet Hoshea (Hosea) declare that Adonai speaks through his prophets using parables?[162]

"That is true" confirmed Ananiah. "Joel, I believe you are correct in saying that this is a gentle yet remarkable man".

---

[156] Matthew 5: 21-26
[157] Matthew 5: 27-32
[158] Matthew 5: 33-37
[159] Matthew 5: 38-42
[160] Matthew 5: 43-47
[161] Matthew 13:10-15
[162] Hosea 12:10; Psalm 78:1-4

— *Chapter Twenty-Four* —

THE FEAST OF THE TABERNACLES

The meetings in the Sanhedrin seemed to be getting longer and longer in their duration and often when the meeting was called at night-time members would not leave the Royal Stoa until the early hours of the morning. One time, when it seemed that the cock would be crowing before the meeting disbanded, it was disrupted by a temple messenger running quickly across the Royal Stoa floor to the President of the Meeting. As Caiaphas, the High Priest, took the parchment from the messenger's hand the apse was filled with silence.

"Well, well, well!" he was heard to say. Dismissing the messenger, Caiaphas looked around the room and spoke. "Gentlemen, I believe we may delete the next and final item on our agenda tonight. It seems that unruly rogue who called himself 'Yochanan the Immerser' has talked too much about things that don't pertain to him and yesterday Herod ordered his imprisonment. He is now in the dungeons awaiting his fate!"

"Why, that's exactly what you said would happen!" said one man, speaking as he rose from his chair. Rapturous laughter and applause followed. At least that would be one less item to discuss and it would seem, a possible problem would be eliminated without any Jewish intervention!

When the meeting closed, as a small group of four walked down the stairs at the eastern end of the Royal Stoa one was heard to say to Caiaphas "Well it seems that the Immerser has come and gone but I think he proved to be just a fly in the ointment. I believe a bigger fly is currently buzzing around the district bringing strange teachings and threatening our sacred roles as leaders of our people".

Caiaphas immediately stopped and turned to the Pharisee who had been speaking and asked him for clarification. "There is a man who calls himself 'Yeshua of Nazareth' who is reportedly doing great and miraculous things, healing many people of their sicknesses and diseases. He, like the Immerser before him, is claiming that the Kingdom of Heaven is near[163]. Like the Immerser he is gaining many followers[164]."

"Nazareth? Nazareth?" responded Caiaphas raising his arms in the air. "Name me one good thing that has come out of Nazareth![165]"

"But Nazareth means 'branch' and doesn't Yesha'yahu (Isaiah) tell us that a branch shall come out of Jesse?[166] Moreover, do not the prophets tell us that he shall be called a Nazarene?[167]" one man in the small group asked.

Turning to face the man who had just spoken, Caiaphas replied angrily "Just to whom have you been speaking?" Surprisingly, Zév did not falter

---

[163] Mark 1:15; Luke 4:43
[164] Matthew 4:25
[165] John 1:46
[166] Isaiah 11:1
[167] Matthew 2:23

but replied, "To Adonai, of course! Who else speaks the truth and knows all things?"

≈   ≈   ≈

The Feast of the Tabernacles was always a busy time in Yerushalayim but this year, a large crowd of travellers and worshippers flocked to the city. Although the followers of the man Yeshua from Nazareth were told he would not be attending the festival that year[168], his own brothers encouraged him to go. Leaving the man in Galilee, his disciples and followers came to Yerushalayim for the feast. Seth had been selected to report back to his father all that they had witnessed over the past months. As it was the day before the Sabbath, Seth knew it was his father's custom to visit his brother Jethro in his baker's shop which was on the main thoroughfare of the city's streets. However, as he entered the city, Seth was overwhelmed at the size of the crowd making its way from the gate towards the marketplace – its pace was laboriously slow and sluggish somewhat like a simmering stream of lava. Finally, when he arrived at the marketplace, which was just as crowded, he peered across the heads of those in front of him to see if he could see his family's stall. Amid all the noise and busyness of the markets with buyers calling out to the people and the chatter of the crowd, he saw his mother and a few of his aunts selling the farm's produce at a stall at the back of the markets.

When Rachael first saw the smiling face of her son coming towards her, her heart greatly rejoiced. Fighting her way through the crowd she laboriously made her way to her son, embracing him warmly. Moving towards the back of the family stall, the two spoke to each other – it was much easier

---

[168] John 7:1-9

to hear there, than amidst the surging crowds. Seth explained that he was wanting to go to Jethro's bakery where he believed he would find his father, but it appeared that the crowds were just too thick, and it would take quite some time before he would reach the bakery. It was apparent that the crowd was moving towards the Temple but as the store was almost halfway down the main thoroughfare, Seth was not sure what he should do. His mother suggested that he go to his brother Joel, who was scribing at the time but to take the back way to the Temple as few people chose to go that way for it encroached the poorer sectors of Yerushalayim. A route which was seldom taken by travellers for the route revealed the oppressive poverty and over-whelming deprivation many of the city's poor inhabitants, endured.

Taking his mother's advice, Seth made his way to the back streets of Yerushalayim. As he entered the poorer sectors, the crowd numbers reduced but there were others who had thought of the same solution to avoiding the congestion of the main thoroughfare. As he moved through the narrow lanes where houses were squashed narrowly side by side, children played in the street and old men sat in their doorways looking aimlessly out into the street. A very bad stench grew as Joel ventured deep within the subdivision of the city. It was difficult to determine its source, but it smelt stale with a hint of urine and death. Seth placed his headcover across his face and took in little breaths as he moved quickly through the constricted lanes. Sighting the Temple ahead, Seth noticed the slow-moving crowd making its way towards the southern temple gate. Veering towards his left, he swiftly made his way to the Synagogue and the place where his brother scribed. As he approached the Synagogue, Seth saw his brother sitting in the shade of the large shittah tree growing in the centre of the courtyard that surrounded the school nearby. Taking a break from his head scribing duties, Joel took time to sit in the shade of the beautiful tree under which he had spent many a time in deepest reflection.

Pleased to see his brother and realizing that there would be more informa-tion about the man Yeshua, Joel arose from the wooden seat and embraced him. Sitting down in the shade the two brothers spoke at length about the man who had come into their lives and so quickly enthralled them. "We have heard so many rumours about the miracles this man has reported to have performed" Joel informed his brother. "There are incredible stories about him healing many people, even lepers[169]. Can these all be true?"

"Everything you have heard is true and I can honestly say that some of these miracles we have seen for ourselves and others have been reported back to us. But while the miracles are amazing, it is what this man says and the way he acts, that draws us to him". Seth reported that after following the man for a few months, he had chosen twelve men from the crowd accompanying him, to be his disciples. The twelve men he had chosen were mostly unlearned and mostly fishermen by trade. In fact, one of the chosen disciples said that the man Yeshua promised to make them fish-ers of men![170] Looking somewhat disappointed, Seth said that Nosh's son Tomas had decided to leave the group when he was not chosen to be part of the selected twelve. Disillusioned because he had spent many hours and weeks following the man Yeshua, Tomas believed that he should have been chosen. The fact that many of the chosen men were of low degree and unlearned, frustrated him and so, he left.

"And what about you? Were you disappointed that none of the three of you were selected?" asked Joel.

"Only for a moment" his brother responded. "When Daniel immedi-ately stated he was pleased he was not selected because that would mean further time away from his family whom he greatly misses, we realised that

---

[169] Mark 1:40-45
[170] Matthew 4:19

we had the best of both worlds for we can follow this man and return to our families as well".

"Good answer!" his brother replied.

Seth continued. While the chosen twelve may have been an unusual selection for discipleship there was one however, Seth felt uncertain about, but he did not mention a name. After the selection, the chosen ones were sent out two by two into Galilee where the man Yeshua wanted to go. Giving them specific directions as to what they could take with them and what they should do in each town, the disciples went eagerly[171]. When they returned, they reported many exciting things that had happened. In their travels, the man Yeshua spent most of his time with his chosen disciples and always when they travelled, large crowds closely accompanied him.

One time, a chosen disciple had told Seth that the group of twelve and the man were crossing the Sea of Galilee when a tremendous storm came, tossing the boat around in the tallest of waves. So exhausted from all their travelling the man Yeshua was asleep in the boat and even the tremulous sea and storms failed to awaken him. Fearing that they were all going to drown, the disciples woke him. He simply got up and commanded the winds and sea to be still. The sea and winds immediately became calm! What kind of man is this the disciples asked themselves that even the wind and the sea obey him?[172]

Joel's face froze for a second and then without realising, he found himself saying out aloud "He made the storm be still and waves of the sea were hushed!"[173] He knew he had written those words when scribing, but could it be another Dabar Promise that had been overlooked? Was it a prediction

---

of the Messiah who was to come? Just for a moment the two brothers looked at one another, stunned in the stillness by what Joel had just stated.

Seth told his brother of another time when the brothers were following the man Yeshua. They were part of a large crowd of men, women and children and after following the man for many hours, they came to a very desolate place. Tired and hungry, yet so captivated by what the man was saying, they refused to leave and so it was that although there were over 5,000 men counted, the man Yeshua told his disciples to have them all sit down in groups of fifty. Amazingly, he blessed five loaves and two fishes someone had offered and then shared it around. Everyone had ample sufficiency and when the disciples collected the food that was left over, it filled twelve baskets![174] Seth said that if he, his brothers, and his friends had not been there themselves, they would not believe it.

Moreover, he explained that the Teacher[175] (for he taught with such authority) often continued to use parables in his teaching and often, when talking about the Kingdom of Heaven, he would use earthly analogies. For example, he referred to the Kingdom like that of a man who scatters seed on the ground, some survives, and some does not[176]; it is also like a mustard seed which starts so small but ends up as the biggest of trees[177]; a woman who loses a coin and searches meticulously for it, finds it and rejoices[178]. Although the disciples often did not fully understand each parable, the Teacher would reveal its true meaning to them when they were alone. Sharing these explanations with his brother, Seth deeply sighed and said "Despite this wonderful opportunity I have been given in following this amazing man, I do miss my wife and my children, whom I believe may

---

[174] Mark 6:35-44
[175] Mark 1:22; Mark 4: 38
[176] Mark 4:1-20
[177] Mark 4:30-34
[178] Luke 15: 8-10

not recognise me. It hasn't been such a long time since I saw them last, but it seems forever".

"Then go and greet them, Seth" replied Joel "and enjoy the short time you can spend with them. I shall go and tell father everything that you have told me today. Go! And give my love to your family".

Anxious to get to his family Seth swiftly departed, whilst Joel quickly went upstairs to the scribing room and informed the acting head scribe he would not be returning to duty for family concerns had arisen. Swiftly he made his way towards Jethro's shop. Knowing the back streets of the city so well, Joel did not go to his brother's house via the poorer section of the city, but rather he took various back streets within the eastern side of the city. At the corner of many of the streets' intersections, he caught glimpses of the trailing crowds endlessly making their way to the Temple. It wasn't long before he took the final back street which led him to the main thoroughfare. As Jethro's bakery was only three shops down, it was difficult, but he finally managed to enter the shop which, at this stage, appeared to be almost sold-out of the buns and loaves so lovingly made by his brother.

Sighting his father and his sister seated at the back wall of the shop, Joel greeted them warmly and then related Seth's news to them. Jethro also listened in keenly for he had found the news of the man who healed so many people, of immense interest. Their father's face appeared to lighten as the news was relayed to him. With every passing day, Ananiah felt with increasing assurance, that the days of the Messiah had come to Isra'el and when he heard the wonderful stories his sons revealed to him about this Yeshua of Nazareth, he found great peace within his heart.

"What a shame he has not come to the Feast" remarked Abigail. While the others agreed with her, Joel affirmed the sentiments of his brothers that while the miracles this man performed were in themselves amazing, he felt a stronger attraction to what the man was saying about Adonai and the way His people should go. Joel declared that the more he learned about the man Yeshua, the more he believed that the words the man speaks concern man's spiritual well-being. In fact, he believed that the Kingdom of Heaven which all Isra'el was expecting and looking so forward to, was not a physical place restricted by size and area but rather was a spiritual place where there were no boundaries.

"While you were relating the tales of my sons about this man" replied Ananiah, "particularly about him commanding the waves and winds to be stilled, a verse from the Tilhilim (Psalms) came to me. Now how does the wording go?"

"He stilled the storm to a whisper the waves of the seas were hushed"[179] quoted Joel.

"Yes!" exclaimed Ananiah. "That's the one!"

"The words came to my mind too father when Seth related the story to me. This man who by his voice commands demon spirits to leave, for sicknesses to recede and winds and storms to abate, must have Divine authority and therefore, must have been sent with Adonai's blessing and enabling!"

All of them were in awe of the news. The crowd by this stage had lessened somewhat and Abagail thought that at last both she and her father could return home. Joel, too, believed it was now safe to leave and he was the first to go. Next, Abigail took her father's arm and gently led him down the street leaving Jethro alone with his two young sons who had been amusing themselves near the ovens in the bakehouse. Jethro was quite happy for them to amuse themselves in the separated oven area of the shop for he believed that while young children who are out of sight, they were also out of mind. (Not many parents would necessarily agree with him).

---

[179] Psalm 107:29

As he was about to gather his unsold wares to his complete surprise, he thought he saw the man they had just been talking about making his way with the crowd walking towards the Temple. "Eli! Come here quickly! There is a man that I need to follow! Come here quickly!" Eli came quickly - only eight years old he was very confident for his age. "I need to follow a man I have just seen so you and your brother can look after the shop. After all the goods are sold, lock up the shop and go home. Do you understand?"

"Yes, father!" replied Eli. "I understand".

"Good! Do as I say!" commanded Jethro as he left the shop. Following in the stream of the crowd, because of his small statue, he could be seen by his sons bopping up and down, hoping to sight the man he thought he had just seen. The two young boys looked at each other.

"What does this mean?" asked the younger.

"It means" said his older brother puffing out his chest, "that I am in charge!"

— *Chapter Twenty-Five* —

THE QUICKLY TURNING TIDE

J ethro busily served his customers in his bakery as the Feast of the Tabernacles and all the celebrations began. It was always a profitable time for the retailers in Yerushalayim when the religious festivals came yet for some reason, this specific Feast proved to be extremely popular. Serving his customers quickly, it wasn't long before his goods were depleted and the shelves entirely bare. As he waited for the last of his customers to come into his shop, he could not understand why he was so sure that the man he saw in the crowd passing his shop just a few days ago, was in fact the man his brothers were following. Despite his effort to follow the man he thought was Yeshua of Nazareth, it didn't take him long to realize that he must have been mistaken. After all, didn't his brothers tell him, the man had not chosen to come to the Feast despite his family urging him to do so?

Eli and his younger brother played in their usual place at the back of the store quite contented with one another's company. Just as he sold the last loaf he had to his final customer, Jethro looked out into the crowd passing his shop outside when, to his dismay, he recognised the face of the man from Nazareth! This time he knew he was not mistaken! Quickly he turned to his elder son and told him to close the shop and return home to their mother. Eli once again puffed out his chest; being in charge held such responsibilities!

≈ ≈ ≈

Once again, because of his small stature, Jethro bounced up and down as he fought his way through the crowd, managing to get brief glimpses of the man who had steadfastly made his way to the Temple. Being short in height had its advantages and disadvantages: it was easy to blend into the crowd when volunteers for a difficult or unpleasant task were called for but it was always difficult trying to see the centre of attention when enveloped in the density of a crowd. Nevertheless, Jethro followed the man right into the Temple and when they were in the Court of Isra'el, the man began to speak.

How Jethro longed to catch sight of the man speaking but all he could do was to remain still and listen to the man's every word. Jethro's heart skipped a beat! It was so true what his brothers had reported, this man spoke with such authority and wisdom. Moreover, every word the man spoke pierced into Jethro's very soul convincing him that this was no ordinary man. The man claimed his teaching was not his own but came from the one who sent him and then started to address some of the criticism about him that had come from the Pharisees. He asked why he himself was being severely criticized for healing a person on the Sabbath, and yet the Pharisees and the Sadducees could perform circumcisions on that day (though this law did not come from Mosesh (Moses) but the patriarchs themselves)?[180]

To Jethro's amazement the man speaking in the temple then directly asked the Pharisees present why they were trying to kill him[181]. Some people in the crowd were unsure as to what the man meant by this, whilst others knew of the increasing animosity to the man on the part of the chief priests, Pharisees and Sadducees. What a strange notion that was, thought Jethro to himself. Who would want to kill this man? Immediately Jethro turned around and saw a small group of Pharisees standing at the back of the crowd overseeing all that had happened yet they made no effort to intervene[182]. Their faces were glum and somewhat expressionless and Jethro felt as if his heart stopped momentarily. One of the Pharisees did not remain there much longer but immediately ran off towards the Royal Stoa.

As Jethro's attention returned to the man from Nazareth, the crowd seemed to move quickly forwards to the place where the man was speaking. It was almost as if the crowd was trying to seize him but it was to no avail for the man had somehow slipped through the crowd safely.[183] Despite trying to find Yeshua within the crowd, Jethro could find no trace of him. He felt somewhat relieved for he felt very unsettled that the emotions of a crowd could become negative so quickly. What a weak and foolish creature is man, that his emotions can change at the twinkling of an eye or at the murmur of a crowd! With these thoughts swimming around in his head, he immediately made his way towards the Synagogue where his brother Joel worked as a scribe. Maybe, Joel might be able to make sense of what had

---

[180] John 7:21-24
[181] John 7:19
[182] John 7:25-26
[183] John 7:30-31

just transpired. Maybe he might be able to provide some enlightenment on what had caused the people's feelings to change so dramatically.

≈   ≈   ≈

Meanwhile, across the Temple grounds on the top floor of the Royal Stoa, the Sanhedrin were deep in conversation. It seemed that over the past few weeks there were seas of rumours circulating about a man from Nazareth who was doing great and mighty miracles. There was also a growing number of people claiming that this man, who also spoke with authority and grace, could very well be the Messiah, the promised one of Adonai. Some were concerned that this type of sentiment might cause an upsurgeance by the people against the Roman authorities, and therefore would mean ever harsher treatment by the occupying power. Many feared that the Romans could take away their current leadership powers. It seemed that this man's influence on the people of Isra'el was becoming more effective than their own. Surely the situation needed to be addressed and if necessary, nipped in the bud?

Calling for people to speak one at a time, Caiaphas called for decorum so that an accurate direction may be taken by the committee. The first man to rise to his feet to speak stated that he had seen some of the many miracles the man Yeshua of Nazareth had been reported as performing. In his whole life, he reported that he had never seen such miraculous happenings, the expulsion of demons[184], healing of the lame[185], the blind[186], the deaf[187],

---

[184] Matthew 8: 28-34; Mark 1:34; Luke 8:2
[185] Mark 2:3-5; Luke 13:10-13
[186] Matthew 9:27-31
[187] Mark 7:31-37

the sick[188]. Surely, he concluded that this man must be a man appointed by Adonai?

The next man to speak rose and questioned the statement of the man before him. "Doesn't my colleague remember that in the days of Moshe (Moses) when he was sent by Adonai to Pharaoh, the Egyptian magicians often could duplicate the miraculous sign Moshe performed. Moreover, there was not just one snake but several! Beelzebub can also perform similar 'miracles'".

Rising to his feet another man proclaimed. "Might I remind my colleague that in the story he quotes, he forgot to mention that the several snakes the Egyptian magicians created came to a very abrupt end by the power of Adonai's one snake![189] Besides, if this man Yeshua is from Beelzebub, how can Beelzebul drive out evil spirits?[190]"

Yet another man rose up to say that he had heard this man and his disciples did many unlawful things such as not washing their hands before they ate[191]; picking grain on the Sabbath[192] and dining with sinners[193]. He also has the audacity to heal on the Sabbath[194] and what was more unbelievable was that he had been heard to tell people their sins were forgiven![195] Who but Adonai can forgive sins? Weren't the man's statements of forgiveness, blasphemous?

Another man reported to the group that he had seen this man teach and perform miracles but when he, together with other Pharisees asked for

---

[188] Matthew 8:14-17; Matthew 12:15;
[189] Exodus 7:8-13
[190] Matthew 12:24
[191] Mark 7:1-13
[192] Luke 6:1-2
[193] Matthew 9:9-12
[194] Luke 6:6-11
[195] Matthew 9:2-8

a miracle, the man was extremely rude and unresponsive[196]. From many sources he had also heard that the man often preached against the teaching of the Pharisees, contradicting the many laws that had to be made because of the people's stubbornness.[197] Surely this man was a rebel, defying Adonai's teaching and turning the people against their leaders?

The discussions went on and on until, unnoticed by the group, a temple messenger came up to Caiaphas and whispered in his ears. Nodding his head, he told the messenger to remain for a moment and rising from his chair, he moved his hands to hush the meeting and waited till silence filled the apse. "Gentlemen, it seems that the man in question is now teaching in the Temple grounds and so I propose we call the Temple Guards to go and bring this man to us. In the meantime, let us proceed onto the next item on our agenda[198]".

The temple messenger was then dismissed and went to arrange for five Temple Guards to be sent to the Court of Isra'el to bring the one who was talking there back to the Chief Priests and Pharisees. When they arrived in the Court of Isra'el they found that the man was no longer there and so they decided that as the Feast would continue for a few more days, they would keep watch on the temple grounds to find the man as he was bound to return.

≈   ≈   ≈

As Head Scribe, it was Joel's responsibility to check all the submitted work by carefully adding up all letters, lines, spaces and words to ensure these concurred with the correct tallies of the letter, lines and spaces of

---

196 Mark 8:11-12
197 Matthew 5-7
198 John 7:32

the original text. Everything had to be perfect as the submitted work recorded the words and laws of Adonai. Today, as he began his counting for some unknown reason, when it came to counting the number of words in the transcript, he found himself saying each word out loud. Correcting himself, he would start the task again only to find that a few words into the passage he would once again be saying the written words instead of counting. Becoming quite infuriated with himself, he stopped and started several times.

Wondering what was happening he stopped and thought "Maybe I will just read the words to see if there is any reason why this is happening to me". So, reading from right to left he began reading the passage and as his fingers steadily worked their way across the parchment, they soon began to tremor. Although he had written and read this passage from the prophet Yesha'yahu (Isaiah) many times, for some reason the words did not spring out and catch his attention like they were doing at that very moment. It was as if a huge veil had been removed and the words seemed to jump off the page and etch their meaning into Joel's heart. The future Messiah was going to be despised and rejected by the people! He would be a man familiar with suffering and grief![199]. In his suffering, it was going to appear as if he was stricken by Adonai himself and that on this Messiah, all sin would be laid![200] The concepts worried Joel deeply. How and why should someone who is good and holy in Adonai's sight, become so un-comely and unholy? While there seemed to be truth in what the words were saying, the exact meaning was complex and difficult to understand.

Continuing to read the manuscript before him, the script proclaimed that the Messiah would be led like a lamb to the slaughter, silent and surrendering to death and upon his death, he was to be assigned a grave with

---

[199] Isaiah 53: 3-5
[200] Isaiah 53: 4-6

the wicked[201]. The words concurred with the concerns of his father and his great-grandfather who believed that there could be some form of rejection by the people. However, the consequence of this rejection was unknown until now and as he read the passage over and over, he knew in his heart, that the presence of the coming Messiah was to herald in a new way to return to Adonai which centred on the forgiveness of sin.

Severely shaken by this realisation, he excused himself when another chief scribe took over his task. Heading towards the large tree in the school courtyard, Joel concentrated on his breathing. Could what he had just read be true? What lay ahead for this man Yeshua of Nazareth? What would his father think of what he had just learnt? These thoughts went over and over in his mind and feeling totally overwhelmed from these, Joel found the concept of such horror, difficult to comprehend.

Just as he was musing over these things, he looked up to see his younger brother Jethro coming quickly towards him. Jethro too, had the appearance as if something was on his mind and as the two men embraced they sat down side by side on the wooden seat near the tree.

"Is father all right?" asked Joel anxiously.

Jethro nodded his head and slightly out of breath said, "Something strange just happened - I don't know where to start!"

Gaining his composure, Jethro related to his brother how he saw the man Yeshua of Nazareth go past his shop so he quickly followed in the huge crowd making its way to the Temple. While he was there as he listened to the man speaking, he could not understand why his heart was excited by everything the man was saying. Then, in conversation with someone in the crowd the man Yeshua asked why people were trying to kill him! The thought that anyone was attempting to kill this man seemed incred-

---

[201] Isaiah 53: 7-9

ulous but the man Yeshua really believed this was happening. Wondering who would want such a thing, Jethro looked at the faces of the crowd surrounding the court and when his eyes beheld a small group of stern-faced Pharisees with hatred in their eyes, he immediately thought they were up to no good. Then, the crowd which appeared to be divided between those who thought Yeshua was the Messiah and those who did not, started to merge towards the man Yeshua in what looked like an attempt to seize him.

"Did they wish to seize him to make him King immediately[202] or did they want to seize him to bring him harm?"[203] asked Joel.

"That's just it! I couldn't say! It was so strange and the whole situation convinces me that the heart of man is so changeable – it can change from sweetness to bitterness in one single second! Honestly, Joel, it really was quite baffling!"

His brother's description of the crowd at the Temple and the words that had just been inscribed in his heart seemed to affirm that the man whom his father and himself believed to be the Messiah, could in fact be in danger. The path that this man was treading could possibly lead to his death. So, the two brothers agreed that they must go and share what they had learnt that day with Ananiah.

≈   ≈   ≈

Just as the Temple Guards had assumed, the man did return to the Court of Isra'el and it was on the final day of the Festival he spoke again with the crowds[204]. Listening to what the man said, the guards decided they could take no action against this man, who spoke so well and spoke of the need

---

[202] John 6:14-15
[203] Luke 4:28-30
[204] John 7: 37-44

for the Israelite nation to return to Adonai and his laws and ways. So, they returned to the chief priest and the Pharisees who were meeting in the Royal Stoa.

"Why didn't you bring him to us?" the Pharisees asked?

"No one ever spoke the way this man does" the guards declared.

"You mean he has deceived you also?" the Pharisees retorted[205].

"This man needs to be condemned for the wrong he is doing" said Caiaphas. "Surely, he must die for it is better for one man to die than have a whole nation destroyed. He is eradicating the foundations we have laid over the years. Surely, he must be condemned!"[206]

Nichodemus, who was also present, immediately protested the law insisted before a man is to be judged, he must have the opportunity to state his case. After his protestations, his peers immediately inquired if he, like this protagonist came from Galilee and that it was very clear in all Adonai's promises, the Messiah would not come from Galilee[207]. It seemed the hostility towards this man of Nazareth had somehow boiled into such a cancerous loathing, the fate that lay ahead for him, was black and foreboding.

---

[205] John 7: 45-47
[206] John 11:49-53
[207] John 7:50-52

— *Chapter Twenty-Six* —

SOUND YET
FORGOTTEN ADVICE

S itting on the front porch of the farmhouse, Ananiah found himself in deepest reflection; recalling many of the in-depth discussions
he had with his father and great-grandfather on the very porch on
which he was sitting. How these discussions would enthral him! It seemed
so long ago almost in a past and forgotten world. So much had happened
over the years and although as his sight deteriorated as the colours of the
world faded before him, he always felt that because of the mercy of Adonai
on that fatal day in the catacombs, he had deep within himself a brighter
place where he felt at peace with the world. But alas, times were different
and changing for the worse. Contemplating if what his sons Jethro and Joel
had told him about the man from Nazareth was true, he felt a tinge of fear
invade his soul; the place where he had found such inner peace.

What was happening to the world? Surely the man they had found was indeed the coming Messiah! Yet there were rumours of people trying to kill him! In the past, the prophets of Adonai had suffered horrific deaths at the hands of Adonai's people, yet this man was no ordinary prophet: he was the one promised so many generations ago, in fact from the very beginning of time[208], and he was the one who would restore Isra'el to Adonai! Ananiah felt himself slipping downwards in his thoughts and without hesitation he spoke to the One who had befriended him and who had been so faithful over the years.

"El-roi, El-roi! You delivered your people from the waves of the Red Sea and from the scorn of Egypt, deliver me for fear is looming within my soul and all seems doomed! O my Friend and Deliverer, how faithful You have been to me since that wondrous day when You poured out Your mercy on a rebellious and unruly child, at the point of death in a desolate place. You have welcomed me as a friend and so graciously given me bountiful blessings; a loving family who seeks to serve you; a wonderful wife and eight beautiful children: two of whom were cruelly taken away when they were so young and innocent. Yet I know, that in that dreadful calamity, You were in control for all things were coming together for Your purpose as You foretold us in Your word how the women would weep. And wept they did! Yet even in that darkest hour, Your word prevailed and in doing so You gave me hope.

---

[208] Genesis 3:15

Then, in the shelter of your Holy Place, You graciously spoke to me and promised me that I would see the Messiah not with my own eyes but my very soul. My soul feels darkened by the recent news I have heard and I am finding it difficult to see through the darkness and the maze of what is happening in the world this day. Strengthen my spiritual eyes so that they may see Your handiwork and uplift my soul that I may praise You for what You are doing and for who You are.

My forefathers before me have always believed that Your Plan in restoring Isra'el through Your promised Messiah has a much deeper meaning. Over the years, I am convinced that You have shown me Your ways are higher and greater than man's [209]. Keep the eyes of my soul alert so that they may see You and encourage my spirit so that I may still please You and know Your Plan, even though I am old and frail.

This man Yeshua of Nazareth is, I believe, a Godly man for he speaks of You, of Your love, and of Your forgiveness. Moreover, he heals with great mercy and compassion and the whole person is renewed. Yet what he tells us relates to Your Kingdom and I believe, like my sons, that Your Kingdom is not of this world but of a higher order. It comes from an awareness of Your existence, but there are many men whose spiritual eyes are like my failing physical eyes. They are blinded by their pride and their own arrogance. Please help your stubborn people, to remove the scales of disbelief that cover their eyes and reveal Your truth to them.

---

[209] Isaiah 55:8-9

El-roi, El-roi! How great are You for even in my devastation, talking to You encourages me and lifts my soul! Please help to keep my eyes fixed upward for the only way out of this pit of darkness lies within the light which shines above me. Continue to strengthen me that I may be faithful to You, for You, my God and Deliverer, have been so faithful and kind to me."

Almost immediately as Ananiah finished praying, Rachael came out of the house to tell him that he had two visitors. His friend Kaleb, who like himself, had aged over the years; his black curly hair had become grey and almost completely receded; his hands wrinkled and hardened by his trade; his body bent and his gait like a duck. He was so different from the young boy with whom Ananiah played in days gone by yet the friendship remained strong and as he waddled onto the porch he told Ananiah he had brought a friend with him.

When Ananiah heard the greeting of the man accompanying his friend, a smile brightened his face. Rachael was pleased to see this as for some time now, she had often observed her husband in deepest thought but the smile that she loved was not always there and that troubled her. "Zév! How wonderful to see you!" exclaimed Ananiah who then quickly retorted "Well, not quite see but it is good to have you here!" Zév's feeble frame edged its way onto the porch when Rachael went inside to get another chair for Kaleb to sit on. Nobody knew Zév's correct age but he must have been well into his late eighties or early nineties but he was, nevertheless, very alert and spritely and still highly revered by the people.

Zév sat down on the chair opposite Ananiah while Kaleb waited for Rachael to bring the other chair from the house. As he sat down on this, Rachael went inside to get the men some refreshments for she could see that their faces were hot and flustered. "My sincerest apologies to you,

Ananiah" Zév remarked, "for I have intended to come and see you for quite some time now but we have been extremely busy in the Sanhedrin of late. How life can become so busy; sometimes you do not even have time to scratch yourself." The last remark caused by Ananiah and Kaleb to gasp but then, Zév continued.

"Ever since we last spoke returning from the river when Yochanan the Immerser spoke, I have been going over and over the conversation we had and there are several things I wanted to ask you. Do you really believe that Yochanan the Immerser was the Messenger Adonai promised?" he asked.

"What do you mean 'was'? Yes, I believe he is", stated Ananiah.

"Haven't you heard the news?" Zév replied. "Yochanan the Immerser was beheaded while imprisoned[210]. There are many rumours circulating but it is felt that Herodias had some input into his death but as you know, rumours run rife."

"Beheaded!" exclaimed Ananiah – the concept brought back the memory of two young boys who had cruelly and innocently suffered the same fate. "Another man of Adonai murdered for what reason? How long must Adonai's followers suffer from the cruel hand of man?"

The men paused in silence for a moment as Abagail brought them mugs of water dashed with wine. Serving the guests first, she then lifted the final drinking vessel and placed this in her father's hands. Leaving the group, she was aware that they were in deep discussion and although she wanted to stand behind the door and listen to what they were saying, she returned to her mother in the kitchen.

"I don't know if you recall the conversations we had as we were travelling home from the Yarden River? Remember, you so kindly gave me the provision of your donkey, Zimra?" asked Zév.

---

[210] Matthew 14:3-12

"Zimra!" exclaimed Ananiah. "Ah Zimra! Our trusted steed!"

Kaleb laughed out raucously. "I trust you were advised about the three rules of Zimra!" he laughingly inquired.

Zév's face was blank. Ignorant of the 'rules of Zimra' he continued. "When we were returning home, I thought you commented that you believed that the Messiah was there among the group of people gathered at the river. When I asked who he was, your daughter made a comment which suggested I wouldn't know him if I saw him. I have been thinking over and over in my head just who was at the river that day and it dawned on me a few months later, that the man from Nazareth was there. I vaguely remember seeing him but I am not sure if my memory is correct so I wanted to come and see you to clarify this and appease my old and tired mind. Was the man of Nazareth there and if he was, do you believe that he is the promised Messiah?"

"Yes, and yes" replied Ananiah.

"Are you aware that there has been a lot of discussion about this man in the Sanhedrin – most of it is not positive?" asked Zév.

"Yes, and moreover, the man himself believes that there are people trying to kill him!" responded Ananiah.

"Do you really believe that the people would not only kill the messenger but also Adonai's prophet?[211] Surely, that could never happen!" remarked Kaleb.

Kaleb's two friends remained silent for in their hearts they knew that this was a wicked generation and such cruelty and injustice was occurring all around them, and man – man has and always will be fickle and selfish in his dealings with the world.

---

[211] Matthew 21:33-45

"What Joel and I have found quite perturbing is that recently we believe we have come across scripture which foretells that the chosen one of Adonai will be rejected, despised and punished even though he is totally innocent. Furthermore, we believe that he may suffer unfairly and unjustly for it is Adonai's will to crush him and cause him to suffer[212]" Ananiah informed them.

"But why would Adonai, the God of Justice and Truth, allow an innocent man and a man He had ordained, to be treated so?" Kaleb asked.

"I do not know the answer to that, Kaleb" replied Ananiah. "But who can understand the mind and ways of our great living Lord? All I believe is that such things are contained in His promises to His people and that His promises are true and will happen. Nor is there anything that man can do to override His will. Adonai's Will will be done!"

"May Adonai be praised!" exclaimed Zév. "The very words you have spoken to us now, I personally spoke to your father many years ago. I recall your father Nosh was there, Kaleb, as well as your father and great grandfather, Ananiah. Your father had a similar concern and came to me for advice. My advice to him was the advice you have given to us, now! How strange it is, to have your own advice fed back to you by another person's mouth! Adonai is indeed in charge and there is nothing we or anyone else can do to change it!"

All men felt peace within their themselves as they sat on the front porch of the farmhouse. Just as they were leaving, Kaleb placed his hand on Ananiah's shoulder and told his friend that the friendship they had was there for life and that if there was anything troubling him, to send for him right away and he would come as quickly as he could.

---

[212] Isaiah 53:10-11

"Oh, Ananiah, have you heard my son Rafe has returned home from following the man Yeshua? He tells us that his teaching has become very strange claiming that he is the bread of life for all mankind. Moreover, if we eat his flesh which is the bread and drink his blood, we will have eternal life[213]. Believing this as somewhat cannibalistic, Rafe said he had to leave. I am sorry that two of my sons have decided not to follow this man Yeshua but Tomas always thought of himself more highly than he should and Rafe -if what you are saying doesn't fit into his understanding, then he chooses to pay no attention at all. They must take after their mother in this regard – those genes did not come from me!"

---

[213] John 6:51-66

— Chapter Twenty-Seven —

PREVAILING WISDOM

S inging and humming to herself, Abagail busily completed her chores. How she loved the freedom and fresh air of the farm and its pleasant rural surroundings! By daily feeding the farm animals, Abagail felt as if she was contributing to the family business and just like all her brothers, cousins, and uncles, she was part of a larger concern. Being the youngest child and the only daughter there were times, particularly when all her elder brothers had married and left the farmhouse, when she felt alone. However, as all her siblings lived nearby, it also was a happy occasion when they visited their parents, and it was then Abagail would enjoy their company once more. Now aged fifteen, she had blossomed into a beautiful young woman. Sadly, her father's failing eyes were unable to see this, but it was noticed by all her family, especially her mother, who knew in her heart there would come a time when her only daughter would leave and become some fortunate man's wife. With her daughter, Rachael thought to herself, some man would be gaining a treasured possession.

Just as she was completing her chores, she heard her mother call her from the farmhouse. Jethro had popped in for a visit and had brought some Abagail bun with him. She urged her daughter to finish her chores and join them in the house for some refreshments. Abagail was pleased. Of all her brothers, Jethro was the one with whom she felt the closest. Unlike her other siblings, who were tall and fine looking, Jethro appeared to be the physical runt of the family. Small and robust in stature with curly auburn hair (which seemed to become less and less over the years) it was not just Jethro's smile that she enjoyed seeing but also, his warm welcoming hugs which were so strong and sincere, so reassuring to her that she was truly loved. Those hugs were the most precious of all!

Her chores completed Abagail washed her hands in the basin of cool water placed on a table outside of the house. Thoroughly cleaning these, she shook them vigorously in the air to dry as she went into the house. Upon her entrance, Jethro rose from his seat and moving across the room, embraced his sister hugging her in the way she loved. Then, bringing her to the table, Jethro and Abagail sat down next to their father and mother. When he informed them that he had come because of his conversation with his wife Rebecca (a snare) the night before, Rachael took a hesitant breath. Of all her daughters-in-law, Rebecca was the most demanding. A tall thin woman, she appeared in both statue and personality to be the opposite of her son. Yet, as Ananiah would continually remind her, Jethro chose her, and the marriage was Jethro's choice. When she first met Rebecca, Rachael knew just who would be the overseer of her son's family for Jethro was such an easy-going person, wanting to please all and offending none. Rebecca, on the other hand, knew only one way – her way- and quickly would bring on child-like tantrums if she was not obtaining it.

Jethro shared with them that when he had left his older eight-year-old son in charge of the bakery to follow the man Yeshua, Rebecca was rightfully not pleased as an eight-year-old child should never be given such responsibility. If Jethro wanted to leave the bakery surely there should be someone older left in charge? It was Rebecca's suggestion that Abagail might come and work in the bakery so that if Jethro had to leave, at least some one more appropriate remained in the shop.

"But surely", remarked Rachael, "the most appropriate person to work with the baker, would be the baker's wife?" Ananiah reaching his hand towards his wife's arm and tapping this gently to motion her to let her son speak, waited for his son to continue.

"No", replied Jethro. "She has to visit her elderly parents each day to look after them. They find the boys are a little rambunctious and noisy so that is why they stay with me at the shop".

"We all have families to look after" replied his mother. "Where would we be if we left our children to go and look after our elderly parents?"

"Unfortunately, in a place I am not yet ready to be!" said Ananiah causing his daughter to laugh out loud.

Jethro continued, aware that his dear mother often had different views to that of his wife, stating that he was there to ask Abagail if she would come and work for him in the bakery.

"But what about my work on the farm?" Abagail asked. "And what about father? Who would look after him?"

"I am still in the land of the living! I'm still here!" Ananiah reminded them.

"You can still do your farm chores and mother has looked after him before" replied Jethro. Rachael believed that the very words her son was using came not from his own mouth, but someone else's.

"Isn't your mother elderly?" Rachael asked her son.

Ananiah turned to his daughter and said that the decision to be made, would have to come from her. What did she wish to do? The group were silent as Abagail thought the suggestion over. Like her mother, she could see how this suggestion might help her sister-in-law whose rightful place was beside the husband who loved her and having her young sister-in-law completing her task served no-one but Rebecca. Thinking quickly and gifted with the wisdom of her father, Abagail turned to her brother and spoke.

"Thank you, Jethro for thinking of me but I am sorry, but my answer is 'no and yes'".

Everyone looked confused. "First, I will not come and work for you in your shop each day for my place is here at home with my dear *elderly* mother *and* father. What I will do however, is this: I will come and work in your shop during the three festive times when the man Yeshua comes to Yerushalayim and attends the Temple. This will release you and enable you to do as our brothers Daniel, Seth and Jabin are doing in following this man and seeking to learn more about him. In fact, when they are visiting their families while they are home, you will be able to witness what this man does yourself and do as you have done, report this back to father and Joel. Enabling you to do this for us all will be part of my contribution as a family member for following and observing this man is a family responsibility and therefore, I am happy to do this for you under these terms".

Ananiah was pleased. He knew that as a young woman, Abigail could not accompany the man Yeshua as closely as his sons for as a female, she could not follow the man into the Temple. Courts in the Temple for the women folk were separated from the men. Also, he knew how his daughter loved to feel she belonged and that she was helpful to others. So, her decision was a wise one for she was completing the task under her own terms and not the terms of someone else, whose agenda might be considered selfish and inconsiderate.

Jethro appeared happy with the suggestion and believed that this would please all parties.

Over the passing weeks and months rumours ran rampant through the city. The terrible demise of Yochanan the Immerser and his beheading was superseded by the rumours of the many miracles of the man they call Yeshua of Nazareth who, together with his disciples and an ever-increasing number of followers was reported to be travelling around Galilee[214], Decapolis[215] and even through Samaria[216]. Moreover, it was reported that many of the miracles this man performed were completed in the very sight of the Pharisees[217] whom it was rumoured were becoming progressively antagonistic towards him. As the Passover Feast was approaching, there was some speculation whether the man would return to Yerushalayim. As many believed that he might be the coming messiah promised so long ago by the prophets, they hoped that he would be coming to the city to finally restore Isra'el to its former glory. It was this specific rumour that angered the Pharisees and the chief priests most of all. It was becoming increasingly obvious to them that this man was attracting the people's attention for all the wrong reasons and as he had on many occasions, spoke publicly to them in harsh terms, it was time to nip this problem in the bud so that it would not intensify. Just how the bud was to be nipped and what steps should be taken were continuously raised and furiously debated during the meetings of the Sanhedrin and other gatherings.

---

[214] John 4:4-26
[215] Matthew 4:25; Mark 5:1-20
[216] Luke 17:11
[217] Mark 3:1-6

On the day before Passover, Rachael received a wonderful surprise. There, standing in the doorway of her home was her youngest son Jabin. He had been chosen by the three brothers to tell his father about all that had happened during the time they had been following the man Yeshua. At first the brothers were happy just to be able to report all they had learned back to their father but as the weeks went by and they observed more and more miracles, the brothers agreed that there was something else that drew them to this man. Whilst Daniel and Seth were not sure as to what this attraction could be, Jabin was certain he knew exactly what the attraction was.

After receiving a long embrace from his mother, he looked up to see his father enter the house from the door off the front porch. "Didn't I just hear Jabin's voice?" Ananiah inquired. There before him was his father, who had aged greatly and by the expression of his face and the laziness of his eyes, had now become totally blind. Jabin's heart sank. How his father had changed! Warmly embracing his father, Jabin could see that his father's spirits were immediately raised by his presence and he believed that the news he had come to tell him would bring his father further cheer. Then, it was Abigail's turn to greet her brother. She had been hanging out washing to dry when she heard excited voices coming from the house. Stopping what she was doing she ran immediately inside where to her delight she recognised the tall form of her brother Jabin.

Jabin also saw a change in his younger sister – how she had grown! She was now changing into a beautiful woman and just like her mother, she had the same gentle nature, the same eyes, and the same smile. Everything had changed so much since he had last seen his family, it was if he and his brothers had been living the past months and year in another world. "I have so much to tell you about the master" he said as his family sat around the table as Jabin continued. "No doubt you have heard of his many miracles and the wondrous things that he has done. We know this for as we travel around, we find that the people know all about him before he arrives in their towns and villages. These wonderful things are true for the three of us have often seen them with our very eyes as we travel in the crowds that follow him. Sometimes we hear from his disciples what he has said and done".

"A few weeks ago, when we were quite a way from any villages and towns in the Decapolis, once again the master turned a few small fishes and seven loaves of bread into a great banquet where over 4,000 men were satisfied. Moreover, when everyone had eaten and had self-sufficiency, there were seven baskets filled with uneaten pieces![218] Just as he had done on the north-eastern shore of the Lake before, he felt compassion for the people and although the crowd was smaller than the previous one, many of the people in this crowd were believed to be Gentile! To me, it was if his compassion knows no bounds!"

Jabin took a moment to collect his thoughts; there was so much he wanted to tell his family about the wonderful things he had seen this man do but there was something more urgent that lay on his heart. "The people who follow him seem to be drawn to the miracles he does but unfortunately, they cannot seem to see past these. They get food in their stomach; their sicknesses and diseases are gone, and they still follow him demanding more[219]. They seem to have scales on their eyes which prevent them from seeing who the man is, and wax in their ears that stops them from hearing what he is saying".

"It is what this man is teaching us, I find even more amazing than the miracles in all their perplexities and complexities. This man is a teacher from Adonai and yet many of those following him stubbornly refuse to see him for who he truly is" Jabin said.

---

[218] Mark 8:1-21
[219] Mark 8:11-12

Ananiah's ears were immediately pricked by the words Jabin had used, causing him to immediately ask "What do you mean 'for whom he truly is'?"

"Father, this is no ordinary man! What man tells the sea and storm to be calm[220]? What man can instruct demons to come out of another[221]? What man can walk on water?[222] Yeshua does all these things! Moreover, he knows the scriptures intimately quoting them correctly and explaining many things. This is no ordinary man! I believe this man knows Adonai so well - in fact when he is teaching, my heart leaps and I feel as if I need to listen forever, for the words he speaks are so refreshing to the soul."

"What are his teachings?" inquired Abagail.

"His teachings!" exclaimed Jabin, "These are most exciting and enlightening!"

"First, he refers to Adonai as 'our loving heavenly father' - *father*! There are many different words we Jews use that describe the greatness of Adonai but 'father' is not one of them![223]" The word itself tells us that Adonai wants a deep and personal relationship with us. What deity do you know desires such a relationship with his creation? Moreover, He has such deep love for all his creation despite what they may feel towards Him yet He loves them regardless. In fact, Yeshua told us that Adonai's kindness and love is given to all[224]. What deity is there who loves his people regardless of what they have done? Yeshua urges us, as Yochanan the Immerser did, to repent of our sins and turn back to the living God[225]. He has promised that if we do this,

---

[220] Mark 4: 39
[221] Luke 4: 41
[222] John 6: 16-21
[223] www.smilegodlovesyou.org
[224] Matthew 5:45
[225] Matthew 4:17

not only will our sins be forgiven[226], they shall be remembered no more![227] Which deity offers such gracious mercy to his people?"

"But the repentance must be sincere and come from a heart that is willing to change. It's no good at all, to ask for forgiveness and keep on doing the same sin. Rather there is a submission required of giving yourself to Him completely, surrendering your will, yourself, and your life to Him, not holding anything back or keeping some of the treasures laid aside for later pleasure[228]. Complete compliance is what he desires of his followers. Adonai's love is freely available to all those who seek it even though our lives have led us down a sinful path away from Him and His loving presence. But no matter how far we have moved, we are never beyond hope[229]".

Jabin went on to explain how Yeshua had said that the most important thing we can do is to love Adonai with all our heart, soul, strength, and mind[230] and Jabin had identified from the master's teaching different ways in which we can express and demonstrate that love. The first was to know and be obedient to Adonai's commands[231]; this would mean that we obey Adonai's laws as well as Yeshua's teachings[232]. The second required us to trust in Adonai and Yeshua; this involved maintaining our faith in the most difficult times of our lives when we face criticisms, cynicism and sufferings. Such are unfortunately just part of life and we must rise above them. We can only do this by having peace with our Creator, with one another and within ourselves. Thirdly, we need to put Adonai above all things in this world; we cannot serve two masters – Adonai must always come first.[233]

---

[226] Mark 3:28-29
[227] Isaiah 43:25
[228] Matthew 11:28-30
[229] Taken from www.christianbiblereference.org/jteach.htm
[230] Deuteronomy 6: 4-5; Mark 12:30
[231] Luke 18:28
[232] John 8:31,51
[233] Luke 16:13

Fourthly, we must be committed to what we believe. Our faith needs to take root in the soil, be watered and nurtured by the ways of Adonai. We need to grow like the mustard seed[234] so that our lives are useful to Adonai. Fifthly, we must be humble before Adonai and others[235]. Humility, Jabin stated, was the very essence of the man Yeshua who assumed no arrogance or egocentricity in his character. Of course, being humble means that we concentrate less on our own character and more on the character of Adonai Himself. Finally, we must take time to pray. Jabin informed the others that he had often sighted the man Yeshua rise early in the day, to go to a solitary place where he believed, the man spoke with Adonai[236].

Furthermore, Yeshua had given the people a sample of a daily prayer. Jabin had memorised this in his heart and analysed its structure carefully; Open with praise to Adonai by calling Him affectionately 'father' and praise his holy name; ask that His will be done on earth and in our lives; ask Him to give the things we need, but don't ask for things we merely desire; ask for forgiveness for our sins and acknowledge that we must also forgive those who sin against us; Finally ask for strength to resist temptation and not follow the path of evil[237].

"I find it perplexing" Jabin said, "that while the people tirelessly follow him for the miracles they do not see or feel the depth of his instructions which surely equip the body for godly service and a life of goodness. But, of course, this generation is like the ones before it and sadly like the ones to come; all the people behold only that which is good for themselves and fail to see what the needs are of their brothers, sisters, friends or strangers; for self is reigning supremely on the thrones of their hearts."

---

[234] Mark 4: 30-32
[235] Romans 12:3
[236] Mark 1:35; Luke 4:42
[237] www.christianbiblereference.org/jlovegod.htm; Matthew 6: 9-13

— Chapter Twenty-Eight —

A BIRD'S EYE VIEW

As usual, the Feast of Passover was a busy time in Yerushalayim as people from far and wide across the country poured their way into the city. To many each festival seemed to attract more and more people for it wasn't only the Jewish people who came to the city but gentile converts as well. Just as she had said she would do, Abagail went to work with her brother during the festival and having her assist him in the shop was a great blessing for as it has been said 'two pairs of hands work better than one'. While they were busily serving customers in Jethro's shop, a customer popped his head through the door and informed Jethro that the man they had been talking about recently was now teaching in the Temple Court yards. Obtaining a nod and a smile from Abagail, Jethro quickly left the shop making his way through the crowds in the main thoroughfare and headed straight to the Temple.

Once again in the Court of Isra'el he found the man Yeshua teaching the people. Because he was so frustrated with his small stature, he was determined to find a position where he could witness the man speaking. But alas, Yeshua was sitting down[238] as he was teaching the crowd around him and this made Jethro's task to find a higher place where he could see the man speaking more difficult. Hence, Jethro made his way around the perimeter of the crowds until he came to a tall column at the side of the court. Pulling himself upwards with his arms and his legs, he scaled the column as if it was a palm tree. His small hands were extremely strong, and he was so determined to have a good view of the man. Wrapping himself securely around the diameter of the column, he managed to rise above the crowd, securing a perfect bird's eye view of the temple. He must have looked a sight but he didn't care for at least he could see everything that was going on.

The man Yeshua spoke as he had before of the necessity to stop living life selfishly and repent - to turn back and worship the living God. Just as he was preaching, Jethro noticed there seemed to be a disturbance within the crowd as a smaller group of people moved like a large school of fish sprawling through the crowd progressing towards the teacher. Once they had reached the place where Yeshua was now standing, Jethro realised that they were all Pharisees who roughly had in tow a woman who was sobbing and crying loudly. Without hesitation, they threw her cruelly down on the floor of the Temple. In frigid fear, the woman wept bitterly, her head lowered in complete shame. Forcing her to stand before the Teacher the Pharisees explained that this woman had been caught in the act of adultery and stated that the Law of Mosesh (Moses) commanded this woman to be stoned[239]. Then, they asked the Teacher what did he have to say about her punishment? Their sarcastic tone made it evident to the whole crowd exactly what their intention was.

---

[238] John 8:2
[239] Leviticus 20:10; Deuteronomy 22:22

It was obvious to Jethro and to the rest of the crowd that the whole situation (and possibly the predicament of the woman) was a trap for Yeshua. If he once again forgave the woman as he was reported to have done many times to the sinners who crossed his path, he would be in complete contradiction to the law of Moshes (Moses). Furthermore, by forgiving the woman, the Pharisees would accuse him of not being from Adonai even though the man had been reported as saying everything he did, the miracles and his teaching all came from Adonai Himself[240]. Consequently, if the man did not support the law, he would prove to be a false teacher and this revelation to the people watching in the Temple, would publicly seal his fate.

Jethro watched carefully as the man Yeshua stooped down and appeared to be writing something on the temple floor; then he rose and standing erect he spoke to those accusing the woman of adultery. He stated that if any one of them was without sin, he should be the first to throw a stone at her[241]. Then, he lowered himself again and wrote again on the temple floor.

Jethro and the crowd watched in dismay as silence filled the court. All eyes were on the faces of the Pharisees to see what each would do but not one made a move to stone the woman who continued to sob uncontrollably. Their faces were cold and expressionless. Everyone in the crowd watched as each of the Pharisees who had brought the woman before Yeshua, withdrew from the scene. When all the Pharisees had left, Yeshua stood up and asked the woman where her accusers were; wasn't there anyone who condemned her? The woman told him "No one, Sir" to which the man replied that neither did he and told her to leave her life of sin and go.

The whole incident brought tears to Jethro's eyes as the compassion of the man as foretold by his brothers seemed to be boundless and available to all regardless of the severity of the sin that had been committed. The

---

[240] John 5:16-23
[241] John 8: 2-11

cruelty of the harsh judgement of the Pharisees was dispelled swiftly by the merciful forgiveness of the man Yeshua. "What a wise judge!" Jethro thought to himself. Then, not without reason, he wondered "What did he write on the temple floor"?

The Pharisees who had brought the woman in their ruse to the man Yeshua expecting him to be completed shamed in front of the people, had the tables turned on their actions and the prospective outcome. As each left the court, the initial feeling of honest self-appraisal rapidly spiralled into a deep resentment that each had been publicly belittled in front of the crowd. How could such a plan back-fire? Instead of themselves, it was the man Yeshua who had proved his point and made each Pharisee appear a fool. Needless-to say, their feelings of embarrassment plummeted into intense feelings of hatred; something had to be done with this man and whatever it would take to stop him from turning the people against Isra'el's leaders would have to be instigated and quickly, too.

During the festival Jethro would leave home early each day and head up towards the Temple where he anticipated the man Yeshua would be speaking again. His heart stirred within him as he reflected upon all he had heard the teacher say. It was obvious to Jethro that this was no ordinary man. He had such humility, such compassion and such love for Adonai and His people and yet for some reason, the Pharisees seemed very antagonistic towards him. Of course, there were times when replying to their criticism of him, his response would have greatly provoked them for the known arrogance of the Pharisees was superseded by the gentle humility of this man.

Moreover, Jethro believed that when he spoke, this man spoke of higher things which some of the people failed to understand. Many saw his teaching as advice for sound daily living whilst other saw a deeper meaning and extended purpose beyond just living godly from day to day. How that deeper meaning entranced him but Jethro failed to understand how people

could so stubbornly refuse to see beyond the boundaries of their own comfort. On the Sabbath day of the Passover, the main thoroughfare was filled
with travellers slowly making their way to the temple so Jethro crossed to
the eastern part of the city to avoid the crush of the crowd. Just as he was
passing the Pool of Siloam the people in the street excitedly were talking
to one another. Jethro realised something unusual had transpired and so
he asked a man sitting on the doorstep of his house, what had happened
to cause such a stir in the city. "Apparently, a man who was born blind can
now see again. They say a man healed him – must have been that miracle
worker from Galilee. Quite remarkable, isn't it?" the man said to Jethro.

As he moved by the people talking in the street, he heard people asking, "Isn't this the same man who used to sit and beg?[242]" Some said he
was and others replied it just could not be. "Where is this man?" Jethro
asked excitedly.

"He has been taken to the Pharisees" said a man. So, Jethro stepped up
his pace and went to the Temple as quickly as he could.

As it was the Sabbath and the Sanhedrin would meet on any day except
the Sabbath and Holy Days, a large group of Pharisees were talking on
the lower floor of the Royal Stoa. Suddenly a group of men came rushing
towards them. "This man can now see! This man can now see!" the group
were heard to say. Within the centre of the group was a man who had a
huge smile on his face.

"What do you mean he can now see?" Ezra asked.

"I was begging in the streets when a man came up to me. I heard him
spitting on the ground and then he put something on my eyes, told me to
go to wash my eyes in the Pool of Siloam. As I finished washing my eyes as
the man had told me, I suddenly realised that I could see![243]"

---

[242] John 9: 1-9
[243] John 9: 11-34

Ezra turned to his peers and with his back to the small group of men, rolled his eyes - "Guess who?" he whispered. Turning around Ezra said to the men before him "This man is not from Adonai because he does not keep the Sabbath".

Zév then asked, "How can a sinner do such miraculous signs?" Quite a lot of discussion transpired and the conversations back and forth were often argumentative and angry.

≈   ≈   ≈

Kaleb guided his best friend into the Court of Isra'el as he had done for over forty years. There, together with other men, they worshipped their God with thankful hearts. Rachael and Abagail, together with Kaleb's wife did likewise in the segregated Women's Court. This was a tradition in which all the Jewish people partook every Holy Festival and this Sabbath of Passover was no different. Each Sabbath when it was a Holy Festival, Ananiah secretly hoped in his heart that the man Yeshua might be there for it was well known he often taught in the Temple during the holy times. Ananiah was delighted that his sons were able to report back to him about what the man was doing but deep down in his heart, he longed for an opportunity to hear the man speak as he was convinced that this man was indeed the one who had been promised to the generations before. So, his secret desire was just that; a secret that no-one else need know.

Once their worship had finished, they all met one another on the steps of the Golden Gate. It was there they saw Jethro moving quickly towards them. Excitedly he told them all that he had heard and observed during the past few days as they all listened intently. Jethro said that he intended to go into the Temple to see if the man Yeshua was there. When they told him they had not seen the man, Jethro went inside regardless as he wanted to worship Adonai like the others.

Saying goodbye to Kaleb and his wife, Ananiah, Rachael and Abigail made their way through the busy streets towards Joel's house. While going towards the Temple was always a slow meander, coming home against the crowds was always a little difficult. It used to amaze Abagail how people would stare at her father as she led him homewards. Of course, her father was blind and within the city and indeed the land there was a stigma against anyone who incurred a disability but Ananiah was also well known and respected in the city. Sadly, it seemed that some were not willing to disregard the disability and acknowledge Ananiah's reputation as a learned scholar. Rather, they perceived Ananiah to be different from the rest of society. Abagail felt this was very unfair for her father was a human being, just like the rest of the population of the land. It was not his choice that he had become disabled and despite his disability, Abagail saw her father for the man she loved. His blindness was not what made him whom he was, but rather his loving heart and gentle ways.

As usual, Joel's wife Zohar had invited them to her house for refreshments after they had visited the temple. As it was the Sabbath, Joel was also home. Greeting one another warmly, the small party went into the house and sat down at the large table in the kitchen. Joel's five sons now aged between three and ten eagerly came down the stairs to greet their grandparents and their aunt, who over the past ten years would often play with them. As five boisterous boys always make a lot of noise, Zohar told her sons to take some fruit from the bowl on the kitchen table and go upstairs. She would bring some refreshments up to them soon. Quickly taking a piece of fruit from the table, the boys ran noisily up the stairs.

After the adults had finished their repast and discussed the goings on in Yerushalayim, the women went into the kitchen. Zohar asked Abagail to take a tray with prepared treats and some water up to the boys who had been playing quietly upstairs. Upon Abagail leaving the kitchen with the tray, Zohar turned to her mother-in-law and said: "Now mother, what is troubling you?"

"I am not sure what you mean" replied Rachael.

"I have known you for twelve years" replied Zohar "and I know when your heart is quiet, you are worrying about something. Please share it with me, woman to woman".

Rachael smiled at her daughter-in-law. "Well," she said "I am becoming quite concerned about Ananiah. He is now completely blind and yet he still manages the family farm. Not that I begrudge him for that as it keeps his mind active and very much alert. If I suggest that he gives it up, he will be quite devastated and it will deeply hurt him. I can see how Ananiah has become quite dependent on Abagail. Furthermore, each day I look at my daughter and see how much she has grown. She should be married soon and her future should not include looking after her elderly blind father. I fear his blindness is taking her down an alternative path on which she should not go. I'm concerned that should I discuss my thoughts with him he will be greatly upset; but not to say anything at all, dooms Abagail for an unfulfilling life!"

Gently placing her hand on Rachael's shoulder Zohar said, "Mother, mother, why spend an hour of your day worrying about tomorrow when all that you are worrying about might never be. Today is the day you are living - live it with thankfulness and joy. Adonai knows our thoughts, our concerns, and our deepest worries. He knows our every need and will be there for us no matter what. Worrying about something that may never happen only adds grey hairs and stress to a weary soul."

Rachael smiled and kissed her daughter-in-law on the cheek.

"Now I know why my son married you, you are so wise", she said.

"Oh dear!" exclaimed Zohar with a laugh "and I thought it was for my good looks."

≈   ≈   ≈

After worshipping in the Temple, Jethro looked around the complex to see if he might see the man Yeshua but it was to no avail. However, as he moved outside of the Court of Isra'el, he glanced across the grounds and saw that on the lower level of the Royal Stoa, a small group of Pharisees seemed to be having an animated discussion and then to his amazement, he saw a man being thrown out of the group[244]. The man stumbled for a moment and then moved quickly out of the Royal Stoa and made his way to the Golden Gate, passing Jethro on his way.

Jethro immediately followed the man and was only a short distance behind him. Outside of the Temple the man named Yeshua came up to the formerly blind man, placing his hands on his shoulders and asking him if the man believed in the Son of man. "Who is he, sir?" Jethro heard the man ask. "Tell me so that I may believe in him".

When Yeshua told him, he was the Son of man, the man Jethro had been following fell to his knees and worshipped him. Yeshua told the man that he had come into the world so that the blind will see and those that are sighted will become blind. Jethro knew he was talking about spiritual rather than physical sight but a small group of Pharisees standing nearby watching the situation, could not see this at all. As leaders of the people, they should know Adonai and his laws yet, selfishly, they looked to the laws they themselves had made for the people and in doing so, had sadly wandered far from the truth. Consequently, and with a hint of resentment,

---

[244] John 9: 34

they quite indignantly asked if Yeshua was inferring that they were blind too. Yeshua replied stating because they claimed they could see; they were in fact blinded to the truth[245].

"Ouch!" Jethro thought to himself.

---

[245] John 9: 35-41

— Chapter Twenty-Nine —

AN UNEXPECTED
JOURNEY

J oel stared at the six parchments of paper of the Dabar Promises
before him. He had laid these carefully on the kitchen table so that
he might gain an overall view of all the promises he, his father, his
grandfather and the men before them had gained over the years. It was
a clever idea to write these down on the separate parchments for as each
promise was written down, Joel noticed certain themes emerging. There
was, however, a matter that troubled Joel greatly.

After many years of faithfully scribing the collection of promises, there
was one blank sheet of parchment on the table. Wondering if there were no
more promises to come or whether there were many more that had been
completely overlooked, he scrutinized each parchment carefully.

The parchment which contained the most promises related to the restoration of Isra'el and most, if not all the promises before him were well

known by the people and provided a hope for a future no longer under tyrannical leadership. On the second sheet of paper, there were quite a few promises which identified the genealogy of the Messiah. The third parchment revealed disturbing signs that the promised Messiah was to be rejected and betrayed as did the fourth parchment which indicated that the precious Promise by Adonai would be subjected to suffering and pain. The fifth parchment recorded what the ministry of the Messiah would be like. Then there was the sixth parchment: the one which was completely blank.

Over the months as the man Yeshua travelled the countryside, Joel's brothers would excitedly return to Yerushalayim and share with his father and himself, what they had witnessed when following this man. Often, as they spoke, a promise would come to mind and Joel would carefully place each new promise on a specific sheet of parchment. The blank sheet, however, seemed to indicate that either there were no more promises or there were promises which had been completely overlooked. A perfectionist at heart, Joel felt quite uneasy about the parchment that currently contained no promises at all.

Placing the parchments together, he gently rolled them securing them with a leather strap. Placing these under his arm, he made his way towards his father's house. He would share his findings with his father and see if he had any ideas as to what had been overlooked in their investigations.

Sharing his findings with his father and mother and Abagail he was somewhat relieved to hear his father comment that they had not recorded all the promises for there were bound to be others which would reveal themselves at the proper moment. As they were pondering the promises before them lain out on the kitchen table again, silence filled the room. This was interrupted when Rachael let out a gasp of surprise for there, unexpectedly standing at the door, was Daniel!

As it had been several months since they had last seen their son, both Ananiah and Rebecca were delighted to see Daniel looking so well. Puffing as if he had been running a long way, Daniel excitedly told his family how the master had sent out seventy-two men to do exactly as the twelve disciples had done before but covering a much broader area. The men were told to go and prepare the places for Yeshua's message. Daniel had been partnered with Seth and Jabin with Nosh's son Micah and each pair went ahead of the master as instructed. Telling the good news to different towns, the men had seen many people repenting and changing their ways. How it gladdened their hearts when people changed and when to their astonishment, many were healed from their diseases. When they returned to the master, the others who had been sent out also had similar tales[246]!

As Daniel gathered his breath, he said it finally dawned on the three sons that they should come and get their father and take him to the master to be healed. This was something they should have done when they first began to follow the man. Why they had left this for so long, they did not know! So, Daniel left the group as they followed the master on his travels to return home to collect their father and take him to K'far-Nachan where the master was expected to be in a few days' time.

Both Abagail and her mother rose to their feet agreeing totally with this decision and eager for Ananiah to travel with his son to K'far-Nachan. "I will go too", replied Abigail. "As will I" said Joel.

"No" replied his father. "Your work is with the scribes and you unfortunately cannot leave on such a whim. I will be perfectly alright with Daniel and Abagail. Your responsibility is here in Yerushalayim". Rachael then realised the enormity of the task – how could it be possible to get Ananiah

---

[246] Luke 10: 1-17

who was completely blind to K'far-Nachan in just a few days after all K'far-Nachan was over one hundred kilometres from Yerushalayim?

Daniel revealed that the three brothers had given this considerable thought. They believed that there were different ways in which the journey might be undertaken. They could take one of the farm's working horses and attach this to a small dray. Daniel could steer this with his father seated alongside of him whilst Abagail sat in the back of the dray with the group's belongings. The group could travel via Jericho and traverse across the regions of Peraea and the Decapolis, safely travelling along the western side of the Yarden River. As they reached Tiberius where many of Rachael's relatives lived, they could make their way around Lake Galilee to K'far-Nachan. This trip could possibly take six days or more.

The other ways involved the more direct route of travelling through Samaria and although this was not a popular route for the Jewish people, it was often taken by the gentiles. Nosh's son Micah had told them that their father had some business acquaintances who were involved in the large camel trains that brought goods travelling north and south through Yerushalayim. Apparently, because travelling across country was often perilous, there were some people who would pay a small fee to travel with the caravan and trail behind them. There were also some people who would pay extra money and travel by camel with the caravan itself. Either way provided a safer and quicker journey through Samaria.

Furthermore, Daniel explained, there were two options on the types of camels that are used. Most of the traders use two humped camels for these could carry over one hundred and eighty kilograms in weight and would usually travel about forty-eight kilometres each day. The dromedaries had longer legs and therefore travelled more quickly and within 24 hours travelled more than a hundred kilometres. Most caravans used two hump camels in the train, though the workers would often ride on dromedaries.

With so many travel alternatives racing through their minds, there was a prolonged period of silence. It was Ananiah who first spoke. "I suggest that we investigate immediately when the next caravan is due to see if we might hire three dromedaries to travel with the train through Samaria. If there is no train available, I suggest we purchase a young steed to draw our smallest dray for our farm horses are old now and the journey would be too great for any of them. We would then take the slower trip by travelling via Jericho through Peraea and the Decapolis."

"If you go by camel train, how would you get home?" asked Rachael.

"Maybe we could return the same way or even purchase a new horse and dray at K'far-Nachan" Daniel replied. "Either way, we will bring your man home, Mother" he warmly assured her. Swiftly they prepared for the trip: Daniel and Joel immediately went into the city to find out when the next camel train was due whilst Rachael and Abagail packed all the things they believed were needed as well as food provision for the travellers. Ananiah carefully counted out all the coins needed for the trip as an expectant air filled the house while each person moved busily within it.

Daniel and Joel returned to report there was a camel train departing Yerushalayim at the ninth hour that day, so they had booked two drome-daries to travel with the caravan for they were informed that travelling on these was more comfortable than travelling on camels with two humps. Daniel would travel with his father on one and Abagail on another with their luggage. Daniel was informed that the train should reach K'far-Nachan by the following afternoon.

Not long after Daniel and Joel returned, the women had finished the pack-ing and Ananiah grew excited as he considered that at long last, he would finally meet the man for whom his relatives had so eagerly waited. Securing all their belongings on Zimra, with an air of optimism and hope, the four began to say goodbye to Rachael. "I will return Zimra after the train leaves" Joel said to his mother whose smile was fighting the feelings ranging within her.

"God speed" said Rachael to the three travellers as she kissed each one good bye but when she came to her daughter, she hugged her a little longer than the others only for Abigail to sense that her mother was pressing something into her hand. As they travelled towards the city, Abagail glanced down and saw a small bag which she realised was full of coins. Glancing back through her tears, Abigail saw her mother smiling and waving. Wondering if this could be the answer to all concerns about her husband, Rachael felt as if she mustn't get her hopes too high for everything is always in Adonai's hand. "If only" she thought to herself "If only!"

The camel train of fourteen two humped camels was being loaded just outside the Governor's Gate near the market place. Six dromedaries were nearby, two with very fine saddles. "I do hope those are ours", Daniel remarked to his sister as he pointed to the animals at the back of the train. Walking up to the man in charge, Daniel said in Aramaic that he wished to pay for the two dromedaries he had ordered that morning but the man shook his head and said that although he was very tempted to take Daniel's money, the cost for the two beasts had already been paid by the gentleman standing near the hides stall in the market. Glancing to his left, Daniel saw the smiling face of Kaleb who, upon catching his eye, waddled quickly towards them. "Your trip is on me, dear friend" he said to Ananiah. "Do not worry about the cost for I know these people and after hearing that you were going to K'far-Nachan, I secured a good price for your trip and it is my pleasure to pay for you all knowing that you will be safe in these men's company. I have given them orders that you and your family will be well looked after and I can see by the quality of the saddles and the beasts they have proved that as always, they are true to their word".

Neither Ananiah, nor Daniel nor Abagail had ridden on a camel before so the whole trip proved to be an exciting venture for them. When it was time for the train to leave, the travellers said farewell to Joel who wished them Adonai's blessing and a safe return. Two camels were kneeling on the ground as Daniel was told to get into the saddle first. Some of the train workers then tried to lift Ananiah up off the ground and onto the beast but he protested loudly telling them to put him down and just tell him what he had to do, and he would do it. It was rather comical as the men did not speak Hebrew but broken Aramaic and so following their very strange accents and loud broken speech, Daniel instructed his father what to do. It didn't take Ananiah long before he confidently stepped into the saddle behind his son and then, as requested he could either hold onto the straps on each side of the saddle or clasp his hands around his son's waist. Ananiah's hands moved swiftly across the sides of the saddle to find the location of the leather straps. Not finding them, he simply put his arms around Daniel's waist holding tightly as he did. "Oh Father! I love you too!" Daniel joked. "I have no idea what you mean" his father replied.

Observing what her brother and father had done in climbing up onto the beast, Abagail mounted the camel as if she had done it many times before. The seat was surprisingly comfortable and when all the animals were raised up on their feet, she was amazed at what she could see from this height. Walking through the city towards the western gate, the whole city took upon itself a different perspective. Moving steadily through the gates and towards the long road ahead, Abagail felt sure that she was going on an unexpected adventure and that something very exciting, was waiting for them at the end of the trip.

As the camel train moved down the exiting road travelling northward to Galilee, Daniel chatted busily to his father informing him where the train was now located and what was observed on his left and right-hand side. It wasn't long into the journey before Daniel began talking about the master and all the wonderful miracles the brothers had observed while following him across the country. Although Ananiah had heard many reports of these before, he never tired of hearing the tales recalled. Passages which had been recorded in Scripture and in the list of Dabar Promises, sprung to his mind as his son spoke; this man was certainly fulfilling the promises in many ways. It did not take long however, as the train travelled onward, for Ananiah to inwardly recognise that Daniel, unlike his brothers Seth and Jabin, seemed to be overly drawn to the miracles of the man for whenever Ananiah questioned about the man's character and his teaching, Daniel would be preoccupied and relate yet another miracle the man had performed.

Abagail trailed immediately behind her brother and father observing the mechanics of the train and the responsibilities of the people accompanying them. The head man spoke fluent Aramaic and rode on his dromedary at the beginning of the train. His six helpers who could only speak broken Aramaic but communicated well with each other using a strange language and hand gestures, would walk or run beside the camels. The helpers could not have been as old as Abagail for they were very small in stature but very strong when handling the beasts. Their skin was the darkest black and they had deep brown eyes. It amused Abagail that when they talked and smiled, flashes of brilliantly white teeth could be seen. Walking along side of the camels the workers never seemed to tire though later in the journey, Abagail noticed that some of the young boys would take a break by climbing up onto the backs of the three remaining dromedaries and rode comfortably on these for a time. Sometimes, when all the dromedary camels had a helper resting on them, the head man would yell at them and one or more of the helpers would quickly dismount the camel and walk alongside the train.

Sometime into the journey, she heard the head men yell something to Daniel in Aramaic and immediately after this, Daniel turned his head back to his sister and told her they were now in Samaria. "Samaria!" thought Abagail to herself. Who would have thought that she would ever enter this unfriendly and unwelcoming place! It was well known that the Samaritan and Jewish people did not get along because although both believed in Adonai, the Samaritan people only believed in parts of the Pentateuch and this was written in their own Aramaic language. Many years ago, they had built their own temple on Mount Gerizim (instead of Yerushalayim) and this act had brought much tension and hostility between the two races. So much so, that the Jews later destroyed the temple furthering more resentment on the part of the Samaritan people. It was also believed that these stupid and arrogant people could never receive Adonai's favour.

In the distance, Abagail could see that the train was approaching a mountain pass and once again, the head man yelled more information to Daniel who then told his sister that they would soon be entering the mountain pass between Mount Gerizim and Mount Ebal. Just before entering the pass they came to a small village which had a large well located on its outskirts. Suddenly, the head man gestured the train to stop and made his way towards Daniel and Ananiah. They seemed deep in conversation before Daniel turned his camel towards his sister and told her that the well before them was Ya'akov's (Jacob's) well. The head man believed that this well was known by the Jewish people as a sacred site and was wondering if they wanted to obtain some water from the well. Abigail could see that there were several women with empty jars on their heads heading towards the well where, a queue of women waited to fill their vessels. Abigail said that she would be happy to get some water for them and translating this to the head man, Daniel then asked Abigail if there was a vessel for the water in their belongings.

Abigail replied that the bowl they had would not be large enough for all of them and she wondered if the men accompanying them had a larger vessel. When the head man heard this request translated to him by Daniel, he was very surprised. He thought that the three-people accompanying him might like to taste the water for themselves and to think that they would do so with all the company of the train was quite uncommon, yet very kind. In Aramaic, the head man yelled directions at the accompanying boys. Two came over and brought Abigail's camel down onto its knees. Her young bones were stiff and tired after sitting for so long, but she managed to dismount from the beast. Another young boy ran up to her with a tall jar which she took and made her way to the well. Queuing with the ladies, she patiently waited her turn. She daren't not speak for it was well known that Samaritan people were often rude and unfriendly.

Just before it was her turn, the woman in front of her filled her own jar and then, turning to Abagail motioned her to place her vessel on the ground. Complying with the woman's request, Abagail was touched when the woman filled her jar right to the brim with the water she had drawn. "Thank you so much" replied Abigail "That is very kind of you". She was so pleased to see the woman smile.

With the water jug resting on her head, Abigail returned to the train. Carrying water on her head was something she often did on the farm and so the skill of keeping such a heavy load on her head was not new to her. At first, she went to the head man, who shaking his head and gesturing widely, motioned her to give her father and brother a drink of the water. So, approaching her camel, she placed the vessel down on the ground, and leaned across the belongings strapped to the beast from where she removed a medium sized bowl. Filling this with the water, she then approached her brother and father whose camel had also been brought to its knees and the two had dismounted to stretch their legs. Ananiah took the first sips and the cool water was so refreshing to his parched mouth. What pleased him even more was to know that this water came from the very well Adonai had given Ya'akov (Jacob). Daniel drank next and then Abagail sipped the pleasant water eagerly. Then, taking the tall vessel, she gave this to the head man, who was still seated on his camel, who then nodded his head and drank from the vessel. After he had quenched his thirst, he summoned the others to come and drink the water. The six boys eagerly ran and waited as each satisfied their thirst on such a hot day.

Stopping at Ya'akov's Well was not the only respite the travellers had on the journey that day but the stops wherever they were, were always welcomed. As the sun began to recede, the sky was filled in a canopy of red, purple and golden clouds. This was a beautiful and peaceful scene for the travellers and as the camels moved slowly into the darkening twilight, Abagail looked forward to the day her father would be able to see again the marvel of Adonai's creation. As the evening replaced the day, a full moon beamed radiantly in the night sky clearly revealing the earth's terrain. Shortly afterwards, the train stopped and the head man once again began yelling at the young men who assisted him. The young men brought the camels to their knees allowing the travellers to finally dismount. After he had dismounted, Daniel helped his father down from their beast and after Ananiah had regained his land legs, Daniel went over to his sister's camel and helped her down.

The head man walked over to Daniel and spoke to him in Aramaic pointing in the direction of a large tree nearby and then to the opposite direction to the tree. Daniel told his co-travellers that they would sleep on this side of the camel train under the tree while the other men would sleep further away. Unpacking a few essentials Daniel made a small camp near the tree as Abagail prepared a repast for the weary travellers. While she was doing so, one of the young men came towards them carrying a large flat wooden scoop upon which was a huge pile of fresh camel dung. This he threw down on the ground. "Is that what I think it is!" remarked Abagail.

The young man had a small piece of flint in his hand and picking up a nearby stone, proceeded to strike the flint repeatedly against this until a spark arose and the pile of dung lit. "I refuse to cook on that!" protested Abagail but her brother assured her that it would be alright. Taking a flat stone griddle, his mother had packed, Daniel put this on the fire. "And now cook" he asked, "what do you have for us weary travellers to eat?"

The heated remnants of the left-over Abagail bun were a much-welcomed delicacy and the leftover water from Ya'akov's Well which had been placed in a bottle, finished off the repast. Exhausted from their travelling, the three lay down on the large blanket Daniel had spread on the ground. Abagail was instructed to sleep between her brother and father and as they covered themselves with another large blanket, the fire continued to flicker in the night sky. "Oh Father" Abagail said, "It is a beautiful night with a large full moon in the sky which reveals so clearly everything that surrounds us and as for the night sky, it is filled with thousands and thousands of bright shining stars! There are so many of them! They must be uncountable!" she shared.

"To us Abagail, but not to Adonai" her father replied. "Not only does he know the exact number, he calls them each by name[247]".

"All glory to Adonai!" said Daniel as he rolled onto his side, and wearily closed his eyes.

---

[247] Psalm 147:4

Chapter Thirty

A MEETING IN
K'FAR-NACHAN

As the morning sun greeted the new day, Daniel opened his eyes only to feel as if something was not quite right. Turning to his right he saw his father still sound asleep and gently snoring, but alas, between himself and his father was an empty space. Realising that his sister was not present, he immediately sat up and looked anxiously around the field where they had stopped the evening before. The young men employed by the head man were tending the camels and from the makeshift bed Daniel looked across the field nearby to find his sister walking briskly towards their campsite. Hugely relieved, he waited for his sister to return before chiding her vehemently for leaving either her father or his company while they were travelling. This was an unpleasant place and despite the re-assurance she may have felt in the recent day's travel, this was no place for a woman to be by herself.

Abagail listened to her brother and realised that it was out of love and concern that he spoke to her so harshly and despite his tone of disappointment in her, she was pleased to think that he now regarded her as a woman. Just two years ago, she was a young girl in his eyes. But there were some things that just had to be kept private and her morning ablutions were of no concern to her brother. Ananiah woke up and Abagail greeted him, telling him that all the camp was busily preparing for the day. There was some fruit to eat if he was hungry and once again, the family sat together devouring the refreshing fruit Rachael had included.

It didn't take long for their belongings to be packed away and loaded onto their camels. One of the young men took their luggage and secured it once more onto Abagail's camel. The head man making his way across the grassy field from the other side, yelled instructions rapidly at the young men. The young men busily complied. Sighting his passengers, he raised his hand in greeting to them while two of the men came over to Daniel's camel. Slapping the camel's knees with a stick and giving the beast the command to kneel, the animal gently lowered itself down to the ground. Once more Daniel mounted and secured himself safely in the saddle before he told his father to mount the beast. By this stage, Ananiah had become quite adept at feeling the side of the beast, the location of the stirrup and the straps that enabled him to grasp and pull himself up and across the animal. It was obvious that the young men found this a sight to behold- a man who was blind mounting a camel so quickly and ably.

When Abagail mounted her beast that had also been forced to kneel by the two young men, she mounted as gracefully as she could. When the camels rose to their feet, the head man yelled his orders and once again, the train moved onward across the grassy field into the countryside. The morning sun shone brightly as the train travelled through fields and tracks. Morning dew sparked on the grass and leaves of the trees and all travellers felt excited about the coming day and the long-awaited meeting that would take place. At the start of the journey, it was obvious that the three travellers were pre-occupied in their thoughts for not much was said during the initial stages, but it wasn't long before the train was travelling beside a small brook and the head man once again in Aramaic called out to Daniel.

When informed by the head man that they the train would soon be crossing the Kishom River, a huge smile was observed on Ananiah's face. "Why this is where D'vorah (Deborah) and Barak led Isra'el into victory over the Canaanite hosts of Yavin (Jabin) under the commander Sisra (Sisera)[248]!" he exclaimed. Ananiah then told them that in wintertime the stream was a rushing river and could only be crossed at certain points. Fortunately, the river at this time of the year was a shallow stream in most parts and once a suitable passage was found, the train moved across to the other side.

As the train traversed the countryside, there were several farms on which farmers could be seen tilling the soil, walking alongside their animals pulling their ploughing instruments. Women could be seen scattering seed over the tilled soil. Once again, the head man was heard to call out to Daniel who then turned to his sister and said, "Welcome Abagail to Galilee!" "Galilee!" she thought to herself. "This is where the man comes from!" To be honest there was little difference in the countryside in terms of scenery. Again, the train travelled through farms where men were busily tilling the soil and women were sowing seeds. Abigail, pleased to be in a safer land, waved to the women in the field but to her dismay, while the women stopped what they were doing and examined the train moving across the fields, they neither smiled nor waved. This was the reception she received each time the

---

[248] Judges 4 & 5

train passed workers in the field and it made her think of contrasting cold, indifferent responses from her own people and that of the welcoming smile and kindness of the Samaritan woman at the well.

It was mid-morning when the train finally stopped for a respite break and the six young men were the recipients of many orders from the head man. Some of the young men responded and once again caused the camels on which the travellers were riding, to lower themselves to the ground so that the riders could dismount and stretch their legs. Two of the young men ran to the head man who appeared to place something in their hands, and they ran quickly off to the nearby village.

It was not a large village but strangely there was a large gate in the middle of the road into the village itself. Abagail thought it strange that there was not just a large gate, but a gate present with no surrounding walls to the village at all.

"Maybe we should buy something to eat" said Abagail but as she started to make her way into the village , one of the young men came after her shouting in Aramaic "No! No! No!" When Daniel went to his sister's aide, the young man pointed towards the head man who had dismounted his camel and was standing in the shade of a nearby tree. After a long exchange, Daniel then reported back to the travellers that the head man had sent the two young men into the village to buy something to eat for them all. Just as Abagail was willing to share the water gathered at the well, he wanted to show his appreciation for her kindness by returning the compliment and buy some food for them. Abigail thought to herself, how strange it is, that one act of kindness can often be unexpectedly returned.

"The head man told me that the village here is Na'im (Nain). He did not want to take the train through the village but prefers to go around it. I don't know why, but I had completely forgotten that this is the very village where the master did a miraculous thing at the beginning of his ministry" Daniel told them.

Daniel recalled how he, his brothers and friends and a large group of followers were astonished when they came to this village with the master. As they approached the town's gate which was not far from where they were standing, a funeral procession came out from the village. A widow's only son had died and there was much weeping and wailing. The master was so touched by the people's sadness that he told the woman not to cry; and then he went up to the bier and told the man to get up. To everyone's amazement, the dead son sat up and began to talk![249]

"You forgot a miracle that brings a dead person back to life! How could you forget such a thing?" queried Abagail.

"How miraculous and strange!" replied Ananiah. "The scrolls report that Eliyahu (Elijah) also raised a poor woman's only son who was believed to be dead[250]. How great is this man who voice commands nature, the spirits and even death to obey him! When has a mere man ever been able to do such things?"

Some hours into the afternoon, Abagail could see a large town on the horizon and beside it, a large lake. "This must be the lake where he commanded the wind and waves"[251] she thought. Gradually, the train drew closer and closer and once again, the head man in Aramaic, called out to Daniel. Speaking loudly so that Abagail could hear him she heard him say, "Thanks be to Adonai, the town ahead is K'far-Nachan!"

As the train approached the city sprawled widely across the banks of Lake Galilee, the sight of people coming and going in the streets was accompanied by the noise of habitation and daily activities. K'far-Nachan was an

[249] Luke 7: 11-17
[250] 1Kings 17: 17-24
[251] Mark 4:35-41

expanding town for it was situated in a key position which enabled traders to come from the south, north, east, and west. Although a fishing village, the traders had brought many reasons for people of different professions to live and work in the town. Passing a Roman Garrison, a small station which housed a company of soldiers situated on the outskirts of the town, the streets became full of houses and buildings as the cobbled streets of the town began to echo with the sound of camel's hooves. Towards the centre of the town, on the left-hand side of the street, was an elegant Synagogue which had three separate doors at the front. Abagail remembered that her brothers had told her that a Roman centurion, whose servant was very ill, had financially contributed to the completion of the building. How strange it was for a Roman to be willing to pay for the expenses of building such as a place of Jewish worship. That servant lived because of the healing power of the master who had shown such compassion to all – even those not of the Jewish race[252]. This was the very place where so many miracles had taken place! This was the place where they would finally meet this man – the man they had learnt so much about.

By the time the train had come to the marketplace, much smaller than the Yerushalayim market but just as busy, the travellers were pleased when the whole train stopped. Dismounting from their camels which had been brought to their knees by the train's assistants, Daniel, Ananiah and Abagail dismounted. Just as her second foot touched the ground, Abagail was grabbed by someone behind her who spoke in a gruff voice "Well, what a sight for sore eyes! How about giving me a big kiss?"

Fortunately, her raised right-hand which was just about to slap the inquirer's face was intercepted by a very strong and powerful hand. To her dismay when she looked into the face of her abuser, Abagail saw the wel-

---

[252] Luke 7:1-10

coming smile of her elder brother Seth. Thankful that her hand and his face had not connected, Abagail hugged her brother warmly. "One or both of us have been coming to the market every day since we arrived back in K'far-Nachan, after following the master" he said. "Jabin felt certain that you would be coming by camel train though Micah was most anxious that you came in the company of those traders with whom his father had dealings and not with some of the other traders who are quite untrustworthy and avaricious in their business deals. I am so relieved that you have been fortunate in securing passage with good people to lead you. It's so wonderful to see you again".

Immediately Seth went over and embraced his father. As his hands moved over the face and body of his son, Ananiah felt pleased. Although he could not physically see his son, or how he had grown into the handsome man he was, his fingers told him that this was a fit and strong man whose voice revealed satisfaction and contentment with his life.

Seth had told his father, Daniel and Abagail, that suitable accommodation for them had been found which was not far from the marketplace in the guest room of a friend's home. Before leaving for the house, Ananiah wanted to thank the head man for his kindness to them during their trip and so, when Daniel brought him over to the head man who as usual, was giving multiple directions to his team, Ananiah thanked him in perfect Aramaic. "I never knew you could speak Aramaic, father!" Daniel said.

"I learnt it at school, so long ago but just over the past day, as I heard the directions and instructions given to the team, quite a lot of it came back to me."

Picking up their belongings, Daniel, Seth, Ananiah and Abagail were accompanied through the busy marketplace to their accommodation which was only two streets away. The friend's place had three levels and the guest room was located on the second floor. There were two comfortable beds and a table with four chairs in the room and upon the table was a large bowl of fruit. The table was beside a large open window and a warm and pleasant breeze circulated through the room. Being on a high level, the window revealed a spectacular view of the lake and the town.

The landlady brought some refreshments up to the room and these were welcomed by the weary travellers. As they were sitting around the table consuming these, Jabin and Nosh's son Micah came through the door. Embracing all the travellers they then sat down on the two beds nearby as conversations about the long journey and the ministry of the master were exchanged. Jabin told his father what had transpired since they had last met, most of this had been covered by Daniel.

The master continued to do many miracles however, Jabin, Seth and Micah had come to believe that these, though amazing, were excelled by the authority in which the master taught. Throughout their time of following him, the master always spoke of calling the people to forsake their ways and return to the teachings of Adonai. The people had become so selfish in their ways, putting others below themselves and seeking selfish gain for themselves at the expense of others. Calling the people to return to Adonai and seek his forgiveness, the master asked for sincere repentance, always seeking Adonai. He talked of being kind to all and putting other's interest above your own and every time the message was delivered, the master always spoke with authority and conviction.

Seth added that he had come to believe that the master had not come, as he said, to replace the law but to fulfil it. In fact, many of the things he spoke about clarified some of the confusion of Pharisee law. Constantly referring to the Scriptures, which he appeared to know thoroughly, he continued to use parables to illustrate the points he was making.

Micah then said that recently there were statements made by the master, which confused and bewildered his disciples and followers. He talked of having to go away[253] which saddened many who had enjoyed his journey. He also said that he had to be 'lifted up'[254], though what this meant, no-one seemed to know. Then, there were statements from him about the elders rejecting him[255] and most disturbingly, that he was going to die![256] Surely, as the Scriptures stated, the Messiah was going to reign, and live forever? So why would he be going away? And why would he have to suffer and die?

When Ananiah heard these words, his felt as if his heart had been stabbed to the core. All the verses about the suffering servant that had been etched into the parchment compiled over the years ran through his mind. This was most perplexing, and it was difficult to comprehend. Then he heard Seth continue.

"He is beginning to receive a lot of rejection, too. We have witnessed this even from his family[257], from his own town[258], from his followers[259]".

"Are people so blind they cannot see the goodness of this man!" exclaimed Abagail.

"Their eyes have been blinded and their hearts hardened so that they can neither see with their eyes nor understand with their hearts![260]" replied Ananiah, quoting the prophet Yesha'yahu. "By His Hand, these things must be!"

Suddenly a noise from outside the window began to grow as sounds of people laughing and talking could be heard in the streets below. It was apparent a crowd was moving along the streets of the town and Daniel, Seth and Jabin arose exclaiming, "It is the master!" Together the group

---

[253] John 14:28; John 16:7
[254] John 12:32-36
[255] Luke 9:22
[256] Matthew 16: 21-23; Mark 9: 30-32; Luke 18: 31-34
[257] Mark 3: 20-21; Mark 3:31-34
[258] Luke 4: 16-30
[259] John 6: 60-66
[260] Isaiah 6:10

excitedly made their way down the stairs to the lower floor of the house and moved quickly into the streets. Ahead of them was a large group of people making their way to the markets and then, down a narrow street. Following in quick pursuit, both Seth and Daniel took their father's left and right arm and guided him towards the crowd. Ananiah's feet barely touched the ground and now he had to put his trust in his sons. Abagail, Jabin and Micah followed in close pursuit as they too were buffeted by the merging throng. Pushing their way through the crowd, Abagail could see the back of a man whom people seemed to be revering and talking to.

Ananiah's heart start to beat as they made their way through the crowd; something within began to stir and gradually increase. It was somewhat like the sensation he had felt as a child delivered in the desert, but it was so much more. He then recognised it was the total awareness he had felt over thirty years ago, when he fell face down in the Holy Place. What drove him to fall face down to the floor that night, he did not know but he was aware he was in the presence of a being that was far greater and holier than any other and that he, in his sinful nature, could not assume any other position. His joy in this being's presence escalated when he heard the being's voice like the wind. It was then he felt as if he was a vessel and the joy within him, was full to overflowing. That same awareness and feeling began once more to increase steadily and it was then he realised, that at that very moment, once more he was entering the very presence of Holy Adonai himself!

Seth touched the shoulder of the man the crowd was following. "Master", he said "Allow me to introduce you to our father who has long waited for your arrival". Just as the man was about to turn to greet Ananiah, he exclaimed that someone had touched him.

The crowd continued to press in against them. "Master" said one of his disciples "there are people pressing in on us everywhere! It is impossible to know who touched you!"

The master then replied that he knew someone had touched him for he felt the power go out from him. Looking around at the crowd, there bowing at his feet was a woman very fearful and sobbing. She explained how she had suffered a blood disorder for over twelve years and despite going to many doctors and becoming penniless because of this, she had heard about Yeshua. Believing that if she could just touch the hem of his garment, she would be healed, she turned her back upon the laws that prohibited her from entering the town and sought him. She confessed it was she who had touched the hem of his garment and when she touched the garment, she knew she was instantly healed. The master then told her to go in peace and be free from her suffering; her faith had healed her.[261]

Amazed by what had taken place, the crowd with the master pressed on – it seemed like they were going to a specific place but in the turmoil of what had just transpired, the group of travellers and their friends were left behind. Deeply disappointed, Daniel expressed to the group that they needed to press on and follow the crowd so that their father might be healed. But the others said it would be best to wait for another opportunity. This resulted in a heated debate but Abagail, disliking such tension between her brothers was just about to insist they stop their quarrelling when her eyes looked at her father. Never had she seen him smiling so broadly and never, had she seen his blue, but blinded eyes so brilliant.

---

[261] Luke 8: 40-48

— *Chapter Thirty-One* —

RETURNING HOME

Ananiah requested his family to return to the lodgings as he was feeling tired after such a long day. Placing some coins in her hand, he asked Abagail to purchase some food for their evening meal in the marketplace and said that he was looking forward sharing this with them that evening. So, Abagail went off to the markets where she purchased two large fish, some bitter herbs and oil as well as several sheets of unleavened bread. When she returned to their lodgings, she found the young men seated at the table while her father was resting on one of the beds. Her brothers were carefully whispering keeping their voices low and expressed their discontentment with what had transpired. Micah listened carefully.

"I need someone to debone the fishes" Abagail asked, and Micah immediately arose from his chair and offered to help her. Together they made their way downstairs to the kitchen where Micah took a large knife and plate and began filleting the fish outside. Once deboned, Abagail cut the fish into medium sized pieces and placed these in a bowl with some of the oil and bitter herbs she had bought. Allowing these to rest a while, she began heating the leftover oil in a pan on the stove. Thanking Micah for his assistance, she asked him to advise her brothers that the meal would be ready very soon.

After giving thanks for the meal, the men tucked into the meal that Abagail had so lovingly prepared for them - it was a particularly tasty meal and her brothers, Micah and her father enjoyed every morsel. Abagail had correctly assumed they would have hungry appetites, so she had made ample food for them all. The glass of wine the landlady had given them complemented the meal nicely. When the meal concluded, Daniel spoke. "Father," he said, "while you were resting, we decided that we would take you to meet the master early tomorrow, before the crowds start to follow him. We believe, that as his pace was quick this afternoon, that he must have been heading to another place and what with the crowd and the woman who touched him, it is not surprising that he was distracted and therefore unable to cure you". Ananiah sighed. "My dear children", he said, "there is something I must tell you and I ask that you all listen carefully to what I am about to say – I do not wish to trouble the master as he so faithfully goes about doing the work Adonai has sent him to do. Today, even when I was in his presence, I did not need my eyes to see him for my soul affirmed most convincingly to me that this man is indeed Adonai's Messiah. I have never been so convinced about anything in my whole life!"

"Adonai has been so faithful to me ever since he rescued me from death at the hands of those Deliverers bandits many years ago, and I am so grateful for He has greatly blessed my life. He has given me a wonderful wife, and six wonderful children. I have a roof over my head each night, and food in my belly each day. He has surrounded me with such faithful friends, and I have never lacked anything. So richly has He blessed me that I feel unwor-

thy to stretch out my hand now to demand even more! Abundantly satisfied with all He has done it is selfish of me to ask for more and therefore I
would like to return home to Rachael and the farm I love so much. We shall
need to inquire if there are any camel trains heading towards Yerushalayim
in the next few days. If not, we shall have to purchase a sturdy horse for the
journey and a small dray as well".

"To be honest Uncle Ananiah", Micah replied, "father always insisted
that there was only one group of traders whom he considered to be good
and trustworthy men, and you were fortunate to have secured their services
in coming to K'far-Nachan . There may be other trains coming through the
town in the next few days, but they will not be as honourable or reliable
as the people who brought you here. It is probably in your best interest to
take the longer way home by travelling west of the Yarden River for that is
the safer route."

"But father", interrupted Daniel, "you have travelled such a long way
and there is still time for the master to heal you!"

"Have you not heard what I have just told you?" his father replied. "My
life is not dependent on a miracle as I am content with the lot that has
been given to me. To ask for more than what I already have is unnecessarily
selfish and I refuse to use Adonai in such a way! I do not need a miracle to
know who this man is for not with my own eyes have I seen him, but my
very soul!"

The next morning, it was decided that Daniel and Abagail would go
into the town to purchase a sturdy horse to pull a small dray. Being involved
in his father's tanning business, Micah said he knew quite a lot about horses
and would go with them. This allowed Ananiah to spend some more time
with Seth and Jabin while the others traversed the town heading towards
the blacksmiths. As they passed a barn not far from the blacksmith, Abigail
exclaimed, "Just look at that! It's perfect!"

There, at the side of the barn, was a small dray no longer than a meter and a half in length. It had four small strong wheels, two on each side and on the front, there was a bench which allowed two people to sit comfortably as one, the driver, steers the horse pulling the dray. There was a plank of wood at the back of the bench which would support the backs of the two-people travelling in the front. Then, on the other side of the back was another bench on which two more passengers could travel their backs against the direction they were travelling. Completely enclosed around the back seat was a small area in which goods could be stored. "Not only would that be perfect for our trip home, but it would also be perfect to have to take father into Yerushalayim! It could be our own personal cart!"

"Whoa! Steady on!" replied Daniel. "Have you not heard you can't put the cart before the horse! Let's find an animal to pull a dray before we purchase one!"

Asking a man near the barn as to where they might be able to purchase a horse, Daniel was directed to the barn on the opposite side of the road. Entering the small barn, they could see through the outside door two corrals each filled with a small number of horses. When they came to the first corral, three horses, a masterful white Arabian and two beautiful black stallions stood together in the centre whilst the fourth horse, a sturdy chestnut stallion stood apart from the group in the corner of the enclosure.

Both Micah's and Abagail's eyes were drawn to the chestnut horse whose coat shimmered in the sun. The horse stood firm and still, its eyes fixed on the travellers. Greeting the man who approached them, Daniel asked the cost of a horse. The man explained that four of his finest horses were placed in the first corral. Each of the horses had been broken-in and all had individual temperaments. "How much is the chestnut male?" Micah asked.

The man hesitated. He told them of the four horses in the enclosure before them, the chestnut was the most resistant when being broken in.

Even now, he would not associate with the other horses and the man there-fore recommended a horse be chosen from the remaining three. Not really knowing why, Abagail who often tended the horses on the farm, entered slowly into the corral. The three horses in the middle immediately moved away to the opposite side of the enclosure but the chestnut horse remained still looking at Abagail. When she stopped in the middle of the enclosure, she looked at the chestnut stallion and raising her right arm, called him to come to her. The horse remained still.

Raising her right arm again, Abagail called the horse to come to her and the three men watching this, were amazed when the horse gently moved towards her; stopping immediately in front of her, the stallion's eyes remained steadfast on Abagail. Gently, Abagail stroked his forehead, then his nose. "He's beautiful," she remarked, "come and see for yourself."

Daniel and Micah moved into the corral and came up to the front of the beast. Firmly feeling the horse's shoulders, rump and fetlocks, Micah stated that this indeed was a truly fine and strong animal. "Can you give us a good price on this one?" Daniel asked.

As the man and Daniel began to barter, Abagail asked Micah, "Do you think he will be able to pull a dray for us?"

"Definitely, he is a very strong and sturdy horse" remarked Micah.

"Then we shall call you 'Samson'" said Abagail as she stroked Samson's nose and beautiful blonde mane.

After securing a price on which both parties agreed, Daniel shook the man's hand and told him, they would pay for the horse now and collect the stallion later. As he approached Abagail and Micah who were now waiting for him outside of the barn on the road, Daniel explained that while he was pleased with their purchase as the animal was such a fine beast, the price decided, though fair, greatly reduced the balance of the money his father had given him. They would therefore have to buy a second-hand dray as they also needed to have money to purchase food in their travels as well as to cover their accommodation. When Abagail asked how much money was needed for food, Daniel took the remaining coins out of his purse and began separating them; in one pile was the cost of their accommodation at the lodgings and their food, and the remaining coins could be spent on a dray.

"I would still like to find out the price of the small cart we saw" Abagail remarked.

Although Daniel believed that purchasing the cart his sister had set her heart upon was out of the question, he conceded that there was no harm in finding out its price. Taking Micah aside, Abagail asked him to inquire as to how much the cart would cost and pressing the purse her mother had given her into his hands, asked him to barter with the owner and secure a good price with her mother's money.

When they returned to the cart which was still in the same place where they first had sighted it, Micah went up to a man nearby asking him who owned the cart. The man pointed to the barn where they had purchased Samson. Returning to the barn, it wasn't long before Micah came back with man who had sold them the horse. Once again, the bartering process continued. "We have already purchased a good horse from you" Micah told him. "Now it is your turn to give us a good deal on the cart".

Both Abagail and Daniel could see that the acquisition of the cart appeared to be a possibility as the two men bartered vigorously. It wasn't long before Micah returned to Abigail and Daniel, informing them that the man had consented to a reasonable price, and had also agreed to give them a harness and reins for the trip. They had sufficient funds for the purchase so if, they agreed, he would tell the man they had reached a satisfactory deal. Both Daniel and Abagail were pleased and told Micah they would be happy for the transaction to proceed. Removing the exact money agreed upon from the coins in Abigail's purse, Micah gave the purse back to Abagail who, as her fingers pressed against its sides, realized there was still coinage within it. Counting the remaining coins, she realised Micah had masterfully bargained for half the number of coins her mother had given her! "Who gave you that money?" Daniel inquired. "Mother," replied his sister. Daniel smiled – his mother always seemed to know when assistance might be required and here, more than one hundred kilometres from Yerushalayim, her extra coinage ensured that the three would be travelling home with the safest transport.

That afternoon, the threesome went to the markets, purchasing the necessities they needed for their evening meal and their upcoming travel. That evening, just before he retired to bed, Ananiah carefully felt the number and sizes of the coins that remained in his purse. At first, he hesitated and then he took each one out and carefully counted them two times. There was a significant number of coins left in the kitty and he wondered what sort of nag and means of transport the three had bought to take them on the journey home. But Micah had insisted it was a good, strong horse and Ananiah realised, that he would just have to trust the journey to Adonai. After all, they had come to K'far-Nachan safely and Adonai had never left him lacking.

The travellers rose early the next morning and having paid the landlady the night before, prepared for their journey. As they were outside of the residence with their belongings and all their goods wrapped securely and stacked neatly on the street, they heard the sound of a horse's hooves coming towards them. Looking towards the sound, Abagail saw Micah leading Samson down the street, regally pulling the cart behind him. She was so pleased with their purchases the day before and the sight before her caused her to thank Adonai for his ample provision of their needs.

When the horse stopped, Micah helped Daniel load their goods into the cart. Abagail took her father's hand and led him to Samson. "Just feel how strong he is father", she said. "And he's just as handsome, too!" As Ananiah moved his hands gently across the horse's body, his fingers told him that this was an exceptionally strong horse. Stroking Samson gently on his forehead, Ananiah agreed. "Yes, indeed! He is a very fine horse". Farewelling and thanking Micah for all his help, Daniel prepared to mount the cart. "Oh! I nearly forgot!" exclaimed Micah. "When the previous owner heard of your trip, he thought you might like to have this!"

From the back of the dray was a strong, empty wooden box which Micah inverted and placed on the ground. This enabled Ananiah, with Micah's help, to easily step up onto the floor of the front of the cart. Then he removed the box to the back of the cart, so Abagail could gain access to the back section of the dray. With all travellers on board, he replaced the box at the back of the cart and farewelled his friends wishing them a safe journey and God speed. As the cart made its way down the streets towards the lake, Abagail waved back to Micah. "How he has changed!" she thought to herself. "He is no longer the young boy my brothers used to play with: he has become a man, and quite a handsome man, too!"

As the cart moved along the dusty road by Lake Galilee the sun had fully revealed the day. On the lake, fishermen could be seen returning from their night's work whilst others were sitting by the lake cleaning their nets. People were on the road too, making their way towards the city which now appeared behind the travellers. It was a picturesque setting, yet all travellers were quietly reflective in deep and personal thoughts about their short stay in K'far-Nachan. "You are both in deep thought" Ananiah said to his children. "Tell me what's on your mind, Daniel?"

"Father" Daniel replied, "I do have something I want to share with you, and I do ask that you can understand what I am about to say". Daniel confessed that he had given his decision much thought and last night, when he farewelled his brothers, he told them that he would not be returning to follow the master. Their failure to secure the miracle he thought his father so richly deserved, and the fact that each day he seemed to be missing his family more and more, had caused him to make the decision not to continue journeying with the master.

His father re-assured Daniel that he was living his own life and the decisions he made needed to please himself as well as his own family. "You must do what Adonai tells you to do" Ananiah said. Daniel guiltily thought to himself that it wasn't so much what Adonai was saying to him, that caused him to make this decision but rather his heart, which was feeling saddened and alone.

"And what about you, Abagail?" Ananiah asked. "What is causing your mind to ponder so quietly?"

"I'd rather not say" responded Abagail.

"Well, I shared with you both my thoughts" replied Daniel. "It's only fair that you should tell us yours".

"Well, all right!" responded Abagail. Abagail said her thoughts centred on that poor woman who, on the day of their arrival at K'far-Nachan, desperately sought the master despite the cumbersome weight of her illness. Knowing full well that she was an outcast[262]; forbidden because of her condition to go near any town or people, in complete opposition, bravely broke through the barriers of exclusion and in the purest of faith, simply believed that if she could only just touch the hem of his garment, she would be healed! Moreover, the woman knowing that she was defiled because of her illness, bravely reached out to simply touch his hem[263]. The extent of this woman's bravery was extraordinary! She defied her uncleanliness and

---

[262] Leviticus 15:25-27
[263] Leviticus 22:5-6

its consequences and acted entirely on her faith; yet in his compassion, the master healed her, regardless.

The two men nodded. It was an extraordinary situation. As Samson led them on their way, the incident consumed their thoughts. But the deepest insight lay within Ananiah's contemplations. "Could it be", he heard a small soft voice say, "that this is just like a young, anxious father who trespassed into a place where he was totally forbidden; who entered it unclean and unholy yet believed that all he had to do was to ask if a child was safe? Could it be that his faith enabled the forgiveness of the 'trespasses'? Could the enormity of such a perceived unholy sin secure forgiveness as well?"

"Oh, Adonai!" Ananiah privately cried to his God, "could it possibly be that the sin I have carried for so long since that night in Your Temple, has been forgotten by you?"

Ananiah's heart skipped a beat as a small soft voice within him gently asked, "What sin?"[264]

---

[264] Jeremiah 31: 31-34; Hebrews 8: 10-12

— *Chapter Thirty-Two* —

SEEING IS
BELIEVING

A s she had done for the past week or so, ever since her husband, son and daughter went on the long trip to K'far-Nachan, throughout each day Rachael's eyes would scan the northern horizon – the direction from where the travellers would return. She missed the companionship of her husband and the delightful smile of her daughter. Her heart started to long for the day of their return, but she knew in her heart that it was all for her husband's benefit. How wonderful it would be for his sight to return to him, and he could regain all the things he loved doing! But Rachael daren't dream of the future possibility of Ananiah re-gaining his sight for this dream was almost an impossible one – one that depended on a man everyone was talking about and who appeared just too good to be true. So, Rachael turned her thoughts to other matters, and these were often interrupted by the sound of Joel's three boys laughing as they played outside the farmhouse.

Joel had insisted that while his father and sister were away, he would bring his wife and three boys to live on the farm, keeping his mother company. In fact, Rachael was very appreciative for Zohar was a good mother, keeping her boys in check and she looked after them well. Although the house in which they lived in Yerushalayim was satisfactory for the family, the wide-open spaces of the farm, the attraction of the animals and the freedom of playing in different and intriguing areas, somehow seemed to reduce the boisterous and often deafening sound of their play. Everyone seemed at peace here. Joel had also taught the boys how to feed and take care of all the animals on the farm – a task which Abagail would do each day. It was such an interesting challenge for them. It had reached the stage they knew the time of day when the animals must be fed and were so competent in the task, Joel felt as if they could do this completely by themselves.

With deep thoughts in her head, Rachael immediately stopped what she was doing and stared at the northern horizon. There in the distance was the smallest speck which she watched carefully. Someone was approaching the farm and so Rachael left the kitchen and went outside of the house to have a clearer look at what was in the distance. It did not take long for her to realize that a horse drawing a cart was advancing toward the farm and when she realized that this could be her loved ones, Rachael started running towards them. Her heart was beating loudly within her as she gleaned Abagail and Daniel frantically waving their hands and smiling, while her husband was just sitting at the front of the dray grinning widely. "Why isn't he waving?" she wondered. "Can't he see me?"

Then, when the travellers came to where she was standing, Abigail leaped out of the cart and rushed up to her mother and embraced her warmly. "Oh! how wonderful it is to see you again, mother!" she said. Then, while still embracing her daughter, Rachael could see across her daughter's shoulder Daniel go to the back of the cart and get a wooden box for his father who, with Daniel's help, dismounted and walked towards his wife. It was then Rachael realized that Ananiah had not been healed.

The joy in seeing and being with her husband once more overrode the disappointment Rachael had momentarily felt. Kissing him on his forehead, cheeks, and lips, she told him how much she had missed him. "I never thought I would say this Ananiah", she said, "but I truly missed your snoring!"

"But I don't snore!" insisted Ananiah.

"Yes, you do!" exclaimed Daniel and Abagail in unison.

"And," added Abagail, turning to her brother "so do you!"

"And you!" Ananiah and Daniel laughingly replied.

After greeting one another, the group showed Rachael the results of their wonderful purchases in the small cart and the strong horse, Samson. Rachael stated that she thought the cart would be most suitable for driving into both the markets and the city as well as the fact it would be perfect for taking Ananiah anywhere he wanted to go. When Rachael saw how fine and strong the horse was, she turned to her daughter and whispered, "Was there enough money?" To this Abagail quietly informed her there was ample and pressed the tiny purse unobtrusively back into her mother's hands.

When Joel's boys who were playing in a nearby field saw their grandfather, uncle and aunt had returned, they happily left their game and ran quickly to greet the travellers. "Can you see Grandpa, can you see?" asked one of the boys. "Not with these sad old eyes of mine" replied Ananiah, "but with these old wrinkly hands of mine, I can feel that you are all growing up so fast and becoming so tall, just like your father". His face, beaming widely, Ananiah gently moved his hands across the faces and bodies of his three grandsons who giggled as he tickled them.

The three boys immediately hopped into the back of the cart and sat on the back seat as Daniel mounted and drove the cart towards the farmhouse. Their arms wrapped around one another, Rachael, Ananiah and Abagail walked besides the cart. It was such a wonderful feeling being home again. Home is always a wonderful place to be after a long and tiring journey.

That evening, when Joel returned home from his scribing duties, he was greeted by his three sons excited that the travellers had returned safely but when Joel entered the room where his family had congregated, his father's eyes failed to look his way and Joel realised the traveller's purpose for their trek had not been fulfilled. Yet there was a brightness in his father's eyes that Joel had not seen before. Greeting his father, brother, and sister, he sensed his father's and sister's contentment about the trip, but his brother Daniel was much more reserved as if there was something troubling him. It was after the evening meal when Joel and his father were sitting on the front porch enjoying the quietness of a disappearing day, when Joel spoke honestly to his father.

"There is something I would like to suggest to you father, and I want you to listen carefully to what I say" he began.

"That sentence must be in the genes of this family!" Ananiah thought to himself but inwardly he knew what ever was going to be spoken, had received careful thought and consideration.

"Father", Joel began, "My family has had such a lovely time here at the farm. It has been wonderful looking after mother and I believe she has enjoyed having us here, too. The boys have behaved well, and they have thoroughly enjoyed the responsibilities living on the land can bring. Both Zohar and I realise that while you have been able to manage the farm despite your disability, some tasks must be getting rather difficult for you. I have been considering giving up my scribing duties and becoming the manager of the farm, with your blessing of course."

"But who will scribe for the family so as to not break the family's commitment to Adonai?" inquired Ananiah.

"My eldest son has displayed excellent talent in his writing so much so, that he is helping me with the six sheets of parchment on which we record the Dabar Promises. He is quite enthusiastic in this task and I feel that he will be able to continue on scribing just as I, you, grandfather and our forefathers have done" replied Joel.

"But you know so very little about farming or managing a farm!" his father replied.

"I am a fast learner, and I am sure my uncles can teach me" Joel answered.

Fully knowing what the honest answer was to his next question, Ananiah asked his oldest son, "Wouldn't you miss reading and recording the word of Adonai?"

Joel did not answer for he knew what the answer was and to disclose this to his father, would make them both feel unhappy.

"Joel," his father said "you are my oldest son and you have always been perceptive and kind to both your mother and to me. You have been given an extraordinary talent which must be used for Adonai's glory, and His alone. You are correct is saying that you are not a farmer yet no doubt you would quickly learn. Over the past few days, I have given the farm a lot of thought and I have come to a decision. On your way to work tomorrow, would you mind asking your uncles Adam, Tomas, and Bogdan to visit me after work? There is something I wish to tell them."

The next day Abagail had three willing helpers assist her when feeding the farm animals but the animal the boys loved most of all was Samson. Daniel had made a strong stall at the back of the barn where the horse had protection from the cold night wind and rain. The boys were delighted that their father had granted their request for the family to remain a few more nights at the farm and their happiness was most apparent in their rowdy outbursts and laughter. So, the day began, as it usually did, with lots of chores and activities.

Late that afternoon after all the work on the farm had been completed, Ananiah's brothers Adam, Tomas and Bogdan walked briskly across the fields to the farmhouse, a little unsure as to what their brother was going to say. When they were all seated around the kitchen table, (which often was used as a board room/conference room) Ananiah spoke openly to his brothers. He thanked them for all their support and hard work over the past years, but particularly the last three. Telling them that once he realised his sight was deteriorating, he was determined not to let this affect his enjoyment of life and so he persevered as hard as he could to ensure his life was useful and productive. Management of the family farm had been a real blessing to him but he was now concerned that his disability was affecting the productivity of the farm itself and so it was for this reason, he had decided it was not fair to all the family for him to continue in this role and therefore, he intended to resign as farm manager.

"Your wisdom and guidance have greatly assisted our productivity over the years" Adam said. "Who will be able to fill your shoes?"

Ananiah replied that over the last few days he had given this considerable thought and wanted to ensure that the person who would take over from him would be someone who had not only worked on the farm but was fully aware of its difficulties and the needs of the people who worked there. It was then announced that the person who would fill the role of Manager was in fact, now standing in the doorway. As the people in the room turned their heads and looked towards the doorway, standing in the middle of this, was Daniel.

Daniel also thanked his uncles for all the work they had done in contributing to the farm and he assured them that he would be returning to the farm working side by side with them through every season. He expressed his gratitude to his uncles for the care and concern they had shown for all the workers and wanted to reassure them, that he too had everyone's best interest at heart. To illustrate this, Daniel had realised that not all the women workers on the farm were being paid. The women who made the lunches for the workers (the cost of which was now paid by the workers to the Manager) usually came from relatives and families of those present within the room. But they had never been paid or even allocated a wage for their work. It was for this reason, Daniel had decided that the women who prepared and delivered the meals given to the farm workers, will now be paid. However, as they would not be working the whole day, the women's wages will be half the amount paid to the workers for the season, and the workers would only have to pay 2.5% for their lunches.

Daniel stressed that the first people who would have to be paid are the family members working on the farm. In the event of a poor year, no hired women workers would be employed. But the family members and the women folk who made their meals, would always be paid, their wage naturally dependent on the crop's productivity.

Daniel had always believed, as did many others who worked on the farm, that the land surrounding the barn was extremely fertile and therefore, he had decided that different vegetables would be grown around the perimeter of three of the barn walls. These could be planted and managed by the children and grandchildren of the broader family, making this a family concern. It was important to give the children an insight into the purpose and productivity of the farm and so, the products grown there by the children would be reaped by the children and their families. In the event of there being any surplus, this could be sold at the marketplace in the city.

Daniel's insight into the farm pleased not only his uncles and his father but also his sister who was listening to the conversation. Pulling her mother to one side she whispered, "Isn't that wonderful mother, we are going to be paid for our work!"

Rachael did not answer.

"Mother!" cried Abagail. "The women folk are finally going to be paid for their assistance on the farm!"

"Abagail!" her mother whispered. "Where did you think the money I gave you for K'far-Nachan came from?"

"You mean father was paying you to do the meals?"

Rachael nodded.

"And what about me? Did he ever pay me?"

"Since your fourteenth birthday - some of the money I gave you for the cart was yours!"

"Drat!" replied Abagail. "I should have bought the horse! Samson could have been mine!"

≈　　≈　　≈

Weeks quickly passed by and the next Passover Festival was only a month away. Whilst working in the markets, selling the farm's produce Rachael had heard some disturbing news. A faithful customer's brother had fallen seriously ill and while Rachael had noticed that her customer hadn't come to the markets for some time, she was saddened to hear that the woman's brother had just died. Feeling as if she would like to visit her customer, she informed the family that following the Sabbath, which was the next day, she would take Samson and the cart to visit her friend. Although she did not know the lady all that well, she felt in her heart that she was a good person who must be beside herself in grief at the passing of her only brother.

Abagail said that she would accompany her mother and following the Sabbath, the two set forth for Beit-Anyah (Bethany) which was only two kilometres south east of Yerushalayim. Small bags of flour, vegetables and other provisions had been placed in the back of the cart as the women journeyed to the small village. It did not take them long to reach the village which was still filled with mourners comforting the bereaved family. When they arrived at the woman's home, they took their gifts with them and entered the dwelling. The woman who was in deep grief did not recognise Rachael at first but when she realised who she was, the woman ran up to her and wept. "My poor sister has taken our brother's death so hard" she said. "Would you mind staying with her a while?"

Rachael and Abagail could hear a woman loudly sobbing, almost inconsolably. "It's OK to cry" comforted Rachael, "but you will see your brother again!" The woman nodded her head and sat silently in her grief. Suddenly, she began crying loudly.

The woman who was a good customer came quickly into the house and said something to her sister who then, quickly got up and ran outside of the dwelling. "She must have gone to the burial site!" someone exclaimed and all the people in the house including Rachael and Abigail ran after her.

Following the grieving women right through to the northern entrance of the village, Abagail was astounded when she recognised the man the woman was talking to. "Mother", she whispered, "that is the man Seth, Jabin and Micah have been following!" Although they could not hear the entire conversation, they swiftly followed the man and the grieving women and found themselves in front of a stone white tomb sealed by a large stone. Standing in front of the tomb, the man wept bitter tears. "See how much he loved him!" someone said whilst another said, "Surely if he can open the eyes of the blind, he could have saved his friend from death!"

Prevailing against his tears, the man asked that the large stone be rolled away but the woman whose brother had died, protested saying that it was four days since the man's death and his body would be in a stinking state of decay. But the man insisted and then looking up to heaven, the people heard him pray, calling upon his Heavenly Father. Rachael could not believe the command that the man then gave to the deceased body of El'azar (Lazarus) – to come forth out of the tomb!

Almost immediately, there standing in the entrance of the open tomb was the man, his funeral cloths all bound around him! Gasps of disbelief echoed amongst the people gathered there as the man called Yeshua commanded that the grave clothes be removed[265].

Everyone in the crowd had looks of incredulity etched firmly on their faces, even the woman and her sister. The only face that did not reveal such scepticism was Abagail's. "Is there anything this man cannot do!" she exclaimed to her mother whose eyes were drenched in tears. For Rachael, her soul's eyes, like those of her husband's, had been fully opened and she was consumed with such joy knowing that everything Ananiah believed about this man from Nazareth, was true. Realising that she had just witnessed a magnificent miracle, she also knew that she was in the presence of Adonai himself. Her heart was so filled with overflowing joy, and fervently she praised her God. "Surely," she said to herself "this man must come from Adonai! Who else can command the dead to rise?"

Her joy was interrupted by a strong hand and a voice which asked, "Mother! What are you doing here?" There beside her were her two sons Seth and Jabin. "How could anyone not believe in this man?" Rachael asked wiping away her tears. "Who has ever commanded death to flee[266]? Everything your father says about this man, is true! Praise be to Adonai who has so graciously allowed our eyes and souls to witness for ourselves the miracles performed before us!"

---

[265] John 11:17-44
[266] Isaiah 25:8; Hosea 13:14

Never in her life had Rachael seen a contrasting change of emotions flow so spectacularly. The tears flowing from the deepness of the sorrow of the death of the loved brother, the intense gloom and extreme sadness that hovers steadfastly over the human heart, in a matter of seconds had dramatically changed into tears of overwhelming joy and gladness, relinquished relief and never ceasing happiness. Such were the emotions of the weeping sisters and the crowd around them. Who else but Adonai could turn such sadness into pure joy?[267]

Rachael's ears were now fully opened as the two brothers who were accompanied by Micah exchanged what their master had been doing. For the first time, the words they spoke rang in her heart and her love and interest in the man she had just seen perform a great miracle, streamed to the point of overflowing[268]. Of course, there were more incidences of witnessing people being healed. Yet, as they had stated many times before, the men recalled the most intriguing thing to them was what the master had been saying.

Disturbingly, he had told his disciples that he would be going up to Yerushalayim to die[269]. However, there were many in the group of followers who hoped that when he travelled to Yerushalayim during the coming Passover, he would assume his rightful reign. There were some, Jabin reported, who were so deeply concerned about the prospect of others trying to murder the master, they urged him to stay away from Yerushalayim because of the emerging and expanding hatred of the Pharisees and rulers of the Sanhedrin. Yet the men recalled that even at the beginning of his ministry, the master had said that no prophet can be killed outside of Yerushalayim[270].

---

[267] Psalm 30:11
[268] Psalm 23:5
[269] Mark 10:32-33
[270] Luke 13:33

≈   ≈   ≈

Although it was usually their custom to spend some time before going to sleep to talk about events of their day, that night, as they lay in bed, Ananiah and Rachael talked incessantly about the man from Nazareth. Ananiah explained how many of the Dabar Promises written on the sheets of parchment appeared to be fulfilled in the life of this man. The couple soon realised that not only were they united in a loving marriage, but they now also shared in the exciting fulfilment of Adonai's long-awaited promises. Although previously Ananiah had felt supported by his great-grandfather, father, and his sons, he felt so much stronger and contented now his views were also shared by his wife.

Chapter Thirty-Three

A LONG
AWAITED DAY

Staring at the ceiling above him, Joel laid wide awake as the prospect of a good night sleep had forsaken and abandoned him. Like many nights before, the Dabar Promises found within the Scriptures wandered through his mind and not only was there confusion present, but conflict as well. Particularly confusing was the prospect that the Messiah would have to suffer[271] and indeed be betrayed[272]. Who would be so foolish and evil to betray the promised Messiah? Most conflicting and perplexing was the belief that the Messiah would not only die suffering a cruel, lonely death, he would be abandoned by his family, his friends and his God[273]. Surely, this could not be?

---

[271] Isaiah 53: 10
[272] Psalm 55:12-14
[273] Psalm 22:1

Yet the Dabar Promises passed down through the ages foretold there would be a Messiah who would not die[274] but rather would come and restore his people, reigning forever[275]. These conflicting notions argued amongst themselves in Joel's head and he could not find any comfort, just total confusion. Realising that he needed to have a break from these thoughts, Joel quietly rose from his bed so as not to awake his sleeping wife, and lighting an oil lamp beside his bed, he went down the stairs to the kitchen table. Gathering the six sheets of parchment where the Dabar Promises had been faithfully recorded, he spread these out, side by side across the kitchen table. Placing the oil lamp in the middle of the row, he once again prayed for wisdom[276]; his eyes once more gleaned over the words before him.

On the extreme left side of the table lay many of the promises handed down to the Jewish people through the ages and these related to the restoration of Isra'el to its fullest glory whilst on the extreme right was the vacant, empty page. He placed all the promises relating to the restoration of Israe'l collectively together. As he glanced across the remaining pages, Joel realised that these related to the Messiah Himself, his genealogy, his rejection, his suffering and his death. It was then he placed all these pages in the middle of the line on top of one another, making another pile.

There were now three piles before him, two with pages neatly packed and the one uncompleted page. Recalling a saying by the man Yeshua his brother Jabin had reported, (though a quandary at the time it was shared), for no reason sprang into his mind; "The first shall be last"[277]. Jabin removed the pile of promises which foretold of the restoration of Isra'el, he placed this at the right-hand side of the empty sheet. Gazing at the three piles

---

274 Psalm 16:10
275 Psalm 146:10
276 Proverbs 2:6; Proverbs 3:13
277 Matthew 19:30

in-front of him, he gasped to see the revelation before him. The first pile now documented the ministry of the coming Messiah, many promises were already revealed in the ministry of the man Yeshua. Several sheets included in this pile reported that His ministry would end in his cruel death.

The other pile on the right indicated after the Messiah's death there would be a second return which would be an eternal one as promised by Adonai in the prophets. But what lay between the Messiah's death and his return was at that moment, a blank and empty page!

Joel's heart leapt as he remembered his brothers telling him that the Messiah said that he was going away but he promised them he would return[278]. Surely his return would be his second coming? But what promises pertained to the vacant page? What must take place as a result of the Messiah's dying, to enable his triumphant coming a second time? Although this was an even greater mystery, there appeared to be clarity where there was once confusion, and there was assurance, where there once was uncertainty.

When Zohar awoke the next day, she found an empty space beside her. Coming down to the kitchen she found her husband lying slumped over three piles of parchment and lightly snoring. As she glanced at the three piles, she carefully picked each pile up trying not to awaken Joel but unfortunately, he woke just as she was doing so. "There were three piles!" he exclaimed "I hope you haven't mixed them up!"

"And good morning to you, too" replied his wife. "No, I haven't, here are the three piles as you had them." Placing the three piles in front of her husband, Zohar commented that it was wonderful how the first pile composed of information about the man Yeshua of Nazareth and all the wonderful things he had been doing, whilst the final pile related to the millennium rule as described by the prophet Daniel[279]. As to the promises

---

[278] John 14:28
[279] Daniel 8 - 12

on the middle blank page, although Adonai had not revealed them yet, she felt certain that they would be revealed soon.

Startled, Joel looked at his wife. "It took me the whole night to come to that conclusion and you deduce this in such a short time!" Zohar did not answer – there are some times when men unfortunately reveal that they do not understand women at all.

It was the week before Passover when Kaleb hurriedly came through the back door of the farmhouse. Standing beside Ananiah, Rachael was pleased to see her husband's friend and wondered what message he was going to bring them. She knew it must have been important for it was obvious that despite his aging years Kaleb had made every attempt to get to the farm as quickly as possible. Panting, Kaleb paused to gain his breath before telling them that Yerushalayim was ablaze with rumours that the man everyone had been talking about was making his final return! With this visit there was extreme excitement for many people who believed the man from Nazareth was Adonai's chosen one and this was the final visit that the prophets of old foretold. There was high speculation and rejoicing by the people who now believed Isra'el was to be released from the Roman authorities. At last, the day that generations of Adonai's people had longed for was finally here! The whole city was in turmoil as stories about the long-awaited Messiah spread through the homes and the streets. The people were jubilant that this was the day when Adonai would finally answer the people's prayers! The whole city was ablaze with gossip and the news was circulating fast around the surrounding region beyond the extremities of the city.

At Beit-Pagei (Bethpage), not far from Beit-Anyah, it was reported the man from Nazareth had told his disciples to go to the village and bring back a donkey and her colt[280]. The man had attracted many people who

---

[280] Matthew 21:1-6

were accompanying him to Yerushalayim and the latest rumour reported they would shortly be at the eastern gate of the city. Excited by the news that Kaleb had brought them, Rachael quickly called Abigail and together they hastily prepared Samson and the cart and then with Ananiah seated beside his wife, the three of them made their way to the eastern city gate.

As they arrived at the city gate, they could see a large crowd of people in the distance and the approaching sounds of laughter and singing quickly grew louder as the procession advanced towards the city. At the front of the procession a large group of people joyfully shouted "Hosanna to the Son of David! Blessed is he who comes in the name of the Lord! Hosanna in the highest!" Then, followed the man Yeshua, sitting on the colt of the donkey. Some people lay their cloaks on the road before the donkey whilst others had cut branches from the trees and lay these in the wake of the Messiah. As Abagail described to her father the scene that was before them, Ananiah found himself saying aloud "Say to the Daughter of Zion, see your king comes to you, gentle and riding on a donkey, on a colt, the foal of a donkey".[281]

"Could this really be happening?" asked Rachael. "The long-awaited Messiah has finally come and entered our great city to claim his kingdom! What a privilege to be here and see this for ourselves!". While Rachael's and Abagail's hearts beat excitedly, Ananiah's heart was confused. There were so many Dabar Promises that suggested this may not be the time for the Messiah's rule and yet there was such overwhelming joy within his heart and the assurance that someone special was riding by. Indeed, the reappearance of that feeling of a powerful presence, experienced so long ago in the Holy Place, surged within him causing his heart to feel full and overflowing.

---

[281] Zechariah 9:9; Matthew 21:7-11

Following the crowd, Rachael drove the cart with its passengers through the city gates as the celebration continued. Some of the people watching the procession smiled and waved whilst others simply stared at the goings on. Children began singing and dancing and there was such a euphoric atmosphere that seemed to engulf the city as the procession moved past the marketplace and into the main thoroughfare. As the crowd appeared to grow the people pressed closely against the dray and enclose themselves completely around Samson who appeared to become increasingly agitated, for he was not used to such loud commotion. Rachael became aware of his stress and after what seemed an eternity eased him towards the outside edge of the crowd.

Passing by Jethro's shop, Abagail turned to wave to her brother who was watching the procession from the shop's door. Sighting the family in the dray, Jethro waved frantically and just as Abagail prepared to alight from the dray, she saw her brother hold his hand high in the air shouting to her to remain in the dray. As Jethro left the shop and made his way towards the moving dray, Abagail sighted a stone-faced Rebecca busily serving customers in the shop.

It was soon evident that the pressing crowd was unsettling the horse so Rachael made a quick decision to turn into a narrow street on their right-hand side. Moving away from the noise and frivolity of the people, the horse appeared to calm down as Abagail alighted from the dray and coming up to his side, re-assured him that all was well. "That was a little scary", Rachael was heard to remark.

"Rachael" Ananiah said, "Would you mind terribly if we do not continue? It is obvious that the horse is uneasy when moving in such a large crowd and it would be too difficult for me to walk with you as I am overwhelmed with tiredness. Perhaps Abagail could catch up with her brothers but as for me, despite the waiting for this momentous day, I am finding it difficult to keep my eyes open!"

Rachael looked at her husband and she knew in her heart that there were many times when she felt that he needed to rest because of his tiredness, but he would insist he was fine and carry on regardless. Yet on this long-awaited day, it was he himself who suggested that they not continue and for him to do so, meant he must have been feeling out of sorts. "It's probably wise for me not to go," Abagail responded. "The man most probably will be going to the Court of Isra'el in the Temple and I won't be able to go there". Jethro said that he would follow the crowd to see what the Master was going to do and farewelling the group, he joined the procession making its way to the Temple grounds.

Taking the back streets, the cart moved in the opposite direction and made its way back to the city gates. Although Abagail was disappointed that they would not be present when the promised one would restore the city, she was deeply concerned for her father whose health appeared to be declining; whose strength appeared to be waning before their very eyes.

— *Chapter Thirty-Four* —

THE COST OF
FULFILMENT

S amson pulled the little cart being driven by Rachael towards the
eastern gates of Yerushalayim. As usual, Ananiah was seated in
the front of the cart with his wife, whilst Abagail sat at the back.
Attached by a rope at the back of the dray, Zimra moved quickly to keep
in pace with Samson. Rachael had decided to bring the donkey just in case
a large crowd prevented the group from moving alongside of the man they
were seeking, as happened only a few days before. With Ananiah seated on
the back of Zimra, it would be possible to travel with the crowd and keep
up with the man from Galilee.

Although Ananiah and his family had come to believe that the kingdom
the man from Galilee talked about was a spiritual rather than a physical
kingdom, they also believed that this man was the indeed the promised
Messiah. Their hearts were filled with great hope, excitement, and antici-

pation. Only a few days before they had witnessed the man from Nazareth entering the great city and the joyous memory of the crowd's happy singing and jubilant rejoicing occupied their minds. As no mention of the man upsurging the Roman authorities was reported they wondered if this would be the day when he would finally establish his kingdom?

As they entered the city, they were astonished to find that the streets of the city were deadly quiet – a complete contrast to the joyous refrains of their previous encounter with the man from Galilee. Instead, only Samson's and Zimra's hooves and the turning wheels of the dray could be heard on the street's cobbled stones. It was an uneasy stillness that greeted them though they thought they heard crowd voices drifting from the Governor's Palace. Alighting from the cart at Joel's house, Rachael tethered Samson to an outside post, and went into the house with Ananiah and Abagail.

A stone faced, and anxious Zohar greeted them and when they saw that both Jabin and Seth were also present in the house, they noticed that their faces were drawn and serious. "What has happened?" Rachael immediately inquired and when Seth began to speak, his words chilled their blood and they all stood still like stone.

"The Master has been betrayed by one of his disciples and has been handed over to the Roman Authorities!" he told them.

"But how can this be?" inquired Abagail.

Jabin told them that last night after the disciples had shared the Passover Meal with the Master in Yerushalayim[282], they went to the Gat-Sh'manim (the Garden of Gethsemane) on the Mount of Olives to pray and it was there that one of the disciples came up to Yeshua with a group of Roman soldiers. Betraying the Master by kissing him so that the soldiers knew which man to seize[283], Y'hudah forsook the Master and all his good teach-

---

[282] Mark 14:13-26
[283] Mark 14:43-50

ings and handed him over to the Roman authorities. "There was something about that man Y'hudah that I just did not like" added Jabin. "I have always had a somewhat disturbing feeling about him!"

Jabin continued to say that they believed the Master was first taken to the Sanhedrin where he was harshly cross-examined and people with false testimonies lied about him[284]. Then he was taken to Governor Pilate who upon hearing that the man came from Galilee, sent him to Herod who was in Yerushalayim at the time[285]. Herod returned him to Pilate in the early hours of the morning. It was believed the Master had been cruelly beaten, mocked, and tortured during the time he was buffeted to and from the different authorities[286]. He was kept in prison overnight.

"When we heard what had happened, we came straight to Joel's house. He and Jethro have gone to the Governor's Palace where we believe most of the city is assembled. We dare not go ourselves, for we fear that like his disciples, we shall be arrested too".

Ananiah sighed. "Everything you have told us fulfils many of the Dabar Promises!" he exclaimed. "It seems that they are being unveiled before our eyes! Many of these promises we have faithfully written down on six pieces of parchment, sometimes not knowing exactly how they would be fulfilled. But my heart knows the man from Galilee has fulfilled them faithfully." Moreover, Ananiah continued to tell them, scripture came to his mind just as Jabin was speaking; that the Messiah would be falsely accused and there would be people who would give false testimonies about him[287]. He would be silent before his accusers[288], spat upon and struck[289] and, he would be

---

[284] Mark 14:53-65
[285] Luke 23:1-12
[286] Luke 22:63-65
[287] Psalm 109:2-4
[288] Isaiah 53:7
[289] Isaiah 50:6

judged[290]. But where, they wondered, would he be given a fair trial when the world appears to be clearly against him?

Just as they were thinking this, Joel and Jethro came through the door. Their faces white, in disbelief, they told the group that they had just come from the courtyard of the Governor's Place where Pilate had tried to persuade the people not to condemn the man from Galilee, whom he regarded, was completely innocent. But the people appeared rebellious and antagonistic towards the man Yeshua despite Pilate's pleading. So, in line with the custom of releasing one criminal during the Feast, Pilate offered the crowd a choice between the man from Galilee and Bar-Abba, a notorious and unpopular criminal. But the crowd chose the infamous criminal! When Pilate asked the crowd, what should be done with Christ, the man from Galilee, the angry crowd shouted, "Crucify him!"

"But crucifixion is the price felons pay for their sinfulness!" Abagail cried. "This man is a man from Adonai and totally innocent of any crime. How can one who is godly, and innocent be made to die in such a cruel way?"

"I was thinking that myself, too" replied Joel "but then, I remember reading the prophet Yesha'yahu saying that the Messiah would die the death of a wicked man[291]. I completely disregarded this because I thought this could never be! But here it is, happening, right before our very eyes!"

"Where is he now?" asked Ananiah.

"They have made him carry his own cross and drag this to Gulgolta (Golgotha)", Seth replied.

"We must go and be with him", pleaded Rachael.

"Absolutely not!" exclaimed Ananiah. "Gulgolta is no place for a woman! You must stay here with Abagail and Zohar. Jethro, Joel, and I will take Zimra and remain with the man during this terrible time. Please stay

---

[290] Isaiah 53:8
[291] Isaiah 53:9

here and pray for us, and pray also for that poor man himself, who is only doing Adonai's work and is innocent of all the accusations against him!"

As Ananiah perched on Zimra's back, Joel and Jethro made their way to the western gate of the city, they did not say a word to each other. Completely lost in their own thoughts concerning the terror of the moment, their minds pondered many questions with disbelief that what was transpiring was real and not imagined. Most of the crowd that had assembled in the Governor's Palace courtyard had dispersed and the streets again appeared empty and deserted.

Heading to the cold, barren hill of Gulgolta there were only small groups of people scattered there and it seemed that the large crowd which so eagerly demanded the crucifixion of the man from Galilee were not as eager to watch him die. It seemed this man who had gathered such a large following over the past three years, was now facing death rejected and alone. Jethro heard the loud sound of hammering as they came to the hill of Gulgolta and then a cruel sound of three thumps as three crosses with strong ropes around them, were dropped heavily into their stands. Each thump seemed to vibrate through Jethro's body and echo across the stone quarry.

There before them were three men; their hands and feet nailed to three cold, hard wooden crosses. The man from Galilee had been placed in the middle of the other two criminals and at the top of his cross, written in both Aramaic, Latin, and Greek[292] was a sign which said, "King of the Jews". Below the three men were a small number of Roman soldiers who had the terrible task of crucifying the three 'guilty' men. Jethro felt that he could smell alcohol coming from the men who seemed to be completing their assignment task as if it was a daily routine. Glancing across to his

---

[292] John 19: 19-22

father, he could see tears falling steadily down Ananiah's face and it was as if his father's eyes were seeing the horrific sight in front of them.

"What is it father?" he asked placing his right arm around his father's shoulder.

"The feeling of Adonai's presence though strong, seems to be dissipating; it seems to be being pulled down by an overwhelming heaviness which I cannot fathom. Please tell me what is happening. I need to know what is happening to the man Adonai has sent us!"

There were a few passers-by who scoffed at the man in the middle and even the two men with whom he was crucified, tormented him as well[293].

"Oh!" exclaimed Ananiah, "He is in absolute pain and agony, yet they continue to cruelly mock him!"

Jethro began to explain the terrible scene before them and as he was describing what was happening, both Ananiah and Joel recalled the Dabar Promises, most of which had either been overlooked in their recording or included on the parchments but without full understanding. They were stunned by what was happening before them and could not comprehend how and why such a terrible thing was occurring.

Explaining that the soldiers at the foot of the cross were casting lots for his clothing[294] Ananiah recalled the scripture which said this would happen[295]. Then, the man in the middle cried out "Forgive them Father, for they know not what they are doing!"[296]

"What compassion! Even in his pain and anguish, he prays for the sins of those who are murdering him!"[297] Ananiah thought to himself.

---

[293] Matthew 27:39-44
[294] John 19:23-24
[295] Psalm 22:18
[296] Luke 23:34
[297] Psalm 109:4

Time passed slowly and occasionally the silence was broken by the groans of men on the crosses. One of the men beseeched Yeshua to save them from their anguish and pain but the other, who had previously scoffed at the man in the middle was heard to ask, "Yeshua remember me when you come into your kingdom"[298]. Yeshua answered him, re-assuring him that very day, they would be together in paradise.[299]

"What mercy! What reassurance!" thought Jethro. "Not once has this man cursed yet if anyone needs to curse, surely he should because of his pain! But no! He does not curse but offers comfort and assurance!"

Sometime later the man in the middle looked at the people surrounding the cross and there to one side was a small group of women with a man. Despite his pain with blood streaming down from his brow Yeshua looked at one of the women crying there and said, "Dear woman, here is your son"; and to the man, he said, "Here is your mother".[300]

"Such love!" thought Ananiah. "Surely this cannot come from a man dying on a cross – surely these words of compassion and great love must come from Adonai!"

As the sky began to darken, the man in the middle was heard to exclaim "I am thirsty!" One of the soldiers dipped a sponge into a jar of vinegar wine, put this on a hyssop stick and lifted it to Yeshua's lips[301]. As Jethro was describing this to his father, Joel exclaimed "They put gall in my food and give me vinegar for my thirst!"[302] Not long after this, the man in the middle was heard to exclaim: "Eloi, Eloi, lama sabchthani! (My God, my God, why have you forsaken me?)" Ananiah and Joel knew that these words came

---

[298] Luke 23:39-42
[299] Luke 23:43
[300] John 19:25-27
[301] John 19: 28-29
[302] Psalm 69:21

from the Tehillim (Psalms)[303] . They continued to be overwhelmed by what was happening. As the skies grew ever darker, the man in the middle gave a final cry; "Father into your hands I commit my spirit!"[304] and with a loud cry shouted, "It is finished!"[305]

Upon the man's final words, the sky became completely dark, and thunder (but no lightning) rumbled loudly through the sky. The earth tremored at the sound[306] and it seemed to those at the scene, Adonai was not at all pleased. One centurion exclaimed that truly, this must have been the son of Adonai[307] whilst all of those watching, beat their breasts in utter shame[308].

As the day ended, the soldiers had been ordered to take the three bodies down from the crosses as the following day was a Jewish holy day, and bodies were not permitted to hang there during that time.[309] To ensure that the crucified men would be dead, the centurions broke the bones of the thief on the right and the thief on the left of the man in the middle. But seeing that he was already dead, a soldier pieced Yeshua's body with his spear[310]. Approaching the hill from a distance, Jethro saw two men who came and collected the body of Yeshua. "Why, that's Nichodemus!" whispered Jethro to his father.

"I believe the other man is Yosef of Ramatayim;[311] he is a good man who is very wealthy and a member of the Sanhedrin council, like Nichodemus!" stated Joel in astonishment.

"Both members of the Sanhedrin council?" replied Jethro. "The very people who caused his death, come to bury him as well!"

---

[303] Psalm 22:1
[304] Luke 23:46
[305] John 19:30
[306] Matthew 27:54
[307] ibid
[308] Luke 23:48
[309] Deuteronomy 21:22-23
[310] John 19:31-37
[311] Luke 23:50-56

"Do not believe that everyone who serves on the Sanhedrin is a corrupt person" Ananiah said, rebuking his son. "Don't forget your grandfather served Adonai faithfully for many years on the council and a godlier man I have yet to meet".

Too often rash words can be spoken in judgement, without knowing all the facts and without realizing that the words themselves are so far from the truth; they reveal not only the arrogance of the speaker but his ignorance as well.

≈　≈　≈

Early the next morning Joel heard loud knocking on his front door. Peering into the street, he saw Zév who pleaded that he come quickly for there was something he just had to see. Quickly putting on his outer garments, Joel went down the stairs to his front door. When he asked what was the cause for all the noise, Zév replied, "Just come!"

The men moved sprightly through the narrow streets of the city which, at the time of the morning were empty for as the dawn had just broken, not many people were up and about. For an old man, Zév was still very agile, and Joel had to make a concerted effort to keep up with him. "Did we really give him a ride on Zimra that day three years ago' at the Yarden River?" Joel asked himself. When they reached the Temple complex, they went down the stairs in the eastern colonnade into the lower corridors and hallways of the underground section of the Temple. Making their way through these, they went up a set of stairs and found themselves in the Court of the Priests. "I am not too sure I should be here!" Joel protested as Zév beckoned him towards the Holy Place. Inside the Holy Place were a group of priests, including Caiaphas and Ezra.

"Why! It is just like they said!" one priest was heard to exclaim. "But how could this possibly be? This just cannot be!"

"In my whole life of serving Adonai" another was heard to comment, "I have never seen the Holy Place in such a state!"

When Joel approached the Holy Place, which appeared to be dark and unwelcoming, he saw that the strong veil that led into the Holiest of Holiest had been completely torn from the top to the bottom. The height and weight of the curtain made it impossible for a man to tear, yet there it was, completely torn apart. "It is believed" said one of the priests, "that this occurred the very moment the man Yeshua died on the cross! Moreover, many have said that when the earthquake occurred at the time of his death, tombs of many of the saints, were opened! What does it all mean?"

"In hazarding a guess" replied Zév, "I would assume that Adonai is not at all happy with what you have so cruelly and unfairly done to His prophet".

"What are you two doing here?" Ezra asked. "This is a Holy Place!"

"It doesn't seem too holy to me" commented Joel. "It appears completely deserted".

"Bring the Lamp which never goes out over here" Caiaphas ordered, "so we can examine the curtain more closely".

It was then everybody stood still. Glancing over to the menorah, they realised that there was no light in the room at all because all the lamp's oil was completely extinguished. Moreover, when Joel looked towards the twelve loaves of bread on the showbread table, in the darkened shadows all the pieces appeared as if they were full of mould and completely stale.

"When are you going to realise that you have done an innocent man a great injustice?" Zév demanded. "When are you going to realise that like your fathers before you, you murdered a man Adonai has sent us?"

"If you truly know the word given to us by Adonai" Caiaphas said, "you would know that we are instructed to kill all false prophets"[312].

"But this man was not a false prophet!" replied Zév.

"And he did not turn the people away from Adonai but showed the people that Adonai is a gentle and loving God who wishes His people to repent. He was from Adonai and was therefore not a false prophet!" Joel argued.

"The god he preached was not the God we know!" interjected Ezra. "So, he was a false prophet and he needed to be killed. We have done no wrong! No wrong at all"

"You've done no wrong? You not only killed an innocent man, but you also killed a prophet of the most-high God!" replied Joel.

"Get out of here before I get the temple guards to arrest you!" threatened Ezra.

"Are you all that blind?" replied Joel. "Can't you physically see that Adonai has left the building?" Then, after saying this, Joel and Zév returned to their homes.

Sadly, we live in a world that distorts the truth for its own benefit, makes its own rules and turns its back on the Living God. We rebel against Him and place the individual on the throne of the human heart. We live for self and not to serve. Openly rejecting His truth, the world lives for selfish pleasure and not for selfless gain.

---

[312] Deuteronomy 13:1-5

—— *Chapter Thirty-Five* ——

DEEPEST INSIGHTS

T he day following the crucifixion of the man called Yeshua of Nazareth, found Rachael quite concerned about her husband. Over the last few months. she had noticed he was tiring easily and complained about a lack of energy. His energy appeared to be quickly zapped when the couple with Abagail went on short trips to Yerushalayim. Their journey to Yerushalayim following the joyous procession accompanying the man Yeshua into the city, resulted in Ananiah staying in bed the following day. Although the previous day spent on the lonely hill of Gulgolta had taken its toll on all the family members, Ananiah was the one who appeared waxed and waned in deepest thoughts. Whereas Abagail and herself could complete their daily chores and keep themselves busy, Ananiah could not for his blindness had handicapped him and confined him to a chair. There, he would just sit and think. It grieved her to see him in this state and despite his unwillingness to get out of bed that morning, she insisted he got up and dressed himself. She was delighted when she heard her grandchildren's laughter outside and as she looked out of the window, she saw Zohar walking towards the farm with her three boys running around her.

"I hope you don't mind us coming, mother" Zohar said as she greeted Rachael "but there is such an oppressive and uneasy atmosphere in the city today, so I thought I would get the boys out of the house and give their father some peace".

"Is Joel alright?" Rachael asked. Like the others, Joel had been shocked by all that had happened, but Zohar said that all through the night and the early hours of the day, he was conscientiously writing on the six sheets of parchments that contained the Dabar Promises. It was almost, Zohar explained, as if he was obsessed with the accuracy of what was being written down. Apparently, he had left the house for a short time before she had woken but by the time the children were up, he had returned to the house and to the parchments of paper. Still writing when she and the children left, Joel promised that once he had finished, he would join them on the farm.

"You don't mind, do you?" Zohar asked.

"Of course not!" Rachael replied. "You are all like a fresh breeze to us!"

As Ananiah sat on the front porch, he could hear the laughter and voices of his grandchildren playing in the fields nearby. "Oh, Adonai!" he prayed. "Could what I am thinking now be true? It is so difficult to understand. If it is true, how can it be explained? I can barely comprehend this mystery myself so how might I explain this so that my family might understand?" Just as he was praying, Joel's youngest boy ran up to the porch and excitedly exclaimed "Grandfather! Grandfather! I have a present for you! Hold out your hand!" Stretching his right hand out, Ananiah felt the wheat stalk in his hand. "Where did you get this?" he asked for the harvest season was long gone and new seed had just been planted in the soil. "I found it lying on the ground" was the reply.

Transferring this to his left hand, the fingers of his right hand moved gently up the slender stalk until they came to a husky seed. Rolling the shell of the seed back and forth in his fingers, he gently removed the husk and transferred this to his left hand. Then in his right hand, he rolled the smooth seed around his thumb and forefingers. "Of course!" he exclaimed. "Of course! This is how! This is how!"

Rachael came out of the house to see what the commotion was all about. "Where's Joel? Where's Joel?" Ananiah anxiously inquired.

"Why, he's coming across the fields now!" Rachael replied as she viewed Joel running briskly towards the farmhouse carrying the rolled parchments in his hand. "Father! Father!" Joel cried "I believe I have found the reason the Messiah had to die!"

"I too, have come to a realisation" replied Ananiah.

The two men talked for what seemed ages. Joel said that when he was observing the cruel death of the man on the cross, he remembered the very first words spoken by Yochanan the Immerser when they had first encountered the man from Nazareth by the Yarden River. "Do you remember what he said when he saw Yeshua coming to be baptised?" Joel asked. His father shook his head.

"He said '*Behold the Lamb of God who takes away the sins of the world*'! The Lamb of God! Hanging on the cross before us yesterday was God's one and only sacrificial lamb!"

Joel explained that the lamb sacrificed every year in the Temple was a temporary atonement which only endured for a short period of time, for man so easily falls into sin. So sinful was man, a lamb had to be sacrificed every year. Yet Adonai had a plan that would redeem man to Himself by offering His messenger as the one and only lamb that is without blemish, whose blood is pure and whose life is holy[313]. Only holy blood can remove man's sins and the sins of the world. "Whilst I watched his tormented body as he hung there yesterday" Joel continued, "the words of the prophet Yesha'yahu came to me and the very meaning of the words were revealed right in front of me.

*He had no beauty and majesty to attract us to him, nothing in his appearance that we should desire him. He was despised and rejected by men. A man of sorrows familiar with suffering. Like one from whom men hide their faces. He was despised and we esteemed him not. Surely, he took upon himself our infirmities and carried our sorrows, yet we consider him stricken by God, smitten by him, and afflicted. But he was pierced for our transgressions, he was crushed for our iniquities; the punishment that brought us peace was upon him, and by his wounds we are healed. We all like sheep have gone astray, each of us has turned to his own way; and the Lord has laid on him, the iniquity of us all. He was oppressed and afflicted yet he did not open his mouth; he was led like a lamb to the slaughter, and as a sheep before her shearers is silent, so he did not open his mouth. By oppression and judgment, he was taken away and who can speak of his descendants? For he was cut off from the land of the living; for the transgressions of my people, he was stricken. He was assigned a grave with the wicked and with the rich in his death, though he had done no violence nor was there any deceit in his mouth. **Yet it was the Lord's will to crush him and cause him to suffer,***

---

[313] Isaiah 53:10

and through the Lord his life a guilt offering, *(emphasis added) he will see his offspring and prolong his days, and the will of the Lord will prosper in his hands".*[314]

"Of course! Of course!" shouted Ananiah. "His life was the cornerstone that man has rejected!"[315]

Ananiah rejoiced with his son as they recalled all the Dabar Promises. "But tell me father", Joel asked, "What is your realisation?"

Ananiah smiled. "How strange it was, that you should remember the words of Yochanan the Immerser" he said, "for I too have been thinking of the very words I heard that same day. Whilst the man Yeshua was coming out of the water after being baptised, I heard a voice say, 'This is my beloved Son; in him I am well pleased'. His Son! His Son! Not His messenger, nor His prophet, but His Son! The man from Nazareth, was not just the Lamb of God as Yochanan called him, he was the Son of Adonai; so, the lamb that hung willingly on that cross yesterday, was the one and only Son of the Living God!"

"This is just incredible!" replied Joel. "We must share this with the others". Immediately, they went inside and shared what they had found, and the sadness of the times was mixed with bitter, sweet rejoicing as the Dabar Promises were graciously revealed.

Following their family discussions about the Promises, Ananiah said that he was feeling very tired and would have to rest for a while. Retreating to their bedroom at the back of the house, he lay down on the bed and closed his eyes. There he stayed for the whole afternoon and the evening. His body so lacking its former strength, he found that breathing required the biggest of efforts. During the night, his laborious breathing worried

---

[314] Isaiah 53:2-10
[315] Isaiah 28:16; Psalm 118:22

Rachael so much so she could not sleep. Praying to her Lord, she asked that Adonai would be a comforter to her husband and ease the pain he was daily baring.

Ananiah's breathing seemed to become shallower with each passing hour, so at the break of day the next morning, Rachael woke Abagail and asked her to go into the city and get word to her brothers that their father was not well and to come to the farmhouse immediately. Meticulous in her thoughts, as she rode Sampson towards the city, Abigail had decided to go to Joel's house first so that his sons might be able to go to Jabin and Seth's houses as they lived close to each other. Joel could inform Jethro and she would go quickly to Daniel's house near the farm and return home to be with her mother whom she could see was most anxious.

It wasn't long before the whole family were gathered around the bedside of their father whose breathing had now become so quiet, it was only by the raising of his chest that they could see their beloved father was still with them. Ananiah stirred and opening his eyes, he asked "Who's there?"

"All the family is here, darling" Rachael said as she comforted her husband. "What for?" asked Ananiah.

"To tell you we love you" was all Rachael could say.

The solemn moment was suddenly broken as Kaleb appeared in the doorway of the bedroom. "Ananiah! Ananiah!" Kaleb breathlessly exclaimed. "He is alive! He is alive! He has risen!"

—— Chapter Thirty-Six ——

OPENED EYES

Silence once more filled the room. Kaleb explained that Micah had just visited him, telling him the most extraordinary story. The man's disciples had told Micah that early that morning two of the women went alone to the tomb of the Master to anoint his body for burial but when they had arrived at the tomb, they found that the large stone which had sealed the tomb, had been rolled away. Upon entering the tomb, they could not see his body and suddenly two men in shining robes stood beside them, asking them why were they seeking the living among the dead. The men told the women that the Master had risen![316]

At first, when the women and the disciples heard this they did not believe but one of the women saw him in the garden and mistaking him for the gardener asked him where the soldiers had put the master's body. It

---

[316] Luke 24:1-12.

was only when he spoke to her, did she realise it was the Master himself.[317] The Master is alive!

"But we were there and watched him die and also when the soldier pierced his side! He was definitely dead!" refuted Jethro.

"He has been resurrected! He has shown us that we can, and shall be resurrected as Adonai has promised!" exclaimed Joel. The final page of the six parchments could now be completed!

Immediately Rachael shared with her family, "After we witnessed the calling of El'azar (Lazarus) Beit-Anyah from the grave, didn't the Master say that he was the resurrection and the life? Did He also say that who believes in him will live, even though he dies; and he who lives and believes in him will never die?[318]"

Ananiah eyes sparkled. "And the scriptures say" he added, "You will not abandon me to the grave, nor will you let your Holy One see decay![319] We did see him die but the grave has no hold on the sinless Son of God. He could not rot in the grave because he no longer is dead! What other god bring such refreshing hope to his people?"

"But not just His own people!" Joel continued. "When Yochanan the Immerser identified him when were present at the River Yarden, he didn't just describe the Master as the Lamb of God, he called him the Lamb of God **who will take away the sins of the world**". "The Lamb of God was not just for the Israelite people, but came to atone for the sins of the whole world! Therefore, this wonderful promise of a Messiah was not just for the Israelite people, though this is what we Jews have selfishly believed over the years. I have just realised that the Dabar Promises we have so meticulously and carefully collected over the years are Adonai's promises that were not

---

[317] John 20:11-16
[318] John 11:25-26
[319] Psalm 16:10

just for the restoration of a nation, but rather they are promises which relate to the restoration of creation!"

Those assembled around the room were convinced that everything that had been promised by Adonai over the years had been fulfilled in the life of one man, but not an ordinary man, a special man sent by Adonai Himself. "He lived to die, and died to be resurrected!" Kaleb exclaimed. "What a marvellous mystery! Who would be able to complete such a plan?"

"Only the Son of God!" proclaimed Jabin.

"Not just the Son of God!" replied Ananiah, "But God Himself!"

The people in the room stared at Ananiah, who had become animated by the news and the discussion. But what he was saying now, was this a sign of delusion? Then, weakly reaching out to the bedside table with his left hand, Ananiah fingers searched for the piece of wheat his grandson had given him. Joel and Daniel helped raised their father's upper body so that he was sitting comfortably in the bed. With full assurance in his voice, Ananiah begun to speak.

"We all know that Adonai has many names and these cover many aspects of His great being and character. He is so mighty we cannot describe Him in just one single word. Did not the man Yeshua call Adonai, His 'Father', and did he not say He was His Father's 'Son'? And has not Adonai spoken to man throughout time by His 'Spirit'?; Father, Son and Spirit- one in three and three in one! But man cannot comprehend such complexity, and fails to understand that each is an individual yet each is part of the other".

"Yesterday, as I was trying to make sense of this myself, one of my grandchildren came up and placed this plant in my hand and as I felt its texture and substance, it dawned on me that one in three and three in one, is not such a complex concept. Tell me what is this I have in my hand?" Ananiah asked.

"It is wheat" the family responded.

"Yes, it is wheat for that is what we call it. Let us say the wheat represents 'Adonai'" continued Ananiah.

"And what is this?" asked Ananiah gently bringing us fingers up and down the stalk.

"The stalk!" replied the group.

"Let us say the stalk represents the 'Father'" Ananiah explained.

"And what is this?" he asked rubbing the husk between his fingers.

"The husk!" the group responded in unison.

"Let us say the husk represents 'The Spirit'", Ananiah continued. "And what is this?" he asked exposing the seed.

"The seed!" was the family's response.

"Let us say the seed represents 'The Son'. And there we have it – wheat comprises of a stalk, the husk and the seed. Three in one and one in three; each equally important and necessary for the wheat to grow yet unable to do so without the other two. That is how I can understand that Adonai is God the Father, God the Son and God the Holy Spirit. It is apt that the seed is The Son for surely a seed must die before it can live!"[320]

What had just been revealed to the group gave them great joy – all except Daniel who stated that he found it difficult to believe a dead man could be resurrected. Such a statement was beyond sound and logical reasoning. Daniel could not believe that this man was who his family believed him to be. He could, however, see that his loved ones did believe in this man Yeshua and stated he respected them for this.

Gathered around their father's bed, most of those present rejoiced in the revelations before them. Just then, Micah came through the door explaining that the disciples had decided to make their way to Galilee as the Master had told them to do as well as the angels present at the tomb that morning.

---

[320] John 12:24

He wanted to say farewell to his father before leaving Yerushalayim and so he rushed to the farmhouse to say goodbye to Kaleb. Upon hearing this news, both Seth and Jabin stated that they also wanted to return to Galilee with the disciples because they remembered the Lord promising he would return there after the Passover. Ananiah asked his two younger sons to come to him and when they did, he blest them and told them he was pleased and proud of all they had done over the years and encouraged them to continue on with the challenges that would be before them. Then, he asked for Daniel to come forth.

Holding his son's hand, Ananiah told him that he was also pleased that Daniel had turned into a fine young man whose recent skills of management had reassured Ananiah, the family would have a sound source of income for the current and future generations. Daniel assured his father, that while he was not going with his brothers, he promised that as long as he was manager of the farm, there would always be an income set aside from the five percent taxes of the workers, to allow his brothers to complete their discipleship for Adonai. There would also be money set aside for the continuation of family members who wanted to be a scribe, thus continuing their forefathers' agreement with Adonai. Hearing his son's promise pleased Ananiah who blessed him as well.

Summoning Jethro, Ananiah thanked his son for his faithfulness to his mother's family and Ananiah told him of his admiration of Jethro's loving character. Speaking kindly to his son, he blessed him as he had done Jethro's brothers.

Then, turning to Joel, he asked Joel what he wanted to do now that the fulfilment of Dabar Promises was completed. "But not all the promises have been fulfilled father" Joel stated. "The Messiah promised that He was going to return and that his followers must be ready for him when he does[321]. Only then, will the promises that were given to the prophet Daniel be fulfilled. He <u>will</u> ride into the city and he <u>will</u> assume His rule and there <u>will be</u> a time of peace[322]. However, until that time, the world would suffer many problems and hardships but the people who believe in the Master must be strong and wait for His return".

"So, there is now an urgency to spread this news across the nations" said Rachael. "Before He returns, Adonai's message of hope and restoration must be taken to the world![323]"

Once again. Ananiah asked his son what he wanted to do. Then Ananiah added, "Please be truthful in what you say".

"Oh father" exclaimed Joel. "Now that all these truths have been revealed to me, I really have no interest in old prophets' promises. It is like the Master said, "Why put new wine into old skins?[324] What I have learnt about the Son of God over the past three years excites me so much, and I still long to know more. I would love so much to be with my brothers as they return to Galilee where I could learn much more than I already know".

Ananiah placed his hands upon his son's head and said, "Then, go in peace and look after your brothers. But don't forget your mother or your sister; remember fondly the journey we have taken together over the past three years or so".

"And what about you, Abagail, what is it you want to do with your life? Please be honest like your brother".

"I will stay with you, father" replied Abagail.

---

[321] Matthew 25:1-13
[322] Isaiah 32:18; Isaiah 55:12
[323] Mark 16:15-16
[324] Mark 2:22

"Haven't you realised by now that your father can tell when you are not being completely truthful? Once more I shall ask you, what is it you want to do with your life?"

"I have always wanted to be with my brothers who have been following the Master" Abagail replied.

"Right from the beginning of His Ministry, there have always been a small group of women who have faithfully followed the Master and helped the disciples"[325] insisted Jabin. "Furthermore, we shall keep her safe, father – this we promise you". Joel and Seth heartily agreed as did Micah, who was still in the room.

"Then go in peace" Ananiah said to his family. Summoning Kaleb, he took his friend's hand and thanked him for his friendship and companionship over the years. The two had grown up to be the best and finest of friends and Ananiah felt fortunate to have such a loyal friend as Kaleb. Leaving the room one by one, the family left to go on a new journey leaving Ananiah alone with Rachael.

≈   ≈   ≈

"Rachael, there is one question that has not been answered. Are you able to answer it for me?"

"What's the question?" Rachael asked.

"Why did Adonai choose me, over all the other seven boys to rescue from the catacombs?"

"Oh, I knew the answer to that question even before I met you" Rachael answered.

---

[325] Luke 8:1-4

"The reason Adonai saved you, my darling so many years ago, is because He is all knowing and He knows just how special you are!" Kissing him passionately on his forehead, she told him to have a rest for it had been a most tiring but memorable morning.

≈   ≈   ≈

With all the family gone, the house was quiet and somewhat vacant. Whenever she felt the need to look in on her sleeping husband, Rachael would enter the bedroom, move over to the bed and place her hand on her husband's brow. Often, she would sit on the side of the bed and hold his hand – his hands were now aged and wrinkled. She remembered as a young girl holding Ananiah's hand which always felt strong and secure. Now, his hands were old and feeble. Once when she was sitting by his bed, Ananiah was stirred from his sleeping and feeling the comfort of his wife's hand in his, he smiled, nodded his head and went back to sleep.

It was sometime in the afternoon when Ananiah awoke and unknowingly put his hand into the pocket of his outer garment. Grasping an object within the pocket, he pulled this out and rotating this around with his fingers, he realised that this was the small wooden block his great-grandfather had handed to him so many years ago when he first heard about the Dabar Promises. Remembering that his great-grandfather explained Adonai's boundless deity and power to him, his thoughts went even further back to that day in the catacombs.

"Oh Adonai! My Lord, my Saviour and my God, how gracious have You been to your servant Ananiah. Despite my stupidity and selfishness, you overlooked my flaws and in your great mercy, you looked upon me with such grace and

favour. Rescuing a stubborn child from certain death, you have faithfully walked with me through my life, bestowing upon me such boundless blessings; a loving wife and children who know You. I have so much to be thankful for. Yet, Lord, I am so tired and I can scarcely talk to You but there are two things which I must thank You for."

"There are so many Dabar Promises you have revealed to my family over the past generations and I am so grateful that you have allowed us to have a glimpse into the plan You designed so long ago. Included within the Dabar Promises which have been such a blessing to me, are the ones You gave to me in the Holy Place so many years ago. You said that I shall not see Your Messiah with my own eyes but with my very soul and this by Your Grace, I have seen. Though my tired eyes are weary, my soul is not, and even now I can rejoice in the knowledge of You. Then, You promised me that after all had come to pass, I would see Your Messiah for who He truly was and is. He came, lived and died for You, with You and in You. This is a marvellous mystery. May there be many more people in this world and in the generations to come, who also come to know You, Your Son and Your Spirit".

"The second thing I am so grateful for is this: when you chose to save me on that fatal day, it was not because you wanted me to do something great for You. Although many thought I would be ascribed a great task, that was not to be. Rather, You graciously saved me because You simply desired me to know and love You. **That is what you desire for all**

your creation. How loving are You, my God and Saviour! How wonderful are You my gracious Lord, to want to be the faithful, loving and loyal friend of such a foolish and ignorant man!"

Exhausted, Ananiah closed his eyes and a warm breeze blew through the shuttered window of the room. All Ananiah could do was rest. His body was tired. Sometimes he would stir out of his slumber but he would immediately return to his rest, breathing laboriously. For a moment, he thought he heard someone call his name, and stirring from his sleep he opened his eyes. Tears were flowing down his face and suddenly, Ananiah realised that there was a light within the room. Attempting to blink through his tears, he strained to see the source of the light which seemed to grow larger and larger. There, before him, were rays of brilliant light which formed a glowing aura around a blurred figure in its centre. Peering even more intently, Ananiah saw in the middle of the light, the appearance of a man dressed in a brilliant white robe and whose arms were extending outward welcoming him. Once more, he heard the voice which sounded like a rushing wind and causing his soul to feel brimmed to overflowing. "Ananiah," the voice said, "Come!"

For God shows and clearly proves His (own) love for us by the fact that while we were still sinners, Christ (the Messiah, the Anointed One) died for us

(Romans 5:8 Amplified Bible Classic Edition)